THEY HUNT

THEY HUNT

CLAIRE FRAISE

Sabertooth
Press

To Andrew,
for being the best plot consultant a girl could ask for.

PART 1
Ghost Hunters

1

Shiloh

I didn't exactly have high hopes for my life, but I still never thought I'd end up in jail. Seriously. If someone had asked me before Max went missing if it was more likely that I'd get stabbed to death by the masked guy from *Scream* or if I'd spend the rest of my life behind bars, I would've put money on the *Scream* thing. But I guess I was wrong.

The heavy door of the juvenile detention center closes behind me. Squinting against the bright ceiling lights, I let the police officer guide me toward the main desk. A sign above it reads: INTAKE.

The cop handcuffs my wrists to the counter. Tight. Like he thinks I belong in them.

He drops a folder on the counter. The uniformed woman behind the desk looks up.

"I called from the road," the officer says. "This is Shiloh Oleson."

The woman opens the folder and thumbs through, taking a long slurp from her McDonald's iced coffee like this is just another morning and not the worst day of my life. She's pushing forty and looks appropriately tired for being up this early. Her braids are falling out of her messy bun, and the brown skin around her eyes is puffy.

Close to a minute goes by before she returns her attention to me. "This is your first time here?"

I feel like she should already know the answer. She literally just read my file, so I don't know why she asked, but I suck it up and say, "Yes, ma'am."

"Okay." The woman sets down her cup of coffee. "I'm going to start the intake process. You need to answer a couple of questions and sign a few things, okay?"

I glance at the cop standing behind me. He doesn't look scared. Just ready. Like he expects me to do something or make a break for it. I wish I could, but I know there's no escaping this place.

One way in. No way out.

The woman clears her throat. I look back at her.

"Yes, ma'am," I say. "Sorry."

She double-clicks her mouse. "Do you understand why you're here?"

I nod. Of course I understand why I'm here. I didn't answer any questions at the station because I didn't know what I was supposed to say. Telling the truth about how ghosts are real would get me thrown in an asylum, but it's hard to argue that I'm innocent with all the blood that's on me right now. It's caked under my fingernails. It's all over my camo print sweatshirt, in my blonde hair, and on the rubber toes of my Converse. I might have gone a little overboard with how many times I smashed Leonard's head in, but I don't regret doing it. That asshole deserved it.

I doubt this woman wants to hear that right now. So again, I just say, "Yes, ma'am."

She asks about my clothes and where I'm from. I try hard to focus on what she's saying and not on the police officer standing behind me, or how unsteady the floor feels under my feet. It's been four hours since I was arrested, and the adrenaline from the fight with Leonard has worn off. Everything hurts. Under my arms. My knee. The cuts on my hands. I can still taste the acrid smoke on my tongue, clinging to my clothes and making my lungs burn. My nose is still very much broken and, as much as I was trying to ignore my concussion, it's hard to ignore the pain pulsing behind my eyeballs right now.

But it's okay. Leonard is dead. All of this was worth it.

I try to hold on to that as the woman points a camera at my face. I give the lens a blank stare as the flash goes off.

She scans my fingerprints. I can hear a clock somewhere in the room. Every tick of the secondhand sounds louder than the last, like it's counting down to something bad.

I force out a long breath. I'm not going to hyperventilate. I will hold myself together.

With a grunt, the woman lowers herself back into her chair. The springs creak like the chair is grunting, too.

"You were in a house fire, correct?" She jiggles her mouse, smacking her lips together like she couldn't care less about the conversation we're having right now. The cool glow of the computer screen reflects onto her face. "Last night?"

I nod. That's not something I can hide. Miles arrested me right outside the burning house, and there's so much smoke on my clothes that it makes my stomach queasy.

"Did you start the fire?" she asks.

I purse my lips. The cops already asked me this at the station. I said nothing then, and I won't say anything now.

"Were you with your friends?" she tries again. "Who were you with?"

There's no way I'm going to bring my friends into this. The whole point of Miles arresting me was so I could take the fall for them. "Just me."

The woman types something into the computer. "How did the fire start?"

I open my mouth to tell her, but close it, because the real answer is not something I can say.

My friend hurled a Molotov cocktail at me because an evil ghost drugged him and told him to kill me.

Insane Asylum, ticket for one.

"Are you hurt?" the woman asks.

"I'm fine."

"There's a lot of blood on your clothes."

"It isn't mine."

She raises her eyes to the officer behind me. Was I not supposed to say that? I'm too tired to think clearly.

The woman points at my face. "Did you hurt your nose?"

I go to touch the strip of tape on my nose, but the handcuffs stop me. "I broke it last week."

"How did that happen?"

Pain pulses through my temples. The corners of my vision blur, so I close my eyes and lean onto the counter, resting my forehead on the inner part of my elbow. "Can I have some Tylenol?"

"Our nurse will take a look at you." More typing. "To see if anything's wrong."

"I have a concussion," I say, coughing on the words. "I just need Tylenol and to go to sleep."

"You seem angry," the woman says. "Do you feel angry right now?"

I'm angry that she's not giving me Tylenol. When she doesn't move on, I raise my head to look at her and rest my chin on my arm. She raises one of her drawn-on eyebrows.

Is she seriously asking me if I'm angry? Of course I'm angry. I'm going to spend the rest of my life being treated like a murderer for saving my friends and family from an undead lunatic.

The woman waits for a reply. I have nothing to lose, so I tell her the truth.

"Yes."

She peels back the corner of my file. "It says here you killed a man with a stolen firearm."

The memory hits me like a slap in the face. The smell of urine and hay. The dim lamp that barely lit up Max's limp body. I pepper-sprayed Leonard in the face. He clawed at his streaming eyes as I told him to get away from my brother. A low laugh rumbled out of him.

There's no point in tryin', he said. *See, Max is already gone from this world.*

I raised the gun so fast. Shots split the air as I blew holes through Leonard's long, green trench coat. I shot him until I couldn't shoot him anymore. Until there weren't any bullets left.

Max was already dead when I shot Leonard. It wasn't self-defense. It was retaliation.

But the police don't know about Max being dead. For all they know, Leonard was trying to kill Max when I shot him. Could I argue it was self-defense?

Clenching my fists so hard my nails bite into my palms, I try to keep my voice steady. "I was protecting my brother."

"You were also brought in on charges of assault and battery," she says. "Do you think it's right that you were arrested?"

"Davey and Scotty are bullies."

She peers at one of the papers. "I heard you broke the boy's knee."

"What else does it tell you in that form?" I snap. "My star sign? What I had for breakfast yesterday?"

The woman glares at me. Deeper in the building, I hear a door close with dull finality. I try to push down the panic that's rising in my throat.

The woman gathers the forms and taps them against her desk. "Because of the severity of your charges, you'll be held without bail. Have you decided who you want to call? Maybe your mom or dad?"

I twist my wrists in the cuffs until metal digs into my skin. There's no way this woman would know that Mom is dead, and that her body is currently possessed by Leonard's psychotic mother. The only person I want to talk to is Max, so I can tell him I'm okay and that I love him, but he's still with Handy, and I don't know how to reach him. Even if I did, calling him would give the police a way to find him, which I don't want either because then they'd bring him right back to my grandparents. I can't call Miles. He's Officer Zweering now, and probably out getting beer poured down his shirt by the other Bethany cops to congratulate him for putting me behind bars. Jonah hasn't come down from the foolery yet. If I called him, all he'd be able to think about is how much he wanted to kill me, which wouldn't be all that comforting.

There's no one I can call. The only person who knows I'm here is Miles, but he can't get me out.

I'm alone.

I glance back at the door guarded by the police officer. Even if I could somehow get out of these handcuffs, I couldn't get through him and out of the building. All these people might believe I'm dangerous, but I'm not. I was just trying to save Max. I didn't mean for any of this to happen.

Call it desperation. Call it a psychotic break. But I need someone to know I'm in here, even if that somebody is one of the last people in the world I trust.

Doing my best to press down the bile rising in my throat, I give the woman Dad's cell phone number and listen as the phone rings on speaker.

He picks up after a couple of seconds. "Hello?"

The woman glances at me, but I shake my head and point at the phone, so she clears her throat.

"Hi," the woman says. "Is this Ernest Oleson?"

"Speaking."

"This is Tamica Bellview at the Gordon T. Richardson Juvenile Correctional Facility calling in regard to your daughter, Shiloh Oleson. She was brought in by the Cincinnati Police Department on charges of assault, battery, and second-degree murder, and is being held without bail. She will have her detention hearing on Tuesday, October 8th at two PM. Will you be able to attend?"

The line goes dead. For a second, I think Dad might have hung up, but then I hear his ragged breathing. I picture him in his new apartment—undecorated and messy because he's never had to clean up after himself a day in his life. In my head, he has a dumb and half-awake look on his face, and a few empty beer cans on the floor by his brand-new La-Z-Boy recliner.

He can't be that surprised to get this call. He didn't lift a finger to help me when I was being questioned by those stupid detectives. One of the last times I saw him, I cut him with a kitchen knife, so he probably thinks I belong here. Come to think of it, he's probably glad I've been arrested, because I'm the one who told the FBI about the abuse, and if everyone in Bethany thinks I'm unstable, he'll have an easy time convincing everyone I was lying.

Oh my God. Calling him was a mistake. He won't do anything to help me.

"Shiloh?" His voice is hoarse from the early-morning wake-up call. "Goddamn it, is she there? Can I speak to her?"

Only I can hear how much he's hamming it up over the phone. I shake my head at the woman.

She takes a second to respond, like her brain is lagging. "She does not want to speak to anyone, sir."

He mutters an expletive. There's a clink on the other end of the phone, like he's putting down a cup. Or maybe a glass.

"This is ridiculous. Shiloh, honey, if you can hear me, this is going to be okay. I will get you a lawyer. He will come see you today, and you will do as he says, you hear me?"

"Sir—"

"It's all going to be okay." Dad raises his voice. "Him and me, we'll get you through this."

"Sir, I'm going to hang up now, you—"

"I love you, Shiloh." Dad's voice is urgent. I hate how sincere the words sound, even though they mean nothing. You don't throw lowball glasses at people you love. You don't backhand them or tell them they're worthless or push them down the stairs just because you're mad. "This is going to be okay. I promise you that."

"Goodbye, sir."

The woman hangs up. The click of the phone is sharp and final. I turn my eyes up to the panels of light and close my eyes.

Is Dad actually going to send me a lawyer? Is he sending me a lawyer because he cares, or because it's better for his image to come across as a loving parent instead of an abusive alcoholic who's happy that his daughter's in jail? I shouldn't trust a word that comes out of his mouth, but I want to because I've never felt so small and alone in my entire life.

"You'll finish the rest of the intake process inside," the woman says. "Go with Officer Robinson here, okay?"

A new officer comes to undo my handcuffs. She's short. Even shorter than Francesca, which is saying something. Her blonde hair is slicked back in a neat bun. There is a hardened expression on her face, like she's had this job for too long and nothing I do could ever surprise her.

Officer Robinson pins my wrists behind my back and leads me out of the room, down an unmarked hallway with concrete walls painted glossy white. She guides me into a bathroom. Dampness lingers in the air like someone showered in here not too long ago. I can smell the faint aroma of cleaning products. She stops me in front of a shower stall barely big enough for me to stand in.

"I'm going to pat you down," she says, all business. "Raise your arms above your head."

I do what she tells me. She snaps on a pair of latex gloves and runs her firm hands down the sides of my zip-up sweatshirt. Keeping my eyes on the wall, I try not to pay attention to her hands pressing against my skin, or how she's touching me when I don't want her to.

I need to go numb. I need to not feel anything if I'm going to stand any chance of getting through this.

Officer Robinson fits keys into my handcuffs and unlocks them. "Please remove your clothes."

A chill runs up my spine.

I want you to take your clothes off.

That's what Dad used to say to me when he was mad. It was code for "I'm about to hit you with a belt so hard you'll wish you'd never been born." Or worse.

I try to calm myself down. Officer Robinson is not going to hit me with a belt. She's going to search me to make sure I'm not carrying anything. Because it's her job.

I turn my back to her and peel everything off. My jeans are stiff with dry sweat. The smell of smoke stings my nose as I pull my T-shirt over my head and drop it on the floor.

Officer Robinson gets me to hold my arms above my head, then at my sides. She makes me squat in weird positions, which would be uncomfortable enough even if it weren't so cold in here.

She has me turn around again. I focus on the floor as she runs her eyes over my body. It feels wrong to stand naked in front of a total stranger. I wonder if she notices the scars from where Dad hit me. Or the marks on my lower back left by the belt. If she does, she says nothing. I'd guess she's seen worse.

She bags up my clothes and tells me to shower, leaving me alone in the room. I don't know what the point of modesty is now that she's literally looked inside my butthole, but I'm just going to do what I'm told.

I turn on the shower. Water comes out as a thin spray. It stays cold no matter how much I play with the dial, so I grit my teeth, pull the elastic out of my hair, and step barefoot under the icy water. It hurts like hell, but also soothes my bruises, quiets the throbbing in my temples, and loosens the tape covering my broken nose. I removed most of the bandages and packing a few days ago. This tape is the only thing still on it, but my cartilage has healed enough that I doubt the tape is doing much. At this point, my nose will heal crooked no matter what I do, so I peel off the tape and drop the bloody strip onto the shower pan.

Using the bar of soap on the floor, I wash all the blood off my face and out from under my fingernails. Officer Robinson bangs on the door before I can get to my hair, but I'm not trying to impress anyone in here, so whatever.

I wrap myself in a towel. Officer Robinson comes back in with a bag of clothes containing new underwear, a bra, two pairs of socks, two long-sleeved white shirts, one gray hoodie, and a folded beige jumpsuit.

"Put these on," she says.

I hold up the scratchy uniform. "I thought jumpsuits are supposed to be orange. In all the movies, they're orange."

Officer Robinson glares at me. Go figure. The fabric is rough, and the jumpsuit is too big on me, but at least it smells clean, and it's not giving me a headache like my old ones were. She re-secures my handcuffs, and then two men in uniforms and baseball caps come to take over from her. Seeing them makes me almost want to laugh at how ridiculous this situation is. Do these people really think they need two grown men to keep me under control, when I'm barely 130lbs soaking wet and couldn't take even one of them without way more energy and some kind of weapon?

Jonah would laugh about this if he were here. Picturing his easy-going smile as he calls the officers my security detail makes a tiny coin of warmth bloom in the middle of my chest.

But he wouldn't laugh about it right now. Because he's on foolery and tried to kill me.

The men keep one hand on each of my arms as they lead me through the building. The walls are all white. Every door is green. Some have windows in them. I try to peek through to see if there are any people in there, but the glass is too narrow and I'm walking too fast.

I wonder if the foolery has worn off Jonah by now. Probably not. Leonard gave him so much, and when Jonah looked at me, it was like he had forgotten everything about me. I can still see the anger burning behind his blue eyes when he lunged at me with the knife. He was going to stab me. He *wanted* to stab me. Until I told him I loved him.

I can't believe I said that. I don't even know if I meant it. Those words … the only reason I said them was because I thought he was about to kill me, and I was trying to get him to stop.

Do I love Jonah? I never thought I could love anyone other than Max. I thought Dad screwed me up too much to let another person in, but it's easy with Jonah. He gets me. Nothing I say scares him away, so I don't need to hide anything from him, but is that love?

It doesn't matter. Not anymore, because I'm never going to see him again.

One officer unlocks a door labeled HOLDING 4. He leads me into a wing with a bunch of closed doors, opens one, and steps out of the way. My knees jam up.

The cell is a quarter of the size of my room at home. Just big enough for the essentials. A metal toilet and sink combo. A cracked mirror. A stool bolted into the floor, and a mattress pad on a concrete slab against the far wall. There's a pillow and blanket. Some toiletries in a plastic bag.

No part of me wants to go in there, but the man shoves me, and I stumble into the middle of the room.

The officers undo my handcuffs. I turn around.

"Am I in here alone?" I ask, my voice trembling. "What happens now? Can I have something to e—?"

The door slams. I press my nose against the window and watch the two officers walk away, scanning their IDs and letting themselves out of the wing.

My breath fogs up the glass. I glance at the other cell doors and see a girl's face staring back at me. She widens her eyes until they bug out of her head, then drags her finger across her throat.

This can't be happening. This can't be real.

The corners of my vision spot. So much pain stabs through my temple that I can't stand anymore, and I barely make it to the mattress before collapsing on my side. The pad is thin. Concrete presses hard into my shoulder, sending a dull ache through my bones. I bury my face in the pillow. What was that breathing exercise Miles said he did when he felt a panic attack coming on?

Breathe in for three seconds. Hold for five seconds. Breathe out for seven seconds.

I do that for a couple of minutes, but I feel as bad as I did before. My head throbs. So does my nose. I was so focused on killing Leonard and so hopped up on adrenaline that I could ignore the pain for a few days, but now that Leonard is dead, it's like my body is making up for lost time.

I close my eyes. The room spins around me like I'm locked in the cabin of a boat. I pull the blanket over my body. The lights are on and so bright that they turn my eyelids pink, but I'm too tired and nauseated to care. In a couple of minutes, sleep pulls me under.

I can hear my teeth chattering before I wake up. My body shivers under the blanket.

I open my eyes. The lights are still on. Cold air stings the tip of my swollen nose. A breath slips through my lips. It comes out as a misty fog.

Is it seriously so cold in here that I can see my own breath?

I drag my aching legs over the side of the bed. It was cold in here when I arrived. I'm not sure how long I slept, but it's not normal for a room to be this cold. Not even a jail cell, because I bet there are regulations against temperatures like this. This feels like I'm in a freezer with an ice cube pressing against the base of my skull.

Something moves in the corner of my eye. I turn to the sink and watch the mirror fog up like I'm taking a shower.

I step closer to it. So much condensation covers the surface that I can't see my reflection anymore.

A line streaks down it. What the hell?

There's another line. Then one across. Oh my God. Those aren't random squiggles.

They're letters.

My breathing quickens. I glance over my shoulder, but nothing is behind me, so I focus on the words. I can't breathe. I can't move. I can't even think until the entire message has been written. I stumble away from the mirror and press my back against the wall, staring at the words because they're all I can see:

I FOUND YOU

2
Shiloh

I grab my pillow, clutching it to my chest for a second before dropping it. What the hell am I thinking? A pillow can't protect me from whatever wrote that message.

Or whoever.

It has to be a ghost. Nothing else would make sense.

I found you. Who the hell has found me in here?

I only know one ghost angry enough to come looking for me.

The fog fades from the mirror. The words disappear, leaving the cracked mirror looking as depressing as it did before.

I wrap my arms around my stomach and grit my teeth to stop them from chattering. It's still way too cold in here, but at least the cold at the base of my skull is not there anymore. I glance around for anything that might be moving toward me, but there's not much that can move in here except the blanket and pillow. Everything else is bolted to the floor. For security reasons. Because I'm in jail. I imagine Leonard's ghost putting the blanket over itself and rushing toward me like something out of Scooby Doo, but it's not funny, so I don't laugh.

That message was a warning. Leonard wants revenge on me

because I killed him. How did he escape from the other side so fast? Sending him there was supposed to trap him there forever. Or at least longer than a few hours.

I found you.

Is Leonard going to kill me as a ghost? Is that even possible? Probably. The ghost at Ella Ruggles's house touched stuff. It made the room cold and was powerful enough to throw books around. If ghosts can throw books around, who's to say Leonard couldn't drive a toothbrush into my eye, or find a plastic knife and stick it in my neck?

Oh my God. I can't even see ghosts. How the hell am I supposed to defend myself against something I can't see?

The air gets thin. I grip the neckline of my jumpsuit like that could help me breathe.

I'm going to die in here. In this tiny cell in a juvenile detention center where nobody can come to save me.

I push the thought away. No. I will not die in here. Right now, the ghost of Leonard's mom is possessing my mom's body, and Max is alone. He needs me. Nobody has found me guilty of anything. Even though it goes against everything in me to believe anything Dad says, he's sending me a lawyer, and that lawyer might help me get out of here.

I just need to survive until he does.

I walk over to the mirror, gripping the corners of the sink and staring at my warped reflection. Oh, boy. I look like crap. Blonde hairs stick to my forehead and temples, still wet from the shower. The bruises under my eyes have turned a sickly yellow and brown, and a web of red veins creeps through the whites of my eyes. I need to go back to sleep. I also need to make a plan, which requires some thinking, and thinking is hard when I'm running on only a couple of hours of sleep. But I can't go to sleep if Leonard is still around watching me, so I do my best to string together some logical thoughts.

There has to be something that repels ghosts. I saw a movie once where people drove away angry spirits with salt. Or maybe I'm thinking of slugs. I'm pretty sure ghosts can only touch things in the real world if they're old and powerful. Francesca said something about that once. I only ever knew one old and powerful ghost, and that was the one at Ella Ruggles's house. She threw books at us. Made chandeliers rock. Typical haunted house stuff. She was angry with Ella, but she never killed her. Maybe she didn't want to. Or maybe ghosts aren't strong enough to do things like choke or stab people with their bare hands. I don't know which one of these is true, but I can't talk to Ella and ask her, so I'm going to go with option B.

How could Leonard kill me? Could he wrap the blanket around my neck and strangle me with it? He could push me out a window, but something tells me I won't be going near many windows in here. He could punt a bar of soap at my face fast enough for it to re-break my nose, but I'd take a broken nose over being dead.

If Leonard can't kill me with his bare hands, that means he needs to use a weapon. Getting rid of everything in the cell would mean he had nothing to turn into a weapon.

So that's what I do. In less than a minute, I strip the sheets off the foam pad and pile them by the door. The pillow and blanket go, too. I get rid of the toiletries in case Leonard could make a shiv out of a toothbrush, but I keep the soap. Leonard can't kill me with a bar of soap. I'm going to smell gross if I can't brush my teeth, but at least I can wash my hands.

I decide to keep the mattress pad because I'll be sleeping on top of it and weighing it down enough that Leonard couldn't use it to suffocate me with. Once all that's left is either the mattress pad or bolted to the floor, I bang on the door.

"Hello?" I angle my face to peer through the window, but the block is empty. "Can somebody come get this stuff out of my room?"

No one answers. I glance around the cell, and my eyes land on a beady security camera perched high in the corner. Of course they're watching me. Those Big Brother jerks.

I climb on top of the mattress and wave my arms above my head.

"Hello?" The camera stares back at me like an unfeeling eye. "Do you watch me pee through that thing? Is there any privacy in here at all?"

There is no privacy. This shouldn't surprise me.

"Hey!" I yell. "One of you perverts needs to come take this stuff out of my room right now."

Nobody comes. After a couple of minutes of screaming at the top of my lungs and threatening to drive a toothbrush into my eye, a woman's face appears at the window of my cell door. She looks pissed.

I plaster on a smile. "Hi. Sorry to bother you, but I have some stuff in here I need you to get rid of."

She blinks. Says nothing.

"It's nothing bad," I say, in case she thinks it's something bad. "Just my bed sheets and the pillow."

She blinks again. Like she's processing. "You want me to get rid of your pillow?"

"Yes." I try to come up with a reason to justify this. "I don't like sleeping in sheets."

"You don't like sleeping in sheets," she echoes.

"No, ma'am. I … get night sweats."

Her eyebrows knit together. This must not be a request she hears every day. I bite my pinky nail. She barks something into her walkie-talkie and orders me to put my hands against the wall. I press my palms against the smooth concrete. I hear a scraping sound, and some clinking that might be keys. The door closes.

I turn around. My stuff is gone. Now, I can go to sleep.

I lie back down on the mattress pad, burying my hands in my sleeves and tucking my knees to my chest to get warm. Giving up the blanket was the right thing to do, but it's so cold in here that right now I'd cut off my pinky toe to get it back. I hope I'm cold because whoever is in charge of the thermostat is a heartless son of a bitch and not because Leonard is in here watching me sleep like some kind of ghost version of that vampire from Twilight everyone in my school thought was so hot. I close my eyes. My lids are pink against the overhead light. Something tells me that if I have no say in the temperature they keep this place at, I will also have no say in when the lights go off.

I'm so tired from last night that I can feel the exhaustion in my bones, but this mattress is so uncomfortable, and my body won't stop shivering. I picture my room at home, and how many blankets I used to pile onto it in the winter. I wonder if I'll ever get to sleep in it again.

I don't know how much time passes before someone knocks on the door. There's a loud bang, like a bolt moving. A man's voice barks something that I don't understand, and a tray of food slides through a slot in the door.

I sit up. Every muscle in my body aches at me to lie back down, and my head is throbbing so much that my vision spins. I need some Tylenol, but I need food even more.

Carrying the tray over to my bed, I grab the flimsy plastic spork and dig in. I spoon the sticky oatmeal into my mouth, bite a chunk out of the sausage patty, and then eat the entire waffle. Crumbs spill onto my legs. If my mom could see me right now, she'd be horrified at the way I was eating, but she's not here.

Once I've finished the whole plate, I lean back on my hands. A burp rises from my stomach.

My eyes linger on the packet of salt. In case salt really does repel ghosts, I tuck it under the mattress pad. Could Leonard kill me with a spork? I guess he could scoop an eye out. So I snap the spork into pieces and hold them in my hand until an officer comes to take my tray away. A small smile tugs at the corner of my mouth.

Leonard might think he can kill me, but that cocky asshole has another thing coming.

Local Teen Arrested as Murder Suspect: Shock Grips Community

BETHANY, Ohio - The community of Bethany is in shock as 16-year-old Shiloh Oleson, a junior at Bethany High School, has been arrested for the alleged murder of 92-year-old Patrick De Beauvoir.

Oleson was taken into custody by Cincinnati police on Monday. She is currently in juvenile custody awaiting her detention hearing, according to a City of Cincinnati spokesperson.

The incident occurred on Saturday, September 21, 2019, close to the intersection between River Rd and Green St in Mount Keenan, Ohio. De Beauvoir was shot nine times and died at the scene. The motive behind the crime appears to be connected to the kidnapping of Oleson's younger brother, which deeply affected the community. No further details have so far been released.

More updates on the case will be provided as information becomes available.

3

Miles

When Shiloh suggested I arrest her, I should have taken a second to think it through. Because if I'd done that, maybe I would've realized that the first thing every police officer in the city would want to know is how I found her, and I have no idea what I'm supposed to tell them.

"There's something about this whole situation I still don't understand." Chief Schnebly says, and I resist the urge to reply, *You and me both*. "How did you know Shiloh Oleson would be in that house tonight?"

I shrug my shoulders up to my ears, then drop them when I realize how exaggerated the motion is. How *did* I know Shiloh would be in that house? That is an excellent question. It's definitely not because I was in there with her, because Shiloh is my ex-girlfriend, or because I'm a dead 16-year-old boy playing the most terrifying game of dress-up known to man.

"Uh …" I try to think of an appropriate answer to Schnebly's question, my mind racing as I weigh the consequences of my words. Am I supposed to lie and tell him what he wants to hear?

Spin some kind of story about my A+ detective work worthy of a Sherlock Holmes novel? I don't want to accidentally say something that would incriminate Shiloh and increase her chances of getting convicted for a crime she didn't commit, but I can't stand here and say nothing. I ultimately settle on: "I g-got an anonymous t-tip saying she was hiding at the old farmhouse on the Monroe property."

Chief Schnebly hums. He and I are standing at the main entrance of the Cincinnati Police Department, where I followed Shiloh after arresting her. The real officers took her to the detention center an hour ago. I tried to excuse myself without looking suspicious, but I got stuck answering questions, pretending to write a report, and taking trips to the water cooler every few minutes to keep myself hydrated because I was sweating so much that I was in serious danger of passing out. I've been here so long that the sun has risen. Soft morning light filters through tall windows and glass double doors, casting a gentle glow on the polished linoleum floors. Big city officers walk with purpose behind the reception desk. Urgent fingers drum on computer keyboards. The smell of fresh coffee drifts in from a nearby room, mixing in with the aroma of paper and ink and the house fire smoke still on my clothes. Every distant ring of a phone sends a spike of dread through my body.

Did someone discover the bodies in the burned house?

Has Richie recognized me as the police officer who was keeping him prisoner with Shiloh and Jonah?

Did someone find security camera footage of me with Shiloh and discover that I'm a complete fraud?

My damp uniform clings to my skin. I hope Schnebly can't see how much I'm sweating. This uniform feels like it just came out of the washing machine. It needs to go in the washing machine after last night. *I* need to go in the washing machine after last night.

Another officer joins us. I have never seen him before in my life. His piercing eyes look like they can see right through people, so I remind myself to keep breathing so he can't see through me.

"It was a p-popular spot for kids at the high school to break into," I say, then when a strange look flashes across the Cincinnati officer's face, I add: "Like our old friend Jonah Weatherby."

I shouldn't be throwing Jonah under the bus, but I have to play the part. Jonah's name gets a confused look from the Cincinnati officer and a knowing grunt from Schnebly.

"There's a warrant out for his arrest, too." Chief Schnebly leans closer to the other officer. "He's a local kid on probation for drug proliferation, and last week he sent a boy to the hospital."

I bite down on my tongue to prevent myself from screaming. Davey and Scotty were about to throw me off a bridge. If it weren't for Shiloh and Jonah coming to save me, I could have died.

The officer cocks his head to the side. "Same as this Shiloh girl?"

Chief Schnebly nods. "The same incident, at least. Say, Randy, was Jonah hiding in the farmhouse with her?"

My brain short-circuits, like all the hamsters running on the wheels in my head die at the same time.

"I d-didn't s-see him in there," I stutter.

Chief Schnebly would need to be deaf not to notice the tremor in my voice, but he doesn't let on.

"Worth checking, anyhow," he says. "I'll stop by and remind Lydia to replace that broken door. I wonder if Shiloh knows what happened to Talulah."

A drop of sweat runs down my upper lip and into my mouth. I wipe it away. Chief Schnebly glances past me. I turn to where he's looking and see Lindsey sitting on a plastic chair with her arms crossed over her chest like a kid on a time-out. Even though she has been awake for as long as I have, her eyes are alert. Her brown skin is warm even in the sterile light of the station, but that's about the only thing about her that is warm right now. She's looking at me like she wants to cut my head off.

I won't wait around here long enough to give her the opportunity.

"I'm actually not feeling well, sir," I say. "I breathed in too much smoke from that house, and I need to get myself checked out at the hospital."

Schnebly's face knits in concern. "You need me to drive you?"

"No," I say. "Thank you."

"You let me know if you need anything, you hear?"

Oh, I'm going to a depressing part of the other side for lying to this poor old man.

Backing away, I push through the glass doors, embracing the cool morning air. The wind beats against my face and cuts through my uniform like it wants to blow right through me, and I wish I could let it.

But that's not possible, so I hurry to my squad car. The door to the station opens and closes.

"How did you do it?" Lindsey demands.

I turn around. Up close, she looks exhausted. So aggressively pretty, but exhausted, with veins in the whites of her eyes. Lindsey is scary when she's angry, and she's so pretty that I can't seem to form a single coherent thought around her. The only thing I can do is play dumb.

I pull my sunglasses over my eyes and thrust my hands deep into my pockets. "Do what?"

"Get everyone to believe you."

"I arrested Shiloh Oleson," I say, raising my voice to keep it from trembling. "You watched me do it."

She shoves my shoulder. I stagger backward.

"I know you're helping her," Lindsey says. "I knew it the second I saw that sketch. You only arrested Shiloh to make yourself look less guilty. Hell, she could have told you to arrest her." The blood drains from her face. "Oh my God, are you sleeping with a sixteen-year-old, Randall?"

A jolt of panic runs through me. "I am *not* sleeping with Shiloh Oleson."

"I can't believe I ever thought you were my best friend."

Lindsey's words hang in the air between us. *Best friend*. I didn't know that Lindsey and Randall were best friends, I knew they were friendly, but I was so wrapped up in trying not to be found out that I didn't spend a lot of time thinking about how well they knew each other. It would explain her fixation on me. She knew Randall well enough to know when he was acting weird. I stole someone else's life, and now I'm going around messing everything up.

As much as I wish I could fix things with her, I wouldn't even know where to start. It's not like I can tell her the truth.

Lindsey narrows her eyes at my chest. Stepping forward, she grabs a piece of my uniform. "Is that blood?"

I glance down at the streak marring the navy fabric. It's there, but not red enough for Schnebly to have noticed.

I push her hand away, trying hard to maintain my composure.

She laughs. "You got your ass kicked by a teenage girl?"

The blood is not mine. It's also not Shiloh's. Some of Phil's blood must have gotten on me when I carried him through the house after Shiloh's mom stabbed him.

Fiona brought him to the hospital. Francesca is there, too. I need to find out how they're doing.

But I need to get Lindsey to go away first. I don't know how Lindsey knows all this stuff, but she's onto me, and if I show even an ounce of fear, she's going to pounce on it.

Pulling my shoulders back, I step toward her.

"I'm not helping Shiloh," I say. "I arrested her because I'm good at doing my job."

"You're such a liar."

"So what if I am?" I ask, not knowing if this is the right strategy but just going for it. "Seriously. So what, Lindsey? You can't prove anything. All they have is your word against mine, and your word isn't looking all that good after you led the chief across the state trying to pin this on me. Stop accusing me of things you know nothing about. If I were you, I'd go back in there and do a little groveling because that might be the only way you'll save your job."

I have never seen another human being look so mad. Her eyebrows pinch, and her eyes narrow into slits. If she were a cartoon, her head would balloon to four times its normal size and wisps of smoke would come out of her ears.

I walk back to my car, spinning my keys around my finger like the cool guys do in movies.

"I'm going to prove you're helping those kids," Lindsey calls after me, her voice straining to be heard over the howling wind. "You might have arrested Shiloh to cover your tracks, and now I bet you think you can get her out, but I'm going to be watching you."

"By putting another tracker on my car?" I don't dare look back at her so she can't see how pale I am. "Did you get a warrant for that, or is that something else I need to tell the chief?"

"I swear." Her words are icy. "I'm going to get you thrown in jail."

The station door slams. The sound echoes in the near-empty parking lot.

My heart pounds so hard it clogs my throat. I need to get out of here. Dropping to my knees behind the car, I run my hand over the bumper. The surface is cold and rough against the pads of my fingers. In a matter of seconds, I find the tracking device hidden just out of view.

I rip it off the bumper and crush it under my boot. The plastic casing shatters. I stomp again, smashing the thing until the wires stick up at odd angles and sparks wink at me. Kicking the tangled mess of wires and plastic onto the mulch bed, I get into my car and drive away.

I drum my fingers on the steering wheel and try to remember how to breathe. The weight of the situation bears down on me, making it almost impossible to catch my breath. Shiloh is in jail.

Lindsey is out for blood. She knows I was helping Shiloh. Whether that's a lucky guess or good policing instincts, I don't know, but she's the best officer on the force, so I'd put my money on the latter.

What does this mean for me now? Lindsey said she's going to be watching me. She wants to prove I'm helping Shiloh, which means the smart thing for me to do would be to lie low and not do anything that makes her suspicious, but I can't do that. Shiloh doesn't deserve to stay in jail. I used to blame her for what happened to me. I spent so much time when I was on benmjöl hating her, but at the end of the day, my death wasn't her fault. I'd only known her a few weeks. I didn't have to help her look for Max if I didn't want to. I made my choice. So I can't leave her alone in there. She has no one, and she must be so scared. I couldn't live with myself if I didn't at least try to clear her name. And on top of it all, Jonah's still high on foolery. There's a warrant out for his arrest, and Francesca has nobody looking out for her. They need me.

I hate everything about this. I didn't want to die, but if I had gotten a 30-second trailer of what my new life would be like when Francesca was strangling me, I don't know if I would have gone through with it.

I'll just have to be smart if I want to keep Lindsey from following me. I book myself a room at a Holiday Inn Express, where I'm finally able to get out of the uniform that has been threatening to drown me in my own sweat. I turn on the shower and make the water as hot as it will go. The sound of rushing water drowns out the car horns outside. I step under the stream and audibly wince as the burning droplets hit my skin. The scalding water makes me feel weak and small, but one glance in the mirror through the fogged-up glass tells me I'm neither of those things. Randall Zweering is everything Miles Barot-Renaud was not. Tall. Broad-shouldered. Muscular. Dare I say handsome? In my old body, I used to dream of being built like this instead of the lanky and badly-strung puppet I used to be, but it's hard to enjoy it when this body is not mine. Being happy with the way I look feels wrong, so I focus on scrubbing the grime from my arms and face with the citrus-scented soap.

I change into the everyday clothes I threw in the duffel bag filled with weapons in case something like this happened. Every part of me wants to collapse in that bed and stay there for the rest of my life, but I can't sleep until I know if Francesca and Jonah are OK, so I throw on a baseball cap, brew myself a cup of instant coffee from the mini bar, and walk out the door.

Fiona never told me which hospital she was going to. Unfortunately for me but fortunately for the people of Cincinnati, there's more than one hospital in the city, which means I need to go between a couple of them to see if Francesca is there. In an ideal world, I could lie under that hotel comforter and call each place, but I'm too tired to stay awake if I lie down.

By the time I get to Marchand Memorial Hospital, I have finished my tiny cup of coffee. It did nothing to revive me. Not even coffee can bring you back to life when you're half-dead.

I stroll up to the woman at the main desk. I'm still wearing my sunglasses, so I take them off.

"Good morning," I say, reciting the words I'd rehearsed on my walk here. "I'm looking for my missing sister and I'm wondering if you could tell me if she's at this hospital."

"Sure, I can help you with that." The woman moves her bleached hair to one side of her neck. I catch a whiff of hairspray lingering around her. "What's your sister's name?"

"Francesca Russo," I say. "She's fifteen, and has black curly hair … or actually, it's white now, and she looks older than fifteen, but that's because her skin got wrinkled and started to sag." I try to pull myself together. "Is she here?"

There is a sluggish moment of silence as the woman looks it up on the computer.

"Mm-hmm," she says. "She was brought into our emergency room last night and is now in the ICU."

"Can I see her?"

"General visiting hours don't start until nine, but if you'd like, I can print you out a pass and you can wait until then."

I glance down at my watch. It's only ten minutes until nine. "I can do that."

She asks me for a photo ID. I clam up since I bet all the visitors IDs are on record and Lindsey could find out that I was here, but I don't think she'd look here, and I need to go see Francesca.

I hand the woman Zweering's driver's license. She examines it, her fingers brushing against the laminated surface. I can't tell if her expression is suspicion or something else.

"We're half-siblings," I say, hoping that will be enough to justify why "Russo" and "Zweering" sound nothing alike.

I give her a winning smile, painfully aware of how tense the muscles in my cheeks are. She smiles back at me, then hands me a paper pass along with my ID.

"Second floor, down the hallway on your right," she says. "You can't miss it."

The elevator moves so slowly that standing in it feels like it's physically aging me. A woman stands beside me holding flowers. Peonies. Their sweet fragrance mingles with the sterile smell of antiseptic. When the elevator dings, I walk out, following the instructions to find a reception area with plain blue couches, fabric-backed chairs, and a TV on mute in the corner. The only other person here is a gray-bearded man in overalls and the kind of weathered skin you can only get from spending your life in the sun.

I wonder if any of the others are in this hospital. Phil and the house sitter are probably here. Talulah, too. Or, I mean, whichever ghost is possessing her body.

Could Jonah be here as well? I doubt it. He had so much foolery in his system that the doctors would have brought him straight to the psych ward.

In ten minutes, a doctor comes up to me. A stethoscope dangles around her neck, glinting against the overhead lights.

"Are you here for Francesca Russo?" she asks, and I nod. "Are you the brother?" I nod again. "Do you have a parent here?"

"It's just me." The words stick in my mouth like glue.

The doctor nods, her expression understanding, and gestures down the hall. "Right this way."

I follow her into a patient room and past the bed of an unconscious middle-aged man on life support. I have a mental picture of what I'm expecting Francesca to look like, but when the doctor pulls back the curtain, all the air leaves my lungs.

Francesca is lying in a hospital bed, hauntingly still. Her eyes are closed. A pale blue gown is draped over her body, and every inch of exposed skin is covered in tape and bandages. A breathing tube runs into her mouth. A big machine like the one I had in the hospital after being shot monitors every beat of her heart. Fluids run into her arm through an IV and a neck brace keeps her spine aligned, and white curls fan out over her shoulders. So much gauze covers her left hand that she looks like she's wearing a boxing glove, but only four fingertips stick out of it. In the harsh light, the wrinkles in her face look even more defined than they did in the basement.

My mouth drops open. I turn to the doctor, who is closing the door to her room behind us.

"She was unconscious when she arrived, and missing the ring finger on her left hand," she says. "It appeared to have been severed and field dressed. She's lucky we caught the infection in time."

The words "severed" and "finger" send a chill up my spine. Did Leonard do that to her? Even imagining how much pain she would have been in, or the ways he could have tortured her, makes it hard for me to speak. "Is she in a c-coma?"

"Francesca is in a comatose state, yes, which means she's unresponsive and unaware of her surroundings."

"What does that mean?" I ask, my voice trembling. "W-what are you g-going to do for her, now?"

"Her body is extremely weak, so we're trying to help her rebuild her strength by allowing her to rest and giving her plenty of fluids. We have placed her on life support to ensure her vital functions are maintained while her body recovers. Beyond that, I'm afraid there is not much else we can do."

My stomach drops. "What do you mean not much else you can do?"

"I'm so sorry," the doctor says. "All that's left to do at this point is to utter a prayer and hope that she wakes up."

4

FrANCeSCA

In my life, I have found myself stuck in quite a few unexpected places. In the trunk of my father's car while playing hide-and-seek. Underneath the living room couch when trying to retrieve a marble. But neither one of these places was as frightening as being trapped on the other side.

I scream Shiloh's name. My voice bounces off the trees, echoing back at me and sending a chill down my ghostly spine. I continue to call for Shiloh, again and again, but before long, my pleas begin to sound less like her name and more like screams.

A dense fog envelops me. One tree appears to lean closer to me. So does the one beside it. Branches reach out for me like fingers, eager to ensnare me and hold me here forever.

I will not let them.

With a tingling sensation spreading through my chest, I weave through the branches. Gray bark and charred lichen brush against my shoulders, somehow tangible and intangible at the same time. Small particles hover in the air and pass through my body as though I am not even here. There must be an end to this forest. If only there was a clue, some sort of signpost to help me escape, but the trees appear to go on forever.

I drift to a stop and cover my face with my hands. Every time I have ventured to the other side before, there has always been somebody in the real world to pull me back to reality. Shiloh yanked my head out of the cooking pot at the old farmhouse. Leonard always removed the brass helmet before I drowned, and the sudden rush of cold water would jolt me back to my senses.

Could I be … dead? Is that why I cannot wake up?

I glance down at my palms. They are pale and wispy, difficult to see, unlike those that belong to the other souls on this side of the veil who glow so brightly they could be lanterns in the shadows. I must not be dead. If I were, wouldn't I glow more brightly, as well?

Closing my eyes, I strain to hear any voice or sound coming from the real world. Something—anything—to indicate that I am still alive.

A beeping sound reaches my ear. It is mechanical. A manufactured echo against the silence of the forest. Its beats are rhythmic, almost as though it is beating in time with my heart.

A pang of recognition hits me. Oh my goodness. A heart monitor. That is what I am listening to. Miles had one connected to him when I went to visit him in the hospital. That must be where my body is. If I am connected to a machine, that means I am not dead.

I still need to return to my body. Leonard said he was going to kill my friends, and none of them will be expecting it because they believe he is dead. I imagine Leonard causing an engine malfunction in Miles's car, making it wrap around a telephone pole. I can nearly hear the screech of metal and smell the burning rubber. Leonard could leave the gas on in Shiloh's house when she is sleeping and make the entire structure go up in flames. All it would take is a simple shove to push Jonah through an upstairs window and onto his driveway. His bones would break. Blood would pour from the back of his head. And Evangeline …

Leonard will want revenge on her most of all, because he loved her, and she chose to be friends with me instead. The thought of her being in danger is like a punch in the stomach. The pain is sharp and very, very real.

I must warn them. They are all defenseless against Leonard. None of them can see souls, let alone touch them. Without me there to help, they are as good as dead already.

I calm my breathing, focusing on the numb rhythm of my chest rising and falling as I try to figure out where I am. Unfortunately, all the trees look alike and there is not one single soul in sight.

A car horn blares in the distance. I go toward it.

I glide through the colorless forest for a long time before the trees thin. The gaps between them become bigger, and I approach a narrow road, which I follow into what appears to be a fairly ordinary neighborhood. This place does not resemble any place I have been before on the other side. I would have assumed I would bring Leonard's soul to his childhood home, but this more closely resembles Bethany, although with fewer cornfields.

In the distance, there is a loud trumpeting sound. I pause.

Is that …? No, that could not be an elephant. This is a heavily populated area, not the plains where I found Ola.

The noise sounds again. Curiosity propels me to the end of the road, where a gasp catches in the back of my throat.

A park stretches over multiple city blocks. There is a big archway hanging over the entrance, decorated with a banner reading: "DURAND BROS CIRCUS."

This must be their winter quarters. There is no big tent, or banners advertising shows. I do not experience smells the same way on the other side, it is as though my brain tells me what things should smell like as I see them, but sounds … there are so many of them here. The rumble of train cars. Loud conversations, and booming laughter. The out-of-tune carousel music makes me want to cover my ears. So many souls whip around me that it is difficult to know what to pay attention to.

There is a big wooden barn with slats that appear to be peeling off. Pens caging animals of all shapes and sizes. A train that stretches all the way to the horizon.

A pair of dead-eyed white horses with feathers between their ears walk past me. I reach out to touch the closest one. Its silky mane makes my fingertips tingle.

Something hard slams against my shoulder. "Out of the way!" a male voice barks.

A man rushes past me as if running away from something. I glance over my shoulder to find a horse carriage trotting toward me at a rapid clip. I roll out of its path moments before misty hooves crush the place I had just been occupying.

A cage on wheels rolls past me. There is a bear inside it, hunched over with its mouth and tongue hanging open like a panting dog. The bear does not glow with the same brightness that Ola did. It is dull. Not like Ola has been.

Could the animals here not be the real souls of animals, but echoes of the surroundings, like the cars and houses? I do hope so, because this is not a good way to spend eternity.

Is this place all that awaits people on the other side? Do happy places on the other side simply not exist?

The bear in the trailer rolls away. I cover my ears, hoping it will drown out that awful music and make it easier for me to think, but my hands do nothing to stop the melody.

Is there a gate back to the real world here? I have found gates hiding in the most peculiar of places, but I am not sure where to begin to look for one here.

The soul of an old man stands in front of one of the animal enclosures, staring at the giraffes. I glide up to him.

"Excuse me, sir," I say. "Do you happen to know which city we are in?"

The man turns to look at me. His gray beard is thin and shaped like a triangle. One side of his skull is caved in, like his head is made of Play-Doh and has been dropped by accident.

"This here?" he asks.

"Yes, sir."

"This here's Cincinnati." He snorts. "Least what's left of it."

Oh. When I brought Leonard's soul across the veil, I must have gone to the place where he died. Shiloh killed him in that old house he was keeping me prisoner in, which means …

I raise my gaze to the houses across the road from the park. One is much taller than the others. Green shingles stick out almost horizontally from its sides. The entire house is lopsided, but it is unclear whether that is a product of shoddy construction or being on the other side.

I point at it. "Whose house is that?"

The man follows my attention. "In my day, that place belonged to Joseph Durand."

"Do you know of a Leonard Gailis?" I say. "Has he ever lived there?"

"Not in my day," he says.

"What about in the past week or so?"

He looks me up and down, then returns his focus to the giraffe. "I've heard rumblings."

Something flutters in my stomach. Perhaps bringing Leonard through to the other side tore open a passageway.

I thank the man for his time and speed across the road, dodging the automobile and pausing at the house's front door. I have still not grown accustomed to moving through objects, so I close my eyes and remind myself that it is not solid before going inside.

A cool tingling sensation passes through me, but my form finds its shape again quite quickly. I pause in the foyer. Every one of the lights is off, but I can see just fine in the shadows. My surroundings rush back to me piece by piece. The black-and-white checkerboard floor tiles. The carved wooden staircase with its burgundy carpet and creaking joints. The dusty crystal chandelier above my head.

This is the right house.

A shudder passes through me. Being back here makes me sick to my stomach, but I must stay focused.

The sound of piano keys floats in from the living room,

tinkling like the sound stars would make. I pass through the wall toward the sound.

A girl sits at a grand piano, stroking the keys with a careful tenderness that only a musician would possess. She has her chin tucked down and her head tilted to the side so that her dark ringlets fall into her eyes. I recognize the song. It is the one that Dorothy sings at the beginning of *The Wizard of Oz*. My mother used to sing it to me when I was a little girl.

But this girl is not singing. She is playing the melody in a slow and melancholic fashion, causing all the hope to bleed out of the song.

I do not believe she sees me. In any other circumstance, I would not want to jar her out of her trance, but I am rather desperate for somebody to help me, so I clear my throat.

The girl shoots up from the bench. The melody cuts out mid-note, the sound echoing strangely in the air.

"I am so sorry to startle you," I say, "but I am trying to find a passageway to the real world. Do you know of any that have opened close to here?"

The girl furrows her eyebrows. She has rather stern features that make her look older than her puffy floral dress tells me she is. "A passageway?"

"An opening," I say. "To re-enter the world of the living."

"If I knew that, do you think I'd still be here?" She rolls her eyes and sinks back down onto the bench, the old wood not making a sound under her weightless figure.

I open my mouth to ask her another question, but she plays the melody again. Her fingers plod along the keys.

"Please," I say, straining to be heard over the music. The girl plays louder. "I am only trying to return to my friends—"

She plays a deep discord and looks up as if to tell me not to talk to her anymore. I have seen that expression enough times in my life to understand she will not help me. I will need to find an opening myself.

I rush back into the foyer, pulling photo frames off the walls and throwing them on the floor. Each clatter echoes through the empty space. I go to the kitchen, ripping pots and pans off the stove and throwing them into the air, watching them tumble upward in the opposite direction that gravity would usually take them. Used tea bags sit on the countertop. I am not sure who could have used them. Evangeline told me that souls cannot eat. Even if they could, nothing tastes like anything here. I go inside the oven, open the kettle, and even rush into the horrible cellar and peer into each of the cardboard boxes, but there are no membranes between the worlds to be found.

My breathing quickens. The sensation of cold air rushing in and out of my nonexistent lungs makes me feel as though creepy-crawly things are scuttling over my arms.

Perhaps there is a place to get through in the forest where I first appeared. I retrace my steps as quickly as possible, scouring the trees and the bulbous plants that resemble cabbage to search for a passageway, but there is nothing. I cannot be trapped here. I must warn Shiloh that Leonard is coming for her. Leonard has taken enough from my friends. I will not let him kill them when I am here and can do nothing about it.

An unusual piece of bark catches my eye. It bulges out from the side of the tree and pulses as though it were alive. With desperate fingers, I grab hold of the slippery bark and peel it away, revealing a wormhole embedded in the tree.

It is no bigger than a coaster. I press my eye to the membrane and peer through the veins stretching across it. All I can see are trees. They are made of colorful yellows and browns, with no particles hanging in the air or rotting bark peeling off the trunks.

Could I even fit through this opening? Gather the strength to squeeze myself back into my world through this tiny aperture like some sort of spectral toothpaste?

I push my fingers against the elastic membrane. It stretches like a sheet of plastic wrap, but does not break. I pinch the spongy film between my fingers and try to rip it apart, but it slips from my grip and snaps back into place. Using my mind, I try to puncture a hole through it, but all I can do is get the membrane to wobble.

There is a rustling sound behind me. I turn to find the soul of an old woman hovering a couple of feet off the ground.

"Did you find a way through?" she whispers.

"There is a membrane here," I say, "but I cannot get it to open."

With a sigh, she sinks onto the cabbage and settles among the muddy roots, sending up a small billow of particles. "I wonder how long we'll have to wait this time."

A knot of dread forms in the pit of my stomach. "How long do you usually have to wait for openings to form?"

"God, it can be years, and that's if they open at all, but what's there that's better to do? Watch those fake animals?"

She trains her eyes on the wormhole, and a resigned expression comes over her face like she is preparing to wait for a long time. I do not have time to wait. I certainly do not have time to wait years. Leonard could have found a way back to the real world by now. I did not think there were many ways to escape from the other side, but Leonard presumably knows more about the other side than I do. Perhaps he can open gates himself, or perhaps there is a special way to find them, like using the map that the Soothsayer had in her circus trailer when we first met her.

Something occurs to me. Something I cannot believe I had not thought of before.

The Soothsayer could tell me herself.

I imagine she would know how to get back to the real world. It is an indisputable fact that she knows a lot about souls because she talks to them in her glass ball.

Wilma Robinson is dead, so she must be here, on the other side. Perhaps her soul is still in the place she died. With a newfound sense of hope, I say goodbye to the waiting soul and soar off back toward the road.

5

Francesca

As it turns out, the other side is not above abiding by earthly traffic rules. I would have imagined being able to bypass traffic or the rules of the road would be one of the few good things about being a soul, but I am coming to discover there are not many good things about the other side.

I wander through this otherworldly city for quite a while in search of a highway. Even though my surroundings resemble the real world, this is not the version of the world as I know it. The road signs are confusing. Everything appears to be dated, as though it is from a time different from my own. I remember Ella Ruggles explaining how the other side exists on top of our world like a piece of plastic wrap that has been laid on it. Perhaps that is what is happening here, with every time period laid out on top of the previous one like the layers of an onion, and I am in the layer belonging to an older era. I wonder if souls are trapped inside their own onion layers, or if they can move between them. They must move between them. Usually, a person's life spans multiple time periods and is not limited to only one.

Is the other side a real place? It must be real if every soul comes here. Unless it is an imaginary place shared by everybody's imagination. I am not sure such a thing could exist, but simply because something is imaginary does not mean it is not real.

After quite a long time of searching, I find a sign that says Columbus and follow it to a main road. Ghostly automobiles hum along the concrete ribbon in an orderly procession. I glide above them, so quickly that the cars blur together. The wind whips through me, but I am not cold. It is as though I am part of the air. Or as if I am flying.

Because that is exactly what I am doing. I had been so focused on getting out of the other side as fast as possible each time I had visited before that I had not been paying attention to the fact that I could quite literally soar through the air. I extend my arms in either direction. Laughter bubbles out of me, and I do a somersault like I used to do while swimming as a child.

There are other souls hovering above the cars. Dreary-eyed and gloomy, they drag themselves forward with their arms hanging down. Some have their mouths open. For some silly reason, they remind me of fish.

One woman does not appear to be moving at all. She is still as other souls move around her.

I drop down in front of her. "Hello, ma'am. Would you like me to help bring you along?"

The woman stares through me. There is no acknowledgment that I said anything.

I am trying to think of other ways to help her when a distant beep of a heart monitor pulls me back to reality. I must find the Soothsayer. And quickly. So I abandon the ghostly woman and charge forward as fast as I can in the city's direction.

By the time I reach Columbus, an odd feeling of depletion has taken hold of me. I am not exactly tired, just quite a lot weaker, like my ghostly presence is evaporating. Perhaps the old woman back there was tired. I wonder if people rest on this side of the veil. The souls in the cemetery do not sleep. Do souls sleep here?

I do not have time to find out, so I glide upward to get a better view of the city and it unfurls below me. I am not very good with maps, but I recognize the fairground where I came to see the Soothsayer perform with the circus not too long ago.

I drop into the fairground and drift among its perimeter. On the day I met the Soothsayer, it was crawling with activity, but now, the entire place is empty. I am trying not to get too worried when something shimmers in an old building's windowpane. I stop. The glass ripples, like the surface of a still forest pool, and I am not the only figure reflected in it. A man with long hair and a graphic T-shirt is reflected behind me. So is a blonde woman jumping up and down in front of a stage, pumping her fist in time with an unheard beat. But when I look over my shoulder, there are no such souls around.

How peculiar. I reach out to touch the window. My fingertips pass through the glass, so I push my entire body through, feeling a cooling sensation wash over me as if I am passing through a liquid curtain.

I emerge into the fairground of my memory. Or, at least, as similar as anything on the other side can be to its real world counterpart. I am not at all sure how the reflection transported me between time periods, but I am too nervous about finding the Soothsayer to think too much about it. A big music stage stretches across the empty field. Bone-rattling bass and guitar thrum from the speakers. The air around me vibrates from the rhythmic pulse of unseen drumbeats. I remember disliking how much screaming there was in this music when I heard it in the real world, but it is even worse on the other side because covering my ears does not prevent me from having to listen to it.

I pass a see-through stand selling alcohol, but nobody is inside it, because souls do not eat. The grass on the main part of this field has been reduced to nubs, which I find odd because souls glide above the ground and do not tread on the grass.

There is a big top tent beside the parking lot. The knot in my chest undoes itself. That is where the Soothsayer died, and so that must be where I can find her.

I glide past the posters of the three-eyed faces with their mouths and tongues hanging out and pass through the flaps of the tent. It is much quieter in here. The canvas is solid. I cannot see through it, which must mean it is keeping out some of the noise, but there is not a soul in here.

I slip underneath the tent flap and go to the buses parked behind. In real life, the sun beat down on us as we walked toward the trailer, but now, there is no sun, and there is mud all over the ground. The dressing room trailer where we met the Soothsayer has rusted, and it is bent out of shape like it's been beaten with an enormous hammer.

This is the place where the Soothsayer died. Right here, in this very trailer.

I did not see her body after she died. Jonah was the one who found her, but his description of her was enough to burn an image into my brain and cement it there forever.

She had knitting needles sticking out of her eyes.

I wonder if Leonard stuck them in there before or after cutting her throat. I sure hope it happened after, but knowing Leonard, he would have wanted her to feel it.

There is a burning sensation behind my eyes, like I am about to cry. I know souls can cry because I have seen it happen, but if I am going to talk to the Soothsayer, I cannot cry. I must be strong if I have any chance of convincing her to help me.

Before I can talk myself out of it, I enter the trailer.

It is dark. So dark that it is immediately clear that there are no souls in here. Where could the Soothsayer be?

I close my eyes, doing my best to ignore the rapid pounding of my heart. All I can hear is a distant moan, and a buzzing sound so quiet that I could be imagining it.

I close my eyes even tighter, doing my best to quiet my thoughts and allow myself to sink onto the floor of the trailer. I am already numb. I can feel nothing but the texture of the uneven ground and the chill I can never quite seem to shake, even though I do not feel cold.

Where are you, Wilma?

I listen hard for her. Perhaps harder than I have ever listened for anything before.

Music blares into my ears, making me jump in fright. It's scratchy. Disjointed. Like monkeys banging on instruments.

Not this again. I open my eyes. The music quiets, but I can still hear it in the distance, like the faint memory of a nightmare that lingers after you wake up. Only it isn't a memory. I can hear it.

I go back across the short grass. My eyes settle on a band playing instruments on the stage I passed only minutes ago.

Perhaps the Soothsayer is over there. It is unclear why she would want to be over there. Even from where I stand, the clashing melody hurts my ears, but I venture through the crowd of souls anyway and sure enough, I find her, standing far too close to the stage and watching the band bang on instruments that appear to be falling apart. Or perhaps the band is breaking them on purpose. I wonder if they are the same band as the ones that were playing on the day of the Soothsayer's death. It cannot be, since I doubt they all died on the same day the Soothsayer did, but they sure do look like they would fit into that world.

The Soothsayer is wearing the same clothes she was on the day I met her. A ragged shawl hangs over her shoulders like a bat's wing. Her dreadlocks run down her back and shoulders like pieces of fluffy white yarn.

I come up beside her and clear my throat loud enough to be heard over the mournful trumpet. "Excuse me, Ms. Wilma?"

On the day that I met her, she had told me not to call her the Soothsayer, and instead to call her Wilma. Calling a woman of her age and mysticism by her first name felt strange to me, so I chose Ms. Wilma instead.

Ms. Wilma looks at me. All the air leaves my lungs as if somebody punched me in the stomach. There are gaping holes where her eyes should be, like they are mere sockets in her skull.

I try not to appear shocked because I do not wish to be rude. I suppose it makes sense that she would still have the holes in her eyes, as the marks of trauma stay with a soul if they died a traumatic death. If Ms. Wilma's death was not traumatic, I am not sure what trauma is.

She does not say a word, so I decide to speak first.

"You may not remember me," I say, "but my name is Francesca. I came to speak to you about Leonard on the day that you … er …"

She smiles. "On the day that he killed me?"

I am not sure what to say to that. "Well …"

"It is all right, darling," she says. "You can say the word. I won't be offended."

Blood streams down from her empty eye sockets. I move closer to her, and her head follows me.

I cannot stop the question before it leaves my lips. "Does it hurt?"

"Not anymore."

"But you can still see me," I say. "How?"

"That all depends on what you mean by see. If you mean do I know you are a girl of no more than sixteen, that you have white hair that looks like it belongs to a woman my age, and that you wear an expression on your face like you are maybe a bit afraid, then yes, darling. I can see you."

The band stops playing for a moment, only to pick up playing a similarly unpleasant tune as if they had never stopped. Ms. Wilma sways to the beat of the otherworldly music.

Listening to it is beginning to hurt my head. I do not understand how she can. "Do you find this music pleasant?"

"Lord no," Ms. Wilma says, "but it's more interesting than listening to nothing."

"I would prefer to listen to nothing."

"Surely you did not seek me out to criticize my taste in music," she says. "Come, darling, out with it."

"I need your help to return to the real world."

She furrows her brow. "You mean to tell me you're needing to bring yourself back to life?"

"No, because I am not dead."

I tell her about the astral projection, and how I can travel to the other side without dying. I share how I tried to find an opening in the forest, and how I could not tear through the membrane. When I tell her about Leonard's threat to kill my friends, bitter laughter erupts from her.

"That boy does not know when to quit." Blood runs into her mouth and stains her teeth. Because it has no color, it looks an awful lot like tar. "Am I mistaken in assuming that you've already tried to rip through the barrier with your hands?"

"I tried, but I could not break through."

"That must be because you are not rightly dead." Ms. Wilma drifts backward, away from the stage. "Come, darling, come with me."

I do as I am told, more than happy to escape the terrible music. Ms. Wilma goes across the fairgrounds and passes through the wall of her dressing room trailer. I have passed through objects that appear to be solid a few times already today, but it is still very strange, so I close my eyes out of habit before assuming my form again inside.

Ms. Wilma opens an old leather chest. "Since you cannot get through the membrane yourself, your only option is to wait for a gate to appear, but you don't have enough time for that, especially since I'd bet that bastard has already broken his way through. I can open a gate for you. Or at least, I could while I was alive, but if Leonard can retain his capabilities in death, then I'd assume I can too. I just need to find that book."

"Which book?"

Ms. Wilma lowers her face through the chest as if peering through the surface of a pool, then moves on to a flimsy cardboard box. I do not understand how she can see, but she can, if not through her eyes, then in some other way.

"What are you looking for?" I ask again.

"Soothsaying is an ancient art that can only be passed down

from mentor to apprentice, and our tomes hold the secrets of our trade," she says. "The binding procedures. The manipulation of the veil."

"Can anybody practice soothsaying?"

"Every seer must have the ear, like you and I have. Having the sight like you do is even better, but I do not have that power. In another life, you would have been quite the apprentice. You, my darling, contain more power in your pinky finger than I do in my entire body."

Ms. Wilma produces a book from the box. It is the size of a photo album, one of the big ones where the pictures take up entire pages, with a hard cover wrapped in black leather. Rot eats away at it, causing the edges to furl and peel away. I suspect the book would smell rather unpleasant if this were not the other side and I could still smell things.

"Our binding spell depends on manipulating the veil," Ms. Wilma says. "When a Seer binds a person's soul to her globe, she changes that soul's journey so that they no longer go through the veil when they die. Instead, they come straight to her globe. But if a soul goes rogue, there is a way for her to create an opening in the veil so she can retrieve them."

She lets go of the book. It hovers in the air as if sitting on an invisible music stand.

"I do hope the procedure is the same," she says, flipping through the crusty pages. "It's been a long time since I've done one of these, and I could send you to a layer of this place you would not want to go to."

She grabs my hand and pulls me closer to her. Her fingers are firm around mine. A chill runs up my arm.

"This ritual does not call for bloodletting," she says. "Some incantations in this book require blood or bone, but I wouldn't want to ask you for any more fingers."

She does not say it as a joke. I glance down at the stump where my finger used to be. One good thing about being on the other side is that my finger does not hurt so much anymore.

Ms. Wilma removes a cushion from the bench, revealing a

small patch of membrane underneath. She closes her eyes. Tilts her face back. Presses her palm against the wormhole.

She begins to chant. Her words speed up and blend into one another. I try to make out what she is saying, but she is talking too fast and muttering in a language I do not understand.

She chants faster. Wind whooshes around us like it is gathering us up in a small tornado. Her soul glows like a lantern in shadow, far brighter than any light I have ever seen. I am sure it would hurt my eyes if I had the ability to feel pain in the same way.

There is a sizzling sound. Ms. Wilma's palm burns against the membrane, causing white vapor to rise around her.

With a cry, she pushes down hard on the membrane and breaks through to the other side. I let go of her and rush over to see her pull her hand out of the hole she created. The sides of the membrane are curled and charred like Ms. Wilma set them on fire. A wave of something that feels an awful lot like nausea comes over me. I press my fist against my mouth, even though souls are incapable of throwing up.

Ms. Wilma opens her eyes. She is not glowing anymore.

"Lordy, it's been a while since I last did that," she says, shaking her hand out.

I have never seen anything like that before. "I thought magic was the stuff of stories."

"This is no magic, darling," she says. "There is energy lying dormant all around us. All I've done is harness it."

An uneasy feeling comes over me. "Does the book say anything about how to kill a soul?"

Ms. Wilma laughs. "Darling, you cannot kill a soul. It's not possible."

"What do you mean, it is not possible?"

"Nobody has ever done it," she says. "You cannot kill somebody who is already dead."

"So how am I supposed to stop Leonard?"

"If it were me, I would trap him," she says. "Put him in a box, throw away the key, and spend the rest of my days praying he never finds a way out. But darling, I am glad it is not me."

I peer through the scorched hole in the membrane. I can see sunlight streaking across a dusty floor.

"Go on," she says. "Go through and pray he never sends you back."

"Thank you for your help," I say. "Really, I cannot tell you how much I appreciate it."

She waves me away like she would rather not hear it. Closing my eyes, I drift to the opening and push my hand through it. I do not know how to fit my body through an opening that small, so I focus on going forward, and all at once, the world twists away.

Light presses against my closed eyes. I open them to find a much more real version of the dressing room trailer, sitting empty with the sun coming in through its small windows.

"Francesca."

I glance around for Ms. Wilma. It takes me a moment to find the hole in the couch, and I press my nose close to it so I can see through to her.

"Tread carefully, darling," she says, from the other side. "You never know what your friends could be hiding."

I am so startled by her words that it is a couple of seconds before I can reply. "What are you talking about?"

It is too late. The gap in the membrane disappears as the other side gobbles the Soothsayer up.

6

FrANCeSCA

I stare at the membrane for nearly a minute after the hole has closed.

What did the Soothsayer mean? Could my friends be hiding something from me?

It is not possible. I may not have known Shiloh for very long, but I have a feeling deep inside my stomach that she is a good person and would not do me any harm. She believed I could see souls when nobody else would. She came to rescue me from Leonard. After all we have gone through, she would not hide anything from me, especially not something that could put me in danger.

Neither would Miles. He is easily worried about things and does not seem like the kind of person to keep secrets. Jonah keeps many secrets, but he has a good heart, even though he would rather people not know it.

Could the Soothsayer have been talking about Evangeline?

I have known Evangeline for the shortest amount of time, but I feel as though I know her better than anybody else. She had been Leonard's best friend in the entire world until he accidentally killed her during his circus act and she faded to the other side. He had brought her back from the dead inside the body of a girl he kidnapped from my school, and she helped him in the beginning, but changed her mind once she learned about all the people he had killed. She betrayed him to help me. Even though she knew nothing about the modern world and had only known who I was for a couple of days, she turned on the only person she knew from her childhood and trusted me.

I remember how gentle her hands felt going through my hair when I was coming down from the foolery, or the warmth with which she comforted me when I was quaking with fear. In those quiet moments in the cage, only the two of us existed.

She would not hide anything from me. I do not believe it.

The Soothsayer must be wrong. I do not believe she can see into the future. I am not entirely sure how she can see into the past either, because souls trapped in her orb should not be capable of knowing what is going on outside of it. I must remain focused on returning to my friends instead of allowing the Soothsayer to unsettle me this way.

I glance around the dressing room trailer. On the other side, it had been void of any color or life, but the real version is full of color. Pallets of makeup and face paint lie open on the tables. Some of the open pots have dried out. Leather jackets and puffy clown pants have been draped over the backs of chairs. Only one mirror station is neat. I peer at the name tag on the glass: PHIL. I remember Phil. He was the older man who helped rescue me from the cellar. Oh dear, he must be extremely stressed, surrounded by all this mess.

There is a familiar name taped to the mirror beside the door. The Soothsayer's mirror has not been touched. Everything is exactly where it had been on the other side.

I stare into the mirror. My wispy figure flickers and glows brighter. I am much more visible than I was when I first came to the other side. Does that mean I am dying?

I must return to my body. And quickly.

I pass through the side of the trailer. There are no other

vehicles in the parking lot except for a red school bus with cartoons of circus performers painted on the side. Small clouds of dust billow across the asphalt, sending tiny pieces of gravel into the bus with small pinging sounds. This is quite an angry wind, but it does not appear to affect me. I do not feel the wind at all. Or the temperature.

I soar around to the front of the building, past a sign reading the Lazy-U Motel. I am trying to figure out where I could be when a woman walks out of a door, untangling her wet jet-black hair.

I recognize her immediately. She also helped rescue me from that big house. She is the woman who jumped through the roof with Jonah.

She is wearing different clothes from the ones she had on when I met her. Instead of the form-fitting black top and yoga pants resembling the ones certain women in Bethany wear to exercise, she now has on baggy jeans sitting right on her hips and a tiny jacket that shows a sliver of her stomach. She must have returned to the motel after the rescue. I am not sure why she is wearing this outfit when it is so windy outside. She must be extremely cold.

There is a tote bag in her hand, and a cell phone wedged between her ear and shoulder. She fishes a key out of her tiny jacket and unlocks a green car that is dented in a couple of places.

"What do you mean, weird activity?" she says into the phone. "How much activity can she do if she's in a coma?"

I drift closer to the woman, but her eyes pass over me as they roll up to the sky. She climbs into the car, and I pass through the passenger-side door, creeping close enough to the phone to hear the voice coming from the other end. It belongs to a man. Each one of his words blends into the last as he stutters and trips over his sentences. There is something familiar about the voice, but not familiar enough for me to know who is speaking.

"Slow down." The woman flips down the sunshade, puckering her lips in the vanity mirror and dabbing on some lip gloss. "Please speak slowly so my tired old lady brain can understand what you're saying."

"You need to come back," the man says. "The doctors are asking me questions I don't know the answers to. I'm trying to be the adult in this situation, but—"

"You *are* an adult."

"I'm not an adult," the man says. "Or at least not a real one. I need an adultier adult."

"You're not the only one who's stressed right now, okay? Phil just got out of surgery, and I had to run back here because I guarantee you one of the first things he's going to ask for when he wakes up is his Merino wool slippers, and I'm not going to show up empty-handed."

"Fiona, *please.*"

"I'm in the car right now, okay? I'll be there in an hour."

The woman, whose name must be Fiona, hangs up the phone and tosses it through my torso onto the passenger seat. She goes to put the key in the ignition, then pauses. Without warning, she lets out a high-pitched scream that makes me wish I could cover my ears, before hanging her head, running a hand down her face, and starting the car. She watches over her shoulder as she pulls out of the parking spot. The car rolls away, leaving me hovering above the asphalt.

I am too stunned to do anything for a couple of seconds but, before the small green vehicle can escape my sight, I go after it.

By the time we reach the hospital, I have the same depleted feeling I had when I traveled along the highway on the other side, as though my soul is evaporating faster than usual even though I do not exactly exist.

The green car pulls into a parking garage and winds up each level until Fiona finds a space beside the elevator. She hurries out of the car, her gait switching between an accelerated walk and a graceful half-jog. I follow her into the elevator, but instead of riding with her, the metal can goes down without me, leaving me hovering in the space it was just occupying. I must say, being a soul is rather discombobulating. I drop after it and poke my shoulders through the roof so I can see Fiona again because I must not lose sight of her.

The elevator stops. With a ding, the doors open, and I follow Fiona down a hallway with sad beige walls with no pictures on them. As soon as she enters the waiting area, a man rushes over to her. And he is not just any man.

He is Miles.

I did not recognize Miles at first when I saw him in the cellar, but I will not make that same mistake again. He does not look at all like the version of Miles he used to be. His new body is large and appears to be quite strong. It looks capable of lifting both Shiloh and me in each of his arms and carrying us for a very long time, which he certainly could not do before. He does look quite sleepy. He has traded his police uniform for a red T-shirt and striped athletic pants that appear to be soft but not very warm. Perhaps I was mistaken and it is not cold outside after all. I simply assumed it was chilly because of how angry the wind seemed, but I suppose the wind could have been playful. Simply because something is strong does not mean it is unkind.

Before he even speaks, I know it was Miles's voice I'd been listening to on Fiona's cell phone.

"Something is wrong with her," Miles says, pointing over his shoulder. "The heart monitor is going crazy."

Fiona wraps her tiny denim jacket around her torso. "Did you tell the doctors?"

Miles narrows his eyes in a way that appears to say, *Did you really need to ask me that question?* I can see his old face in this expression. It is the same one he used to give Jonah when Jonah asked him a silly question that Miles already knew the answer to. But the look is only there for a moment.

"The nurses are in there now." He takes a step back, beckoning Fiona to follow him. "Come on."

Miles leads Fiona down the hallway with long strides and gestures at an open door. I go in with them.

A man lies in a hospital bed. He is connected to so many machines that I did not know there were so many bodily functions to monitor. The faintest spot of light flickers inside his chest as though his soul is detaching from his body but has not done so yet.

Because Miles is not there to see the man, he goes around a pale blue curtain in the back of the room. I come to an ungraceful stop.

There is a body in a hospital bed. Or … no. Is it … could that be *my* body in the hospital bed?

The body in the bed does not resemble my body. Its hair is stark white. Wrinkles are etched into its papery skin. A breathing tube runs out of its mouth, connected to a gigantic machine that appears to be forcing air in and out of its lungs. If I did not know better, I would say this could be the body of Mrs. Lewis or somebody even older. Not mine.

But it is, so I go to it. A pain stops me. It stabs through my chest like a screwdriver being driven through my ribcage. I gasp, clutching at my chest even though nothing is there.

A high-pitched tone emits from one machine. The line goes flat.

Miles yells for help. Two nurses push a cart into the room, barking at Miles to get out of the way. He presses his back against the wall and wraps his arms around his stomach as he begins to breathe too fast.

I want to tell him that I am all right and there is no need to panic, but the pain in my chest is making it hard for me to move. The nurse's voices ring in my ears.

Bag her.

Start chest compressions.

Put the pads on her.

The pain turns into pressure. I let out a strangled cry. What is happening to me?

A nurse rubs two paddles together. As she places them on my

body's chest, I see a glimmer of light underneath its skin. My eyes narrow. I charge forward, gaping at the shimmering light worming around inside me. Oh my goodness. It is a soul.

There is a soul inside my body.

The soul shifts around. Raising my hands, I reach out to the soul with my mind. Once I feel the hum of energy against my palms, I close my fists and yank the soul toward me.

A ball of light shoots out of my body's chest. It rises above the nurses' heads, casting a harsh light on their hair. The soul stretches. A leg forms from the light. Then an arm. I watch as it assumes the shape of a human.

Oh no. No no no.

Guilherme glances around the room, wide-eyed, as if trying to figure out what has happened to him. He is a very small soul, with arms and legs hardly thicker than twigs and a big hole in the side of his head. Guilherme was one of the souls that Leonard asked me to bring back from the dead when he was keeping me prisoner in the house. On the other side, I found Guilherme in the center of a miserable scene of ridicule. He had a difficult life, and his afterlife did not bring him any peace. I understand why he was so excited about the possibility of having a second chance, but he was so focused on holding onto that chance that he fought my friends when they came to rescue me and nearly killed them, so Shiloh put an axe through his head. I thought he had gone back to the other side. Clearly, he did not.

His eyes find mine. They narrow into slits.

"You, you were supposed to be across the veil," he says in a heavy European accent. "How did you make the return?"

Before I can reply, Guilherme drops back toward my body. I stop him with my mind. He strains against me. Holding him makes my palms ripple and flicker, but I do not waver.

"Are you trying to possess my body?" I ask, my voice thin from the effort of keeping him at bay.

Guilherme spits at me. The glob disappears like a puff of

smoke. "Leonard, he told me that by taking hold, I could make your heart cease."

"Why would you do such a thing?"

"Because of you," he says. "My second chance … you took away. Leonard promised to repair what you had destroyed. He will give me one body of yours if I help in your killing, so that is what I will do."

He presses down toward me. His figure elongates and stretches. He is more powerful than I am. I curl my fingers with the effort to keep him at bay. I cannot let him go. If I release him, he will drop back into my body, and I will not be able to get inside. I am not even sure how to bring myself back from the dead. I have never done it before.

But I must do something. With a cry, I hurl Guilherme through the window. Glass showers around him as he breaks through it and flies out of the building.

Every person in the room stops what they are doing and stares at the window, which, as far as they can see, has shattered of its own accord. I do not stop to stare at anything.

I rush to my body and sink down inside it, stretching out my arms and legs so they are mostly in line with the corpse the way I have seen Leonard do many times before.

Please, disappear.

Nothing happens. I do not have much time before Guilherme returns, but the nurses are still looking around at the broken window.

"Use the paddles!" I shout, even though they do not hear me. "Please, you must hurry!"

One of them charges the paddles and places them on my chest. Guilherme appears in the window, face distorted through the shards of broken glass jutting out from the frame.

A jolt of pain runs through me. My back arches, and everything goes dark.

I open my eyes. Blurry faces hover above me. I blink twice to dispel the haze, and little by little, I begin to make out the features of the nurses. A blonde girl with a small dimple on her upper lip. A middle-aged woman with a mole in between her eyebrows. I search for Miles. In a couple of seconds, his brand-new face appears. His unfamiliar eyes brim with hope.

"Francesca?" he asks. "Can you hear me?"

"Hi," I try to say, but there is something blocking my throat. I gag against it, then cough.

One nurse tells me to hold still. Miles grips my hand so firmly that I cannot tell if he is doing it to comfort himself or me, but I am glad he is here just the same.

"Okay." A nurse rests a hand on my back. "I need you to let out a strong exhale for me on the count of three. Ready, honey? One … two …"

I breathe out on three. She pulls the tube out of my throat, and I cough hard, my throat burning as I buckle over with the effort. Miles wraps his arms around me and guides my head onto his massive shoulder. His arms are big and heavy. Being in them makes me feel safe.

"Oh my God," he says. "You were … I thought you were gone."

I was not gone. Even if I had died, I would not have been gone, but that does not matter right now. I am alive. He is alive.

Perhaps not for long. I release him and glance around the room. It looks the same as the one I was in before, but it is not because the window is intact. There is no glass on the floor. An old woman sits in the bed beside mine, spooning red Jell-O into her mouth and swallowing it without chewing because she does not have any teeth. I wonder if there is any pudding here I could eat.

I curse myself for being so easily distracted. Pudding does not matter when Guilherme is here, trying to kill me. His soul is nowhere to be seen, but that does not mean that he is not somewhere in this hospital.

I grip Miles's arm. He must see the look in my eyes because his smile disappears.

"You are in danger," I say. "All of us … Leonard is going to kill us."

Miles's eyebrows draw together. They are dark and rather bushy, like caterpillars. "I thought Leonard was dead. Shiloh said—"

"Being a ghost does not mean he cannot kill us," I say. "Have you sensed anything unusual around you today?"

"Aside from the window breaking out of nowhere and getting us moved to a different room?"

"I smashed that window."

"Of course you did." Miles exhales a sharp puff of air from his nose. I suppose he has witnessed enough unbelievable things that nothing surprises him anymore. He thinks for a moment, but shakes his head. "Nothing has happened to me."

"And to Jonah?"

"Jonah is at the motel," Miles says. "Fiona said he was sleeping when she left this morning, and I feel like she would have mentioned something like a ghost attack."

"What about Shiloh?" I ask. "Is she with Jonah at this motel as well?"

Miles's eyes widen. A stab of regret runs through me. Oh. I should have thought before speaking. Shiloh's feelings for Jonah are not something Miles enjoys hearing about, but the look in his eyes is genuine fear. He would not look afraid if he were simply uncomfortable with Shiloh's feelings for Jonah.

"Why do you look like somebody has told you that you have sprouted a tail?" I ask.

"Shiloh's in jail," Miles says, and my stomach drops as though the bed has disappeared and I am falling through the air. "If Leonard's going to kill us, I bet he's going to start with her."

7

Shiloh

Once I'm done with breakfast, two officers come to bring me to the infirmary. I get my medical evaluation done and the nurse says—surprise, surprise—I still have a concussion, but that I got lucky and didn't inhale that much smoke from the fire. She gives me Tylenol and has me sit there breathing from an oxygen mask for a couple of hours until she says I can go.

I feel better after doing that, so I have no problem going right to sleep. I sleep for the rest of the morning. Or, at least, what feels like it. There's no clock on the wall, which makes it impossible to keep track of time, but the assholes who control the light switches keep them on for the entire time.

I wake up to banging on my door and voices barking at me to put my arms where they can see them. Rubbing the back of my neck to ease the tension in my muscles, I haul my bruised body off the mattress pad and lean my palms against the concrete. Rough hands snap cuffs around my wrists and push me out of my cell, through the holding area and through the door that keeps us in here. My toes drag against the speckled floor tiles. I'm too tired to pick up my feet or worry about where they might be taking me. That is, until the officers open the door to what looks like an interrogation room, and I forget what it feels like to be tired.

Dad stands up. I haven't seen him since the day of the homecoming dance when the FBI agents arrested him, but he hasn't changed at all. He still has buzzed hair, that beer belly, and hands big enough to crush my skull like an egg until my brain oozes out like yolk between his fingers.

My knees jam up. I try to back up into the officers, but they block the door. He doesn't say my name. He doesn't fake concern. I'm not sure that he could. All he can do is stare at me and eventually say: "What happened to your face?"

I go for blood. "You mad it wasn't you this time?"

Dad winces. Like my words actually hurt him. Like Dad is capable of feeling real human emotion.

The officers take off my handcuffs and walk out the door, leaving us alone in here. So much for protection.

"Shiloh." Dad's voice is measured like he's doing his best not to raise it. "What the hell happened to your face?"

"I got punched."

Dad sits down across from me and braces his forearms on the wooden table. "By whom?"

Why does he want to know? So he can drive back to Bethany with the lights in his squad car flashing and arrest Richie Russo for bashing his daughter's face in? Imagining it feels ridiculous. Because it is ridiculous. Dad doesn't care about my face being punched in because he's done it himself more than once.

But he's looking at me with so much worry that, suddenly, my fear doesn't feel so real anymore. He won't do anything to me in here. Not with the officers right outside and the security camera up in the corner. I cross my arms over my chest and narrow my eyes at him.

"How can you even be here right now?" I snap. "Mom got a restraining order against you."

I hear someone clear their throat. For the first time, I notice the man standing behind Dad.

He's old. Or old-ish, but he looks like one of those guys who's trying too hard to age well. He has silver hair, a fancy-looking watch, and is wearing a three-piece suit that looks professionally tailored. There's an amused expression on his face. Not like he's trying to psychoanalyze a potential murderer, but instead like he's trying to psychoanalyze a hamster. He's not scared of me.

I pull a face at him. Even though I don't know who he is, I'm not scared of him either.

"If I may," he begins, side-eying Dad. "The restraining order your mother petitioned for was a temporary ex-parte order which expired after ten days. Your mother failed to appear at the hearing scheduled for last Thursday, so the judge dismissed the case."

I blink at him. His words bounce around in my brain for a second before hitting me. My fists curl into my baggy pants.

Mom didn't *fail to appear at the hearing*. She was busy. Being murdered.

But saying that won't help me. The man reaches his hand out to me. I ignore it, so he turns the gesture into a shrug.

"My name is Caleb Caldwell." He takes a seat next to Dad. "I'm a defense attorney, and a longtime friend of your father's."

"He was the best running back the Bucks have ever seen," Dad says.

Caleb waves off the compliment, but a slight upturn at the corner of his mouth makes it clear that he appreciated it. "I'm sorry to hear about what happened to you," he tells me. "I've reviewed the details of your case and find it absolutely criminal."

My stomach knots. Absolutely criminal is not the way you want to hear a lawyer describe your case. "So you're saying I'm screwed?"

"No," he says. "I'm saying they're screwed for locking you up in here."

The knot in my stomach loosens. Caleb has to see the relief on my face, because he smiles.

"Miss Oleson." Caleb pauses. "Can I call you Shiloh?" I nod. "Shiloh, you shooting that man was self-defense. Period. End of story. The man you shot kidnapped and tortured your brother, and you shot him because you were afraid for your brother's life. Isn't that right?"

Not exactly. Leonard had just told me he'd killed Max when I shot him. I pulled the trigger because I was angry. But the idea of going back to my cell and waiting around for Leonard's ghost to come and kill me sends a chill down my spine. I can't do that. I can't stay here. So I nod.

Caleb mirrors my nod. "You saved your brother's life. You're a good sister, and your brother is very lucky to have you."

His words fill my entire body with warmth. Until I catch Dad nodding along, and I clench my teeth.

Dad came for me. He came, and he brought a lawyer. Why? I guess this public show of family love and support could help his case against the abuse, but is there anything more? Could there be anything more? I doubt it. What kind of father would he have looked like if he had left me in here?

"Your father is not pressing charges for the borrowed firearm," Caleb says. "Honestly, I'd be shocked if the DA prosecutes you for any of this."

"But ..." This doesn't make any sense. "Detective Babin accused me of shooting my boyfriend ... or I guess ex-boyfriend. Miles."

"Kyle Babin is awful at his job," Caleb says, side-eying Dad because he just insulted one of his officers, but Dad doesn't look like he cares. "I'd guess he was trying to scare you. Miles Barot-Renaud gave a statement to the police telling them this Patrick De Beauvoir was the one who shot him, not you, so this will actually help your case. As for the other charges, there's not a shred of physical evidence."

I'd be lying if I said I wasn't relieved to hear him say that. "I broke Davey's knee."

Caleb laughs, turning to Dad. "Oh, Ernest, you weren't mincing your words about this one. She's a doll." He turns back to me. "I've been doing this a long time, Shiloh, and have gotten much guiltier people out of far worse charges. You might have to do a few hours of community service, pick up a little trash or walk someone's dog, but that's the worst-case scenario. You're a good girl from a good family, and those young men are bullies who all have preexisting records. In the grand scheme of things, this is a blip. I'll have you out of here and back with your family before you can get used to the food."

I try to ignore the bubble of warmth that bursts in my chest. I'm overwhelmed by how much I want to trust Caleb. I don't know if I have ever wanted to trust someone more in my entire life. When I told Miles to arrest me, I put on a brave face, but the idea of being locked in this place for the rest of my life for shooting the man who kidnapped, tortured, starved, and murdered my little brother is too much for me to accept.

Is it possible that, for once in his life, Dad came through for me?

"Okay," I say, trying not to let the desperation into my voice. "Thank you."

Caleb smiles the cool and confident smile of someone who's not used to losing.

"All right." Caleb takes out a ballpoint pen from the inside pocket of his suit. "Your detention hearing is set for Wednesday. That's when we'll learn which charges, if any, the prosecutors intend to pursue. But I'm confident I can put an end to this before we get to that stage. I'll find out who's assigned to your case and discuss the charges with them, but in order to do that, I'm going to need you to tell me everything that happened to you in as much detail as you can. Remember, I'm on your side, Shiloh, and I'm going to get you out of this, so you don't need to hide anything from me. Tell me everything you feel will help your case."

He uncaps his pen and holds it at the ready. I glance at Dad, who gives me an encouraging smile. Coming from Dad, not a lot can be encouraging, and I shouldn't trust a single thing he does, but right now, this is my only hope of getting out of here. So I take a deep breath and start talking.

I don't tell him everything. I doubt Caleb will respond well to the whole ghost thing, so I tell him a mostly true version of the story that doesn't include the supernatural. I tell him that Francesca came to me with information about where Max was being kept. I say we found the trailer in the woods when looking around the tent city, and that Leonard—or Patrick De Beauvoir, as they know him—shot Miles before trying to shoot Max, which is when I shot him. It was a heat-of-the-moment thing. He'd just shot my boyfriend and was about to kill my brother, and the urge to protect Max blinded me. I tell Caleb that Davey and Scotty were beating up Miles when we found them (which is true). I tell him that they had bullied Miles for years leading up to that day, and that they even pulled a knife on him once (also true).

When Caleb has gotten enough out of me, he tucks both the pen and the spiral notepad into his suit.

"I'll be in touch as soon as I find out anything," he says, more to Dad than to me. He reaches out my hand. "It was a real pleasure to meet you, Shiloh."

This time, I take his hand and try not to wince at the pressure of his grip rubbing against the fresh cuts on my palms. "Thanks."

"You should thank your father," Caleb says. "He loves you, kiddo. He's trying to make things right."

Dad nods. I wonder if that's true, and that's the reason he brought Caleb here. Does he really want to try to fix things with us? He doesn't have a bulge in his jaw. No sign that he's trying to contain himself and not blow up at me. He just looks like Dad. The version of him I remember from before Uncle Jim died, the one who would read to me before bed and play hide-and-seek with me in the backyard and believed his little girl was someone who deserved to be loved and protected.

But it's not real. He's not that person anymore. I don't care if he believes he can change. Even if he can, some things are unforgivable.

So I say nothing, and the detention officers bring me back to my cell. My heart pounds as the heavy door locks me inside.

I sleep some more after that and only wake up when my lunch comes through the slot in the cell door. On the menu today is mashed potatoes, chili, an apple, and some sort of grayish mystery vegetable.

I know Caleb said that jail food is gross, but it tastes fine to me, and I finish the entire tray in minutes. It's funny. I'm eating better and sleeping more than I have in weeks. This is like my very own government-sanctioned wellness retreat.

Someone comes to take away my tray. I try to go to sleep, but it's impossible.

I know they put people in here who commit actual crimes, but you know what else is criminal? Putting a teenager in solitary confinement with nothing to do. I hope I won't be alone like this forever. If a judge ends up deciding I'm a danger to society and belong in here, I hope they at least move me somewhere with other people around. I've never been big on the whole being social thing, but if it was just me and my thoughts day after day, I think I'd actually go insane. Or at least more insane than I already am.

I pace around the room. Count how many floor tiles there are. Try to listen for other people in the cells around me. It's not long until I get so bored that I stare up at the ceiling with my arms behind my head, trying hard not to think about Caleb or Dad because I don't want to get my hopes up that they could get me out of here. I try super hard not to think about

Jonah, which is hard because all I want to do is think about Jonah.

If I close my eyes I can picture him lying next to me, bracing his forearm under his head and looking at me with his blue eyes that are so easy to get lost in. I can almost hear what he'd say:

You know, Scooby, this place ain't half bad. It's got everything a girl could want. A lumpy mattress. A toilet-sink-combo. Free food. Plus, it's got no roaches—not in the fall, at least.

I'd tell him I got a good deal. He'd smile, and it would fill me with so much warmth that I'd forget what it was like to be cold.

I wish he were here right now. I'd give anything to hear his voice again, to hear him call me Scooby one more time. I try to imagine his arm draped over my shoulder and going to sleep listening to the steady rise and fall of his chest.

I'm just about to drift off when I hear a faint creak, like a door opening.

I open my eyes, glancing around the room for something out of the ordinary, but nothing is. The door is still closed. The latch is closed also, so the sound I heard couldn't have been my door opening.

Maybe it was the heating system powering on. Or shutting down. Or a rattle in the pipes.

That would be the logical explanation. But in my experience, the logical explanation for why things happen is not always true.

I slide my hand under the mattress pad, grabbing the packets of salt I saved from breakfast and lunch today. My breathing is loud. Each breath comes out as fog, like it did before Leonard wrote that message in the mirror.

The hair rises on my arms. Leonard's ghost must be here.

So what? He can't do anything to me. I got rid of anything he could use to throw at me.

I go to sit up when something hard closes around my throat.

I gasp against the pressure. No air reaches my lungs. The grip intensifies like invisible hands are wrapped around my throat. Like Leonard's ghostly fingers are trying to choke me to death.

I rip open a salt packet, scattering it onto my face. Tiny

crystals sting my eyes and my chapped lips, but the pressure doesn't go away. So much for that TV show myth. I jump up from the bed, ghostly fingers still wound around my throat. My bare feet pound against the cold floor. I can taste copper on the roof of my mouth. Each gulp of air feels like I'm swallowing shards of glass.

Then the choking stops. I stagger sideways, slumping against the wall as I gulp down air. My hands go to my throat, expecting to find the skin tender, but all I can feel is a racing pulse under my skin.

I spit on the floor and curl my fists, wishing I could see and touch ghosts even for a second so I could grab Leonard by the neck and hurl him against the wall with whatever strength I have left.

He tried to choke me. He actually tried to choke me. Slowly, the warmth returns to the cell. I sit back on the edge of the bed and pull on the gray sweatshirt I got this morning, hiding my hands inside it. The silence is chilling. I try to calm my thoughts, but it's hard not to imagine Leonard's ghost lurking out of sight, making it impossible for me to ignore every creak and noise coming from around me.

8

Miles

I'm not kidding when I say Francesca takes a long time—and I mean a *long* time—to wrap her head around the fact that Shiloh is in jail. I understand why. In Francesca's eyes, Shiloh is still the serious and headstrong girl who listens to Broadway show tunes and has a poster of Justin Bieber on her wall. Imagining Shiloh behind bars is not possible.

Until it is.

Francesca's eyes widen. Her mouth forms a small O.

"We must ask the police to release her," she says. "Leonard will kill her if she remains in there."

"We can't just ask the police to release her," I hiss, remembering the old woman on the other side of the curtain. I don't want her to overhear anything. "That's not how it works."

Francesca lowers her voice, too. "You are a police officer now. Can you tell the other officers to release her?"

"That's not going to work."

"Why not?"

"Because I was the one who arrested her."

Francesca gets an expression on her face like I just reached into her ribcage and ripped out her heart. The way she's looking at me is crushing my own heart, so words tumble out of me.

"I had to," I say. "The police were onto me. They were going to arrest Shiloh anyway. Having me do it was her idea."

Francesca drops her eyes to the blanket pulled over her legs like she can't bear to look at me. Her eyebrows pull together. I can see her turning a thought over in her head, considering the next words she is going to say. When she finally speaks, her voice is thin.

"Shiloh may not have very much time," Francesca says. "Leonard may have already found a way out of the other side."

"We need to kill Leonard's ghost," I say. "Blow him up, blast him with proton packs …"

"Proton packs?" Francesca asks.

Oh right. I forgot she hasn't watched that many movies, and probably hasn't seen Ghostbusters.

"It's a movie," I say.

Francesca frowns. "It is not possible to kill a ghost. You cannot kill things that are already dead."

My stomach twists. Of course ghosts can't die. That would be too easy.

"There has to be something that repels them," I say. "Like salt. Or crucifixes."

"I believe time can destroy souls," Francesca says. "I encountered one soul in the abandoned house that was so old it had lost its human form."

Abandoned house? I didn't go to an abandoned house with her. That must have been when I was dying and too hopped up on benmjöl to remember what day it was. I can still taste the acrid tang on the back of my tongue. Still smell the hot aroma of sweat that lingered in my bedroom and made the air feel humid …

I close my eyes for a second and pull myself back together. Even if time does kill ghosts, there is one teeny tiny problem with that.

"None of us can travel through time," I say. "So we'll need to find another way."

"I already told you—"

"I know," I say, "but there has to be a way. Or at least something Shiloh can use to protect herself until we can get her out."

Francesca looks like she's about to tell me no again, when all the blood rushes out of her face. A clammy pallor comes over her and her skin starts to look waxy. "Where is Evangeline?"

I blink at her. It takes more than a couple of seconds for me to remember who Evangeline is.

"Is that the ghost who's possessing Talulah's body?" I ask. Francesca nods. "Isn't she, like, best friends with Leonard?"

Francesca's eyebrows leap up. "What? No. Not at all. Once she found out what Leonard was doing she wanted no part in it. Did she escape from the burning house?"

"Yes."

"Where is she?"

I barely figured out where Francesca was, let alone every single other person who Fiona drove away in that car, so I shrug.

"Could you find her?" Francesca's eyes burn with urgency. "Please, she will be all alone, and afraid. She died so many years ago. She does not know how things function in our world."

I can only imagine how I'd be feeling if I died and came back to life in a reanimated corpse seventy-five years in the future. Having to deal with operating in a brand-new era as well as in a brand-new body would be overwhelming, to say the least.

"Please?" Francesca begs.

"Okay," I say. "Sure. Yes, I can do that."

"Thank you," she says, slumping back into the pillows. Clearly she cares about Evangeline. More than I would've expected.

I remember seeing Evangeline in the back of Fiona's car, so I assume she was driven here. But that doesn't mean she stayed.

"Was she injured at all?" I ask.

Francesca nods. "She was injured quite badly during our confrontation with Leonard."

Which means she has to be somewhere in this hospital. I give Francesca my phone number. She asks me to write it on her arm in big numbers, so I do, and I tell her to call me if she needs anything when I'm gone. On my way out, I offer an awkward smile to the old woman in the other bed, who's staring at me wide-eyed like she overheard our entire conversation, and I set off in search of Evangeline.

I'm going to start by checking the ER. If my memory serves, Evangeline was awake when she was in that car, so I doubt she would've been rushed into surgery or brought to the ICU. I'm breathing so hard it's making me lightheaded, but I force myself to keep my chin held high as I get in the elevator and go down to the main floor. I have no idea where I'm going or how to get to the ER, but if there's anything I've learned in my short experience as Randall Zweering, it's that good-looking guys can get away with way more than they should by pretending to know what they're doing.

It's just a matter of confidence.

So I pretend to know where I'm going as I walk past the main reception, following the sign pointing toward the ER. I try not to slow my pace as I glance around for the next sign, but there are so many signs in so many languages, and even though I can read fast, I can't read that fast. A nurse notices me. She looks like she's about to ask where I'm going, but a staircase catches my eye and I turn down it before she can say anything.

I go down one flight. As soon as I open the door, the clanging of medical instruments and urgent voices greet me.

I go down to the end of the corridor and pause, taking in the bright lights, the beeping monitors, the murmurs of pain, doctors sprinting out into the ambulance bay, and patient beds against the wall. Some patients are in bays closed off by curtains. Others are on full display, nursing cuts or holding kidney-shaped buckets while their family members sit next to them showing varying degrees of concern. Only one patient is all alone. I recognize her. She glances around at the action with big doe eyes, holding what looks like an ice pack to the side of her face as fluid drips through the IV into her arm.

I really don't want to walk into the chaos of the room because I'm not supposed to be here and I don't know how to explain to anyone what I'm doing here, but I promised Francesca I'd go, so I do.

I move through the crowd, doing my best to look like I have a purpose here, and stop at the foot of her bed.

Evangeline narrows her eyes at me like she has to remember where she knows me from.

I clear my throat. "Uh, hi. Evangeline?"

She nods. The smell of her hits my nose, and I place a closed fist to my lips because good Lord she reeks. The smoke barely masks the aroma of feces and sweat and urine that clings to her and her clothes, and it's all I can do not to gag.

"I'm Miles," I manage, glancing over my shoulder to make sure Lindsey isn't listening in over my shoulder or something, even though logically I know that's completely irrational. "I don't think I ever introduced myself, but I'm friends with Francesca. She asked me to come and make sure you're okay."

Evangeline's eyes widen at the sound of Francesca's name. She lowers the ice pack from her face, and I hiss in a breath through my teeth. A deep red bruise has spread over her cheekbone.

"Is she okay?" she asks.

I nod. "She's awake."

Evangeline's shoulders slump in relief. I wonder what the two of them must have gone through in that trailer together for them to be this worried about each other. They haven't known each other that long. It's a couple of seconds before she speaks again.

"I remember you," she tells me. "You wear the badge."

"Not exactly," I say. "Francesca put me into this body after I died, so I'm just pretending to be a police officer. I didn't look like this before."

"I didn't always look this way either," she says. "A friend of mine … well, he's not much of a friend anymore, but he put me in this body. I … I'm not sure I want to be here."

A strange spot of warmth presses into my chest. She gets it. In the midst of all this, I don't think I've ever had a conversation with anyone else who's going through this strange thing like me.

"Can I see Francesca?" Evangeline asks.

I tell her no, because I had to sneak down here to see her, and I don't think I'd be able to sneak her upstairs to see Francesca with no one noticing. It's too much sneaking for me.

Something else occurs to me. A chill runs up my spine.

Talulah was fifteen when she died. She was also reported missing. It's only a matter of time before someone figures out who she is, and Talulah's parents come get her.

That would be a problem for Evangeline. I need to get her out of here before anyone figures out who she is.

Unless someone has already figured that out. "Have you told anyone your name?" I ask, immediately feeling dumb because Evangeline probably doesn't know Talulah's name. "Or talked to any police officers?"

"I told the doctor my name was Evangeline," she says. "Nothing else."

Good. But not that good because it's only a matter of time before someone calls Social Services or cross-checks missing person databases to find her parents, even though I guess it could take longer because she said she was Evangeline and didn't say her name was Talulah. But it's not going to be long before some random person comes around asking for more details.

"There are some people looking for the girl whose body you're … you know, using," I explain. "I need to get you out of here before anyone figures out who you are. Can you walk?"

She nods, resting the ice pack on the bed. I glance at the nearby nurses and doctors. They are too preoccupied to be paying much attention to us. If I lead Evangeline like I know where I'm going it might just be good enough.

I tell her to pull the IV out of her arm. She does, wincing as the tape rips up some of her baby hairs. Placing one hand on her shoulder, I help her onto her feet, and she clings to my arm, swaying for a couple of seconds before stepping forward. Together, we weave through the ER, moving cautiously but quickly. Every step makes my heart race faster. A security camera sits up in the corner and I lower my head so that my baseball cap shields my face.

We reach the stairwell. I hold her hand as we go through the reception area on the first floor, then back out to the parking lot.

I could cry with relief at how happy I am to be out of there. Evangeline stops walking.

"Are you okay?" I ask.

She shakes her head, looking up at me with a deer-in-headlights sort of expression. She barely knows me. She probably doesn't love the idea of entering the modern world for the first time with a total stranger.

But she doesn't have a choice. "I promise, it's not that scary. I'm going to bring you to the hotel where we are all staying, and you can get a shower and some sleep there. Sound good?"

Evangeline says she would like to sleep. I don't blame her. That's exactly what I plan on doing.

She keeps a firm grip on my hand as we step onto the sidewalk. The sun is high, which is understandable because it's one in the afternoon now. I pull the visor of my baseball cap down over my face because who knows who could be patrolling these streets? With my luck, Lindsey would drive by on her way back to Bethany and see me walking in normal clothes holding hands with a 15-year-old girl who has been missing for over a week, and that wouldn't be a fantastic look for me.

In the corner of my eye, I can see Evangeline gaping at things. The McDonald's sign. A woman texting while walking. I don't really know what to say to her. I'd be having a culture shock too if I died for seventy-five years and suddenly woke up in 2094 to discover that robots are running the world, or it's like a totally normal thing for people to beam themselves home.

If she were with Francesca, I'd bet she'd be asking a million questions about everything. I guess she doesn't know me well enough yet. So once we get in my car, I pass her my phone. Just as soon as I've cranked the window down, because when I tell you this girl needs a shower ...

She holds it in both hands. "What is this?"

"A phone."

"A telephone? Really? Where is the wire?"

"It doesn't need one. It has a touch screen," I say. She gives me a confused look, so I enter my password and open Safari. "This is the internet. You can type anything you want to know into this search bar, and it will give you an answer."

"I can ask it anything in the world?"

"Anything you want."

"Holy mackerel."

I start the engine as she examines the screen. If I'm remembering correctly, Evangeline died in 1944, which means she grew up in the 30s and 40s and the phones or televisions they had back then were not what they are today. The way she stares at the tiny screen makes it look unlikely that she will ever turn her eyes away.

But she does when I pull into the McDonald's drive-thru and tap her on the shoulder. "Are you hungry?" I ask.

She nods. Unsurprisingly, she doesn't know what a drive-thru is, or what her options are in terms of ordering, but I play it safe and order her chicken nuggets and fries, realizing only after the fact that I didn't think to ask if she had any allergies. I doubt she'd be able to tell me if her body did have allergies because she probably doesn't know. Come to think of it, her body could have something like epilepsy or diabetes, and she'd have no way of knowing about it. Putting people inside of bodies they don't know about is super irresponsible. Did Randall have any allergies or illnesses I should know about?

Evangeline takes a chicken nugget out of the carton and

examines it. I wonder if they had chicken nuggets in the 1940s. She doesn't wait that long before biting into it.

"What do you think?" I ask.

"The taste is rather uninteresting, if I'm honest, but it's not unpleasant."

She devours the rest of the box in a couple of minutes and then moves on to the fries. She shoves three or four into her mouth at a time while punching her pointer finger into my phone's keypad to type each individual letter like my grand-mère used to do even though she had all the text zoomed in so much you could see it from space. I'm pulling onto the highway when she gasps.

"Is *that* the photograph of me they printed in the papers after I died?" she asks. "Golly, why do I look so washed out in this photo? I look downright peaked."

Evangeline is quiet again for a couple of minutes, chewing on her fries, before gasping again.

"Edmund looks so much prettier in his photo," she says, like I'm supposed to know who Edmund is. "I'm glad he's not here, or I'd never hear the end of this. It's not right. Everyone is going to remember him as being so handsome when he wasn't, really. He was going off to war. Everyone looks more handsome when they go off to war."

I guess asking would give me the opportunity to get to know her better. "Who is Edmund?"

"My brother." Her voice comes garbled through a mouthful of fries. "He died in the war and liked to play chess with me on the other side of the veil."

Oh, right. Because that's a totally normal thing to say.

"Eddie looks so upright in this picture." She flashes me the phone screen, showing me a black-and-white photo of a boy in his early twenties with big ears sticking out from under his neat comb-over. "But he wasn't like that. One time, he played a trick on our older brother, Albert, and swapped out his hair tonic with molasses. Albert didn't realize until his hair was a sticky mess, and all of us had such a good laugh about it."

Evangeline laughs at the memory and eats some more fries. The brightness of her laugh makes me want to smile, too.

"Your brother sounds like he'd be friends with Jonah," I say. "He peed in his sister's humidifier once."

Evangeline's brow wrinkles. Even when I explain what a humidifier is, she still doesn't crack a smile.

"Is that your friend who was injected with foolery?" she asks.

The way she says it—like foolery is code for "poison"— makes a knot form in my stomach. I manage a nod.

"I've seen many folks messed up by foolery before," she says. "Pudsey gave it to me once, and it was no picnic."

My heart hammers in my chest. "Do you think he's going to be okay?"

She shrugs. "Usually, if a person only gets a smidge, they go back to normal in a day or so. It's when they start acting hysterical that you have to watch out. Too much foolery can make a person lose their mind, and I've never seen anyone get as big a dose as your friend did."

Well, that's super comforting. I hadn't been all that worried about Jonah so far this morning because, compared to Shiloh in jail and Francesca in a coma, he seemed pretty safe, but I'm worried about him now. It's all I can do not to flip on my sirens and floor it the rest of the way to the motel.

In case anyone is tracking my police car, I park a ten-minute walk down the road in a grocery store parking lot and walk to the motel. I wish I didn't still have this car. This is the car I drove when we all tried to go kill Leonard, and I haven't done the three-hour drive back to Bethany to return it yet. It wouldn't be impossible for someone to figure out where I was. I'm pretty sure police cars have built-in GPS systems, and Lindsey looked mad enough to go to every single business in a ten-mile radius asking if they'd seen someone fitting my description, but it's not like I can ditch the car, so I try to be as careful as I can.

The purple-haired receptionist at the Lazy-U Motel says we're in luck because they've been completely booked, and a two-person room became available this morning. I pay for two nights in cash in case Lindsey is tracing my credit cards. I don't know where the line is between precaution and paranoia, but I don't intend to find out the hard way.

I open the door to room 13 with an actual key. Evangeline flops onto the closest bed, and in a minute, is snoring. She still smells awful and shouldn't be getting into bed smelling like actual filth, but I don't blame her for being tired and I guess she can shower later. I stare at the other bed longingly. I'm starting to get nauseated by how much I need to sleep, but Evangeline's words about foolery are playing over and over again in my head, and I won't be doing any sleeping until I go see how Jonah is doing.

So instead of going to sleep, I walk over to the room he's staying in and knock on the door.

9

Miles

"Handy?" I say, knocking again. "It's Miles. Are you in there?"

No answer. A gust of wind blows into me from behind, passing through my puffer coat and making me shiver. Handy has to be in there. He was under strict instructions not to leave this room until we got back. I press my ear against the door, but I can't hear anything over the thumping of my heart. It's two thirty in the afternoon. Handy should be awake by now—especially since he's rooming with a six-year-old boy and a brainwashed teenager who's coming down from a murderous rampage.

My next thought hits me like a punch to the stomach. Could Jonah have hurt Handy or Max?

I have never been so scared for my best friend as I was last night after Leonard plunged that needle of foolery into his neck and told him to kill Shiloh. I have also never been so scared *of* him. There was so much hatred on his face when he looked at Shiloh. He wanted to kill her. Even when he was tied up in the back of the car with no weapon, he threw himself at her like he wanted to rip his wrists out of the cuffs and strangle her with his bare hands. If he tried to hurt Max ... Handy swallows swords and juggles chainsaws for a living, which is one of the most badass things I've ever heard, but he still has no legs. I'm not a betting person, but if I had to put money on whether a brainwashed teenager or a man with no legs would win in a fight, I'd have to go with the former.

But picturing Jonah winning a fight with Handy is making me think about Max's body lying limp on the dirty motel carpet, which is making me feel like I'm about to throw up.

"Handy!" I pound both hands on the door. "Open up!"

Still nothing. I clasp my hand to my forehead, trying to stop myself from hyperventilating. Max could be in there right now—unconscious, bloody, or worse. I barely know Handy, but he seemed like a nice guy. Not a guy who deserves to be beaten to death by a crazed lunatic.

I promised Shiloh I'd take care of Max. If anything happened to him, I could stop worrying about Leonard and his ghost pals altogether because she'd be the one to kill me.

"*Handy!*" My voice breaks with desperation. "I swear to God if you don't open this door, I'm going to kick it in."

"I'm comin'!" Handy's voice is muffled through the wood. I slump against the door in relief. "Geez, man. No need for all that yellin'."

The lock slides back. I step away from the door in time for it to swing open and reveal Handy balancing on one hand. From the waist up, Handy looks like an intimidating guy. His shoulders are broad. Muscles bulge under his graphic tee, and tattoo sleeves cover his arms. His beard is long and bushy. He looks like he belongs in a biker gang. Or at least, he would, if he still had legs.

Handy yawns. I'm so relieved to see him I should smile, but anger rises from the pit of my stomach.

"Are you deaf?" I snap.

"Not last time I checked," Handy says in a high-pitched Southern accent that doesn't sound as intimidating as he looks.

"Wish I was. It'd save me from having to listen to all your yammering."

"All my …" I shake my head to clear it. "You can't *do* that."

"Do what?" Handy asks. "Sleep?"

"Not answer the door," I say. "You had me worried that something bad had happened."

"How long do you think it takes for a man with no legs to answer a door?" he asks.

I suddenly feel like a jerk. "Sorry. I'm really stressed right now."

"I'll say." Handy backs into the room, and I step in after him, closing and bolting it behind me. "Is there anything you ain't worried 'bout? I mean, seriously. I ain't never met a man who worries more'n you."

Clenching my teeth to stop myself from saying something I'll regret, I glance around the room. It's gloomy in here, but sort of humid. The curtains are drawn. Every lamp is off, so the only light coming in is a sliver of afternoon sun peeking through the shades. The room's pretty big, and has two queen beds, a tangerine armchair, and a TV that's playing cartoons. The smell of pizza hangs in the air. It's too stale to be from this morning. Handy must have ordered it last night and maybe saved a slice for breakfast. I'm glad I ate that burger on my way because otherwise smelling this would have made it impossible to think of anything except for how much I wanted to eat.

"Make yourself at home." Handy pulls himself onto the armchair like it's easy. "Everybody else has."

Max sits on the bed closer to me, hugging his teddy bear to his chest. He's staring at me with those sad, brown eyes that are identical to Shiloh's, like he's already seen too many bad things in the world and expects to see more. Even though he's wearing a matching set of blue Tonka Truck pajamas and his blond hair is sticking up haphazardly, his eyes are bright, like he's been up for hours. Or maybe they just look bright because the glow from the TV is reflected in them.

He glances at the door, then back at me. "Where is Shiloh?"

I open my mouth to reply, but close it because what am I supposed to say? That his sister is in jail and his mom is dead, but hopefully not for long since Francesca's awake now and could put her ghost back into her body? I promised Shiloh I would protect Max. Am I protecting him by lying about where Shiloh is, or by telling him the truth?

Max's frown deepens. "Did my sister kill the bad man?"

I guess he knows more about our current situation than I thought he did. Shiloh must have given him some details.

Technically, Shiloh did kill the bad man, but if Leonard is haunting us from beyond the grave, we're still in danger. Would Shiloh want me to tell him that the bad man is dead?

Max glares at me. "Is Shiloh okay?"

"Yes," I say, glad to have a question I can finally answer.

"Where is she?" he demands.

I'm too tired to think clearly about what to say. Before I can decide on a course of action, a groan comes from the other bed.

Jonah is sleeping with his back turned to us. Even though he's mostly covered by the blanket, I can tell he's still wearing the black peace sign T-shirt that he was wearing last night, which is gross, but I doubt he was in much of a headspace to shower or do his skincare routine before falling asleep last night.

He doesn't wake up. Because the last image I have of Jonah is the one of him lunging at Shiloh with a knife, I turn to Handy and whisper, "Is Jonah still …"

"Handcuffed?" Handy blurts out. "He sure is. Fiona told me not to take 'em off, and I do what Fiona says."

Under the covers, I spot the rope I tied around his torso last night. "Has he woken up at all?"

"Nope. Not since he got here. You know, now we're talkin' 'bout it, I don't like this one bit. What's he done to get himself all tied up? Why do I got to watch 'im? Is he gonna attack me?"

"He probably won't attack you." I glance at Max, who's hanging off every word that comes out of my mouth. "Could you get Max out of here?"

"Oh, sure, make me the babysitter. Why do I got to be the—"

"Because I'm going to wake Jonah up, and you might not want to be here when I do."

Handy seems to agree. Grumbling, he asks Max if he wants to go to the vending machine, and Max slides off the bed. Handy closes the door, leaving me alone in the room with a sleeping Jonah.

I can hear my breathing. It's loud. So loud it's hard to concentrate on anything else.

Will Jonah try to attack me like he attacked Shiloh? Richie did. He was scared and mad and didn't know where he was, so it didn't matter who he attacked. I'm not scared of Jonah. He's handcuffed, and I'm twice his size now, but I also don't want to fight him, so instead of shaking his shoulder, I flip on the light.

The sudden brightness turns all the furniture into that florescent shade of orange that belongs only on construction vests. Jonah rolls away from the light, still sound asleep. Apparently, I'm going to have to wake him up the old-fashioned way, because nothing in my life is easy.

I approach the bed. Jonah's face has wedged between the pillows. How does he have air in there?

"Psst," I say. "Jonah. You need to wake up."

He doesn't stir. Great. Jonah is a heavy sleeper. One time, in middle school, my mom drove us to an amusement park. On the way home, I was so hopped up on sugar that I couldn't sit still, so my mom put on the radio, and we sang along at the top of our lungs. It wasn't until we got home that I realized Jonah had slept through the entire drive. If he slept through me belting it out to Celine Dion, he's going to sleep through my polite whispers.

So I raise my voice. "Jonah, come on. Wake up."

He turns onto his back. His mouth is open. A snore that sounds more like a snort rumbles through his nose.

This is ridiculous. Being polite won't get me anywhere.

In one sudden motion, I pull the blanket off him. His eyes open. A scream rips from his throat and he sits up, kicking his boots out in front of him as he searches for the source of danger.

When his eyes find me, he stops. He stares at me like he's

trying to figure out who I am. Maybe he thinks I'm Officer Zweering and he's forgotten that I'm really Miles. I go to remind him when he rolls his eyes and scrunches up his face.

"Asshole." His voice is hoarse. Probably from inhaling smoke from the burning house. "That was mean."

He knows me. He remembers who I am. I'm so relieved that I laugh.

Jonah frowns. "You're seriously laughing at me right now?"

I just laugh harder. I guess the foolery hasn't messed up his mind. His body, on the other hand, has seen better days. Soot streaks his face and his greasy black hair hangs over his forehead in clumps. His blue eyes are bloodshot, and the week-old bruises under them have turned a grayish yellow and green. The hem of his jeans is singed and partially gone. There's a raised lump on the side of his neck from where Leonard stabbed him with the needle. He smells so much like smoke it makes me queasy, and of course, there are handcuffs on him, and rope tied around his torso, restricting his movements.

But he's okay. I almost want to hug him, but I remember how Shiloh recoiled when I hugged her in this new body, and Jonah hated Officer Zweering more than she did. He knows it's me, but on some level that stops mattering when I look and feel like someone else.

Jonah catches me staring at him. "What are you looking at?"

"You," I say. "Do you have burns on your ankles?"

"They don't hurt."

"You smell awful."

"Yeah, well, I feel like shit." He slumps back onto the pillows, crushing his handcuffed wrists under him. He gives no indication of having noticed. "Where am I?"

"In the motel."

"Is there any reason you got me up at the crack of dawn?"

"It's two thirty."

Jonah coughs hard. It sounds so painful that I wince on his behalf. "Got any water?"

I glance around the room. There's no fridge or microwave in here, and definitely no minibar. "I can get you some."

"Let's grab something to eat. When I tell you I could fuck up a continental breakfast spread right now …" He pauses. "Wait, what time is it?"

An uneasy feeling fills my stomach. I just told him what the time was. Is his brain really that cloudy that he already forgot?

"It's two thirty in the afternoon."

A hazy look comes over his face. "I missed breakfast?"

Oh no. Maybe I spoke too soon. The foolery must still be in his system. I guess that's to be expected. He only got injected twelve hours ago.

My mind races as I try to figure out how to approach this. Richie was still almost foaming at the mouth when he was on foolery. He wouldn't listen to anything I said, even though Leonard didn't tell him to kill me specifically. Jonah doesn't seem angry at me. He just looks confused.

Maybe I should remind him of what happened. Sitting on the foot of his bed, I gesture at him. "Do you remember why you're wearing those handcuffs?"

The question stuns him. He tries to move his hands, still tied behind his body, and his eyebrows pull together.

I'll take that as a no. "Leonard gave you foolery last night, and you kind of went on a rampage."

The wrinkle between his brows deepens. "I did what?"

"You came with us on a mission to kill Leonard." I do my best to ignore how fast my heart is pounding. "You had him in a headlock, but he broke free, and then he stabbed you with a needle filled with foolery."

"A needle?" Jonah's eyes search the space in front of him, like he's trying to remember. "He stuck me with a *needle*?"

"And told you to kill Shiloh."

He looks at me. Blinks like he wishes he was still asleep.

"I had to," he says.

What? "No, you didn't."

"Shiloh tried to kill me," he says. "It's not her that's in her body. It's one of Leonard's ghosts in there."

Oh no. I do my best to keep my voice from shaking. "That's not true."

He nods, like he's confirming a memory. "Shiloh tried to kill me."

"You're the one who tried to kill her."

"Because she tried to kill me."

I stare at him. Is this seriously the conversation we're having right now? Who started it?

"You're not remembering it correctly," I say. "Leonard gave you foolery and told you to kill Shiloh. It's a mind-control drug."

"I know what foolery is."

"Okay," I say slowly. "So if you remember what foolery is, and you understand you got it, then do you understand that you were the one who attacked Shiloh and she was only defending herself?"

Jonah considers this for a second. But then his eyes bore into mine and my heart sinks.

"She was possessed," he says. "I saw it happen."

"Jonah—"

"Shut up and listen to me!" Jonah snaps. "Shiloh is possessed, and we've got to kill her before she kills us."

He says it with so much conviction. Like there is no doubt in his mind that it is true. A tingling sensation comes over my face and gives me the sneaking suspicion that I'm going to throw up all over the carpet, which I suspect would not make Handy very happy.

I turn away from him and fumble with the doorknob leading out of the room.

"Uh, Miles?" Jonah says. "Where are you going?"

I step out of the room and slam the door. Jonah yells my name, and I lean my back against the door, doing my best to breathe evenly.

This is bad. This is so bad. I had a feeling that it could be bad, but I was hoping it wouldn't be this bad.

He was convinced that Shiloh was possessed. But what's creepy is that even if Shiloh was possessed, that would mean she was dead, and Jonah didn't seem all that broken up about it. In fact, he didn't seem like he cared at all.

I try to slow down my breathing, but it gets faster and faster and faster until I'm hyperventilating, and I can't stop because it's like a runaway train with no brakes that has come off the tracks.

I hear a door open and close next to me. In a couple of seconds, Evangeline appears.

"Are you all right?" she asks. I shake my head. "Did you just speak to your friend on the foolery?"

I nod and continue gasping for air. A crease appears between her eyebrows. With a gentle hand, she leads me over to the curb and tells me to sit. Pulling my long legs up to my chest, I do my best to get enough oxygen to stop myself from passing out.

"I'm sorry," I say, the words sounding more like a wheeze. "I'm trying to process a colossal amount of insane information all at once, and it's making it hard for me to breathe."

She frowns. "I gather your friend is still not right in his mind?"

That's one way to put it. "He remembers who Shiloh is, but he thinks she's possessed and wants to kill her."

"I can only imagine how scary that must have been to see him in that state."

"My ex-girlfriend is in jail," I say. "My friend is in critical condition at the hospital, and now my best friend has lost his mind. I'm … alone in this."

"You aren't on your own," she says. "I'm here, and I know more about foolery than anyone you will find on this side of the veil, so I can help your friend."

I stare at her. She smiles at me, looking shyly optimistic despite the crushing weight of reality closing in around us and the incredibly high probability of us failing and me being killed by Leonard all over again. I suddenly understand why Francesca was so worried about her in the hospital. Being locked in that creepy basement alone would have been terrifying, but the way

Evangeline can smile while staring death in the face is something that I'm sure would get me through even the toughest of times. Come to think of it, Evangeline *has* stared death in the face. She is technically dead and possessing someone else's body. So am I.

I do a breathing exercise and listen as she tells me everything she knows about foolery. When foolery was administered to her friends or other performers in the show, it was only given in small doses, which led people to develop a mild hangover but didn't drastically alter their perception of reality. But if anyone ever got too much, they were never the same again.

"Foolery preys on fear," she says. "It makes people forget good memories and creates new bad ones that justify what the person has been asked to do. If he was asked to kill your friend Shiloh, his brain would need to invent a reason for him to do so."

"So ... what?" I ask. "He thinks she's possessed, because that would give him a reason to kill her?"

Evangeline nods. "I believe so."

"But ..." This still doesn't make any sense. "Why doesn't he care what happened to her?"

"I'm not sure," Evangeline says. "If you want my advice, it would be to give him a bit of time. As the drug works its way out of his system, he will become more like his old self, and then we can figure out how much lasting damage it did to his brain."

"So he's never going to care about Shiloh again?" I ask. "He's always going to want to kill her?"

Evangeline gives me a look that tells me that, once again, she is not sure. "I could go sit with him and bring him some tea, if you'd like."

I nod. Jonah's hungry, so I tell her to bring him some food from the vending machine because I really will throw up if I face him again right now. She goes into the motel room. I bend over my knees, wrapping my arms around my thighs and releasing a shaky breath. All of this ... it's too much. There are too many things to worry about, even for me.

I need to focus on the things I can control. Like finding a way for us to defend ourselves from Leonard's ghost.

Francesca said killing ghosts was impossible, but there must be some way to at least repel them.

I may not be able to see ghosts like Francesca can, but I'm a smart person with good deductive reasoning skills and I got a five on my AP Physics exam. The physics class I took didn't teach me anything about ghost energy, but ghosts have to be made of something. I just need to figure out what it is.

After another five minutes of deep breathing, I pick myself up off the ground and set off to figure out how to kill a ghost.

10

Miles

Because I'm the least qualified person I know to have landed this job, there are only two things I can fall back on: my understanding of high school physics, and my extensive knowledge of movies.

Both of those things involve using my brain. Unfortunately, my brain is not working the way it should be because I've gotten exactly seven hours of sleep in the past 32, so I stop by the motel room for a power nap that turns into a much more serious nap because I go unconscious the second my head hits the pillow. But I manage to pull myself back up after a few hours.

I sit at the desk and do some thinking, trying to reason this through as logically as possible. Ghosts don't exist in physics. There's not supposed to be any such thing as ghost energy, but there has to be, because both Francesca and Leonard can manipulate it. I remember my AP Physics teacher, Mrs. Pichon, talking about the first law of thermodynamics and telling us that energy can neither be created nor destroyed. That must be why ghosts can't be killed.

I can remember the lecture that Mrs. Pichon gave us where

she said that energy is the capacity to do things. She said that there are two main types of energy—kinetic, which is the energy of a moving object, and potential, which is the energy an object possesses due to its position or condition. Francesca told me once that ghosts are cold, and they make the space around them cold. If ghosts released energy, they would make the surrounding space hot, so ghosts must somehow power themselves by absorbing ambient heat and converting it into ghost energy. By this logic, if I made it really cold, they would be able to draw less energy, but I can't meaningfully influence the ambient temperature. There's still a lot of energy in cold air.

I bite on the end of my pencil. If ghosts are continually pulling energy from their surroundings, that means they need to exert that energy in some way to exist. So how do I slow or stop that process of energy conversion?

Science doesn't know ghost energy exists. It doesn't recognize it. I sure don't recognize it, but how did we figure out anything existed? By experimenting. So I need to experiment to figure out what could interfere with the conversion of ghost energy.

Could you image the kind of recognition I could get if I succeed? *High school student proves existence of afterlife.* Or I guess *—Small town cop proves the existence of ghosts.*

But how do I experiment if I can't see or communicate with a ghost? I don't have the monocle anymore, and Francesca is too weak to leave the hospital. I try to remember what the amateur ghost hunters did on those BuzzFeed videos about paranormal investigators. They always had EMF detectors. Some of them used thermal imaging cameras. Oh my God, if ghosts draw energy from their surroundings, I should be able to see them on thermal cameras. They should show up as cold splotches.

Okay. So in theory, I should be able to go find some ghosts using thermal cameras to find cold splotches, then I can see if I can get these cold splotches to go away or to weaken.

I pull a crumpled McDonald's receipt from my pocket and flatten it against the table, jotting down as many ideas as I can for things that could potentially affect ghost energy. None of this makes any sense, so I just write down every single thing I have seen on TV or in ghost movies that has interfered with them. Even though this is a terrifying and daunting prospect and the probability of success is low and I'm having to do all of it on my own, there's a tiny part of me that's … I don't know. Excited? I don't know if that part belongs to me or to Randall Zweering, who must have loved building things because I now possess the knowledge of how to make a potato gun, which wasn't there before. It's becoming hard to differentiate between the Randall parts of me and the Miles parts. Randall Zweering is me. Miles Barot-Renaud stopped existing the second I died, just like Randall Zweering did when he died, and this new person I have become is not really Randall or Miles. I'm just a weird combination of the two.

Once I have made a list, I grab my car keys from the table and take a deep breath.

Okay. Let's go do some ghost hunting.

I can buy a lot of the stuff on the list at Walmart, but some of it isn't so easy. Getting holy water results in one of the most mortifying experiences of my life. I search for a dispenser in the first random church I find, but I don't know if it's holy or not. Is it just water until a priest blesses it, or do churches buy their water pre-blessed? I know less about religious practice than I do about physics, so I just dip a plastic bottle into the font in front of the altar as one or two people sit there and pray, no doubt wondering what I think I'm doing.

I stop at a drive-thru on my way to the cemetery, then park my patrol car on a side street where I finish the last bite of the burrito I picked up. It's my second meal of the day and even that hasn't satisfied the hunger that's gurgling in my stomach. Miles always picked at his food. Randall Zweering has an appetite, which must be a product of all the gym equipment in his apartment. I should learn how to use that. I like being able to lift heavy things, and I don't want to lose my strength.

In a way, switching bodies is kind of a great fitness hack. I can only imagine the pop-up ads:

Doctors hate him! Women love him! Now the power can be yours!

I tell myself to focus and lean over the steering wheel to peer over the crumbling rock wall. There aren't many people here. The sun is setting, and the number of people who enjoy being in cemeteries at night is has to be pretty small, barring Francesca of course, so I grab my shopping bags and get out.

I let myself in through the creaky iron gate. I'm also not a huge fan of being in a cemetery at night, especially now that I know ghosts are real, but unlike the other unwitting visitors I have exactly no choice in the matter. I walk over the hill, side-eyeing a woman kneeling in front of a grave decorated with flowers and passing a couple of kids my age strolling hand-in-hand through the stone angels and weathered tombstones. The sun has dipped below the horizon, turning the sky a navy blue that is getting blacker by the second. I'm hoping that the shadows will provide some cover from any prying eyes, because people are going to pry. I'm acting weird, and this cemetery is in a crowded neighborhood, so I'm glad when I find a quiet spot all the way in the back behind a small mausoleum. I drop my bags on the grass. The building provides a little cover from the rest of the cemetery, which is pretty empty now that it's almost dark, and nobody can see me from the surrounding houses because of the hill and the stone wall bordering the property. I hope those kids aren't looking for a quiet spot to make out among the dead.

I crouch on the damp grass and set up the thermal imaging camera I bought. The camera is built like one of those handheld scanners at the grocery store that let you check prices. I'm not exactly an expert on how any of it works, but I point the camera out at the cemetery and angle the viewing screen up toward me. The lens turns the world into a patchwork of color, some yellow, but mostly green and light blue. I can make out the sharp edges of the gravestones and the stubs of mown grass, but no human shapes.

Which is fine. It makes sense, because if it were that easy to see ghosts, every self-proclaimed ghost hunter in the world could see them, and I know from videos that is not the case.

I need to look for cold splotches. If I'm right, ghosts aren't going to show up as individual human figures, but instead they'll be cold patches where they are drawing heat from the air. The gravestones are pale blue. The grass is a mix of green and yellow, but the air around the stones is navy and kind of hazy.

I pan the camera around. At the edge of the cemetery, the haze thins out and turns turquoise.

I point the camera back at the middle of the cemetery. Squinting at the tiny screen, I try to make out shapes in the blob, but it looks like a cold mist hovering over the gravestones.

Ghosts. It has to be. It can't be fog because it's not foggy right now.

My heart pounds so hard that I can feel it in my fingertips. I place the thermal camera on the ground between my knees and rummage through my shopping bags. Okay, ghosts, let's see if you're a fan of holy water.

Holding the thermal camera in one hand, I walk up to the haze and splash the bottle of holy water onto it. Nothing happens. The cloud doesn't change. I dump out the rest of the bottle, realizing too late that I'm just dumping it onto someone's grave, but I guess that's okay because the water is blessed.

So that was a bust. I rip open the bag of salt I bought at the grocery store and sprinkle it on the cloud. This gets a weird look from a woman across the cemetery getting into her car, and sure enough, it does nothing.

Those urban legends were kind of a stretch anyway. I burn sage and hold it out to the haze, my eyes darting between the screen and the real world to make sure I don't accidentally drop an ember and start a fire because that would be the last thing I need. No cigar.

Resting the thermal camera on the grass, I take a radio out of the plastic Walmart bag and reach for the scanning dial. This one I actually have some hope for. Frequencies can disrupt energy forces. It's a thing. like how high enough frequencies can shatter wine glasses, or whales have trouble communicating with each other because there are a lot of ships in the ocean.

I start with the AM frequencies. All I get is white noise, so I crank up the volume and start playing with the dial. I'm so glad there's no one here, or I might actually die of embarrassment. That's all someone needs. They're visiting a dead relative, and I blare white noise right in their ear. Scratchy voices blare through the gravestones. The blue cloud remains the same. I switch to the FM range and a Bruno Mars song blares from the speakers. The navy cloud flickers, and my heart soars, but even the rest of the song doesn't make it change color on the thermal image, so it was probably a gust of wind or another minor fluctuation.

I turn off the radio and run a hand down my face. This is so dumb. None of this is going to work.

I shove the radio back in the plastic bag and clear my throat. "Be at peace," I call into the blue cloud. Obviously, nothing happens. All the ghosts are probably hovering right above my head, laughing.

What else is used to dispel ghosts in movies? Love? I have enough self-respect not to even try that one.

There's one more thing I have to try. I go back to the mausoleum and get the big red and white horseshoe magnet out of the bag. Walking back out into the middle of the cemetery, I hold the magnet out in front of me and point the thermal camera at the gravestones, leaning back to look through the viewing screen. Nothing happens to the lingering fog.

Please work. Please please please.

One minute goes by. Then another. Slowly, the fog begins to lighten. It's so subtle that I'm sure I'm imagining it at first, but little by little, the fog becomes less hazy as it thins. I blink to reset my eyes. There's a hole in the fog around the magnet. Right where the magnet is, the haze is gone.

I blink at the screen. Well, that makes no sense.

Of all things, did that seriously just work?

I try again, walking with the magnet over to another patch of navy. In a couple of seconds, the haze lifts.

A laugh bursts out of me. I did it. I really did it.

I need to tell Francesca. Gathering everything back into the duffel with trembling hands, I run back to the car and bang a U-turn, driving as fast as I can to the hospital because I'm a freaking police officer and nobody's going to pull me over.

11

FrANCeSCA

Only thirty minutes before visiting hours end, Miles enters my hospital room with a bag slung over his shoulder. Clinking sounds come from inside of it, as if it is filled with cooking pots and pans. I am not sure why he would bring me pots or pans. There is no place for me to use them in here.

"Hi," Miles says, breathing hard. He puts his bag on the ground. "How are you feeling?"

I press a finger to my lips and point to the old woman in the bed beside mine, who appears to be sleeping. Her head is tipped to the side, and her shoulder-length white hair partially covers her face. I have been trying to go to sleep myself all day and have not been having any luck, so I do not wish to disturb her if she has found some peace.

"Could you close the curtain for me?" I ask Miles.

He does as I say, sliding the curtain so slowly that it hardly makes a sound. I like this about Miles. His thoughtfulness appears to have survived in his new incarnation. If my experiences these past couple of weeks have taught me anything, it is that a body is not as important as the soul inside of it.

Miles pulls up a chair beside my bed, bracing his elbows on the mattress. It is completely dark outside. The glass appears to be a navy blue. Only one panel of light above our heads is on, casting harsh shadows onto Miles's face.

"How are you feeling?" he whispers again. The closed curtain may prevent the old woman from seeing us, but it will not stop her from hearing us, so we still must keep our voices down.

In truth, I am in quite a lot of pain. The fear I felt while trapped in the cage made me overlook how much I needed to eat, the aches in my joints, and mostly, the pain in my cut-off finger, which has been throbbing all day, even though it is not there anymore. I can still feel my old finger. Or perhaps the ghost of it, so real that I swear it is still there until I look down and only see four fingertips poking out through the bandage. Every pulse brings the memory of the gardening shears back to me. How the blades bit into my skin moments before they closed.

Telling Miles that is simply going to worry him, and I do not wish to worry him any more than he already is.

"I feel as though I have been whacked all over my body with a giant beaver tail," I say, offering a small smile.

Miles does not return it. My teeth begin to chatter a tiny bit, and Miles removes the puffy coat he is wearing and drapes it over my shoulders. I thread my arms through the sleeves and smile at how good the smooth material feels against my skin, but the coat does not warm me up all the way. The shivery feeling is coming from deep within me.

"Did you find Evangeline?" I ask.

"She's fine," Miles says, prompting a sigh to slip through my lips and my teeth to stop clacking together. "I found her in the emergency room. I got her something to eat, and she's at the motel sleeping."

I imagine Evangeline sleeping on a proper bed underneath a proper blanket and not on the pile of moldy hay at the bottom of the cage. Picturing her comfortable and safe makes me feel warm and tingly all over my body.

She is all right. She is safe and sleeping and all right.

A smile grows on Miles's face. He bounces on his toes, like he is trying to hold back his words. I doubt he is smiling about Evangeline sleeping, so my eyebrows draw together.

"You have something you need to tell me," I say. "Did something happen?"

"I did it." His smile grows even wider. "I really did it."

"What did you do?"

"I figured out how to stop a ghost." Before I can reply, he continues talking. "It's physics. Or, at least, it's based on physics. You know how gravity is a cluster of matter that has power and attraction, and how everything is always pulling on everything else?"

I did not know that, but I was never very good at my science lessons at school. "I suppose so."

"Well, I think ghosts work the same way," he says. "Ghosts power themselves from the energy around them. I'm pretty sure they convert heat energy. That's why they make the spaces they're in so cold. Do you know about the coefficient of friction?" I shake my head. "It explains how ambient energy can be converted to heat. If a surface is slippery, there is less friction, so all I had to do was add more friction to the conversion process to stop the ghosts from drawing energy to power themselves. I came up with some ideas, tested them out at a cemetery, and I did it—I found out how to stop them."

Imagining him testing his ideas at a cemetery puts an uneasy feeling in my stomach. The souls at the cemetery in Bethany were my friends. They are good people. I do not like the thought of somebody forcing them to do things they might not want to do.

Miles does not seem to register the confusion on my face. He reaches into his bag and pulls out a red and white horseshoe magnet that is bigger than my hand.

"Magnets." His smile grows wider. "A powerful magnet makes it harder for ghosts to convert ambient energy from their surroundings."

I peer into the rest of his bag. It is filled to the brim with magnets identical to the one I am holding.

"I bought every magnet they had," he says. "I don't know how or why it works. None of this should be possible, even in theory, but it is."

The meaning behind his words sinks in. "Are you saying that magnets can protect us from Leonard?"

Miles nods. "An ordinary magnet isn't as powerful as an electrically charged one, but I don't think the doctors will be happy if I set that up for you in the hospital, so it's better than nothing."

He tells me to keep the magnet with me at all times. According to him, if I keep the magnet, no ghost can approach me. He says the words with utter certainty. I am not sure how certain he can be when he cannot see souls himself, but he is.

Could he be right? I wish there were souls in here for me to test the magnet on, but the room is empty of anybody except for me, Miles, and the sleeping woman on the other side of the curtain. I hold up the heavy magnet. If Miles is right and this can protect us from Leonard, that would be wonderful. Miles and Jonah could carry one around with them. Evangeline could sleep with one under her pillow. Even though I am fully capable of pushing souls away with my mind, I could sleep holding one like an uncomfortable teddy bear to prevent Guilherme from tampering with my machine or to stop Leonard from attempting to smother me with a pillow. These magnets could save our lives. Leonard would eventually have to give up, because he is not strong enough to get through to us. I am beginning to feel quite optimistic about our chances of surviving his attacks until one thought enters my brain and sends a stab of pain through my heart.

Using magnets may help us, but they will not help Shiloh.

She could not find a magnet in her prison cell. I have never been to prison before, but I imagine it is quite restrictive, not unlike being trapped in a cage, which is something I am unfortunately familiar with.

I inhale a shaky breath. Miles appears to be considering going to find a doctor, but I stop him with one word:

"Shiloh."

The smile drops off Miles's face. He goes a little gray. He had been so excited about his discovery that I doubt he would have considered whether this would end up helping Shiloh.

Miles surely could not bring a magnet in for her. I am sure the guards search the people entering to make sure they do not bring in anything they are not supposed to, and a magnet could be perceived as a weapon. Perhaps they would not search a uniformed police officer, but that officer would need a good reason for being there …

I am so caught up pondering this question that I do not notice the two transparent figures gliding out of the wall behind Miles until they have entered the room. My breath hitches in my throat. I stare at them. The tall boy in the newsboy cap has a timid expression on his face, like he is unsure about whether he should be here. The young woman with the dark curls and a white dress hovers above the floor beside him. Four small, black, and very shiny shoes hang from below her skirt.

Patrick and Maude.

I did not know they were here. I have not seen them since I escaped from the burning house. Leonard snapped Patrick's neck like a dry twig, and his soul disappeared through a window. And Maude … I did not see her die, but I found her host body lying dead on a bed. In the chaos of the day, I completely forgot about them.

I raise my bandaged hand in a wave, wincing as a jolt of pain shoots through my knuckle like a miniature stab of lightning.

There are so many things I could ask them, but the first thing that comes out of my mouth is, "Hello."

Miles registers that I am not speaking to him. He grabs a magnet from the bag and points it in their direction. Maude's whispery figure pales as though some of the energy has been drained from it.

I widen my eyes. Perhaps Miles was right about the magnets. I did not doubt him, but I did not completely believe him either.

"How did you find me?" I ask them.

"I spotted you leaving the house." Maude gives the magnet a wide berth as she comes closer. "Patrick and I, well, we—"

"Followed you," Patrick finishes. He does not look even a tiny bit happy to be having this conversation. I remember the promise I made to him before bringing him back from the other side.

You promise to bring me right back here? he had asked. *To Ola, when it's all done?*

I failed him.

"I am sorry," I say. "About … Ola. I …"

"Do you still have the elephant hair?" he asks.

"I believe so," I say. "I tucked it in the ringmaster's coat, and when Leonard was dying, I took it out and put it in my skirt pocket, so it must still be with my dirty clothes."

Patrick nods. "Could you take me back?"

I would like to, but I am not in any condition to go back to the other side until I have gotten out of the hospital. Bringing Leonard over nearly killed me, and I do not want to die.

But I am not sure how to tell Patrick this. He only agreed to help me stop Leonard because I promised I would bring him back, and I do not like disappointing people. I need to stay alive so that I can stop Leonard, and I cannot do that if I remain trapped on the other side in the endless plains with him and Ola.

The weight of Patrick's expectations and the need to save Shiloh pull at me, but I do not see an easy solution. There is so much pressure. So much urgency. It is enough to make me want to cover my eyes and ears and hide in the hospital bed until an idea enters my head.

Miles may not be able to enter prison with a magnet undetected, but somebody else could.

I doubt Patrick will want to help me again, but I explain our discovery about the magnets to him and Maude anyway, as well as what we believe Leonard is attempting to do to Shiloh. Patrick is stony-faced while listening, but Maude's mouth drops open.

"Shiloh needs a magnet," I say, "but we might need some help to get her one."

A couple of seconds go by before Patrick appears to understand what I am asking. "No."

"Please?" I ask. "You can move things without being noticed. If Miles buys a magnet and drives to the prison fence, could you perhaps float it to Shiloh for us?"

"How am I gonna get that gal a magnet inside the jail?" Patrick asks. "Slippin' it under doors, going up the stairs … it ain't gonna work."

I relay his words to Miles, who turns the idea over in his head for a couple of seconds before suggesting:

"She will have to go outside," he says. "I'm pretty sure they can't legally keep her indoors for longer than twenty-four hours, so they'll need to let her outside for some exercise, and the ghosts can be waiting for her with the magnet when she does. They'll have to keep watch and get her the magnet when they see her."

They might have to wait a long time, but I do not see any better way to do this, so I nod. Patrick does not appear convinced.

"How am I supposed to carry a magnet when I can't even touch it?" Patrick asks.

I pause. That is a good point. Miles asks why I have such a puzzled look on my face, and I tell him what Patrick said. The conundrum stumps Miles for a couple of seconds before he offers a solution.

"I could put it in some kind of packaging," Miles says. "Or attach a long string to it that he can pull."

Patrick considers the idea. "It's got to be feather light."

"It will be small," I assure him.

"Chances are we don't get it to her."

"At least there is a chance," I say, and Miles nods.

"I'll go with him," Maude says. "We can team up."

"You ain't steppin' foot near that place." Patrick points a finger at her. "Leonard could be in there."

Maude gulps. After everything Leonard did to her, I would not blame her if she did not want to go.

But this does not appear to stop her. "I'm going. Besides, we'll be stronger together."

"Why do you even want to help her?" Patrick asks, as though I am not here.

"Because it's the decent thing to do," Maude says. "Leonard has gone nutty, and someone needs to put a stop to it."

Patrick presses his lips into a line. An unreadable emotion crosses his face. I understand that his feelings for Leonard are complicated and that the choices he faces are not as easy for him, but there comes a point when personal feelings stop mattering.

"I want to head back to Ola," Patrick says. "I didn't ask for any of this."

"If you help me with this," I say firmly, "I will take you back across the veil. You will bring Shiloh a magnet, and once I have gone home from the hospital and I am feeling stronger, then I will bring you to Ola."

Patrick turns this idea over in his head. I am not accustomed to giving people ultimatums, but Shiloh's life depends on this, so I am not mincing my words. I remember Evangeline saying that Patrick is a good person and that he has a good heart, but this is not his battle. All he wants to do is go back to his corner of the universe where he finally found peace, and after all he went through when he was alive I cannot blame him for that.

Close to a minute goes by before Patrick hangs his head and nods.

"How am I supposed to find her?" he asks.

I tell him that Miles will lead him to the detention facility in his car, but once they have reached the edge of the property, it will be up to him to get the magnet to Shiloh. She will likely not come outside until morning, so they may have to lurk around the prison for a long time, but it is all right because souls do not sleep anyway, which must mean that they have a higher tolerance for boredom as well. Miles finds a photograph of Shiloh on his phone. He flashes the screen in the opposite direction that Patrick is in, so I twirl my finger to tell him to spin. I glimpse the photo he chose. Shiloh is sitting on the grass outside, in front of what appears to be our school. Her hair is up in the way she normally wears it, but she is smiling, which is more unusual for her. Miles photographed her mid-laugh. Her nose is scrunched up and her eyes are squinting. Even across the room, I can feel the happiness exuding from the photo.

I glance up at Miles. His cheeks flush, and he puts away the phone. That photograph of Shiloh must be his favorite.

Imagining the smiling girl in that photo alone and behind bars creates an ache in my heart. She must be so afraid. It is remarkably unfair that she is a criminal in the eyes of the law when, if it were not for her, Max would not be alive, and I would still be in the cellar. Or on the other side, in a more permanent manner.

Because neither Patrick nor Miles can communicate with each other, I tell Patrick to follow Miles and I tell Miles to verbally explain what he would like Patrick to do at each stage at the process, even though he cannot see him.

"I can feel the ghosts in here," Miles says, his breath coming out as a visible fog. "It got colder after they came in the room."

"Do you need your coat back?" I ask. The smooth material smells of something that is not Miles yet, but will be soon.

He shakes his head. "Keep it. Are you going to be okay? I mean, alone here tonight?"

"I am not alone." With a small smile, I hold up the magnet he gave me. "In the hospital, I am never really alone, am I?"

Miles smiles. He leaves, and both Patrick and Maude trail after him. Clutching the magnet against my stomach, I lean back against the pillow and release a long sigh. I do not feel very strong right now, but one way or another, I must become strong again by morning, so I close my eyes and will myself to sleep.

The old woman in the bed beside me dies during the night. I have witnessed death enough times to recognize it. The finality of those last breaths. In front of my eyes, the woman begins to glow, like her entire body has been dipped in bioluminescent algae.

A ball of light emerges from her. I can hardly breathe as it elongates and stretches into arms ... legs ... a head. I consider greeting her but, as quickly as she appeared, she fades into nothing with nobody there to witness her passing but me.

Seconds later, nurses rush into the room with a rolling cart. One closes the curtain to block off my view. I hear fabric ripping and somebody yells, "Clear!" but it is too late. She is already gone.

The nurses leave. There is a commotion as somebody comes to bring the body away, but after that, it is silent. I grip the magnet under the sheets. I would much rather be in the cemetery alone at night than in the hospital. Generally, I feel much more comfortable in the company of the dead than the living, but it is impossible to sleep over the wailing and crying that is coming from down the hall. Every soul in the hospital is brand new. They are confused at having woken up as a soul, or grieving their own life alongside their family members. By the time souls reach the cemetery, they understand they are dead and have taken the time they need to come to terms with it, but hospitals are places of loss, and the process is often sudden and unexpected.

I toss and turn for another couple of hours. Close to four o'clock in the morning, so much pressure has built in my bladder that I cannot ignore it any longer. There are so many wires and sensors attached to me that I need to call a nurse to disconnect me so that I can stand up. He offers me an arm to lean on and rolls my IV pole as I shuffle across the clean floor in slippers that are too big for my feet. Each step is an agonizing effort. Once I am in the bathroom, the nurse tells me he will wait outside, and I close the door.

Using the IV pole for balance, I lower myself onto the toilet and, afterward, drag myself to the sink. I run my uninjured hand under the water, but I do not clean the bandaged one. Enough gauze and tape are wrapped around it that I can pretend there is still a finger in there somewhere. Or perhaps it is merely the echo of one.

I dry my bare hand off on the front of my gown and use it to cradle my injured one, wishing I could do something to make it stop burning so much. I raise my eyes to my reflection in the mirror. I have never fancied myself as pretty, but every single thing I used to like about my appearance is gone. My dark-brown curls are ivory. So many of them have fallen out in clumps that there are bald patches on my head. My face is sagging, like there is too much skin to fit over my bones and it is bunching up. The color has drained from my brown eyes, as if my irises had been washed with alcohol. The girl I used to be is gone, and in her place is an old witch from a dark fairytale.

It is as my mother said. Everything … *everything* comes at a price.

I always wanted to use my ability to help people, but I did not think the price would be this high.

A hot pressure builds behind my eyes as though I am going to cry, so I turn my eyes away from my reflection and go back into my room. The nurse helps me back to my bed and I eventually do go to sleep, but the sad feeling that has come over me does not go away until morning.

12

Shiloh

It's hard to sleep when I know there's an evil ghost lurking around me. Every single noise wakes me up and makes me jump, and I don't even have a blanket to huddle under.

I slept for most of the day, so I spend the night lying on the mattress and biting my nails, trying to figure out if I'm cold because there's a ghost in here or because the heating in this whole place could be turned up a few degrees. But I am tired when the lights turn on in the morning.

Because my life is one cruel joke, an officer comes to get me just as I'm thinking about falling asleep and marches me through the building to an outdoor yard for some exercise or form of personal enrichment or whatever they call it these days. The small fenced-in area is built like a dog run, with tall fences topped with barbed wire and gravel on the ground. The officer goes back inside. I can see him guarding the other side of the door. I guess he's pretty confident that I can't get out of here, and he's right to be. There's no chance I'm scaling that fence, and it looks like I'm the only one out here, so there's no one to throw me over.

I drop my gaze to the hula hoop on the ground. Is this my government-sponsored exercise for the day?

No way am I doing that. I rub my hands together, breathing on them as I glance around the small yard. The morning sun is high, but it hasn't done much to warm up the air.

How long am I supposed to stay out here? I guess I could go back inside any time I want. Yesterday, I kept fantasizing about going outside and feeling the sun on my face, but all I feel right now is cold, and I'm tired of feeling cold.

I'm about to cave and use the freaking hula hoop when I glimpse movement over my head. I look up.

At first, I don't really understand what I'm looking at. It looks almost like a kite, but it's not a kite, because normal kites fly with their strings hanging down and this thing looks like it's hanging by a string suspended in the air. It floats above the barbed wire like an upside-down balloon, kind of like one of the red ones from *It*, drifting through the sky like a bad omen.

I crane my neck up to stare at it. The thing is too far away for me to figure out what it is—at least, until it looks like it's going to drop on my head.

I leap out of the way. It lands on the ground soundlessly. It looks like … an envelope?

I pick it up. A piece of yarn has been duct-taped to the back of it. Turning my back to the door so that the officer can't see, I rip it open and pull out a flat refrigerator magnet roughly the size of a bookmark. On the front is a cartoon of a wine bottle and a wine glass with googly eyes. They're holding hands. Underneath them is the caption, "PARTNERS IN WINE."

I stare at the words. I feel like this is something I should burst out laughing about because *what the hell is happening right now?* But it's so weird that I don't know how to react.

Partners in wine? Could my friends have somehow sent this to me?

This magnet has Miles written all over it. It's his sense of humor. He loves puns and corny captions like that. I can picture him so easily, choosing this because it made him laugh in the hopes it would also make me laugh.

Why did he give this to me? How?

Did he get a ghost to bring it in for me?

I turn over the magnet, bending it and rolling it between my fingers, trying to find a message. It takes me too long to spot the words written inside the purple lines of the W:

For your ghost problem. - M

Oh my God. I slip the magnet into my shoe before the officer can see me holding anything, then crumple up the envelope and yarn and fit it through the chain-link fence. It blows away on the breeze, bouncing through the scrub on the other side of the fence like a flat tumbleweed. I can't help but smile both at the absurdness of this situation and also at the promise embedded in his words. He's trying to get me out of here. He hasn't given up on me, and neither have I.

I'm not afraid of any ghost. Not when I have friends like these.

I sit there smiling until the officer calls out that my time is up. I try hard to focus on not walking weird so he doesn't think to check my shoe for anything I'm not supposed to have, and I make it back to my room without him saying anything. Lying down on the mattress, I slide the magnet under my shirt, place it on my chest, and close my eyes. Being trapped in here is still scary, but now at least I have a way to protect myself. A light at the end of a very depressing tunnel, and right now that's all I could hope for.

PART 2
Hush, little Jailbird don't SAY A word

13

FRANCESCA

In the morning, I wake up to find a soul hovering at the end of my bed. I startle, feeling around in the covers for the magnet before I wake up enough to realize who it is. My eyes narrow.

"How long have you been watching me like this?" I demand.

Patrick shrugs. The determination in his eyes suggests he has been here for quite a long time. I do hope he has not been watching me all night, but he could have. The dead do not sleep.

When it becomes clear he will not talk, I do.

"Did you get the magnet to Shiloh?" I ask.

He nods. I slump back into the pillows, overcome with relief for only a moment before he says: "You've got to get that girl out of there."

A shivery feeling comes over me. "Is she in danger?"

"I saw him," Patrick says. "He's goin' after her."

I am not sure why his words drain the blood from my face. I already knew that Leonard was trying to hurt Shiloh. He told me as much on the other side, but I suppose it has not been confirmed, and deep down I was holding on to the hope that perhaps I was mistaken and Shiloh was safe after all. That hope is gone now.

I thank Patrick for his help. He nods and, without another word, passes through the wall.

Only a couple of minutes have gone by before the door to my room opens. A doctor comes inside. He is a middle-aged man with salt-and-pepper curls and the beginnings of a mustache that appears to be coming in white.

He uses the clipboard to gesture at me, running it up and down. "I'm not going to lie to you, kid. I'm at a loss. I can't find anything wrong with you. There's no explanation for your symptoms."

By symptoms, he means my physical changes. He may not have an explanation for why this is happening to me, but I do. I wish I could tell him about the other side to reassure him he really is a good doctor and there is no scientific reason for why I look the way I do, but I have spent enough time around people who do not believe in ghosts to know that telling the truth rarely leads to anything good happening if people are incapable of believing it.

He gives me detailed instructions for how I am supposed to change the bandages. I will need to do it once a day when I go home.

I pause on the word. "Home?"

"We got in touch with your father this morning." He smiles, as though this is good news. "He's coming to bring you home."

As the doctor leaves, I reassure myself that he is mistaken. My father is not coming for me. In any normal circumstances, learning that his daughter is in the hospital should prompt him to pay me a visit, but this is the same man who abandoned me in a trailer because he was embarrassed about me, which is not a strong commendation for his character. I am not expecting him to run into my hospital room ninety minutes later, holding a gift bag and wearing a harried expression as though he had been running.

He stops and stares at me. I am so surprised to see him that I lose my ability to think. It has only been six weeks since I last saw my father, but it feels much longer. He looks the same. He is still only an inch or two taller than I am. There is still no hair on his head except for his eyebrows. A bulbous belly pushes against the front of his shirt as if it were testing the strength of the buttons. I, on the other hand, feel completely different.

He appears to think the same thing, because his mouth drops open. "Francesca?"

I raise my bandaged hand in a limp wave. *"Buongiorno, Papà."*

He points at my face. *"Cosa ti è successo al viso?"*

What happened to my face? That is a good question. I try to think of a proper explanation for what happened, something that might satisfy him and not cause him to blame my overactive imagination, but I cannot think of a single thing that could explain this much of a change. My father already believes there is something wrong with my head because I believe in ghosts. Telling him the truth may not change his opinion of me, but it could make him less agreeable and make it more likely that he will ask the doctor to inspect my mind instead of merely my body before I leave this hospital.

If Shiloh were in my position, she would make a joke, so I attempt to do the same.

"I got sunburned quite badly," I say.

My father frowns. I suppose it was not a very good joke.

"Ti porto a casa mia," he says, and the blood drops from my face. *"Adesso."*

He is taking me to his house. I do not want to go to his house. I have only been there two times. Once when he got married last year, and again a couple of months ago to have dinner with his new family. I liked nothing about the house. It smelled too strongly of pineapple and was filled with dolls for a little girl who was not me. His house is the last place I want to go, especially when I still need to discuss with Miles how we are going to free Shiloh from prison.

I choose my words carefully. "Will Elena be angry about that?"

My father flattens his mouth at the sound of his wife's name. *"Tuo fratello vive con me. È stato ferito da alcune persone molto cattive. Ha quasi perso un occhio. Verrete entrambe a vivere con me."*

He talks so fast that it takes my mind a moment or two to understand what he is saying: Richie is already living with him in Columbus. He is hurt, and he may lose an eye.

Uh oh. Did Leonard hurt him?

Shiloh was convinced Richie was Leonard's host body in Bethany. I did not believe her until he broke into Shiloh's house and nearly murdered us all. Clearly, he had not been Leonard's host, but he must have been helping Leonard in some way. Perhaps Leonard became angry with him. Could that be how he hurt his eye?

I force myself to nod. Ever since my father left me in Bethany, I had dreamed of the day when he would finally come back for me, but I never thought I would wish for him to be somewhere else when he did.

"Did the doctor say I could go home?" I ask.

According to my father, the doctor said that so long as I feel okay, I may go home once my father signs the discharge papers. I ask him to do so.

He smiles at me. His eyes are filled with sadness. I do not know what he is sad about. Perhaps he is sad that I was hurt, although he has never paid much attention to whether I was hurt before. Perhaps seeing me hurt is making him regret not being a very good father a lot of the time, especially now that he has Richie living with him again, but he has always liked Richie more than me because he blames me for shaming our family and making the entire town dislike us. I do not believe he will ever see me differently, regardless of how badly he feels about seeing me this way.

He does not treat his new daughter like this. I have seen the cards he sends out on holidays of him smiling and holding her the way he used to hold me before I became something to be embarrassed about.

He places a small paper bag on the foot of my bed and goes out the door. Only when he is gone do I reach through the layers of tissue paper and pull out the teddy bear with shiny pink fur.

I throw the bear on the ground. Is that what he thought I would like? My father does not know me at all.

I cannot go with him, but he is the only person who can discharge me from the hospital, and Miles has not come to see me yet this morning. I trace the smudged phone number on my arm. I could call him and ask him to come and pick me up.

But I would need a phone. Perhaps I could find one in a store outside the hospital. I sit up in bed, wrapping my arms around myself because I do not enjoy lying one bit. It will not take long for my father to sign the forms, get my clothes, and return for me. In that time, I must come up with a way to escape this hospital without being detected.

I glance around the sterile room, my eyes skimming over the blinking machines, stark white floors, and dull pastel walls. There is something moving inside the wall. It is shimmering. Nearly glowing.

"Hello?" I grip the magnet and hold it out in front of myself with a shaky hand. The air around me grows cold. "Is anybody there?"

Maude glides in through the wall. "Only me."

Oh. I drop the magnet on my lap. "Is everything all right?"

"I heard something about you going home today," she says. "Does that mean you are strong enough to bring Patrick back across the veil?"

I understand that she and Patrick would like to go back to where they came from, but I am growing tired of having the same conversation with them. I begin to tell her, once again, that I need more time to rest and to please leave me alone so that I can come up with a plan to escape, when the tiniest glimmer of an idea pops into my head.

Maude's thin eyebrows draw together. "Why are you giving me that look?"

"Because I need your help," I say. "Could you please go find Patrick?"

Patrick is not keen on helping me again. He only just finished helping me by bringing a magnet to Shiloh, and he does not appreciate being used as some invisible butler to do my bidding.

"I cannot bring you back across the veil if I go with my father," I say. "There will be nobody to wake me up. Besides, Evangeline is with my friends. Wouldn't you like to see her again?"

Maude's eyes brighten at the sound of her best friend's name. Even Patrick's expression softens a little.

In a hushed voice, I tell them my plan. It is not a very thorough plan. It is the sort of plan Jonah would come up with. A plan that relies on sheer luck and how fast I can run, which is not very fast, considering how much time it took me to make it to the bathroom during the night. But then, some of Jonah's plans have been successful in the past, have they not?

I am actually not sure. Unfortunately, I do not remember the last time Jonah came up with a plan that was successful.

There is not much time before my father returns, so we must begin our escape immediately. I press the button for a nurse to come in. On my request, she brings me a take-home bag of gauze and bandages to change the dressing on my finger, some written instructions, and my original clothes. I can see the dirt and grime on the fabric through the plastic bag. I have no desire to open the bag up, but if I am going to leave this place, I must do my best not to look like a patient who is running away, so I do.

The aroma assaults my nose. Urine, feces, vomit, sweat, blood, body odor … I have never smelled anything quite so repulsive in my life. There is blood on the front of my skirt from where Leonard cut off my finger. Or perhaps from where he threw those teeth at me. I plug my nose and turn my face away, unsure of how I will stomach wearing these.

But I do not have a choice. Patrick and Maude watch me, unaffected by the smell.

"Do you mind turning around?" I ask.

Both seem startled, as if they did not realize that they had been staring at me. Gathering all my strength, I yank the IV out of my arm. I kick the blanket off my legs and slide onto my unsteady feet, leaning against the mattress as red and black spots pour into the corners of my vision. Running out of this place may not be such a good idea. I can feel the weight in the soles of my feet, feel how it shifts as my body tries to balance itself. If I fall unconscious, the nurses will carry me right back into this room and I will lose my opportunity, but I will not let my father bring me to his house.

I untie the hospital gown with one hand and pull the rotten clothes onto my body. I do my best not to think about how dirty they are or what made them so dirty. Spending all those days locked inside a cage without access to a bathroom is not something I remember fondly. I could not hold it for very long. Evangeline was kind enough to close her eyes and cover her ears when I had to go.

In the pocket of my skirt, my fingers brush Ola's coarse hair. It is still there. The idea of having to go to the other side again makes me lightheaded, but that is not something I need to worry about quite yet. I would have hoped I would be feeling stronger after resting in the hospital. I suppose I need more than one day of rest to feel back to normal.

"All right," I say to Patrick and Maude, causing them to turn around. "Do I look normal?"

The creases that appear on Maude's forehead tell me I do not.

"Well, at least you're clothed." Patrick soars over to the closed door, and I thread my arms through the sleeves of my coat. "All set?"

Dropping the magnet into the bag, I tell him I am. The teddy bear on the floor catches my eye. It looks very sad, lying on the ground, so I put it in the bag as well.

Patrick pushes his head through the door and glances from one side to another. His spectral form blends in with the clinical white surroundings. He tells us the hallway is clear, so I open the door and follow him to the waiting area so as not to attract suspicion.

My heart beats so hard that the tips of my fingers tingle. I am not sure how we will get past the nurses' station without them noticing. There are so many of them, and most of them know I am a patient.

Pressing my shoulder against the wall, I peer around the corner at them. Some are typing on computers. Others are rifling through papers or talking with one another. My father is not there. I wonder where he has gone. Perhaps to the restroom.

Maude sails over the top of the nurses and stops in the mouth of a hallway on the other side of them. A couple of seconds go by. I begin to wonder what she could be planning when she screams.

All the nurses stop talking. The alarm on their faces tells me I am not the only one who heard that scream. I am not used to other people hearing souls. I have always been the only one who can hear them, but I suppose Maude is much more powerful than the souls I grew up knowing.

Maude screams again. Louder this time, as though she is having her skin peeled off her face. I am looking at her and know she is all right, but the sound tears at something deep inside me.

It stirs something within the nurses as well. They abandon the station and rush toward the sound, running through Maude's vaporous figure. She regains her shape and smiles at me.

I hurry through the waiting area and press the elevator button. In seconds, it arrives with a ding.

The doors close me in. Soft instrumental music plays as the elevator carries me down. I lean against the railing on the rear wall. I can no longer see Patrick or Maude, but I trust they are following me. This elevator did not carry me when I was a soul either.

As soon as the doors open to the main floor, I push away from the wall and walk out. Patrick appears in front of me. His form causes an eerie chill as he moves through the bustling reception. People he passes through rub their arms and glance around for the cause of the sudden chill, providing me with enough of a distraction for them not to notice me.

There is a gift shop on my left. On the other side of the window, my father takes out his wallet as a woman bags a pair of pants and a soft pink sweatshirt. I stop walking. Is he buying clothes for me?

It is a tender gesture. One that is so unlike him. My chest fills with unexpected warmth. I wonder what he will think when he discovers I am gone. Will he worry?

"What are you doing, Francesca?" Maude asks. "Why are you stopping?"

My father turns around. Our eyes lock in the crowd. His eyebrows knit in confusion.

Uh oh.

I hasten toward the sliding glass doors. I hear him call my name as I slip into the parking lot.

The sun is blinding and I shield my eyes with my bag. A frigid wind blows against me. It pushes my clothes tighter against my body and makes both of my ghostly companions much paler. I wonder why that happens. Perhaps it has something to do with energy and how souls use it to power themselves, but I cannot remember enough of what Miles told me to explain it. I curl my bare toes into the towel-like material of my slippers.

A bus has stopped on the other side of the parking lot, and some people are climbing in. Perhaps if I hurry, I could get on it.

I weave between cars. Behind me, the hospital doors open.

"Francesca!" I glance over my shoulder to see my father

squinting against the sun. I do not believe he sees me. "*Che diavolo stai facendo?*"

I duck behind a car and continue running while bent over. Every step sends a stab of pain through the sole of my foot, and I can only run for a few paces before I need to stop, balancing on a car's glossy exterior. The asphalt is hard underneath the bottoms of my slippers. They are too big and slap against the pavement like they are threatening to make me trip.

There are only two people in line for the bus. I must keep running if I am going to make it.

"Francesca?" my father calls, making me push off from a car and stumble forward. "Francesca, *bimba,* why are you running?"

I reach the end of the row of cars and run to the bus. My lungs are burning and the corners of my vision are dark. I am not strong enough to run. I am not even sure when the last time I ran like this was.

The bus doors begin to close with a hiss. I catch them.

"Hello," I say, pulling my heavy legs up the stairs. "May I come on the bus as well?"

Giving me a bored stare, the driver points at the fare box. A bright yellow sign reads: $2.

Uh oh. In my urgency to escape the hospital, I forgot that I do not have any money.

"I am really sorry," I say. "But I cannot pay the fare."

The bus driver sighs. "Ah Jesus, you're the third one today. Is this Free Bus Ride Day? Did I miss the memo?"

I rummage through my bag even though I know I will not find two dollars' worth of quarters underneath the gauze, but my hand closes around the teddy bear. I place it on top of the fare box.

"This is all I have."

The driver blinks at the bear as if he is contemplating his entire life leading up to this moment. I hear my father call my name behind me. I hope he does not see me. I hope he does not stop me.

"Please," I beg. "It will not happen again."

"Just … go sit down. And take that goddamn thing with you." The bus driver points at the bear, and I put it back in the bag. "This isn't a habit you want to start, you hear me?"

I thank the driver profusely and find a seat away from any other people so as not to bother them with how badly I smell. As the doors close, I glimpse my father through the window. He has one hand clasped on his forehead, and his phone raised to his ear. There is a lost look on his face. I am not sure what to make of it. He had never been very concerned for me before, so I do not understand why he would care about me now. I consider waving at him as a gesture to tell him I am all right and will tell him about this one day after this is all over, but I cannot bring myself to do so. Instead, I duck below his line of sight as the bus pulls away.

14

FrANCeSCA

I get off the bus after two stops. There are so many people and I do not know where I am, but it does not take me long to find a coffee shop. The line at the counter is long. I wait in it for a number of minutes, resisting the urge to apologize when the woman ahead of me wrinkles her nose at the way I smell before I ask a barista in a green apron if I could borrow her phone. She does not look pleased. I miss Bethany. Even though so many people in town thought that I was not right in the head, I could always find somebody willing to help me when I needed it.

The man standing behind me offers me his cell phone. I thank him as I punch in the number Miles wrote on my arm and pray he picks up. He answers after four rings.

"Hello?"

"Can you come pick me up?" I say, turning to read the name of the coffee shop. "I am at … Starbucks."

Miles pauses. "Which Starbucks?"

"There is more than one?"

"Can you put me on the phone with someone who works there?"

The barista will not appreciate me interrupting the customer ordering, so I hand the phone to the young man whose phone I borrowed, and he explains to Miles where this Starbucks is. He hangs up.

"Your friend is on his way." The young man offers me a smile. "Good luck."

"Thank you so much."

He goes up to order, and I take a seat on an armchair in the corner to wait for Miles. I wonder where Patrick and Maude ended up. Perhaps they grew tired of helping me and are going to busy themselves with something else until I can help them cross to the other side. I could sure use the reprise from being asked, although I do wish I'd had the opportunity to thank them for their help.

In one hour, Miles walks through the door, but he is not alone. There is a girl with him, and it is as though all the air is drawn out of the room.

Evangeline glances around the coffee shop. Her fiery orange hair is not matted into braids anymore like a bedraggled Pippi Longstocking, but is shiny and clean now. The blouse she had been wearing in the cage has been replaced with a black sweatshirt displaying a motorcycle on fire that I very much doubt belongs to her. The ends of her pants have been folded up so that she does not trip on them. There is a bruise on her cheek, but it is not swollen enough to force her eye closed.

Her sea-green eyes meet mine. In the cage, she cried a lot and rarely smiled, but now she is smiling so brightly that my entire body fills with warmth, and I stop being able to see anything else.

She runs over to me. I stand up from the chair in time for her to crash into me, throwing her arms around me, burying her face in my hair. She does not seem to care how it smells.

"I tried to stay by your side," she says. "I tried, but the doctors sent me away. I didn't want to leave you alone."

Her warm arms tighten around me. They are stronger than I

remember. I have never been fond of physical touch. Perhaps it is because I have not received many hugs in my life, but the way Evangeline is holding me, like she is holding me together, makes my stomach turn topsy-turvy.

She pulls away, smiling so widely that I cannot help but smile as well. I press my thumb into the cleft in her chin. I try to think of something to say, but my tongue feels as though it has been tied in a knot.

Evangeline has no such problem. "What are you doing here?" she asks. "You are supposed to be in the hospital."

"I escaped." I notice Miles coming up behind her with a concerned expression on his face. "My father came to bring me back to Columbus, and I did not want to go with him."

The smile drops off Evangeline's face. "So you ran away? Are you strong enough to leave the hospital yet?"

"I feel fine," I lie, still so happy to see her I cannot stop smiling. "All I need is some rest, and I will be good as new."

Evangeline does not look as if she believes it. Neither does Miles, but going back to that hospital would mean going back to my father, and I am not about to let that happen. So I knit the fingers of my good hand through Evangeline's and raise my eyebrows at Miles. "I am ready to go back to your motel now. Can you drive me there?"

Miles hardly makes it out of the city before stopping to buy me some new clothes. I do not blame him. The smell is unbearable, even though I have had a couple of hours to get used to it.

"Get whatever you want," Miles says, plugging his nose and gesturing at the racks of clothes inside the department store. "I don't care as long as it's clean."

I gape at all the options. The majority of the clothes I own are hand-me-downs from Richie, or ones I have chosen with comfort or affordability in mind. I have not gone shopping for clothes enough to know what looks good. Unfortunately, all of Evangeline's suggestions for me contain quite too many … ruffles.

She pulls a dress off a hanger. It is made out of yellow fabric covered in daisies. Both sleeves are puffed.

"What do you think of this?" she asks, her eyes alight.

As much as I would like to wear something she likes, the idea of forcing myself into such a garment when I am already having so much trouble getting comfortable is not appealing, so I shake my head. Evangeline frowns. I did not mean to disappoint her.

"You should buy it for yourself," I suggest. "It would look pretty on you."

She smiles. "You think so?"

"Try it on."

Evangeline finds a dressing room. After a minute, she steps out wearing the dress, and my stomach flips over.

The sunny fabric makes her skin luminous. She looks like she has gathered all the sunshine in the world and put it inside herself. I feel an odd jolt in the pit of my stomach. My heart quickens, jarred to life and racing as though I was nervous, even though I am not sure what I am nervous about.

She twirls around, allowing the fabric to swirl around her legs. I suspect she is accustomed to looking nice in dresses. "Do you like it?"

I try to focus on her face, but all I can see is the way the dress hugs her chest. My fingers itch to touch the fabric. Or perhaps to touch her. The racks of clothes in my peripheral vision blur.

"Is it terrible?" she asks.

"No," I manage, my voice sounding distant to my ears. "It is very nice."

She smiles at me, then turns to face the mirror on the dressing room door. "If only I could find something to do with my hair. Usually, I wore it in curls, but this girl's hair is much too short to make pretty."

I can only nod, hoping my face does not appear as red as it

feels. Something about Evangeline makes me lose my ability to speak.

She goes back into the changing room to put her old clothes on. Once I have regained my composure, I pick out a flannel shirt and a pair of warm pants for myself. Miles comes to tell us to select underwear and toiletries because he does not know how long we will be staying in the motel. He has already gotten some for himself and Jonah. He also found saline solution and sterile gloves for me, because the doctors said I needed it to clean my finger. He found Tylenol as well because, I could not lie, my hand has been hurting progressively more since I left the hospital and I will need to get used to seeing a stump where a finger once was. I can tell how badly he wants to ask me how it happened. Nobody was there when Leonard snipped off my finger except for Talulah Monroe and Leonard himself. But putting that image in Miles's brain will hurt him. He will replay that in his mind and blame himself for not being there, so I say nothing. Some things are impossible to unhear.

"I also thought you might like this," he says, brandishing a purple cane from behind his back. It has a squishy rubber handle that appears to be designed to meld to the palm of somebody's hand.

But not mine. "I am not an old person," I say.

"I know," Miles says. "I just don't want you falling over."

"That is the sort of thing you say to old people."

"Francesca," he says. "You are the most incredible kick-ass-and-take-names person I have ever known, and you've brought enough people back from the dead by now to raise a small army. Until you recover fully, which you will, I thought it might be a good idea to make sure you don't get hurt any worse than you already are. Okay?"

I press my lips into a line. As much as I do not wish to admit it, Miles is right. Using a cane would help me walk faster. I am not sure why the idea of holding a cane gives me such a bad taste in my mouth.

I take the cane from him. When Evangeline bounds out of the changing room, my cheeks burn.

Miles asks if she is ready to go, and we all make our way to the checkout counter. I carry the cane instead of using it, but I have barely made it two paces before Evangeline taps me on the arm.

"I must say," she whispers, "that cane is quite stylish."

Perhaps I did not hear her correctly. "Stylish?"

She smiles. "You look totally chic."

All right. I suppose she does not think it is too embarrassing. She throws an arm around my shoulders as we walk, pulling me against her. Using the cane suddenly does not feel like such a bad idea anymore.

Once we arrive at the motel, Evangeline brings me to a room. She wraps a plastic bag over my bandage and waits outside the bathroom door while I have a shower. I wash with the water as hot as I can bear it, scrubbing all the grime from the cellar out from underneath my fingernails and working shampoo that smells like almonds into my ivory curls. Clumps of hair come out in my fingers. I quickly rinse them from my hands and toss them into the drain.

I dry myself with a towel and change back into my brand-new clothes. There is no laundry machine here, so they still smell like the store, but anything is better than the clothes I wore in the cellar, which are safe inside a trash can outside of the department store.

Evangeline is waiting for me when I step out of the bathroom. She has changed into her dress, and she brightens up the entire room. At least, she would if her eyebrows were not knit as though she is afraid that I will fall and not get back up again. My feet do feel a little wobbly. Red and blue spots creep into the corners of my vision even after the minor exertion of the shower, so as much as I do not want her to think I am weak, I allow her to help me to the bed.

She props a pillow behind my head and smooths the creases out of the blanket over my legs. The mattress sags under my weight.

"Do you want something to eat?" she asks, her eyes scanning the room for anything she could do that could make me more comfortable. "Maybe some water? There's a vending machine outside."

"No," I say. "I am all right."

She frowns. "I'm going to go find you something. Try to go to sleep."

She begins to move toward the door. I grip the edge of the sheets, a sudden tightness forming in my chest. In the cage, I could not sleep unless I was pressed against her, my back so snugly against hers that I could feel her heart beating. I remember her careful fingers in my hair, untangling my curls with the same precision and skill she used to pick locks. The soft part of her upper thigh cushioned my face as I slept. Even though the days in that cage were the worst of my entire life, I had never been so close to another person as I had been then, and I am not sure I ever want to sleep without feeling her body against mine. I am certain I will not sleep right now if she steps out of this room.

"Evangeline." My voice breaks on her name. She stops, turning to me. "Can you stay?"

She searches my eyes, as if trying to understand what could have made me say such a thing. I do not understand what compelled me to either. All I know is that in the cage, when she was with me, I did not feel any pain, and I do not want to feel pain now.

With a small nod, she draws a chair close to the bed. I had been hoping for her to climb onto the bed. I do not believe she could get too close to me if she tried. She braces her elbows on the mattress and takes my hand.

"I'm here," she says. Her thumb draws a careful circle on my knuckle, sending shivers up my arm.

The knot in the middle of my chest loosens. The aching in my body grows more distant. My eyelids grow heavier. She hums an unfamiliar melody, and I fall into a drowsy haze. The room dims. The last thing I remember before I drift away is the gentle squeeze of Evangeline's hand.

15

Shiloh

I'm disgusting. I smell awful. My mouth tastes like something crawled in there and died, and no matter how much water I drink, I can't get the loamy flavor off my tongue. I need a toothbrush. Can I get one back now that I have the magnet?

One glance in the cracked mirror tells me I look as bad as I feel. At least no one's around to see me—that is, until two officers come to my cell to get me after lunch.

They say nothing about how bad I smell. Both are expressionless as they tighten handcuffs on my wrists and lead me down a flight of stairs. I don't bother asking where they're taking me. Nobody has ever answered me before, so I doubt they'd talk now.

When they stop me in front of a door and don't bring me inside, I risk a question: "What's going on?"

No reply. What a surprise. I'm about to ask again when I hear a familiar voice coming from behind the closed door. The door opens, revealing Dad's silver-haired attorney.

"Shiloh," Caleb says. I can see other people in the room over his shoulder. Their voices carry out into the hallway until Caleb cuts them off by closing the door.

I try to swallow the lump in my throat. "What's happening?"

"You're about to have your detention hearing," he says. "It's fine. Just procedure. You're not on trial for anything. The judge is just going to read out your rights and determine what bail will be set at."

My heart hammers. I'm about to go before a judge, someone who is going to determine whether I get to walk out of here, and I didn't even get the chance to brush my teeth?

"Don't I need to prepare something for this?" I ask.

Caleb smiles at me, like I'm a puppy who just barked for the first time. "I'll do most of the talking. Just answer their questions. Do you remember what we talked about?"

"I remember you saying you could get the charges dropped," I say. "You said it would be easy."

"I'm working on it," he says. "Don't you worry your pretty little head about it."

Pretty little … if I didn't think he was my best chance at getting out of here, I'd punch the smug look right off his face. If Caleb notices the scowl I'm giving him, he doesn't let on.

"Just sit there and look cute," Caleb says. "Your dad is in there, so if you get nervous, look at him, and know that everything will be all right."

Is he serious right now? I don't have time to tell him how bad he is at comforting people before another man who must be the bailiff steps out and undoes my handcuffs before leading me through the door.

This is not exactly what I'd call a courtroom, at least not like the ones I've seen on TV. It reminds me of one of the classrooms at my school, with old books on the shelves and a chalkboard on the wall. Instead of desks, three wooden tables have been pressed together in the middle of the room. Dad sits at the one closest to the door. Three other middle-aged adults I have never seen before in my life sit on either side, and all the way in the back of the room, a woman with wispy blond hair in bangs sits in a black robe that looks almost like one you'd wear at a graduation. There's a microphone on the table in front of her.

The bailiff brings me over to Dad. No part of me wants to get near him, but I doubt he's going to do anything with all these people around us, so I do what I'm told. I stand tall, my back rigid, focusing on controlling my shaky breaths. One of the random adults gets me to hold up my right hand and swear that I'm going to tell the truth, the whole truth, and nothing but the truth, so help me God. I sit on a flimsy plastic chair and wring my hands together, rubbing my wrists to get them to feel better after having those handcuffs on.

The judge clears her throat. In my mind, I was picturing the judge to be some old and serious-looking big guy, not a woman barely older than Mom. But the hard look in her eyes tells me she's not one to mess with.

"This is the matter of Shiloh Oleson," she says. "Let the record show that Mrs. Wagle is present from the prosecutor's office. Caleb Morris is the attorney Shiloh has appointed to represent herself in this hearing, and Ms. Rossi is present from the intake department. Your name, please?"

She's looking at me. She just said my name. Does she need me to say it again? I guess so, because she stares at me expectantly, and so does everyone else in the room.

"Shiloh Oleson," I say.

"How old are you, Shiloh?"

"Sixteen."

Her eyes move to Dad. "And your name, sir?"

"Ernest Oleson."

"Are you the child's father?"

His eyes go to me, like he's asking for confirmation. "Yes."

"Have the two of you been advised of your rights?"

Dad nods. So do I.

"Fine," the judge says. "We're here today for charges of assault, battery, and second-degree murder. Is that right?"

Her words lance through me. I barely manage a nod as I drop

my eyes to the scratched wood on the table, digging my fingernails into my palms.

"Okay, Shiloh." The judge writes something down. "Do you want to tell us what happened?"

Me? I glance at Caleb, who gives me an encouraging nod. I thought I wasn't supposed to do any of the talking. Just sit there and look pretty. That's what he told me.

"I …" My voice is hoarse, so I clear the phlegm from my throat and try again: "My brother, Max, was kidnapped. I found out who had him, and I went to rescue him. The man had a knife. He was going to stab Max."

The judge quirks up one eyebrow. "You shot the man nine times, once in the back."

Technically, Jonah was the one who shot Leonard in the back, but I'm not bringing him into this. This will end with me. "The man was trying to kill my brother. He had kept him in a cage for two weeks and barely fed him. If I hadn't been there, Max would be dead."

"And what would you say your relationship with your brother is like?"

"He's my whole world."

She asks Dad how the two of us relate to each other in the house. Dad gives her some generic answer about how we have always been close, and I clench my fists so hard under the table that my nails bite into my skin. Is the judge going to base her assessment of how much I love Max on what Dad says about us? Does she know about the abuse, and does she have access to what I told the FBI? I want to tell her the reason why Max was my whole world, how he had to be my whole world because otherwise there would have been no one to protect him when Dad went on his rampages. But if I tell her that now, Dad would call me crazy. Would the court order a psychological evaluation? Would Dad take Caleb away? I kind of hate Caleb, but he's my best chance of getting out of here.

So I keep my mouth shut and try to figure out if the judge suspects Dad by the way she's looking at him. She has an impressive poker face that gives away nothing. She asks me about Davey and what happened on the bridge. I start to tell her about him using the knife and beating up Miles when a cold finger presses against the base of my skull.

The words catch in the back of my throat. The shivery feeling spreads through my body, raising the baby hairs on my arms and making my mouth feel dry.

Oh my God.

The judge asks another question, but her words don't reach me because all I can see is the fog riding her breath.

She sees it too. Her eyebrows pull together. "Can somebody turn up the heat in here?" she asks.

One of the random adults gets up. I bite my tongue. Turning up the heat won't do anything.

The reason it's cold is because there's a ghost in here.

I glance around the room, which is dumb because it's not like I can see ghosts. I slip my hand into my pocket to grab the magnet, but a lump forms in my throat. The magnet's not here. I left it in my cell.

Is Leonard here? Is he taking advantage of me not having the magnet?

The judge breathes into her hands, then rubs them together. "Mrs. Wagle, do you feel that you have enough evidence to move forward with these charges?"

A heavyset woman wearing an ill-fitting yellow T-shirt holds up a piece of paper. "I feel, given the information that has been provided, this case should be put before a grand jury."

Dad slams his hand on the table, then turns to Caleb. "You said you would handle this," he says.

Caleb holds a hand up to Dad. A heavy feeling comes over me. I know what a jury is, but I don't know what makes one grand. This is moving too fast. Snowballing like an avalanche, ready to bury me alive.

"Grand jury?" I glance at Caleb. "What is that?"

"The jury will review your case and decide whether there is

enough evidence to indict you," the judge says. "Once they reach a decision, you will be notified, and—"

A gust of wind blows into the judge. Her hair blows out of her face and stands on end like she electrocuted herself.

Everyone gasps. Her hair falls back down. The judge runs a hand over her head, smoothing out her bangs and glaring up at the ceiling for a second before the woman in the T-shirt says something about getting the heating unit under control. Behind her, one of the books on the shelf slides forward. A bead of sweat forms on my forehead. Is Leonard really going to attack me here, in this room?

I need to find a magnet. But any sudden movement could be interpreted as me looking for a weapon, and the bailiff would stop me from getting two steps before dragging me back to my cell.

"Because of the severity of the charges, no bail will be set." The judge's voice is hardly audible over how fast my heart is beating. "You will be held in custody pending the outcome of the grand jury."

Dad stands up in his chair. He yells about how absurd this is, and how I'm not a criminal, but I'm not paying attention to him. The book inches forward to the edge of the shelf, right over the judge's head. It has a clear path to me. All it has to do is shoot straight out.

The judge bangs on the table with her gavel. Dad shuts up.

"*Today*," she says, "the court finds probable cause to believe this child has committed delinquent acts, and will refer the matter to the prosecutor's office to present it before a grand jury. The jury will determine if there is sufficient evidence to indict Shiloh Oleson on all pending charges. Because of the severity of the charges, if the jury chooses to indict, she will be bound over to adult court."

Dad starts yelling again. The bailiff takes a step forward, holding out his hands like he's trying to keep peace. I grip the edge of the table. Being tried as an adult is bad. I could face years in prison. Even life.

The book slides off the edge of the shelf, hovering in the air above the judge. I open my mouth to warn her.

The book falls onto her head. She cries out. The gold-trimmed book crashes onto the table, then falls flat with its pages splayed open.

Nobody says a word. The judge whacks the gavel on the table again.

"This hearing is adjourned," she says, rubbing her head. "Thank you everyone."

She stands up and hurries out of the courtroom. Her words linger in the air. As if from far away, Caleb tells me not to worry. He will handle this. The bailiff escorts me from the room. I risk a look at Dad before I go. The anguish in his eyes surprises me. For a second, I see past the anger, the posturing, and the person he's become who scares me, and see the man he used to be before the drinking made him rot. He's looking at me like I'm about to walk in front of a firing squad, or like he's going to lose me, and suddenly, the judge's words rush back to me.

No bail. Grand jury. Bound over to adult court. Indict.

Caleb didn't take care of it like he said he would. My fate will now be in the hands of total strangers. People from Bethany. The same people who believed Dad would never lay a hand on his wife, even when the light hit her face in such a way you could see the bruises through her foundation. The ones who criticized me for dragging their sheriff through the dirt even after I showed the FBI proof.

The door closes, cutting off the sight of Dad's face. I hold back tears as the officers put handcuffs on me and escort me back to my cell, but as soon as the door closes, the tears spill over. I sink onto the cold floor, wrapping my arms around my legs and sobbing into my knees. This serves me right. I should have known better than to trust anything coming out of Dad's mouth. If I'm bound over to adult court and sentenced to years in here, all the magnets in the world aren't going to hold Leonard off. I don't know how this is going to end, but I know one thing. My life is over. It ended the second I pulled that trigger.

16

FrANCeSCA

A finger pokes my shoulder. "Francesca?"

I recognize the voice as Evangeline's, even though I am not entirely awake. She says my name again, although my mind is buzzing with partially-formed thoughts and the remnants of dreams. In her voice, my name sounds like a song, and it feels as though I have been trapped inside a car and another car has pulled up beside me playing much louder music.

Evangeline pokes me again. "Francesca, wake up."

My eyes open. Evangeline's freckled face swims above me, looking almost angelic, backed by the afternoon light coming through the window. I reach out to touch her cheek.

She catches my hand and places it back down on the bed, turning to look over her shoulder. "There's someone here who'd like to see you."

Using my good hand, I prop myself up and peer across the room. Miles is here, but I have already seen Miles, so I do not think Evangeline is talking about him. Somebody else steps out from behind Miles, and I know exactly who Evangeline is talking about.

Jonah stands still with his arms clasped in front of his body. His black hair is drenched with sweat, and he has a sort of sickly sallow look to his skin like he is very unwell.

Miles has his eyes trained on Jonah like he is waiting for him to do something bad. I was there when Leonard injected Jonah with foolery. Every ounce of recognition drained out of his eyes before he lunged at Shiloh with his knife. I am not sure what Miles is expecting Jonah to do, but I am surprised when a timid smile spreads over Jonah's lips.

"I like the gray," Jonah says. "It's very rock and roll."

I smile, touching a piece of my white hair. "Thank you."

Jonah shifts his arms. For the first time, I notice that he is not clasping his hands together voluntarily. His wrists are bound in a pair of shiny aluminum manacles.

Jonah notices me staring. He glances down at the manacles, and the smile drops off his face.

"I'm wearing these because Officer Killjoy here has me down as a security risk," Jonah says. "Apparently, I could snap and murder all of you at any time. So that's fun."

Sarcasm drips from his words. I know they are not true. Shiloh was the one Leonard ordered him to kill, so she is the one he would murder. If Miles thought Jonah would lose his mind and murder all of us, he would not have brought him here.

I cannot find the words to say to Jonah, so he continues speaking to me.

"I don't know how much these guys have told you about what's going on with me," he says, "but my memory has been shot to shit. Officer Genius tells me half the things I remember didn't happen, and I have to believe him, because he's so much smarter than I am—even though he's a cop now."

Miles's jaw bulges. He does not look at all happy that Jonah is here, but he did choose to bring him here. I suppose it is important for Jonah's recovery to carry on as though everything is normal.

I choose my next question carefully. "Do you remember who Shiloh is?"

Miles gives me a warning look. I know this is perhaps the last thing I should be asking Jonah, because his fragile mind is convinced that Shiloh is somebody who needs to be killed, but he does not lash out or scream. He simply nods.

"Yes," he says. "Obviously."

"Do you know she is a person who loves you?" I ask.

"She used to be," Jonah says. "Until she got possessed."

I shake my head gently. "I watched Leonard bring back his friends, and he did not use Shiloh's body."

Jonah pinches the bridge of his nose. "This is all really fucking confusing."

"The foolery tried to alter your mind, but you cannot let it," I tell him. "Please resist it. For Shiloh, and for all of us who love you. Do you think you could do that?"

Jonah nods. He looks so defeated that it drives a needle through my heart. I wonder if he remembers anything about Shiloh. If he remembers how his dimples used to come out when she called him the silly nickname she had for him, or laughed at some joke he made. I hope those are not all tangled up in the false memories the foolery created, but he is not screaming or trying to break free from the manacles, and I take that as a good sign.

I suppose I must carry on as normal, so I turn to Miles.

"Patrick and Maude were successful in bringing Shiloh the magnet," I say, "but she is still not safe. Leonard is trying to kill her in there, so we need to come up with a plan to free her."

Miles sinks into the armchair by the door, and Jonah, not seeming to know where to sit, chooses the empty bed.

"I already told you," Miles says. "We can't just ask the police to release her—"

"I understand that," I say. "But what if we can prove she did not do what they think she has done?"

"Get them to drop the charges?" Miles asks, and I nod. "I guess that could work. If we can provide new evidence that undermines the prosecution, maybe they'd dismiss the case. But how are we going to do that?"

His question hangs in the room. Is there any brand-new evidence that could clear Shiloh of her charges? Would the prosecutor listen to us if we found something? Miles does not appear to think so because an expression of utter despair has come over his face like there is too much noise in his brain that he does not know how to quiet it down. He looks ready to give up hope, but I will never give up hope.

"Miles," I say. "What are all the reasons Shiloh was imprisoned for?"

Jonah side-eyes me. This must be the first he has heard of Shiloh's arrest, but he does not react to it with any emotion.

Miles is the one who speaks. "Technically, Shiloh's in jail, not prison. Prison is where you go after you've actually been convicted of a crime, and jail is where you go when you're waiting for trial."

I blink at him. He shakes his head as if to clear it.

"Uh …" he begins, drumming his foot. "Well, there's the battery charge."

My eyes widen. "Shiloh hit somebody?"

Miles side-eyes Jonah, who is hanging off Miles's every word. "Jonah and Shiloh both did," Miles says. "Richie and his buddies were beating me up. Shiloh and Jonah came to my rescue, but it got messy. Shiloh broke Davey's knee, but Davey was holding a knife to her, so it was all messed up."

I know Richie is not a very nice person. Being mean to people has always made him feel good about himself, even though he is bigger than nearly every person in school and does not need to pick on anybody. I have seen him tormenting Miles enough times to picture how that altercation played out. If Shiloh and Jonah had not stepped in, I am sure it would have ended quite badly for Miles. On the other hand, Shiloh has a rigid view of what is right and wrong, and she would do anything to protect the people she loves—which sometimes leads her to make questionable decisions.

"Shiloh was wrong to break Davey's knee," I say.

"No kidding?" Miles says. "I mean, Davey has made me fear

for my life on more than one occasion, but Shiloh should have been the bigger person, and she's not doing herself any favors."

"Did anybody else see what happened?" I ask.

"Zweering was there," Jonah says. All of us turn to look at him, and some uncertainty comes onto his face. "Wasn't he?"

Miles nods. "Yeah, actually. He came to break up the fight, and we had to run away from him."

My lips turn upward. "Does that mean you could tell the police officers Shiloh did not do anything wrong?"

"I guess so," Miles says. "I'd have to see if the real Officer Zweering ever wrote an official report about what happened. If he didn't, I could write one and say Shiloh and Jonah did nothing wrong."

Something else occurs to me. "Do police officers wear cameras?"

Miles shakes his head. "Some do, but not in Bethany. Our town is too small, and I guess we don't have the budget because no one here wears them. I don't have one."

"That is good for us."

"You can say that again." Miles leans forward over his knees, a brand-new energy in his eyes. "Okay, so what else do they have Shiloh on?"

Jonah speaks again. "The Richie stuff."

"What Richie stuff?" I ask. Miles and Jonah exchange a glance, as though Jonah is having a moment of clarity and knows exactly what he is talking about this time.

"Uh," Miles begins, appearing like he doesn't know what to say. "When we were looking for you, all of us sort of kept Richie in my apartment for a couple of days and didn't let him leave."

My stomach lurches like I am falling. "You kidnapped my brother?"

"Only for a couple of days," Miles says, as though that would make it better. "To be fair, this was after he took the foolery and tried to kill us at the labyrinth, so we couldn't let him go because if we did he'd kill us. We were trying to figure out if he knew where you were. I gave him food and water, and bathroom breaks whenever he asked. I promise, he wasn't poorly treated."

"Shiloh tortured him," Jonah says, in a low voice.

Miles pauses. "Shiloh did … what? Shiloh *tortured* him?"

"I remember it," Jonah says, "but I don't know if the memory's real or just the drug talking."

"I surely hope it is fake," I say.

"Uh, I'm going to say it's fake because the Shiloh I know wouldn't do that," Miles says, then scrunches up his face. "Never mind. I can actually one hundred percent see Shiloh doing that."

A heavy feeling comes over my limbs. Richie may not be very nice most of the time or care much about the things that happen to me, but he is still my brother.

Miles rubs his eyes. "I mean, what evidence do they have? Is Richie's word enough to charge Shiloh with that? Probably not, right?"

Perhaps not, but just in case … "I could talk to him."

"Do you think he'd listen to you?" Miles asks.

"I am not sure," I say, "but it is worth trying because it may be our only option."

Miles pinches the bridge of his nose and nods. "Okay. So that leaves the third crime. The big one."

He does not say the word. Perhaps so as not to trigger Jonah. But I hear it loud and clear, all the same.

Murder.

There does not appear to be a way to discuss this without triggering Jonah, so I simply begin.

"Shiloh shot the man in self-defense," I say. Jonah stares at me with no emotion in his eyes. "Can they really find her guilty of murder?"

"Technically it wasn't self-defense," Miles says, side-eying Jonah. "Her lawyer could argue that in court, but if she pleads not guilty, her case would need to go to trial, which could be a year from now, and …"

"Leonard will kill her before then," I finish.

Miles nods. "There's evidence against her. They have the gun. Her fingerprints are all over it, and all over the casings they found on the floor of Leonard's trailer."

"What if I told the police that Leonard was trying to kill Max?" I say. "I was there."

Miles considers this. "I guess eyewitness accounts are evidence, but I don't know if it'll be enough."

I try to think of anybody else who witnessed the event. By the time Shiloh shot Leonard, Jonah had already begun to carry Miles back to the road. Only Shiloh and I were in the trailer with Leonard. It was Shiloh, Leonard, me …

And Max.

I remember his tiny soul springing up from his dead body after Leonard killed him. He glowed like a bulb in the shadows, smiling when he saw Shiloh and passing straight through her. He tumbled head over heels off the end of the trailer and landed in a heap on the ground. I wonder why souls do not pass straight through the ground. Perhaps the veil stretches out across the dirt and serves as our ground as well as the ceiling on the other side. I am not sure if that is how it works, but there must be some reason why ghosts do not just sink through to the center of the Earth.

Perhaps Max would remember Leonard killing him. He could tell the police that Leonard was trying to kill him, and that Shiloh saved his life. He could also tell them about the things Leonard did to him in the trailer. His eyewitness account is more important than any of ours because he was the one Leonard kidnapped. Leonard held Max captive. He did things to Max that nobody else knows, and his disappearance was a big event in the town. His statement could prove that it was self-defense because he was the one Shiloh was defending.

"Could Max talk to the police?" I ask.

Miles shakes his head. "Shiloh says Max doesn't remember what happened."

"Perhaps that is because he does not understand what he remembers," I say. "If I explain to him about ghosts …"

"You can't tell him about the ghosts," Miles says. "Shiloh would kill me."

"He may not understand what happened to him, but he deserves to know the truth," I say. "Shiloh cannot protect him from everything forever—especially given where she is. In all likelihood, he knows as much about Leonard as I do after being locked in a cage and having to listen to his ramblings."

Miles does not look so sure. Even Evangeline looks to have gotten a bit queasy.

"Where is Max right now?" I ask. "Can you bring me to him?"

Miles does not look happy when he helps me to my feet and hands me the cane. I am not very good at walking with it, but Evangeline shows me and assures me I will grow accustomed to it after a little bit of practice.

The room that Max is staying in is right around the corner. A man with no legs and very strong arms lets us in. Max is behind him, sitting on the bed and watching television.

Seeing me, Max jumps off the bed and runs to me. I lean the cane against the wall and lower myself to his eye level.

"Where is Shiloh?" he asks. He does not smell very good. His pajamas are grimy. So is he. His blond hair is clumped together with grease. There is worry written all over his face.

"She is not here," I say.

In a sudden burst of motion, he slams his hand into his leg. "Where is she?"

I hold out my hands and tell Max to put his in mine. He looks at them, his eyes narrowed into slits, but he does what I ask.

"Shiloh is alive," I say. "She is all right, but she has been arrested and is in prison right now."

Max blinks. "Why did she go to jail?"

"She did not commit a crime," I say, "but the police think she did something bad."

"You can call my daddy," Max says. "He's a police officer, and he can get her out of there."

"It is not that simple. Do you remember Leonard?" I ask, and

Max blinks at me. "He is the old man who kidnapped you and kept you in that cage in the middle of the woods?"

Max drops his eyes. He pulls his bottom lip between his teeth, but I take this as a sign that he knows who I mean.

"On the night we rescued you," I continue, "Leonard wanted to kill you. Do you remember that?"

Max still says nothing. I lower my voice.

"Please, Max," I beg. "It is extremely important that you remember."

Max raises his eyes to look at me. When he speaks, his voice is low. "The bad man said nothing he did was going to hurt me."

Understanding settles painfully in the pit of my stomach. "You were sleeping when we rescued you. Did the bad man give you something to help you sleep?"

Max pulls at his pajamas like he is uncomfortable wearing them. The gesture is similar to the one that Shiloh does.

"He gave me tea," Max says. "I don't like tea, but he said if I didn't drink it, things would hurt a lot more."

I glance at Evangeline and remember what she told me about chamomile tea helping people who have taken too much foolery. Drinking tea is not always soothing. If the taste of Leonard's tea was strong, it may have masked other things that had been slipped into it, such as medication that would make Max go to sleep. Leonard thought he was doing a good thing by reuniting families with their dead children. He did it to redeem himself. He would not have wanted to cause pain to the children he murdered, so I would understand if he put them to sleep before killing them so they wouldn't feel anything.

"The bad man was trying to hurt you, and Shiloh wanted to protect you. She shot him with a gun and the police are angry with her about that, but if she hadn't shot the bad man, the bad man would have killed you."

Max nods. So do I.

"Do you think you could come with me to tell the police that Shiloh was protecting you?" I ask.

Max pulls at his sleeve and snaps it back into place. "Will they let Shiloh go?"

"I think there is a really good chance of that happening," I say.

"Okay."

I smile at him and glance up at Miles, who has a worried look on his face. "What is wrong?" I ask.

"I hate to be the guy with the pragmatics," Miles says, "but what do you think the police will do if you show up in Bethany with Max when they all think he's missing?"

I am confused about why everyone in Bethany thinks Max is missing. Miles appears to register this confusion on my face, because he goes on to explain how when Shiloh's mother came to pick me up, Max had to go stay with his grandparents, and Shiloh did not like that, so she rescued him.

"Max would go back to his grandparents," Miles explains. "Taking him to Bethany is practically handing him to his dad."

I think for a couple of moments before coming up with a solution. Max may not be able to return to Bethany alone, but he could if his mother came with him.

Leaning forward onto my cane, I release a sigh. "I need to bring back Shiloh's mother."

"Are you strong enough?" Miles asks.

I do not know. Quite honestly, I am barely strong enough to walk by myself, and I would like to spend much more time sleeping before attempting a body swap, but there is no time. Shiloh is out of time. I am out of time. We are all out of time. If I wait any longer, Shiloh could die.

I tighten my grip on the cane. "Where is Leonard's mother right now?"

"In the tour bus," Miles says. "Tied up. Fiona told her friend Big Bruce to watch her. He's super strong, or something. Leonard's mom is insane, and she overpowered both Krav Maga black belt Phil and me, so Fiona didn't want to take any chances."

Uh oh. I have only killed once before, and that was Miles,

who was ready to die. In fact, it was necessary for him to die so that I could bring him back. The last look he gave me in his old body was one of acceptance and gratitude as I held my palm over his mouth and pinched his nostrils together. Several people would have to hold Leonard's mother down in order for me to kill her, and the last thing she would be is grateful.

But I have no choice. "May you please bring me to her?"

17
FRANCesca

There are strange cartoons painted on the sides of the bus. All of the figures have short bodies, chubby cheeks, and eyes that are much larger than usual. I am sure they are supposed to be cute, but the style makes me feel much more unsettled than I would like to admit. One looks quite a lot like Fiona. She is exaggerated in a way that Jonah appears to like, judging by the way he is examining the drawing.

Miles remains stony-faced and points at the stairs. "She's in here."

"She has been in here for three days?" I ask. "Has she left at all?"

Miles shakes his head. "Fiona promised she wouldn't lose her, and I guess she thought Bruce was their best form of security."

"Does Big Bruce sleep?" I ask. Miles shrugs.

"Did he even let her out to piss?" Jonah asks. I study his face to see if there is any trace of animosity or confusion on it, given that we are talking about Shiloh's mother, but he looks normal. "All day?"

Miles's expression shows he does not know how to answer that question. I suppose there is only one way to find out.

Miles helps me up the stairs. I had been hoping Leonard's mother had been kept well-restrained. Perhaps wrapped in chains, or behind bars similar to the way I had been locked in the cage. That is not what I find at all. Seated on a sagging couch on the other end of the bus, Leonard's mother appears quite comfortable. She does not look like she has been wetting herself or trapped in here with no opportunity to escape. Her pink cardigan is torn. There is dirt streaking her cheeks, yet her blonde hair is silky and glistens under the gray lighting. I am relieved to find that there are at least handcuffs around her wrists and some rope around her ankles. Playing cards are spread out over the coffee table.

The bald man who must be Big Bruce looks up at us and immediately stands up. I can certainly see why he was chosen as a guard. He is not quite as large as Ivan had been, but he looks stronger, with muscles that bulge out from underneath his leather vest and a beard so long it goes down past his chest.

"Who are you?" Big Bruce asks.

Miles introduces all of us and points at Leonard's mother. "That is our friend's mom. Or at least, it's her body."

Leonard's mother places her cards face-down on the coffee table one at a time. Each card slaps against the wood. My heart races. I do not want to be anywhere close to this woman. Despite inhabiting the body of Shiloh's mother, she does not look anything like Shiloh's mother does. I can see her mean expression and the sharpness behind her eyes, as if I were looking right at her soul.

Beside me, Jonah takes in a sharp breath. He turns away from us, pressing the fleshy parts of his palms to his eyes and breathing much too quickly.

"You okay?" Miles whispers.

Jonah says nothing. He looks back at Shiloh's mother, but something alien has come over his expression.

He steps forward. Miles grabs Jonah's upper arm.

Jonah struggles to get free. "Let me go!"

"I will not do that," Miles says.

"You can't trust her," he spits out. "She's possessed."

"I know," Miles says. "That's literally why we have her tied up."

His words do not reach Jonah. They only imbue him with more strength as he fights to reach Leonard's mother. I suppose it is not only Shiloh who makes Jonah angry. Even her mother's resemblance to her is enough to allow the foolery to take over his brain again.

As Miles drags Jonah out of the bus, a low laugh rises from Leonard's mother.

"Your friend's not doing very well, now, is he?" she asks. "What a shame. Some people are so weak-minded."

"Why are you playing cards with her?" I ask Big Bruce, mostly to divert my attention from the finger of terror that is dragging up my spine.

"Eleanor is teaching me how to play canasta," he says.

"I'm behaving," Leonard's mother says. "Like a good little prisoner."

My throat tightens. Her chin lowers.

"You here to end me, little missy?" she asks.

I must remove Leonard's mother's soul from the body in order to put Shiloh's mother back into it, but Big Bruce does not need to be here for that. So I put on the biggest smile I can muster, given the circumstances.

"Thank you so much for watching her," I say, "but could you give us a little privacy right now?"

Big Bruce stares at me as if there is more that he would like to say or perhaps like he does not believe me, but it does not appear to be worth much of his time because he grabs his coat and walks out of the bus.

Leonard's mother gathers up the cards and reshuffles the deck. "Nice fella. Awful at canasta."

I try to swallow the lump in my throat. I know what I have to do but I am not sure why I am so afraid to do it. I had the opportunity to kill Leonard when the helmet was over his head, and despite knowing that he would drag me back to the cellar and perhaps even kill me, I could not go through with it. Regardless of everything he put me through, I cannot be the one responsible for choosing who lives and who dies, because that is what Leonard does. I will not become like him.

"You do not belong in this world," I say, and she rolls her eyes. "You need to leave this body."

"I'm the one who's in here," she says. "So it's rightly mine."

I grip the cane until my knuckles turn white. "Please. Shiloh and Max … they need their mother."

"And I need my boy, but I don't see you leadin' me to him, now, do I?"

I stare at the old-fashioned manacles clasped around her wrists. A smile curves across her lips.

"If you aim to be rid of me," she says. "You're gonna have to kill me."

Pressure builds behind my eyeballs, blurring my vision. I place my cane on the dusty floor.

"That pitiful boy tried already, you know. I saw him sneak poison into my potatoes. It's a pity, it is. The look on his face when he saw I didn't nibble none. Only poor Maude had herself a taste and, well, you saw what came of her …"

I remember Patrick sneaking a tiny amount of drain cleaner into everybody's food at the house, hoping it would make everybody weaker for when we tried to escape. I had not understood how Leonard's mother could have remained so strong after ingesting it, but it makes sense if she never had a taste.

Nothing about this is right. She cannot continue living like this. My hands tremble as I pick up a length of rope discarded on a nearby folding chair.

Leonard's mother laughs. "You can't kill me. You're too feeble."

"I am not feeble," I say.

Leonard's mother huffs as though she does not believe me. The bus appears to tilt on its side. The corners of my vision spot, pulsing in time with the rapid beating of my heart. I create a loop with the rope and wrap it around the woman's neck. She stares up at me. A glob of spit flies from her mouth and onto my face.

I wipe it away. Her wrists are bound in front of her body so she could reach up and hit me, but she is sitting completely still. The bus feels as though it is spinning. All the blood rushes from my head.

"Francesca?" Miles asks from behind me. I did not hear him come back into the bus. "Are you okay?"

I drop the rope and step away, catching my balance on one of the wooden pedestals.

Miles appears beside me. "Do you feel sick?"

I nod, my insides churning. A flush of clammy heat washes over me, and the world around me loses its clarity. I can hear Leonard's mother's mean laugh as if from far away.

"I am not strong enough," I say, my voice quivering. "I cannot … I …"

A mug of water swims before my eyes. Miles places a hand on my back, and I slump against him, wrapping my hands around the mug and taking a couple of small sips.

"Come on," he says. "I'll help you back to your room."

Miles pulls me to my feet. I can still hear Leonard's mom cackling, but my stomach is swirling too much for me to care. Miles nearly carries me down the stairs. In the parking lot, he gives me my cane.

The chilly wind that beats against my face makes me feel a tiny bit better. Jonah is leaning against the side of the bus, clenching and unclenching his fists like he is trying to stay tethered to reality. I hope he has found it again. Across the parking lot, Max and Evangeline are standing in front of a vending machine. Max feeds a couple of dollar bills into the machine. Evangeline rips open her chocolate bar and takes a big bite, her lips curving into a smile. Shiloh's mother's soul hovers over Max like the opposite of a shadow. Perhaps it is because of the sun shining above her, or perhaps it is because I had not had anything to compare her to when I saw her this morning, but she looks like a wisp of fog that has taken human shape. She is completely see-through. She is barely there. I grip Miles's arm hard enough for him to stop walking.

He stops. "You okay?"

I shake my head. Usually, when a person dies, their soul does not remain on Earth forever and they fade to the other side on their own. Sometimes this takes a long time, like it did for Mrs. Lewis, who stayed in the cemetery for close to ten years. Other times, it is instantaneous, like it was for the old woman in the hospital. Every soul lingers for a different amount of time before fading to the other side. I am not sure what causes one soul to fade faster than another, but the signs are all the same. They become paler. They become nearly impossible to see, until one day they are not visible at all, which means they have gone to the other side for good. It is easy to see when a soul does not have much time left, and Shiloh's mother is getting very close to crossing over. Even closer than she was earlier today.

But I cannot let that happen. "Shiloh's mother is fading away," I tell Miles. "Quickly. If she has faded this much in one day, she may not be here for me to put back into her body if I wait until tomorrow."

"Well then, what do we do?" Miles asks.

I sit down on the steps leading up to the bus. Miles, Jonah, and I are silent as we try to think of ideas.

"You could take a bunch of 5-hour energy shots," Jonah suggests, stepping away from the bus. "One time, a buddy of mine drank ten bottles at once and didn't go to sleep for forty-eight hours."

"I do not believe caffeine could prevent me from falling unconscious," I say.

Jonah shrugs, dropping his gaze. "I'm just spitballing here."

"I will do it now," I say. "I do not have a choice."

"You could die," Miles says.

"I know."

He shakes his head. "You aren't doing that. No way."

"I will not leave Max and Shiloh without a mother," I say. "They have been through too much already."

"There has to be another option," he says.

I do not believe there is. Shiloh's mother's life is in danger, and I am the reason she was killed in the first place. There is no choice. This is something I must do.

I am about to stand up when a light goes off behind Miles's eyes.

He points at Jonah and snaps. "You."

Jonah points at himself, as if to confirm. "Me?"

"You're a genius."

"Yeah? I mean, I always had a feeling that might be the case, deep down."

"Leonard did this his whole life," Miles says, ignoring Jonah. "Right? The bringing people back from the dead thing? In the circus as a kid, he must have done it a bunch of times, and then he kept doing it as an adult."

I suppose that is true. "What are you saying?"

"I mean, he was, what, ninety in his original body?" Miles paces. "He spent his entire childhood bringing people back in the circus, and he must have brought back so many more people before coming to Bethany. Why isn't he the one in the hospital right now?"

I had not thought of that. Miles has a point. It has only been a couple of weeks since I discovered my ability, and I have brought people back to life fewer than ten times. How could Leonard do it for so long and still grow to be old?

Miles stops pacing. He looks up at me, the color draining from his face. "Oh my God."

"What is it?"

"Benmjöl," he says. "He was probably taking it."

That does not make sense. "You took benmjöl for one week, and you died from it."

"I was dying anyway. Benmjöl was never supposed to extend my life. Just slow down the process enough that I could still walk and move around and not be in so much pain. Maybe if Leonard took small doses—microdosed, almost—it could have staved off the aging and other symptoms."

"I know a guy who microdoses shrooms," Jonah remarks.

Miles pauses as though he cannot possibly see how this could be helpful, then shakes his head. "Maybe I'm wrong and he wasn't using benmjöl, but he had to be doing something because he made it to ninety and still kicked our butts when we tried to rescue Max."

"Do you propose going back to his trailer?" I ask.

"I bet it was bagged as evidence and taken to a locker," Miles says. "I can go to evidence storage and get it. Even if he wasn't using benmjöl, he had to be using something."

I am not thrilled about the idea of taking benmjöl, But neither am I thrilled about the idea of dying. I will need to be very careful. I could die from taking benmjöl as easily as I could from going to the other side.

"Is benmjöl very addictive?" I ask. "I do not want to get addicted."

"I won't let that happen," Miles says. "You would take it only before doing the body swap."

I suppose it would not be the worst idea. "I do not particularly want to die yet."

"Good," Miles says, "because we don't want you to, either."

"Are you going to Bethany today?" Jonah asks. "Like, right now?"

"Francesca said it herself. This needs to happen today or we might lose Shiloh's mom," Miles says, and a fog returns to Jonah's expression at the sound of Shiloh's name. He had been acting so normal that I nearly forgot he was still under the influence of the foolery. Miles turns to me. "Will you be okay here until I get back?"

"Yes," I say. "Go, and hurry back."

Miles calls Evangeline to help me back to the motel room. I

tell him I can walk on my own, thank you very much, but when she offers me her arm, so much warmth rises to my face that I forget what I was saying to Miles. She tucks me back into bed and turns off the lights. Even though I know I should sleep, I remain wide awake with my head on the pillow and my heart thumping like I am running a long race.

18

Miles

The drive back to Bethany takes two hours. In the grand scheme of things it's not a long drive, but when I'm trapped in a car alone with no company but my own anxiety, it feels like it will never end.

I replay what I'm going to tell Chief Schnebly over and over again in my head. I called him yesterday to tell him I got a clean bill of health, but that I wanted to take today off to rest. He was super understanding. Say what you will about small towns, but people are really nice here. The chief seems a genuinely caring person, like he really wants to do right by Randall and the others. Every lie I tell him is getting harder. I hate lying. I used to get so stressed out that I'd soak myself in sweat even if I was standing next to Jonah when he lied, but I've had to lie so much these past couple of weeks that what is one more?

The chief isn't expecting me back until tomorrow, but I still stop by the apartment on my way to the police station to change into a uniform. I can't show up at the station wearing rumpled athletic clothes that look like they've been slept in. The chief will think I had a psychotic break.

I take the carpeted stairs two at a time and go straight to the bedroom. There's a staleness in the air that even I can smell. Like the place is dusty. Or needs a good deep clean. The bed is not made. There's laundry on the floor from all the times I've changed in a hurry, and nothing is where it should be. What I need to do is spend a full day getting this place in order, but I haven't had a free second to myself in weeks and I don't know when I'll get one.

I grab the police uniform in my duffel bag and hold it up to my nose, immediately regretting it. Oh my God, gross. The fabric is stiff with the smell of smoke and sweat and something else that's sour like food that's starting to turn. I didn't get much blood on it. Technically, it still looks acceptable to wear, but the smell is getting to be overwhelming. So overwhelming that I don't want to put it on.

Thankfully, there's a clean one in the closet, so I put that one on and examine myself in the mirror. The golden light coming in through the window is gentle on my new face. It warms the color of my cheeks, adds softness to my bone structure, and generally makes me look less ... alien. I stare myself in the eyes. In *my* eyes. So much has been going on that I don't remember when this body started feeling like my own. This police uniform doesn't feel as much like a costume as it did a week ago. When Randall Zweering was sworn in as a police officer, he must have had to take an oath to uphold the law. He believed in the law's rightness more than anything else—and it ended up being the death of him.

In general, laws are good. In general, killing is wrong, and so is breaking someone's knee, but the law doesn't believe in ghosts or necromancy, and the law has been totally fine letting Leonard spend the past 70 years murdering kids and will no doubt turn the other cheek when his ghost kills Shiloh in jail. Sure, Shiloh has made some mistakes, but she shouldn't have to die because the people around her don't believe in something we know to be true.

Am I asserting my personal sense of morality over the law?

Maybe. Am I doing the right thing? I don't know. But I do know that following every law will not help us stop Leonard, and stopping murderers is a good thing to do.

I'm not supposed to go to the station until tomorrow, so I try to play it off as casually as I can, raising my shaky hand to wave at the woman behind the desk and walking around back to Chief Schnebly's office. It's empty. Everyone must be out doing whatever stuff police officers do when nothing big is going on. Like helping old ladies across the street or giving people speeding tickets for going two miles over the limit. I push through the door to the bullpen and find that it's empty too, which is pretty much the best-case scenario considering what I'm about to do.

Because the universe hates me, Randall Zweering's desk is right by the door. The room is quiet, save for the hum of electricity and the occasional gurgle from the water cooler. I sit down at the clean and empty desk. The only sign that it belonged to Randall Zweering is the nametag on it. There are no pictures or mementos. Everything is aggressively neat, which fits with the picture of the man I'm going to have to be for the rest of my life.

I wake up the computer with a wiggle of the mouse. The screen asks me for a passcode. Instead of hyperventilating, I try to clear my head. I know Randall's password. It has to be somewhere in my brain. There are a bunch of things that I've found in there, like the name of my downstairs neighbor Brenda, or which days I'm supposed to take out the trash. They come to me when I need them, almost like muscle memory. I don't know how that happens. I remember nothing from Randall's life, but I guess we have the same brain now. I have a different soul, but the actual neural pathways that have formed in his head are his.

Releasing a long exhale, I watch my fingers type a string of letters and numbers. The computer unlocks.

I smile. Bingo. Unfortunately, the feeling of victory is crushed by the realization that I don't know where police reports might be saved. I don't know how I got away with one entire week of police work without needing to write a single report. I bet that's something Chief Schnebly will have a talk with me about tomorrow morning when I show up for roll call. A web of options spins out on the desktop. I search around on the computer, navigating the sea of unfamiliar icons and software names. Where is the button marked "Reports" when you need it?

I click on an icon that looks vaguely official. Half expecting to be reprimanded by some automated alarm for unauthorized access, I'm presented with a fresh screen of menus and drop-down lists.

A search bar beckons at me from the top of the screen. I type in "battery report Dog Run Rd Bethany Shiloh Oleson," and the screen as a loading wheel spins for a couple of seconds.

A file pops up. I open it and read it, a sinking feeling settling in the pit of my stomach.

The report exists. It already exists.

Randall must have written it before he was killed. I run my eyes over the form at the top, taking in the name of the reporting officer and the date and time of the event. All our names are listed there, as well as Davey's and Scotty's full names, which makes decoding what Randall actually said about the event kind of confusing. He wrote that Richie, Davey, and Scotty were beating me up. He said Davey had a knife. He said that Shiloh jumped on Davey's knee. He said Richie fled the scene. The report is filled with so many details I don't know which one to focus on, but as I pore over his words, one thing becomes clear.

Officer Zweering already wrote the report.

I can't submit a false report clearing Shiloh's name, because a report already exists.

I keep reading and get to the part where Davey says that

Shiloh and Jonah are the ones who started the fight. I pull my bottom lip between my teeth. Davey is such a liar. Those guys are the ones who started the fight. This never would have happened if they hadn't ambushed me in the woods that day, tried to run me over with a car, and almost pushed me off a bridge.

There's a link at the end of the report. I click on it, and it brings me to another report.

My own death report.

I guess they're linked because they happened the same day. Another officer wrote it, which makes sense because I was already possessing Randall at that point. I remember the chief telling me that my death was being treated as a homicide investigation, and that Shiloh and Jonah were the primary suspects. Judging from this report, it doesn't look like Jonah or Shiloh are suspects anymore. Based on interviews and the report of the fight at the bridge, all evidence points to Shiloh and Jonah caring about me and being my friend, not wanting to kill me, and because there is no evidence at the crime scene and they're still waiting for autopsy results, the trail has gone cold.

I wonder what the autopsy is going to say. Will benmjöl come up on a toxicology screen?

I drop my head into my hands. The report clearly states that Shiloh jumped on Davey's knee. I don't know enough about how the system works to go in there and change it, and changing it will result in so many problems for me that I don't even know where to start thinking about them.

This is not fair. I think about all the times Richie slammed my backpack out of my arms in elementary school, or how Scotty used to give me wedgies that made me scream out in pain. Davey threatened me with his knife so many times. The three of them are all older than I am, and they all got bigger before I did. For some completely unnecessary reason, they made it their mission in school to bully me because I liked poetry and I was sensitive and skinny and I didn't tell my teachers. In high school, the bullying took a psychotic turn and went from name-calling to sticking my head in the toilet and flushing it, kicking me until I cried, and even pulling a knife on me one time.

I could have pressed charges against Davey. My parents would have gone straight to the police and rained a storm of fury on Principal Orr for letting it happen, but it would only have made things worse for me. I used to wish I could be strong enough to stand up to those guys. Because of the body change, I finally am, and I'm not going to let Shiloh die in jail because Davey is a whiny baby who finally got what was coming to him.

Suddenly, I know what I have to do. I run Davey's name through the same search engine and sure enough, up he comes. He has a record. Battery. Petty theft. Carrying a concealed weapon. Probably because he brings a knife to school like your not-so-friendly neighborhood sociopath. And there, right there, is his address. I grab the keys to my squad car and shove up from the desk, peeling out of the parking lot in the direction of his house.

19

Miles

Davey lives on the edge of town. I've never been to his house before, but it has a dirt bike in the driveway that I know belongs to Davey because I've seen it before, so it has to be the right house.

I park in the driveway and step out of the car. Curtains twitch in the neighbors' houses. I have spent so much of my life being afraid of Davey. The thought that I'm about to see him makes me feel ill, but I pull my shoulders back. I'm not about to see Davey as Miles Barot-Renaud. Davey is about to meet Officer Zweering, and he will not enjoy a single second of it.

I knock on the door. A middle-aged woman with a mousy expression and an upturned nose greets me. Registering the uniform and badge, her mouth opens.

She opens the door enough to poke her head through. "Can I help you, officer?"

I clear my throat, trying to make my voice sound even deeper than usual. "I'm here to see David Padron."

Her face drops. It must not be the first time the police have shown up and said that.

"David has been in his room all day," she says. "I swear. My husband will tell you. He'll—"

"He's not in any trouble," I say. "I'd like to speak with David about an incident he was involved in a few days ago. You said he's in his room?"

She opens the door to let me inside, pushing a walker out in front of her as she moves away from the door. I pull my sunglasses down and loop one end into the collar of my uniform as I glance around the living room—at the beige carpet on the floor, and the cooking program playing on the TV. Davey's mom pushes empty bottles of Sprite, cans of peanut butter, and takeout containers out of the way with her walker as she moves through the room. She leads me down a short hallway and opens a door without knocking.

"David?" she asks. "Someone is here to see you."

I step inside. Davey is sitting on a twin sized bed, flipping a pocket-knife open and closed on his lap. His overgrown blond mullet falls into his eyes. There's a blue cast wrapped around his knee, which is propped up on a pillow, and crutches lean against the side of the mattress. The cast is edged with dirt and has been signed by a few of his buddies, and there is more than one crude cartoon on it.

Seeing me, he drops the knife and sits up taller in bed, trying to cover it with a blanket. He fails. I stare at the blade. It's the same knife he used to carry with him at school. The same one he used on me that one time.

His mother says she's going to leave the two of us alone and steps out of the room, leaving the door open a crack.

Davey raises his eyebrows at me. "Help you, officer?"

There's no smugness in his voice. He doesn't sound like the Davey I know, the one who called me things like *faggot* and read my poetry like he was trying not to laugh. Still, my body is jamming up, like I'm the Tin Man and my joints need more oil. I can't find my words.

So Davey fills the silence. "You here to ask me more about that Oleson girl? I heard they finally arrested the bitch."

He grins, like he and the law are on the same side and he wants to be my pal.

He's not my pal. Davey doesn't have the power here. I do. I'm the police officer. Not him. I'm in charge here.

I pull the door closed with a soft click, muting the sound of the TV in the other room. Davey's eyes move past me.

"I'm going to say something, and I'm only going to say it once," I say. "You're going to drop the charges against Shiloh Oleson."

Davey blinks. My heart pounds so hard I can hear it in my ears. I can't believe I'm doing this. This is a bad idea, not to mention a risky one, but I promised Shiloh that I wouldn't let her die in jail.

"Wait." Recognition flashes across Davey's face. He points at me. "You're the cop who was there that day."

"That's right," I say. "I saw what you were doing at that bridge. You tried to run over Miles Barot-Renaud with your car."

The color drains from Davey's face. I guess he didn't think anyone would be watching him when he revved the engine of his truck and stepped on the gas. I rolled out of the way, and the bridge railing was the only thing that kept me from going over the edge. I tried to run from them, but Davey and Scotty were out of the car in seconds, waiting for me.

"It was a joke," is all Davey manages to say.

"Was it a joke when you held Miles against the bridge and threatened him with that knife?" I point at the folded blade that's lying on the bed. "And that wasn't the first time, was it?"

Davey no longer looks like he's having a good time. "I didn't mean any harm."

"You were going to kill Miles. That's the only reason Shiloh Oleson and Jonah Weatherby came to help him."

"I wasn't going to kill him!" Davey exclaims. "Just scare him a little."

"So I guess it was pure coincidence that Miles Barot-Renaud was found dead in the woods near the scene a short time later, was it? And I guess it'll be pure coincidence that his DNA will no doubt be found on this knife of yours."

I pick up the knife that's lying on the bed. He flinches from me.

I got him. The rush of power that fills me with is almost intoxicating. My entire body crackles with strength.

"You're a bully." I flip the knife over in my hand. Davey's eyes widen. "You have been a bully for years, and it stops now." I wave the knife at him between my finger and thumb. "Before it turns into, well, I guess aggravated assault with a deadly weapon at best and homicide at worst, wouldn't you say?"

"I didn't kill him," he says. "I had nothing to do with it."

I pull a chair up to the side of his bed, leaning over my knees and lowering my voice. "You have a choice here. Either you drop the charges against Shiloh Oleson, or I vow to make sure you end up in jail for what you did to Miles. I will follow you around. I will watch you. Constantly. Mark my words, you will go down for this. I will put you behind bars for the rest of your goddamn life, so I recommend the first option. Do you understand me?"

The words roll off my tongue, almost like my mouth has said them before. Davey stares at me, open-mouthed. When he speaks, he's blubbering.

"She broke my knee," he says. "She had no right—"

"Oh, you poor kid, you got beat up by a girl." I only say it because I know this will get under his skin. Shiloh is ten times tougher than Davey could ever hope to be and I'm confident she'd get the better of him if this ever happened again, but he doesn't need to know that. "And she had every right, considering what you and your buddies were doing. Consider this a warning. If you haven't dropped the charges by morning, I'll be seeing you again."

I stand up and slam the chair back into his desk. He flinches again. I leave his room before he has time to reply. Saying a quick thank you to his mother, I climb into the patrol car, turning on the ignition with shaking hands.

Oh my God.

I just threatened Davey. I walked into his house and threatened him. It was wrong on so many levels, but he looked so genuinely scared that I'm pretty sure he will drop the charges.

Or maybe he'll tell an actual police officer what I said, and then they'll have a reason to compare Officer Zweering to the sketch they released after Richie talked to the police.

No. Davey's not smart enough for that. I did a good job scaring him. He won't tell anyone.

A couple of minutes go past. The feeling of power that had taken over my body fizzles out and is replaced by guilt. It twists and kneads my stomach like a wad of pizza dough. I should feel better about this. I just stood up to my bully and made him pay for the many years he tortured me, but all I want to do now is throw up.

I need to keep moving forward. Davey will drop the charges against Shiloh, and now I can focus on getting enough evidence to prove she shot Leonard in self-defense. This means I need to get some benmjöl from the evidence locker for Francesca.

I'm pretty sure that evidence is not stored at the police station. I haven't seen any evidence rooms, and I've seen most of the rooms in that place. This means that the only place it can be is somewhere in the sheriff's department. I've never been there before. I'm not even sure that I'm allowed in there, but going places I'm not allowed to go has sort of become my specialty, so I won't let that stop me.

The drive to Mount Keenan takes twenty minutes. I stop at Walmart to buy a couple of things I will need to pull this off, then go to the sheriff's department, getting out of the car and walking up to the woman behind the main desk.

She looks up at me through pink plastic cat-eye glasses. Crow's feet and smile lines cut deep into her skin, barely masked by her caked-on concealer.

"Hello there, officer," she says. "What can I do for you today?"

"Hi," I say. "I'm Officer Zweering, Bethany PD. I need to look at something in the evidence locker pertaining to the Shiloh Oleson case."

The woman's forehead wrinkles. This is where Shiloh's dad works, so I'll bet this woman knows all about Shiloh. By the looks of it, she's pretty sad about the whole thing, or at least doesn't know what to do about it.

"Sure thing. Let me run 'round back and go find Aaron." She stands up and points at a small candy bowl sitting on the ledge. "Care for a butterscotch? I get them shipped here from Peru."

Because I'm stressed out and emotional and really would like some sugar to distract myself from that, I take a plastic-wrapped candy from the bowl. The woman disappears into the back, and I pop the butterscotch into my mouth, running my tongue over the sphere and letting the sugar dissolve. Butterscotch is so good. I never had many candies growing up because my mom kept none at home. She said they'd rot my teeth, and the data backed her up on it. I shouldn't be having this one now, especially with how it's making all the pleasure centers in my brain fire on all cylinders and making me think of nothing else except for how much I want another, but I'm stressed so I'll give myself a pass.

I'm pocketing another one for later when a man opens the door and waves me through.

"Aaron Grogg." He offers his hand to shake. I hope mine's not sticky. "Evidence technician."

I'm glad nobody is asking questions about why I'm here. I'm even gladder that they didn't call Chief Schnebly to verify my reason for being here. I guess I can thank small town policing for that. I follow Aaron down an unmarked hallway that looks pretty similar to the Bethany Police Station, except maybe a little more beige and less cold. Aaron is not wearing a police uniform. His plain black shirt has York County embroidered where the pocket square should be, his khakis are ironed, and his belt has a bunch of gold keys on it. As we walk by, I glance through a window at the bullpen. A couple of uniformed detectives and other deputies sit at desks, but there aren't as many people here as I thought there might be. Probably because they're out patrolling or solving crimes like they should be. Or maybe because it's late in the day and some of them have gone home.

Aaron peers at me from behind his wire-framed glasses. "You're working the Shiloh Oleson case?"

I nod, keeping my eyes trained ahead so he can't see what a bold-faced liar I'm becoming.

"She wasn't the only one there that day," Aaron says. "There's another kid's prints on the gun."

I do my best to digest that piece of information and what it could mean. Before I can come to any conclusions, Aaron stops walking in front of a room labeled EVIDENCE. He punches a code into the keypad. A light flashes green, and he enters.

He points at a box of latex gloves by the door. I put on a pair and take in the room. It's small, and built almost like the annex of a library, but instead of books there are lots of white boxes with bright stickers on the front.

Aaron walks down a shelf against the far wall. I wonder how everything is categorized. Do they catalog things by type or crime scene or case number? Do they store the drugs next to the weapons, or is everything in a separate box?

He points up at a section of the shelf. "Everything from the scene is here."

He pulls a box down and carries it to a table in the corner, removing the lid and letting me peer inside. The contents are stored in individual plastic bags. There is a signature in Sharpie over every seal and each bag is individually numbered. I guess that's there to prevent evidence tampering. Or to refer to evidence as exhibits in the courtroom.

Aaron steps away. "I'll be over there if you need help finding anything."

I give him a nod. He keeps his eyes on me for a lingering moment before disappearing around the shelves. A security camera stares down at me from the ceiling like a giant evil eye.

Doing my best to steady my breathing, I turn my attention

back to the box and lift items out one by one. The plastic film does a good job concealing the items but holding them up to the light still reveals what they are. A blue shirt rag covered in blood. A small glass bottle with a cork in the top. Everything is packed separately. Nothing is grouped together. I spot an old, leather-bound book in one of the bags. As curious as I am to see what kind of scrapbooks Leonard would have kept of his childhood, it's not what I'm looking for, so I put it aside.

One of the evidence bags contains news clippings. They're stacked one on top of the other, so I can only see the one on the top. The headline reads: "12-year-old girl drowns in family pool." The edges of the clipping have curled, and the paper is yellowed with age, but a young girl's face smiles up at me, a hint of mischief in her brown eyes. I run my eyes down the article. The girl's name was Elsie Nguyen. She died in 2013.

I try to catch the headlines of the other clippings, but I can't shift them around enough. Could these be some of Leonard's previous victims?

In one of the plastic bags, there's a child's shoe. I hold it in two hands, feeling a lump form in the back of my throat, when my eyes snag on the small bag of white powder toward the bottom of the box.

Benmjöl.

I don't have to smell it to know what it is, sitting in there and looking a lot like other types of drugs it isn't. Maybe Leonard has been fooling us and this whole time he's been doing cocaine. Jonah would get a good laugh out of that, but something tells me that's not what's happening.

I need to turn my back to the security camera so nobody can see what I'm doing, but I can't make it look like I'm turning my back to the security camera to hide something or that would look suspicious. I pick up a bag with what appears to be a dirty sock in it and hold it up to the light. Putting on my most convincing frown, I turn my back to the camera and hold the bag up to the light again, pretending that this angle is better before putting the item back into the box.

Every pound of my heart is like a punch in the chest. Aaron could come back any second. I can hear him muttering to himself one aisle over, probably going back over his categorization system to pass the time. I peel back the evidence seal as quickly as I can without ripping the plastic or taking the stickiness off it because ripped tape would make it obvious that something had been tampered with. It's only a matter of time before someone realizes, but it's not like I have a choice here, and I want to be long gone from this place before someone catches on.

I shimmy a glass test tube out of my sleeve. With nervous precision, I drop it into the bag of benmjöl and scoop as much of the powder as I can into the tube before removing it, plugging the top, and sliding it back up my sleeve. It's not a lot. Nowhere near as much as I'd had when I was taking it. But Francesca shouldn't take as much as I did, and I don't want to steal so much that it's going to be obvious that some of it is missing. I press the tape back onto the seal and use a Sharpie to trace over the signature before putting the bag back into the box.

A drop of sweat runs down my temple and lands on the plastic bag. I move other bags on top of the benmjöl, ensuring I tucked the end of the test tube into my glove so it doesn't slide down. Once everything is in place, I release a shaky sigh before replacing the box on the shelf.

"Find what you're looking for?" Aaron asks.

I shake my head, peeling off the gloves. All my sweat has glued them to my palms like a second skin, and I toss them into the trash.

"It was a hunch," I say. "Thanks, anyway. I hope you have a great rest of your day."

Before he can see how much I'm sweating, I push through the door and walk out of the building.

It's well into the afternoon now and the sun gives off an almost golden hue, glinting off the shiny exteriors of the patrol cars and warming my skin. I go to pull my sunglasses over my eyes, but pause. The light makes this parking lot so … warm. I used to think of police departments as being cold, but this one isn't. Not right now.

An acorn crunches under my boot. I glance down to find the sidewalk covered in them. Some bend my sole. Others break under my weight with a satisfying pop, kind of like I'm stepping on bubble wrap.

I smile. This is the kind of thing I used to love writing about. There's so much beauty in the quiet moments. The little things in nature that change the way we perceive the world. That's why I love the Romantic poets so much. Wordsworth wrote about how exploring the simple moments in life give you feelings of calm and clarity, and how the most beautiful things are peaceful times in nature.

I haven't wanted to write much since coming back inside this body. I've been busy, you know, trying not to be found out as an imposter, but if I'm being honest, there is a tiny part of me that's scared my love of poetry has gone dormant.

Before I can think too hard about what I'm doing, I pocket the test tube of benmjöl, dig a crinkled receipt out of my pocket, and unclip the pen from my uniform, jotting down the first words that come to mind:

Oaken carpets line the way
As I tread my path today

Each step a cracking, popping chime
Marking seasons' winding time

Fallen treasures, modest treat
Crunchy jewels 'neath my feet

I sigh. It's not my best work, but at least it's something. I'm about to fold it up and put it in my pocket when someone plucks the receipt out of my hands. A choked yelp escapes me, but the sound dies in my throat when I see who it is.

Lindsey unfolds the receipt, smirking as her eyes scan over my words. It's not a playful smirk. It's a mean one. Like the one Richie used to give me at school before he read my poem out loud.

"You writing poetry now, Randall?" Lindsey asks.

I reach for the receipt, but she holds it out of my reach, laughing to herself as she reads.

"I never took you for the sensitive type," she says, then pauses. "Hold on. What were you doing at a Taco Bell in Dayton this morning? I thought you told the chief you were home sick today."

My stomach drops. "I, uh, stopped there on my drive back this morning."

"Why didn't you take 71?" She narrows her eyes. "What are you doing here, anyway?"

I can feel the test tube of benmjöl in my pocket, weighing me down and bulging like it's impossible to miss. The power is slipping through my fingers. I can't let her turn this into an interrogation.

I snatch my poem back and sidestep her, unlocking my car. She takes this as an invitation to carry on talking.

"I'm going to find out what you were doing in Dayton," she says. "Whatever it was."

She's threatened me so often in the past couple of days that they're beginning to sound empty, but I know they aren't. She won't hesitate to take me down the second she gets some kind of proof, and I have not been as careful as I should have been today.

"Go for it," I try to say, but the words come out sounding more like "Gopher." On my way out of the parking lot, I put a second butterscotch into my mouth. It melts on my tongue as I pull out onto the road.

20

Francesca

I lift the payphone off its receiver, my finger hovering over the keypad. I know Richie's phone number by heart. I never had my own cell phone because my father did not buy me one and there was not enough money in the allowance Richie gave me to afford one. Besides, all of my friends were dead, so there were not many people for me to call. So Richie had me memorize his phone number in case of emergencies. I set the sequence to the tune of a song, and the silly eight-note melody is so deeply ingrained in my memory that I suspect I would still remember it if somebody scooped out my brain. The problem is that I simply do not want to call him.

"Would you please dial the number?" Evangeline asks in the phone booth's opening, wrapping her arms around her stomach and bouncing on her toes. "I will freeze solid if we stay out here much longer."

We have been standing out here for ten minutes, but Evangeline's cheeks and the tip of her nose are bright pink. I am not very cold, but I suppose the phone booth blocks quite a lot of the wind and her yellow sundress does not do very much to protect her bare knees.

I would be happy to leave the phone booth, but I cannot leave it until I have called Richie, and I do not want to call Richie because I am afraid. All my life, I have wanted Richie to like me —or at least pretend to. He always treated me like a burden he did not care to have, and no matter how much I tried to do nice things for him or not get in his way, nothing I ever did was good enough. I do not want him to yell at me over the phone or call me Psycho Sis, and he cannot do either of those things if I do not call him.

But he will also never drop the charges against Shiloh if I do not call him. I doubt he will listen to me, but there is no chance he will listen to me if I do not give him something to listen to.

Inhaling deeply, I pick up the handset. A dial tone emits as I drop a quarter into the slot, dial Richie's phone number, and press the cold receiver to my ear. Evangeline gives me two thumbs-up.

The phone rings. I lean against the side of the booth, my heart pounding so hard it mutes the sound of the phone. Perhaps he will not answer. I hope he does not answer, but I hope he does answer because I need something from him and that is the entire reason I am calling him.

Richie's gruff voice answers the phone. "Yeah?"

My heart flips over. I try to remember the words I had practiced, but I cannot remember a single one.

After a couple of seconds of silence, Richie says a bad word. He mumbles something about being sick of these f-word telemarketing calls, and how he is going to hang up.

I find my words. "*Wait.* Please do not hang up. Richie, it's me. It's ... Francesca."

"Francesca?" His voice is tinged with suspicion. "You serious right now?"

"I did not know who else to call," I say. "I ... need your help."

"Why the hell would you call me?" There is a sharp intake of breath on the other end of the phone. I hear a muffled sound, as though he is moving around on a soft surface, such as a bed or a sofa. "Dad told me you ran from him at the hospital. He's pissed as hell, and—whatever, just … you know Dad's going nuts, right?"

He sounds really angry. Not like he is pretending. Perhaps calling him was a mistake. "I am sorry."

"Things are getting all kinds of crazy, you know? Your little crew tried to take out my eye."

"Please, Richie," I say again, hoping he will listen to me. "I am in trouble."

For a couple of agonizing seconds, he is silent. I can picture him lying on the couch, lips pursed, deciding whether listening to me was worth his attention. "What kind of trouble?"

"I was kidnapped." I close my eyes to try and remember the story I had practiced. "By a very bad man."

He scoffs. "Real funny."

"No, Richie," I say. "He tried to kill me, but my friends, Shiloh and Jonah, rescued me."

"Your freaky friends have totally lost it," he says. "You know what they did to me? That bitch Shiloh got my eye all messed up and guess what? They've got a cop in their pocket. Did you know that?"

"You were drugged and tried to kill them," I explain. "Do you remember a man by the name of …" I read off the name that Miles wrote on a piece of paper. "Todd Knudstrop?"

"That name's dumb as shit."

"Search for him on the internet," I say. Richie lets out a grunt, so I raise my voice. "Please. He gave you drugs. That is why you do not remember. The drug changed your memories and made you think that Shiloh and Jonah were trying to hurt you, when actually the drug made you want to hurt them."

Richie goes quiet for nearly a minute. He must be searching like I told him to. "I know this guy. He, uh, sold to me."

"He gave you something bad," I say. "That is why your memory has changed."

"Francesca, this is crap," Richie says, but he has not hung up yet, so perhaps a tiny part of him believes me. "Why would anyone drug me?"

"I cannot explain it now," I say. "But please, believe me. If you have ever cared about me at all, you need to tell the police not to blame Shiloh or Jonah."

"They gouged out my eye."

"I know," I say, "but if you do not do it, I will be in danger, and I need your help. Please, can you do this for me?"

Richie hesitates. "I'm going to need a lot more answers."

"I can give them to you, but not on the phone."

"Where are you?"

"I cannot tell you that."

"Are you in danger? What the hell is going on?"

"I will explain everything to you once this is all over," I say. "I promise, after, I … I will come home."

He demands that I tell him where I am, but I cannot give him that information. He yells for my father. I utter a small "please, Richie," and hang up, my heart pounding so hard that I can feel it in the tips of my fingers.

A hand rests on my shoulder. I am not expecting the touch, so I jump and turn to find Evangeline standing behind me.

"What did he say?" she asks.

"He …" I struggle to find the words, head still spinning from the call. "He sounded like he might talk to the police."

"That's great!"

"He did not say for certain that he would."

"Even so, it turned out better than you thought it would. I told you. Brothers are strange. They pretend we're such a bother, but deep down, they really do care."

"Perhaps the foolery made him nicer."

She smiles. "Maybe. It's quite the miracle worker."

She says it in a tone that would suggest it is a joke, but my chest still feels too tight to find anything funny. Perhaps the foolery did change Richie's brain. Could it have made him more tolerant of me, or perhaps even like me? That may be too much to hope for. But I hope that he will drop the police charges, because I am not sure how else Shiloh will stop looking so guilty.

In the motel room, Evangeline tries to get me to eat a package of M&M's from the vending machine, but I do not have much of an appetite. Every time she reminds me that I need to eat in order to regain my strength, I am forced to remember why I must regain my strength, which takes my appetite away.

Evangeline pours some M&M's into her hands and eats them two at a time. "I do quite like these candies, but I much prefer cake. I would die for a piece of apple cake right now. Do you think we could find a place to buy some?"

I hum, not listening. She stops chewing and tilts her head to one side.

"What are you worried about?" she asks.

I am surprised she can sense my worry without me telling her about it. Perhaps it is because she and I spent so much time alone in the cellar. The times I slept beside her, timing my breaths so they were synchronized with hers, bound us together.

I search for the words before speaking. "Do you think I will be able to kill Leonard's mother?"

"I think you still need to rest," she says. "But once you agree to eat, and sleep some more—"

"I mean emotionally." I drop my gaze to my lap as I try to find the words. "I have not killed anybody who did not give me permission, and I do not want to be like Leonard."

"You are nothing like Leonard."

"I should not choose who lives and who dies."

"You aren't choosing who lives and who dies," Evangeline says without a second of hesitation. "Leonard's mother never should have come back. There's a difference between what Leonard is doing and correcting all the things Leonard has done wrong."

I stare into her sea-green eyes, as beautiful as broken glass or the surface of a swimming pool. But those eyes do not belong to her. Her eyes closed for the final time long ago. I do not know what color they were. When I met Evangeline on the other side, they were as colorless as the rest of her—only a shade or two darker than the rumpled fabric of her blouse. I guessed they might have been blue.

Hearing her say the words makes me wish I could believe them, but the uneasy feeling does not leave my stomach until Miles returns after seven o'clock. He comes in dressed in a police uniform. His black hair is gelled back with careful precision, and not one single strand is out of place. The lines of his uniform are crisp. The fabric is clean. Dressed like this, he hardly resembles the plainclothes version of Miles who visited me in the hospital, let alone the original Miles who is alive now only in my memories of him. The sight of him in uniform makes my body go on alert, as if sensing danger, even though my mind knows who he is.

He gives me a thumbs-up. It is a youthful gesture, and one that appears incongruous with the rest of his appearance. "I got it."

He can only mean the benmjöl. "Did anybody catch you?"

He shakes his head. "I was stealthy. Like a ninja."

I want to ask him how much of it he could get without being noticed, because I do not see how it could be very much, when he holds up a brown paper bag and announces that he brought dinner. Miles goes to fetch Jonah. Evangeline gives me a burrito. Because I want to make her happy more than I want to avoid eating, I take a careful bite and try to avoid dropping crumbs onto the blanket.

Jonah comes in with Miles, who has changed out of his uniform and back into regular clothes. Jonah is not wearing the manacles anymore. I suppose Miles does not believe him to be a danger to us, and so he does not need to wear them. Even from across the room, I can see the sweat beading on his temples and clumping strands of his black hair together. He does not look very healthy. I wonder what he has been up to the entire afternoon. His hair is disheveled. I hope it is from sleeping. But the pallor of his skin and the dark circles underneath his eyes tell me he has not been getting much sleep.

Only after everyone has finished does Miles pull a chair up to the side of the bed and hold up a test tube like the ones that we used in science lab in school.

"This is all I could get," he says. "But you're only going to take a small amount, so it should do the trick."

Evangeline snatches the test tube out of Miles's hands. "Is this what I think it is?"

Miles studies her. "Uh … maybe?"

"You're going to give her benmjöl?" Evangeline steps toward me, as if trying to get in between Miles and me.

I cannot see Miles because Evangeline is blocking my view, so I lay a hand on her shoulder. "It is all right."

"No, it's not all right. You mustn't take benmjöl." She turns back to Miles. "Do you have any inkling of what this substance can do to people?"

"I have a better idea than most," Miles says. Evangeline scoffs. I realize she does not know about Miles's battle with benmjöl and what his addiction put him through. "This will only be a small dose."

Miles holds out his palm for the test tube. Evangeline lifts it out of reach.

Miles glares at her. "Francesca is not strong enough to do this without help. Would you rather she died?"

"I'd rather she did nothing at all," Evangeline snaps.

Miles looks as though he is doing everything in his power not to raise his voice. I am beginning to believe that they have forgotten I am here, so I take the benmjöl from Evangeline's fingers.

"I will take a small dose," I say. Evangeline and Miles turn to look at me. "Will one of you be so kind as to fetch me a glass of water?"

Miles produces a bottle of water, and a crumpled paper cup that resembles one of the ones used to rinse your mouth at the dentist. He has more experience measuring benmjöl than I do, so I give him the test tube and watch as he removes the plastic plug. The bitter smell hits my nose almost immediately. Miles closes his eyes.

Jonah appears behind him, leaning forward and jerking his chin at the tube. "Want me to do it?" he asks.

I suppose Jonah's memories of Shiloh are muddy, but the foolery did not alter his memories of Miles and his addiction.

"It's just … the smell." Miles's voice is hoarse. He keeps his eyes closed. "I remember the smell of it."

With trembling hands, Jonah takes the tube from Miles's fingers. His hands are shaking so forcefully that he is in danger of spilling whatever benmjöl Miles was able to procure, but I suppose it is better for Jonah to do it than for Miles to have to smell it. Miles walks to the other side of the room. Jonah looks at Evangeline for guidance. "How much should I put in?"

Evangeline's lips are turned down at the corners. I give her an encouraging nod, and she lets out a long sigh.

"A tiny amount," she says. "I'm not joking. Tiny. Like this."

She takes the test tube from Jonah and sprinkles a pinch into the cup. Keeping her back turned to me, she pours some water over it and swishes it around like she is a child creating potions out of mud and sand in a playground. She offers the cup to me.

"Drink it all at once," Miles says from the other side of the room, his back still turned. "It hits faster that way."

I curl my hand around the cup and peer inside it. The water does not appear any different from regular water. When I saw Miles drink benmjöl with the Soothsayer, the water was cloudy. I suppose this water appears clear because there is not very much benmjöl in here.

This is good. I would not like to take very much. The last thing I want is to become addicted, but I would rather take a tiny dose of benmjöl and live than die and be trapped on the other side forever.

Evangeline gives me a half-hearted smile. "We will be right here."

I glance past her at Miles. "Will I still understand everything that's happening around me?"

Miles nods. "It doesn't feel bad. Actually, the first time I took it, I felt better than I had in my entire life."

I suppose that is not something I should fear, although Richie once told me that cocaine made him feel that way, and that is not a good thing to take either. Raising the cup to my lips, I drink the entire thing in one gulp.

A bitter sensation overwhelms my taste buds, sticking to every surface in my mouth. I stick out my tongue and point at the water bottle on the nightstand. Evangeline passes it to me. Even drinking the entire thing does not remove the taste from my mouth. I wipe my lips with my hand and wrinkle my nose.

"That is vile."

"Try snorting it next time," Jonah suggests.

Miles smiles, but it does not reach his eyes. He has come back from the other side of the room and is standing beside my bed. "Yeah, it's not the best."

Not the best is a kind way of putting this. The taste makes me wish I could scrape every last taste bud off my tongue.

"How long until it takes effect?" I ask, still pursing my lips.

"Usually a minute or so," Miles says. "It's fast-acting."

I lie still in the bed, paying more attention than I believe I ever have to the way my body feels. How quickly I breathe. How wonderful it is that my body remembers to breathe for me, even when I do not remind it to. As soon as I begin paying attention to my breathing, my body passes the responsibility over to me, so I am careful to keep myself breathing at a normal rate.

I inhale deeply. My ribcage expands. Air presses against the back of my throat like my lungs are full, and I release it, feeling the air roll out of me. I breathe in again. I squeeze the fingers of my unbandaged hand into a fist, then stretch them all the way open. There is no pain or ache in my joints. Quite the opposite. I feel like I could grab hold of the ceiling fan that is spinning above my head and stop it with one hand. The pulsing ache beneath my bandage is gone, as if my finger has miraculously reappeared. I close my eyes and reopen them, finding that no spots mar my vision anymore. The corners of my vision are blurred, but the center is crystal clear. I can see every single loop of carpet, every fiber in the comforter. So much warmth pours into my body it is like my veins are filled with honey heated over the stove. I kick the covers off my legs and slide to my feet. Oh my goodness, there is no pain in my legs. I lean up onto my tiptoes, then jump up and down until I begin to laugh.

Evangeline frowns. So does Miles.

"Please do not worry." I jump again, higher this time. "I do not feel any pain."

"That's the problem." Miles puts the cap on the test tube of benmjöl and slips it back into his pocket. "It won't wear off for a few hours, but it's at its strongest now, so if we're going to do this, we should do it now."

Now would be good. I feel strong and light and not in any pain for the first time since Leonard cut off my finger. Right now, I could do anything.

"Where is Shiloh's mother?" I ask. "Her soul?"

Everybody stares at me, as though this is a question for me rather than them. I suppose it is.

Closing my eyes, I take a deep breath and reach out to her in my mind, the same way I did when I first learned she was dead and tried to find her in the cellar. The base of my neck tingles, as though an invisible force has pressed a cold finger to it. I can feel her. I imagine gripping her hand and pulling her toward me, through cars and walls and over the broken asphalt of the

parking lot, past the unsightly identical doors and all the way to
…

My eyes open. Shiloh's mother hovers before me, hardly visible in the dim light of the room.

I take her hand. A crackling sensation courses through my palm like I am touching a cube of ice, but for a moment, Shiloh's mother's soul glows more brightly.

"Are you ready to go back into your body?" I ask. She nods. I turn to Miles. "Do you have a rope?"

Miles produces a short piece of nylon rope. It is neon green and glossy. Perhaps too thin, but it will do what it needs to. I will have to strangle Leonard's mother to prevent injury to the body. While strangulation can damage the throat and cause significant bruising, it creates the least amount of harm to a body before reuse, which is why Leonard does it. I try not to think about my similarities to Leonard.

Evangeline brings me my cane, but I wave her away. I do not need it. I can walk on my own. Gripping Shiloh's mother's hand, I drag her out the door. The night air is frosty. So is the pavement. I glance down and notice I am not wearing shoes. Silly me. Pebbles dig into the soles of my feet, but the pain is like a distant thing that I know is there but does not affect me very much at this moment. I am protected from pain. No pain can touch me now.

I stop in front of the bus and press my mouth into a determined line. I must do this. Evangeline was right. Allowing Leonard's mother to continue living in Shiloh's mother's body would be a much worse thing to do.

Releasing Shiloh's mother's hand, I push the folding glass door open and climb the stairs onto the bus.

I cup my hand over my mouth.

The bus is a mess. Construction tools are strewn around carelessly. A crinkled tarp lies crumpled on the floor, splattered with paint and half covered by prop boxes stacked on their sides. Scattered nearby are an assortment of costumes, a rusted saw, and some old cooking pots with blackened undersides that do not appear to have been used in years. Rolls of blue and yellow canvas lean in the places where seats would ordinarily be, but that is not what makes my stomach turn inside out.

In the back of the bus, Big Bruce is strung up to the ceiling by his arms. His eyes dart around, and a scream pushes against the playing card taped over his mouth. On his bare chest, written in bright red lipstick, are words. I step closer to read them:

CATCH ME IF YOU CAN

21

FRANCESCA

I peel the tape off Big Bruce's mouth. A few hairs from his beard stick to the tape and rip out with it.

"Mind the beard!" he shouts against the tape. "*Careful!*"

I continue to pull at the tape, but Jonah tears it off in a single movement. Big Bruce releases a high-pitched shriek and shakes his head as though trying to be rid of us.

"Get this damn rope off me!"

Evangeline helps me untie him. Her fingers are quick and skillful, moving with the same careful precision they do when she is picking a lock, always applying the right amount of pressure in the right areas. Once she unties the knots, Big Bruce stumbles forward, shaking his arms out at his sides and smearing the message written in red lipstick down his chest until the makeup has ceased to resemble words and now looks more like costume blood. His face is flushed a similar color, and he looks oh so angry.

Jonah reaches a hand out to the man. "What the hell happened to you?"

"That bitch happened to me." Big Bruce runs a hand over the

top of his bald head, getting lipstick on it. "She tricked me. She untied herself and went all Rambo on my ass."

I am not sure what Rambo means, but now would not be the best time to ask. "Where did she go?"

"How am I supposed to know?" Big Bruce shouts. "She ran out of here a couple of minutes ago."

Oh, thank goodness. Minutes is not a very long time. If she was here only minutes ago, she could not have gotten far.

I climb over a peg board filled with long dull nails to peer out of the window. I can see my reflection, so I press my nose to the glass and shield my eyes. In the cover of night, it is difficult to see anything past the motel sign glowing neon in the shadows. I can see a cornfield across the road, but it has been harvested and all the stalks have been reduced to short stumps, so it would not provide a good place to hide. A line of trees separates this parking lot from whatever lies behind it, but they do not go very far.

If I were Leonard's mother trying to escape, what would I do? Where would I go?

I would not waste time hiding. My only focus would be on finding somebody to help me. All Leonard's mother would need to do is tell somebody to call the police. They would recognize Mrs. Oleson, bring her to Bethany, and keep her safe in her house, where it would be difficult to kill her unnoticed.

The lights are on inside of the main office of the motel. All the blood drains from my face.

"Frankie?" Jonah asks. "What are you thinking right now?"

I run out of the bus, across the parking lot, and through the front doors of the main office. A middle-aged woman with purple hair sits behind the counter, partly concealed by a computer.

She pulls off the plastic glasses resting on her nose. "Help you?" she says.

Her voice resembles the croak of a toad. I glance at the chairs, the television playing in the corner, and the leafy plant sitting next to it, blowing in the warm air coming from the ceiling vent.

None of it seems real. As though if I reached out and touched anything, it would cease to exist. I wonder if this is because of the benmjöl.

Shiloh's mother is not here, but that does not mean she has not been here.

"I am sorry to bother you," I say. "Has a lady come in here in the past couple of minutes?"

The woman blinks at me. Even her eyelids move slowly. She must be tired. I would be sleepy as well if I had to sit behind a computer all day with nobody to talk to except for a plant.

She peers at my feet. Frowning, she points to a sign hanging on the front of the counter.

No shirt. No shoes. No service.

Uh oh. I was in such a hurry to leave the room that I forgot to put on my slippers.

"I am sorry." I curl my bare toes in a silly attempt to hide them. "But I need to know. Have you seen—"

"No one's come through here." She leans back in her chair as if to tell me the conversation is over.

Muttering a small apology, I go back outside to where Evangeline, Miles, and Jonah are waiting for me. I run to the edge of the parking lot and lean onto my toes, glancing in both directions. Cars drive down both sides of the double-striped road. Cones of yellow light up the sidewalks enough to see that they are mostly empty, apart from a shadowy male figure walking away from us on the other side of the road under a light box sign reading *Mary Lou's Diner*.

My stomach drops. Could she have gone into the restaurant?

I hurry toward the diner. I can hear the others behind me, their footsteps pounding against the dirty concrete. Evangeline is speaking, but I cannot understand a word she is saying. It feels as though my ears are trapped inside my head and the only sounds that reach them are the rapid pounding of my heart and each gasping breath I take. Every car that drives by sends a gust of wind onto my face. Once I reach the lit-up sign, I slow my pace to a walk and enter the restaurant.

The savory aroma of hamburgers is the first thing to reach me. I cross the carpet and do my best to ignore how sticky it feels under my bare feet as I glance around the room. Long chrome counters gleam in the overhead light, and cooks stand with their backs turned to us. Every vinyl booth and stool is occupied. The waitstaff wear aprons and carry trays laden with meatloaf, french fries, salads, and bowls of soup. Now that my breathing has slowed, I can discern the sounds of clinking dishes and murmured conversation. I catch the faintest thrum of a rock song coming from the jukebox tucked in the corner.

A woman with long blonde hair slides out of a booth, but as soon as she turns, it is clear that she is not Shiloh's mother. She glares at my bare feet as she walks by and disappears into the restroom. I do not believe I am allowed to be standing in a restaurant without shoes on. My pants are not long enough to hide them.

In the corner of my eye, Jonah walks in and runs his eyes over the dining area. Our eyes meet. He shakes his head.

This is not good. I cannot lose her. I will not be responsible for Shiloh no longer having a mother.

I peer through the window in front of the restaurant. Across the street, there is a grocery store. Several shadowy figures move across the parking lot, either approaching or leaving parked cars. One is moving rather strangely. The figure is small and feminine. She bends over and swings her arms in harsh motions as she runs, leaping out of the way to avoid crashing into somebody's shopping cart before slipping through the doors. In the entrance, I glimpse pale blonde hair blowing out behind her.

Beckoning for Jonah, Miles, and Evangeline to follow me, I cross the road to the grocery store.

The glass doors slide closed behind us. I use my hand to shield my eyes because it is so much brighter in here than outside. So many sounds assail my senses. The wheels of a shopping cart squeak against the floor. Shoppers crowd the shelves of produce, inspecting every vegetable and piece of fruit before putting them in their carts. Every checkout line stretches into the aisles behind. I dislike crowded places. This is exactly the sort of place I would avoid coming to during its busiest hours, although I do not have a choice right now.

Enough people are in each aisle that it will not be easy to find Leonard's mother. I turn to the others.

"We should split up," I say. "Please do not attract attention to yourself and bring her outside as soon as you find her."

"Are we bringing her back to the bus?" Evangeline asks.

I nod. Quite frankly, I do not see any other way to do this. It is not as though I could kill her in the produce aisle.

Jonah points up at a camera above our heads. Miles pulls his baseball cap deeper onto his head as if that could hide him.

Taking a deep breath, I pull back my shoulders and step into the crowd.

I glance from face to face. A bleary-eyed man picks up a zucchini from the refrigerator. He squeezes it once before replacing it. A gray-haired woman puts a carton of strawberries into her cart. It is all so … ordinary. None of these people are concerned about there being a possessed woman among them. They are not holding other people's lives in their hands. They are only shopping. I wish I could be like them, and my primary concern this evening could be which box of strawberries I was going to buy.

Once I reach the back of the store, I count every person I can see, but none of them resemble Shiloh's mother.

I move on to the baking supplies aisle. There is a woman blocking the walkway with her cart as she inspects the tubes of multicolored icing hanging on hooks. On the other side of the cart, a figure in a dirty pink cardigan rounds the corner.

I run to the next aisle and see Shiloh's mother walking parallel to me on the other side, her blonde hair fanning out behind her. I walk parallel to her, keeping pace so I can be sure I don't lose her, but then in the next aisle, she is gone.

Did I lose her? Did she notice me and escape?

I survey the bustling store. Shoppers move to their own inner rhythms, pushing their carts and peering at the shelves. I can see Jonah at the end of an aisle, shaking his head to signal that he has not found her either.

Somebody taps on my shoulder. I turn around to find a young woman with short brown hair and a nose piercing, wearing an employee vest and a disapproving frown on her face.

She points at my feet. "You can't be in here without shoes."

I curse myself for forgetting to put on those slippers. I try to think of an excuse to give this girl, as I am not in possession of any shoes to put on at the moment and there are more important things for me to do than find some, so I do exactly the wrong thing to do in this situation. I run away from her.

The girl calls at me to stop. My heart thumps as I turn down the pet aisle, looking at the pictures of happy cats and dogs on the tins of food. Squeezing past a young girl with headphones on, I round the corner and find Leonard's mother brushing past the ice cream. She is fast. Each step has a purpose.

She weaves around the chest freezers, glancing over her shoulder at me. She is about to turn the corner when Miles appears in front of her, blocking her path.

He presses closer to her. She goes to move around him, but Jonah stops her.

She appears to be considering how to string the two of them up on the ceiling when I catch up to her. I grab hold of her upper arm.

"I caught you," I whisper.

Leonard's mother's eyes narrow at me. When Shiloh's mother was in this body, she always appeared a tiny bit frightened of everything. Her big eyes would dart around, looking at everything as if it could harm her, but those same eyes are looking at me as if she wants to pluck my eyeballs out with her fingers and swallow them whole. She glances around as if trying to consider her options for escape. I begin leading her away before she can come up with any.

"Who do you think you are, marching me off to my death?" she hisses, quiet enough for only me to hear.

I say nothing. People are looking at us. I smile at them as we pass by and tighten my grip on her arm.

Evangeline is waiting for us in the parking lot. Seeing her, Leonard's mother hisses in a breath between her teeth.

"You deceitful little hussy," she says. "After everything my son did for you, this is how you pay him back?"

Evangeline laughs. "Everything he did for me? Is that what we're calling it?"

"Go to hell."

"I'll see you there," Evangeline says. "Your son is a self-righteous prig, and you're no different."

She says the words so sweetly that if I could not understand them, I would think she was talking to a small child, or perhaps telling a kitten how adorable she found it, but Leonard's mother understands them. The muscles in her shoulders tighten. She moves toward Evangeline.

I push her away before she can take another step. I keep a firm hand on her as we walk back toward the motel. I am acutely aware of how adeptly Big Bruce was tied up, and I remember how Phil cupped his side when he said that Leonard's mother had slashed him there with scissors. She could do much worse things to me. She is stronger and more violent than anybody has given her credit for. I wonder if Shiloh's mother secretly had a lot of muscle, or if her strength is the product of pure rage. From what I know about her, I would guess it was the latter. Even though Miles, Jonah, and Evangeline are all walking behind me, I get a nagging feeling in the pit of my stomach that she could kill every single one of us on her own, and nothing would bring her more pleasure.

On the sidewalk beside the cornfield, she stops walking and looks over at me. A toothy smile stretches over her lips.

I do not understand what she is smiling about. She is about to die. I am about to kill her. This is not the smile of somebody who knows they are about to die. It is the smile of somebody who knows something I do not.

Something glints in her hand. I barely have time to jump out of the way before she swipes a blade at me.

I stumble over the curb and into the road. She laughs. Before any of us can react, she runs into the cornfield.

I scream at her to stop. She does not, running with her arms flailing at her sides like she did in the grocery store parking lot, like some kind of crazed animal escaping into the night. I charge into the corn after her.

The sharp stubs dig into my bare feet. It is so painful that I can feel them slicing through the soles of my feet, but I ignore the pain. The cool night air brushes against my face. Passing headlights cast enough light onto the empty field for me to see the shape of Leonard's mother running away, but with every step, she gets deeper into the shadows and becomes harder to see. I go faster. Every muscle in my legs burns as my bare feet pound against the ground. Black spots creep into the corners of my vision until all I can see is the torn pink cardigan flapping out behind her.

I reach out to grab it. My hand curls around the fabric and yanks it backward, slowing Leonard's mother down enough for me to jump on her and tackle her to the ground.

She shrieks. My body slams on top of her. The impact knocks the air out of my lungs. I pause to catch my breath, but the pause gives her enough time to roll on top of me and pin me to the ground.

A smile curves across her lips. Blood stains her teeth, and she runs her tongue over them.

"Did you truly reckon you could stop me?" she says. "You are a puny and pathetic missy."

She holds up the box cutter. I thrash out against her, but she is wiry and strong. The blade glints underneath the pale moonlight as she holds it to my cheek. The pointy end digs into my skin, and a whimper catches in the back of my throat.

She brings her face right down to mine. "If I had more time, I'd do this real slow."

She moves the blade to my throat, but before she can apply any pressure, her weight is pulled off me.

I gasp. So much pain fills every crevice in my body. I try to sit up, but a curtain of darkness is pulled across my vision and I slump back to the ground. I hear Leonard's mother let out a low chuckle. Her words are far away. They drip with anger. I squeeze my eyes shut and do my best to blink the spots away. I can see the pink of the cardigan. The knots in her blonde hair. Leonard's mother brings her hand across Evangeline's face. Evangeline cries out in pain, cupping her cheek and staggering backward. Leonard's mother grabs Evangeline by the front of her shirt. She pulls her close.

Her words are too quiet for me to hear. Evangeline spits in her face. Leonard's mother pulls back the blade.

The world falls away from me. Evangeline's eyes find mine. She mouths my name.

I am not sure where I find the strength, but I do. My hand closes around something half buried in the dirt. I rise onto unsteady feet and lurch forward. Before Leonard's mother can touch Evangeline, I bring the stone down on her head just as hard as I can.

22

Shiloh

Shiloh's mother lies face-down in the soil, unmoving.

Evangeline buckles inward, bracing herself on her elbows and staring at the ground. I grip the rough stone in my hand for a moment before allowing it to slip from my fingers.

"Thank you," Evangeline says. "You saved my life."

I want to tell her she is welcome. I want to wrap my arms around her and promise her I would do it again, but I cannot do anything but stare at Shiloh's mother.

"I was supposed to use a rope." Each word trembles. "I was not supposed to hit her on the head."

Could I have damaged her brain? Will she remain the same once she wakes up, or will she be different? I did not consider this before hitting her. She had Evangeline. She was going to stab her. I had to save Evangeline.

I wait for the body to glow. No soul comes out. In the corner of my eye, Miles and Jonah appear on either side of me.

"Is she dead?" Miles asks.

"I … I am not sure."

Dropping to my knees, I gently turn the body onto its back

and tilt the woman's limp chin to one side. I press my fingers to her neck. A faint pulse thrums beneath my fingers.

She is alive.

So much relief pours over me that I could cry. I hope I did not hit her hard enough to injure her brain too badly, only hard enough to knock her unconscious. There is dirt on her face, and a long scrape on her cheek. Her eyes are closed. She was lucky. If she had fallen face down with her eyes wide open onto these sharp stalks …

"Did anybody bring the rope?" I ask. "Please, Miles, tell me you still have a rope."

Miles shakes his head and tells me he must have forgotten it in the trailer. I suppose that leaves me with only one option for how to kill her. I have done it before, on the day I put Miles into the body of the police officer, but using my bare hands makes the entire thing feel more … intimate. In this field, we are exposed. The cars driving by could see us, although it is too dark for them to discern our faces. I should not be doing this in public, but I do not have a choice, so I must do it quickly.

Passing headlights flash against Jonah's face. He is staring at the body with so much coldness that a chill runs through me. Lying on the ground with all the muscles in her face relaxed, Shiloh's mother bears a strong resemblance to Shiloh. Jonah does not look at all pleased to see her like this, but he does not exactly look displeased either.

It is the foolery. The real Jonah would never be pleased to see this.

If the effects of the foolery never go away, will this version of Jonah become the real one?

Doing my best to press down the nausea churning in my stomach, I crouch beside the woman. Pressure builds behind my eyes.

"I am so sorry," I whisper. "I wish I did not have to do this."

Placing my hand over her mouth, I pinch her nostrils. Everybody watches me, even Miles, whose face has gone a sickly pale, as if he remembers as much about the day I killed him as I do. I try to remind myself that I am not taking a life. Leonard's mother is already dead. I need to do this to give life back to Shiloh's mother, but nothing about this feels right. I force myself not to move or run or vomit as tears blur my vision.

The body begins to glow. I fall back onto my ankles in time for the soul of Leonard's mother to sit up, her hips and legs still inside the corpse's torso. Her long black hair falls over her gaunt shoulders. The bones of her upper ribcage are prominent, as though her skin is the only thing draped over them. She shines brightly. Her form appears to be made of glow sticks, and her light is strong enough to illuminate the surrounding space. I can see Shiloh's mother's body on the ground. Her pale skin is waxy and gray in death. The blood coming down her temple tints her flaxen hair red, in striking contrast to the peaceful expression that has come over her face.

Leonard's mother curls her translucent fingers around the dead woman's wrists. "I'm not leaving. You can't force me."

"Actually, I can."

Narrowing my eyes, I raise my hands and push her away with my mind, sending her soul soaring across the cornfield until she is nothing but a spot on the horizon. Her scream diminishes with distance until it fades away entirely.

Miles's voice pulls me back to reality. "Francesca. Is Shiloh's mom's ghost here?"

I pause. In the commotion of losing Leonard's mother, I stopped paying attention to where Shiloh's mother's soul was. I reach out to her in my mind. I can see her even with my eyes closed, as if she is projected on my closed eyelids. Her legs are wisps of air. Her hands have disappeared. There is a spot of light, waning like a guttering candle in the center of her chest. I have never seen a soul this close to fading away in my entire life. She peers around the bus, waiting for us. I reach an imaginary hand out to her and close it around her wrist, pulling her all the way to me.

When I open my eyes, her soul is in front of me. There is a

perplexed expression on her face, as though she does not understand how I could do what I just did.

She stares down at her corpse. A gasp catches in her throat, and she points at it.

I do not give her time to ask me questions. I extend my hand to her again. She tears her gaze away from the corpse.

"Please do not worry." I manage a smile, even though no part of me wants to smile at the moment. "I will put you back inside your body."

She does not take my hand. "How on Earth will you do that?"

I consider explaining to her how I did this to Max on the night we rescued him from Leonard, and also how I did this for Miles, but I am acutely aware of every passing car and how bad it would be if somebody came over to us now to find us all crowded over a woman I just killed.

"Please, do what I say," I say. "Trust me."

With a tentative nod, she takes my hand, and a distant chill runs up my arm. Perhaps it is because she is so close to fading away, because I have taken some benmjöl, or because I have grown accustomed to the feeling of souls, but holding her right now feels like I am taking a pint of ice cream out of the freezer. It is not painful at all.

I lower Shiloh's mother's soul toward her body and align her arms and legs with her body. I do my best to keep my breathing steady so that I do not get nervous because there are so many things that could go wrong with this. Shiloh's mother could fade away before I can put her back. She may not wake up. I could fall unconscious. I have done quite a lot of running and the benmjöl may not be powerful enough to keep me alive. After everything I have been through, this could be the thing that finally kills me.

But I am not allowed to be afraid right now because Shiloh's mother looks completely terrified and at least one of us must maintain our composure, so I force myself to smile.

"Do your best to relax," I say. "I have done this before."

Calmly but firmly, I push on her transparent chest and press her into her body. She fades to nothing all at once.

Did I do it? I glance down at my hands—one wrapped in frayed and dirty gauze and one bare. Both are trembling, but at least they are made of flesh and bone, and Shiloh's mother's ghost is gone. Replacing her soul was so easy. I hardly had to try.

Shiloh's mother's chest is not rising or falling. I hold a hand underneath her nose, expecting to feel warm air. I feel nothing.

"Come on." I grip her shoulders. "Please, Mrs. Oleson, you must wake up. You must—"

Shiloh's mother opens her eyes. I jump out of the way as she sits up, glancing around with panicked eyes as though she is expecting to find some attacker ready to hurt her, but she only finds me. She looks down at her own hands. At her arms. At her torso. She runs her hands over her eyebrows, the bridge of her nose, her parted lips, her ears …

"Did you do this?" she asks me, gesturing at herself. "Is this all really happening?"

Oh, thank goodness. She can talk. I did not injure her brain so badly that she cannot speak anymore.

I nod. "How does your head feel?"

"Sore." She rubs the back of it where I smashed it with the rock. There is blood coming from somewhere underneath her hair. I hope the cut is not deep. "Very sore, actually."

"You may feel some discomfort," I say. "From what I understand, that is normal, but because this is your own body, it should be the same as putting on a pair of shoes you own but have not worn in a long time. Miles has gone through this before, although the body he is in right now is not his own."

Shiloh's mother nods, but then pauses. "Miles? As in my daughter's boyfriend, Miles?"

Miles raises his hand in a wave. "Ex-boyfriend, technically, but that's not important right now."

Shiloh's mother stares at him for a moment before shaking her head and scrambling away from him. "You are not Miles."

"Actually, I am," he says. "On the inside, anyway. My soul is

Miles, and I still like Star Wars and poetry, but the body is not mine. I died, and Francesca brought me back to life just like she brought you back to life."

Shiloh's mother continues shaking her head. "This is unbelievable. All of this … unbelievable."

"You were a soul," I say. "You know I am telling the truth, because you just experienced it—"

She holds up a hand. "Just … please give me a moment to process this."

We stand around her in the shadows, watching as she rolls her wrists and ankles. Close to a minute goes by before she asks for help standing up, and Miles lifts her to her feet. No soul is with us to act as a light, so we are in complete darkness now. The moon does not give off enough light for me to see where I am going.

"What just happened to me?" Shiloh's mother's voice is taut, like she is doing everything she can to hold herself together.

"The man who ended your life is the same one who took Max," I say. "He has the same ability that I do, to bring people back from the dead, but he has taken many lives to do it … like hers." I point at Evangeline.

Shiloh's mother gapes. "Talulah?"

"I am not Talulah," Evangeline says. "My name is Evangeline, and I died in 1944."

Shiloh's mother's mouth falls open.

"The police arrested Shiloh because they believe she was the one responsible for this man's murders," I say.

"Leonard is a serial killer whose victims don't appear to die," Miles says. "He kills people and reanimates the bodies."

"Which is what he did to you," I say. "Leonard was keeping me prisoner in that house, and when you arrived, he captured you as well. Shiloh saved me and together we killed Leonard, but now he is a ghost—and a very angry one, who is trying to get revenge. We have reason to believe he could be attacking Shiloh in prison right now, so we are trying to rescue her."

"And destroy Leonard's ghost for good so he can't possess any more people," Miles finishes.

Shiloh's mother puts both hands up, palms out toward us. She does not have to say anything.

"I believe we should stop talking now," I tell Miles.

He nods. Jonah glares at Shiloh's mother. He is not watching her like he is concerned about her, or like she is the mother of the girl he loves who just came back from the dead. He is looking at her like she deserved every terrible thing that happened to her. Like he wished he had been the one to do it to her.

He steps toward her. I cry out to warn Miles, who grabs hold of his friend's arm and yanks him backward, dragging him away from us and marching him back toward the road.

Shiloh's mother watches them leave. She did not see Jonah moving toward her with ill intentions. I do not want her asking questions about what is wrong with Jonah, so I continue speaking to return her attention to me.

"I have a plan to get Shiloh released from prison," I say. "I was there when she shot the man, and so was your son, so I believe if we go share our memories with the police, they will let Shiloh go."

This appears to be too much for Shiloh's mother. She stares at me, slack-jawed, gaping like she has forgotten even how to speak. In the exposed cornfield, an icy wind blows over us, flapping open the sides of her cardigan. She must be freezing.

So I give her something to hold onto. "Come, let me take you to see Max."

At the sound of her son's name, clarity breaks through her confusion. I reach my hand out to her, and she takes it, letting me pull her to her feet. She wobbles on unsteady legs.

"Would you like to lean on me as you regain your balance?" I ask.

She drops my hand. "I can walk on my own, thank you very much."

She holds her arms at her sides like a tightrope walker and moves across the crunching corn stumps back to the road.

Evangeline trails after her with her arms outstretched, determined not to let her fall.

Evangeline glances over her shoulder at me. "Are you coming?"

I nod and move toward her, careful to step on the soil instead of the remnants of the stalks. Perhaps the benmjöl is wearing off, but the soles of my feet are hurting badly, and my muscles ache. I realize what I have done and how ill I felt earlier that morning in the hospital, and I wonder how much more of this my body can take.

I knock on a motel room door. In a couple of seconds, the man with no legs answers.

"Yes, I got the kid still, and no, I didn't reckon I'd be keepin' 'im this long," he says. "When I said I'd watch over the kid, I didn't think I'd be signin' up for life with 'im."

I step out of the way to reveal Shiloh's mother, who reaches out her hand to the complaining man.

"Thank you so much for taking care of my son," she says, "but I can take him now."

The man's eyes widen. I do not think he was intending to complain about Max in front of the boy's mother. He does not appear to know how to talk himself out of his previous words, so he simply moves out of the way and calls for Max to come over.

Max appears in the doorway. As soon as he sees his mother, a smile consumes his entire face.

"*Mom!*"

He flings himself into her arms. She picks him up and holds him against her chest, cupping a protective hand over the back of his head and pressing him close to her.

"Oh, honey," she says, her voice breaking. "I'm so sorry."

Max pulls his face away from hers and scrunches up his nose. "You smell bad."

So many tears run from Shiloh's mother's red eyes that I am surprised she has any water left in her body at all. She cups Max's cheek and brushes his blond hair out of his face like she is trying to ensure he is real.

A hand drops on my shoulder. I glance behind me to see Evangeline smiling at me. Her eyes speak for her. I know she is trying to make me feel better and tell me I did a good thing, but all I can think of as I watch them is that this never should have happened. I should never have called Shiloh's mother to help me. All I did was reverse a bad thing that never should have happened in the first place.

Shiloh's mother turns to me, still holding Max. "I will take you to the district attorney tomorrow. Ernest knew him well, so I can arrange a meeting."

I smile at her. "Thank you."

"Can you give me a ride home, too?" Jonah asks.

I am not sure when he came to join us, but here he is. The crazed look is gone from his eyes. He simply looks sad.

I do not think that it is a good idea for Jonah to return to Bethany. According to what Miles told me, both Jonah and Shiloh were running from the police because they wanted to arrest them for hurting Davey and Scotty. I believe Jonah's probation officer was not happy with him and could put him in prison for violating the terms of his probation.

"Are you sure that is a good idea?" I ask.

Miles comes up beside Jonah. Unlike me, he does not seem particularly concerned. "The police will not be looking for him anymore. I got the battery charges dropped."

"I'm not even going to ask how you did that," Jonah says, a hint of his old humor in his voice. "But I want to have your babies."

Miles rolls his eyes. Something about the lightheartedness of the interaction makes me see the two boys they used to be: the skinny, academically minded student with curly hair and glasses, and the long-haired rebel who took nothing in the world too seriously.

"Can I come as well?" Evangeline asks me, her voice sounding shy.

"Everyone in Bethany will think you're Talulah Monroe," Miles cautions. "They'll take you to her family."

There does not appear to be another option. What would she do otherwise, stay here by herself?

"She can hide with me in the trailer," I say. "We will have to be careful not to be seen."

"Talulah, honey, your parents only want what is best for you," Shiloh's mother says. "You may have had your misunderstandings, but they are good people, and they are very worried about you."

Evangeline flinches as though she has been slapped across the face. I remember what she said to me about Talulah Monroe when I met her for the very first time, and how Leonard found Talulah crying at a bus station because her family threw her out of the house after catching her kissing another girl. While misunderstandings do happen, this was more than a simple misunderstanding. There are some things that you cannot come back from.

I would expect Shiloh's mother to know this, but I suppose she endured Shiloh's father's inexcusable behavior for many years and did not do a single thing about it. Shiloh was the one who stopped it.

"She is not Talulah anymore," I say. "She does not want to go to Talulah's parents."

Shiloh's mother pulls her eyebrows together. Her eyes appear far away, and nearly confused, as if she is trying hard to wrap her mind around what I said. She shakes her head.

"You will stay with me," I tell Evangeline. "So long as that is all right with you."

She nods. I will not allow that horrible family to come and take her. She may be Talulah Monroe to the rest of the world, but with me she will be Evangeline, and she will never go home.

I begin to feel unsteady on my feet and glance around for a place to sit down. Evangeline and Miles rush forward, holding me up underneath my arms and taking all the weight off my sore heels. I rest my head on Evangeline's shoulder, and I glimpse her small smile.

"We will leave first thing in the morning," Shiloh's mother says. She pauses, appearing to remember something. "Do any of you, by any chance, know what happened to my car?"

23

Shiloh

Going to sleep is easy now that I have the magnet. As soon as the lights go off for the night, I crawl onto the mattress pad, lay the magnetic strip flat on my chest, and fall asleep a few seconds later.

At some point, Leonard enters my dreams. He takes the form of the old man that he was when I first met him, tall and gray-haired and wearing that long green trench coat, but now he's a ghost. He's in my house, hovering over a sleeping Max. A kitchen knife glints in his ghostly hands. I try to get to Max, try to claw myself across the wooden floor, but every movement is slow, like I'm wading through tar. The blade plunges into Max's stomach. My scream pierces my ears. I reach Max, pushing the hair out of his face, only to find Jonah staring up at me, gasping and sputtering as blood runs out of his mouth.

I wake up with a strangled cry, my teeth chattering even though I'm drenched in sweat. I glance around for any sign of Leonard, but my cell is empty.

I peel the refrigerator magnet out from under my shirt. It's slick with sweat but it's still there. Leonard can't hurt me. I have the magnet, and I bet Jonah and Max do, too.

It was just a dream.

But it woke me up, and it's going to take a while for me to get tired enough to fall asleep again, so I stand up. The quiet hum of the night fills my ears, broken occasionally by the distant clank of metal or muffled voices coming from somewhere deeper in the building. The cell isn't cold—or at least not any colder than usual—so a ghost can't be in here. Hold on. I could ask for my blanket back now. Because I have the magnet, I don't need to worry about Leonard smothering me with the blanket or using it to tie a noose to hang me with.

I probably won't be able to get a blanket until morning, so I pull a gray sweatshirt over my jumpsuit and tuck my hands into the sleeves. I gulp down some tap water from the sink and try to ignore the gross film coating my tongue and the insides of my cheeks.

The mattress pad's rough plastic casing crinkles under my weight. I tuck my knees to my chest to try to get warm, willing myself to think about anything other than my nightmare and just go back to sleep.

I'm not sure how much time has passed before I hear my cell door bolt sliding open.

Opening my eyes, I sit up on the mattress. A sharp pain shoots down my neck, probably from using my arm as a pillow, but I rub it away.

The door creaks open. A man comes into my cell.

Every muscle in my body tenses. The man closes the door behind him. It's too dark in here to see his face, but the scant moonlight coming through the window gives him a hulking silhouette. His arms and shoulders bulge out from under his shirt. He's wearing some kind of uniform that I assume means he works in the building.

He looks like an officer, or a guard of some kind. What is a guard doing in here?

He smiles. Even in the semi-darkness, I can see the whiteness of his teeth. The gleam in his eyes is one I'm familiar with. Dad used to get that look on the nights he came home drunk and decided that he wasn't going to let Mom or me push him around anymore. On the nights he wanted to give us a reminder of how much we were worth. I've seen that look enough times to know what it means.

Oh God.

He reaches for me. I duck under his arm. His shirt grazes my skin as I run to the closed door, ramming my shoulder into the metal. It doesn't budge.

No. Oh, please *no*—

Rough hands yank me backward and slam me into the wall. Concrete smashes against my skull, and I cry out in pain.

The man pins me against the wall, and presses his body against mine. Bile rises in my throat. I struggle against him, but he doesn't budge. He leans in close to my ear, close enough for me to feel the hot breath rolling out of him.

"You're a pretty thing," he says. "Young and pretty, just the way I like 'em."

My stomach drops. I thrash against him with all my strength. His grip is firm.

"Let me go!" I scream. "Get away from m—"

He clamps a callused hand over my mouth, muffling my scream. His laughter sends a shiver down my spine.

"That's right." The peach fuzz clinging to his jaw and upper lip scratches my face. "Be quiet."

His breath is ripe. The nauseating smell washes over my neck and down my shirt, making my entire body jam up. This can't be happening. Not right now. Not like this. He shoves me harder against the wall and takes his hand off my mouth. I scream as hard as I can but he wraps his hand around my throat, cutting off the sound.

I shove him away from me. I twist my body to the side. I drive my knee into his groin, but he doesn't budge. No air reaches my lungs. It's like the signal in my brain doesn't reach my muscles because none of my limbs will move. I'm broken. Like a puppet dangling against the wall.

His face swims in front of my eyes. I've never seen this man before in my life. Why is he trying to kill me?

I raise my eyes to the closed door. Is this how I am going to die? In this cell at the hands of a stranger?

He squeezes my throat. Pain radiates through my temples and eyeballs and lungs and skull until it's so overpowering that I need to scream, but no sound comes out. My entire head is burning. My knees buckle. I raise my eyes to the tiny security camera above me, pleading for help as the strength drains out of me.

Darkness pushes against the corners of my vision. The man chuckles right in my ear.

"You reckoned you could slip away from me," he says. "But I done told you I was gonna find you."

His words hit me like a punch in the stomach. I open my eyes and stare at the amused gleam in the man's eyes, and the sick way he's smiling at me like he's proud of what he's doing.

Oh my God. *Oh my God.*

Has Leonard murdered someone and possessed them just so he could come in here and kill me?

The magnet won't help me now. It may repel ghosts, but Leonard's not a ghost anymore. He's possessing someone, and he's real as I am. He can kill me any way he wants.

This is not how this is going to go. I won't let this asshole have the satisfaction of knowing he killed me, not when he still gets to be alive and everything I went through would have been for nothing.

Gritting my teeth, I bring my knee up as hard as I can and it connects with something soft. Leonard howls and lets me go, allowing me to push him off and run to the door.

"*Help!*" I scream, pounding my fists on the metal. "He's trying to kill me!"

Leonard grabs the back of my shirt and yanks me away. My

knees crash onto the floor. I push through the pain and scramble back onto my feet, ducking under his arms to get to the door again.

I press my face against the window and scream. A girl's face appears in the window across from me. I widen my eyes, pleading, and slap the door even harder.

"Please!" My voice breaks. "Please, you need to help me!"

She stares at me. After a couple of seconds, she screams too and hits her door. I hear another scream from the cell next to mine. Soon, the entire floor is hitting on their doors and screaming.

Leonard grabs my shoulders and leans in so close to my ear that I can feel his lips.

"I'm comin' back for you," he says. "Don't you be sleepin' too deep."

He shoves me to the ground and unlocks my door, letting himself out and shutting it behind him. I collapse onto the floor, hugging my knees to my chest as I gasp for air.

The door opens. I glance up to see the officer who took away my pillow and blanket, standing with one hand on her keys and a concerned expression on her face.

"A man was in here," I choke out. Every word makes my throat burn. "He tried to kill me."

She crouches down next to me. "Breathe. Just breathe. Can you do that for me?"

"He tried to kill me," I say again, the volume of my voice making me cough. "He tried … he was …"

"Can you breathe?" she asks. "Are you hurt?"

Is she not listening to me? "Somebody tried to kill me."

"Okay." She doesn't sound like she's listening to anything I just said. Into her radio, she says: "I need medical support in Holding 4."

She tells me to breathe again, but I can't breathe anymore. Leonard took over somebody's body, and now he's gotten away. Again. It doesn't matter if I remember what he looks like. If I can identify him this time, he'll change hosts next time, and if he's always changing hosts, it's only a matter of time before he kills me for real. And not even the most powerful magnet in the world would stop him.

24

Miles

Because Miles has a good memory and has become quite knowledgeable about police matters, he informs us that Mrs. Oleson's car is probably being held at an impound lot. The police have more than likely seized it and will be using it to investigate Shiloh's mother's disappearance. He is not sure whether she will be able to reclaim the car or even if it will be in any condition to drive—the memory of the sledgehammer coming down against the glass is all too clear—but Shiloh's mother is insistent. She will talk to the police and, depending on the damage, call her insurance company. She only has one car, after all, and she needs to use it.

Miles must be at the police station at 7:15 in the morning, which means that all of us must leave at five if we have any hope of getting him there on time. Mrs. Oleson and Max will take an Uber to the impound lot a couple of hours later as there is no reason for them to arrive before it opens. Once they are there, they will see about Mrs. Oleson's car or find an alternative mode of transportation to Bethany, where they will pick me up and go to the courthouse. Listening to everybody come up with the plan is causing my head to spin. If any of us have any hope of convincing the district attorney of anything in the morning, we must first get some sleep.

Miles and Evangeline help me back to my room and get me into bed. I feel terrible burdening them like this, so I say thank you over and over again until they both laugh. Miles brings me a toothbrush. Evangeline wipes the dirt off the bottoms of my feet and puts some lotion on my cuts and bruises. She runs a comb through my hair as I brush my teeth, and after I finish, Miles gives me a cup to spit into.

Once my teeth are brushed and the blanket has been pulled over my body, Miles wrings his hands together.

"Do you need anything else?" he asks. "How … uh … how are you feeling?"

I understand he is referring to the benmjöl, but I hardly feel its effects anymore. My body is brittle and weightless, as though I am a husk of wheat.

But I do not wish to worry Miles, so I only smile. "Sleepy."

Smiling back, he touches my foot through the covers. He is looking at me in the same sort of way that Shiloh looks at Max sometimes, with a sort of protectiveness usually reserved for brothers and sisters. Nobody has ever looked at me in that way before. Certainly not Richie.

"Get some rest," he says. "I'll see you in the morning."

He walks through the door and leaves Evangeline and me alone.

Evangeline bolts the door and turns to me. For a moment, it looks like she is about to come to sit by me, but then her eyes drop to my bandage.

"You ought to change the bandage on your hand," she says. "The directions call for it to be done daily."

The warm feeling subsides. Admittedly, my bandage is quite dirty. There is dirt caked into the material, presumably from where I fell down in the cornfield, and the gauze underneath is torn. I certainly do not want it to get infected after the doctors at the hospital fixed it up for me.

I pull myself out of bed and shuffle to the bathroom. Evangeline clears the space on the counter beside the sink and dumps out the bag from the hospital, arranging all the bandages and gauze before reading the instructions. The only place to sit in here is on the toilet, but it does not have a lid, and sitting on the toilet seat with my pants on feels a little improper. Unfortunately for me, my wobbly legs will not allow me to stand, so I lean nearly all my body weight on the counter.

Evangeline does not look up from the instructions. Her eyebrows are furrowed. Is she upset she has to do this?

"I can change the bandages on my own," I say. "The nurse at the hospital gave me a lesson."

She holds out a finger. "Hush. I'm good at this."

Once she has finished reading, she washes her hands and comes to stand in front of me, carefully taking my injured hand in hers. I can feel her fingers through the gauze, holding my hand as she slides the cool blade of the scissors underneath the bandage. Her knuckles brush against my wrist. She presses two fingers together and slides them underneath the gauze. I watch as she lifts it up, creating a gap, and prepares to cut the material. I turn my face away, but once I do, the snipping begins to sound less like scissors and more like garden shears, so I need to look back.

The dirty bandage falls away. I keep my fingers still as Evangeline peels the fluffy gauze away from them. When there is only one piece left, she pauses.

"Are you ready for this?" she asks.

I am not ready, but I have to do this, so I nod. She removes the sterile dressing pad, stained a pale yellow from the disinfectant the doctors put onto it. The breath snags in the back of my throat.

There is a stump where my finger used to be. It is swollen and no more than two centimeters long. The dewy white skin covering the cut is being held together by small sutures.

I try to move the stump. It twitches, sending a stab of pain through my hand.

My stomach churns, but I cannot look away. With the gauze on, I could convince myself that I still had a finger underneath all those bandages, but seeing the stump makes it impossible to deny that the finger has gone. This is my hand now. No amount of pretending can change that. Evangeline stares at the wound. She is standing so close to me that I can feel her breath on my hand, warm but still stinging my open flesh.

"I hate that he did this to you." Evangeline's voice is low. It is the same voice that had tethered me to the cage when all I had wanted was to drift to the other side. "Just picturing it turns my stomach."

Does it turn her stomach because Leonard cut off my finger when he was trying to force me to find her on the other side? Or is it because, even after that, she still made excuses for him and tried to stay his friend?

I cannot bring myself to look at her. My eyes stay fixed on my hand. I knew Leonard cut off my finger. That is not a surprise. The pain kept me company while I was inside the cage. But now, seeing the mangled skin stretched over the stump causes pressure to build behind my eyes, as though I am about to cry.

"Why would Leonard do such a thing?" Evangeline asks.

I squeeze my eyes shut because, even after everything, I can still hear his voice:

One squeeze, Leonard had said as the garden shears bit into my skin. *That's all it's gonna take, and everyone will see you for the freak you are. Believe me when I say you don't get over things like that.*

"Because he wanted us to be the same," I say.

Evangeline curses under her breath. "I could kill him. I really could."

She certainly could. I remember listening to her hitting him over the head with a frying pan, and how afraid he had sounded of her. I had never heard Leonard shy away from anybody like he did from her. I did not know anybody could hold that sort of power over him.

She lifts my hand up to examine the wound under the light, but I jerk it away. I do not want her examining me. Not only can

I not walk without help, and my skin sags in places it never had before, but now my finger is a tiny stump that I cannot use for anything. Leonard was right. I will never hold things the same way I used to. Every time I meet somebody new, this will be the first thing they look at and wonder about, and if they gain the courage to ask, I will need to relive the memory of Leonard snipping it off. I will never escape him. Leonard will follow me now. He will follow me wherever I go.

I turn on the faucet, pulling my bottom lip between my teeth as I hold the wound under the steady stream. Evangeline slides the bar of soap closer to me, and I rub some on the wound. The soap burns so badly that I scrunch up my face. I do not want her to see this. I do not want her here.

"Could you please give me some privacy?" I ask.

She stops moving. "Did I do something wrong?"

"No, I … I would simply rather you did not see this."

"See what?"

"This." I gesture at my hand. "It is disgusting and I'd rather you didn't see it, so please, would you mind stepping away?"

Evangeline shuts off the faucet and searches my eyes. She is much taller than I am, especially when I am leaning against the counter. In one gentle motion, she reaches over me and wraps her fingers around my wrist, bringing it around to the front of me.

"This," she says, "is not disgusting."

I wish she would not be so nice to me. On top of caring for me, now she needs to comfort me. This is not the way I want her to see me, like a tiny bird needing to be nurtured.

I go to turn away from her, but she reaches out and touches my face, tilting my chin up to look at her.

"You are not disgusting," she says. "You are beautiful, and I will not tolerate a single harsh word against you."

I draw in a sharp breath. My heart pounds so quickly that it is making me dizzy. I had thought I knew what it was like to long for something, having spent so much of my life excluded from things, but this ache is new. I would like her closer. I want to step into the warmth of her arms and feel her breath on my skin. Even though I have not known her for long, I cried with her, ate lumpy oatmeal with her in the mornings when I could not see her face in the shadows, and laid beside her at night with my back pressed against hers, comforting myself with the sound of her breathing. Nobody had ever been as close to me as she had.

I stare at the freckles on her skin. The warmth of her hair. Her eyes, the color of the lightest parts of the ocean, are easy to get lost in.

"You are … beautiful, as well," I say.

Her smile disappears. She steps backward, dropping her gaze to the floor.

I am so breathless that I take a couple of seconds to catch up to the fact that she is not standing beside me anymore. I feel her absence like a hole in my chest. Here and gone all at once.

"Is everything all right?" I ask.

She nods. "I'm going to get ready for bed."

I go to ask her why, but she is gone before I can form the words, closing the door behind her.

As much as I want to follow Evangeline, I cannot leave without re-bandaging my wound. I dress and wrap my hand on my own, paying careful attention to the instructions so that I do not mess up. Even though it would be easier to keep pressure on the bandage with somebody else holding it, I get it wrapped in under ten minutes before leaving the bathroom.

I pause in the doorway. Evangeline is not in the room.

"Evangeline?"

I do not know why I bother calling out to her. The room is not very big. There are no places she could be hiding in it.

Her shoes are not by the door. She must have gone outside.

Sliding my feet into my oversized hospital slippers and putting on my coat, I walk out of the room.

The cold air nips at my nose and the tips of my bare toes. I glance around for a moment before I see Evangeline staring at a vending machine with her upper lip pulled between her teeth.

I walk up beside her. She does not look at me.

I do not understand why she is upset. Perhaps she is confused about how to use the vending machine.

"You must press the buttons corresponding to the item you would like to purchase," I say.

She rolls her eyes. "I'm well aware of how vending machines operate. I'm not a simpleton."

To demonstrate, she feeds a five-dollar bill into the hungry machine and punches in a code. I watch as the spiral pulls back, allowing a package of M&Ms to tip forward.

"Five dollars for a bag of candy." She shakes her head incredulously and picks it up. "You should go to bed."

Her words are clipped. Not at all how she sounded in the bathroom a few minutes ago.

"Is there something the matter?" I ask.

Pressing her lips into a firm line, she opens the package of M&Ms and sits on a bench, putting a small candy into her mouth and staring out into the parking lot. I sit beside her.

When she does not answer my question, I try asking again: "Could you please tell me what is wrong?"

"I'm not supposed to be here," she says. "In this body. It doesn't belong to me."

Unease churns in the pit of my stomach. "It does."

"No." She speaks as though this is an indisputable fact and not something up for debate. "I don't belong here."

"You do."

"So this poor girl was supposed to die?" Evangeline asks. "Leonard was supposed to do her in and use her body to restore me?"

"I am not saying what he did was right—"

"This girl was not supposed to die, and I was never meant to return," she says. "You returned that poor woman to her rightful body because you could not bear the thought of your friend losing her mother. So, why should this girl's folks be without their daughter, or her brothers and sisters without their sister?"

I cover my ears and try to process her words. "Stop it."

She continues speaking, and I can still hear her through my hands. "I don't want to go back to your town and masquerade in front of this family, pretending to be their daughter when I'm not. It's unfair to them, and to be honest I was quite content with Edmund on the other side. He may be a bit dull, but I enjoyed his company—much more than I did when we were alive, anyway." She looks over at me, her eyes completely serious. Her nose is flushed pink from the cold. "Can you tell me I'm wrong?"

I open my mouth to tell her that she is, but I cannot find the words.

She nods. "After you deal with Leonard," she says. "I want you to give this girl her life back."

She might as well have punched me in the stomach. I no longer have trouble speaking. "No."

"Please." She eats an M&M, as though she is completely unbothered by what she is saying and does not fully understand what she is asking me to do. "It's the proper thing to do."

"I will not do this."

"Why not?"

I do not understand why she is asking this of me. "Are you upset because I called you beautiful?"

"I'm not the one who you think is beautiful." She points at her face. "This does not belong to me."

Heat rises into my face like I am going to be sick. I know this body does not belong to her, but that does not mean I cannot find her beautiful. I saw her on the other side. She was beautiful then, too, shimmering like an angel with a ribbon in her pale ringlets, but I did not get to know her with that face. Those were not the eyes that peered down as she held me when I was coming down from the foolery. Her ringlets were not the strands of hair framing her round face when she tilted her head back and laughed in the sunlight, cake falling out of her mouth and onto her blouse.

I do not find her beautiful because Talulah Monroe was. I find her beautiful in this body because I came to know it when it was hers.

I am not sure if continuing to speak will make her feel better or worse, but I try anyway.

"This body is beautiful because you are the one inside of it," I say. "And I will not bring you back to the other side because I will miss you, and I want you to stay here … with me."

I can feel the words hanging between us. All I want to do is crumple into a ball and hide from them. Usually, I am fairly good at grasping people's emotions based on their facial expressions, but I cannot read hers.

Evangeline sits there, looking at me with a curious glint in her eyes, and for a moment, I completely forget what it feels like to breathe. I am extremely aware of my body and how numb my toes and fingers are … how dry my tongue is … how my hands are sitting limply on my lap like I am some sort of disfigured doll. Sitting beside her, a feeling comes over me that she can see right through me and knows all the things I am not telling her. I simply do not know how to put these feelings into words. I do not want to lose her. There is nobody I enjoy spending time with more than her. No other person has ever understood me as well as she does. The thought of sending her back to the other side makes me feel as though my soul is gone and my entire body has been hollowed out.

If Leonard can choose who lives and who dies, so can I—and once, just this once, I choose her.

Evangeline scoots closer to me on the bench. I pull backward, unsure of what she is doing.

"Will you hold still?" she asks.

She closes the distance between us and presses her lips to mine.

I am so startled I can hardly move. Her lips are soft and full, as smooth as flower petals and just as gentle. She holds them against mine with hardly any pressure for a couple of seconds before pulling back.

My eyes are still closed as I try to process all the information that has flooded my senses. The tingling sensation has reached the tips of my fingers, even the missing one, and has turned every nerve on my face numb and extremely sensitive at the same time.

Opening my eyes, I see her gazing at me with a mix of affection and uncertainty.

"Did I do all right?" she asks softly.

I can only manage a small nod. "Can I … again?"

She rolls her eyes. "Quit being so polite with me."

Our lips touch again. The kiss tastes like the M&M's she had been eating only minutes ago, completely sweet and like I already want another. A fluttering sensation rises through me. It is as if butterflies have broken free from my stomach and are filling every inch of me with their delicate wings, and it is perhaps the warmest and most irresistibly wonderful feeling in the entire world.

25

FraNCeSCA

Curled up with Evangeline, the darkness cocoons us, as if it were a heavy blanket pulled over our heads. Evangeline does not let me out of her arms all night, clinging onto me as if releasing me for even a moment would cause her physical pain. She does not release me when the night reaches its darkest hour, nor does she release me when it is time for us to leave.

"Evangeline." I lift her arm from around me, only for it to spring back into place. "You need to wake up."

"No," she mumbles into my neck.

"It is four thirty in the morning," I say. She lets out an exasperated groan, which makes my belly flutter. "Miles said we need to leave at five."

"Five more minutes."

Those five minutes turn into ten, and then twelve, and only when Miles knocks on the door giving us a fifteen-minute warning does Evangeline let me go. I drag myself to the bathroom on unsteady knees. Yesterday, the benmjöl had made me strong, but today, every one of my joints feels sticky, as though I am an animatronic person and need to bathe in oil to bend again. There are cobwebs in my head, clouding my thoughts, but I suppose all things considered, I do not feel as sick as I did after I took the foolery.

I brush my teeth, comb my hair, and splash my face with cold water to wash away some of the sleep. My clothes are rumpled from sleeping in them. I rarely yearn for nicer clothing, but I am looking forward to being reunited with my usual garments in Bethany. Evangeline slept in her dress. The fabric is wrinkled but, on her, it looks endearing.

I do not have much to bring with me. Only the bandages and the elephant hair belonging to Ola. I have not seen Patrick or Maude since my escape from the hospital. They seem to have a penchant for finding me. I am sure they will seek me out once I am ready to bring them across again. Patrick does not seem likely to forget about my promise to him.

Because we have a couple of minutes before five o'clock and it is so chilly outside, Evangeline brings a half-eaten pack of M&M's to the bed and we eat the candies sitting atop the covers.

"I must say," Evangeline says. "I imagined, upon my return to the living, that I'd be delighted by all the things I could experience again, like eating cake. Not being roused at such an ungodly hour."

"It is quite early in the morning," I say.

"I will not accept this as morning. If the sun hasn't risen, in my book, it's still night." She eats another candy. "But I have to admit, this room is much nicer over than the dreadful cage."

I laugh, snorting and covering my mouth with my hand. Evangeline smiles.

"It also has a bed," I say. "Which the cage did not."

"This bed alone is the same size as that entire cage," she says.

I had not thought of that. When I think back to being in that cage, my memory is filled with the musty hay that made my nose itch, the terrible animal smell, and the dampness that clung to the air, but those are not my only memories. I also remember Evangeline's hands stroking my hair to soothe me, her occasional groans as she tried to get comfortable on the hard floor, and her cold feet finding my legs during the night to steal some warmth. I remember her touch and closeness as much as I remember the unpleasant conditions, so the memories are not all bad.

She leans closer to me. My breath catches in my throat. I watch for any sign that she would like to kiss me again like she had last night, but she wraps her arms around her stomach.

"May I ask you a serious question?" she asks, her voice quiet and unsure.

I nod. She pauses for a moment, considering her words.

"How did taking the benmjöl really feel?" she asks.

"As though all of my pain had gone away," I say. "It was the most miraculous thing. I felt as though nothing mattered anymore, and nothing could hurt me."

Evangeline frowns. I am not sure why she asked if she did not want to hear the answer.

"Is that wrong?" I ask.

"I just want you to be careful," she says. "Benmjöl is not a miraculous thing. It's very dangerous."

"I understand."

"Everyone reckons it's swell until it gets its claws into you and just tears you to pieces."

"I am already torn to pieces."

"You aren't hearing me." Her face is serious, but I am, too. I cannot see a world in which I live very long past Leonard. At the rate my body is deteriorating, I do not think that I have very much time left in it. "Can you promise me you will not take it again?"

I cannot promise her that. If I had not taken benmjöl last night, putting Mrs. Oleson into her body may very well have killed me, and if doing that will kill me, I can only imagine how much power it will take to kill Leonard. But I do not need to worry about that right now, and neither does she, so I do the only thing I can think of to make her drop this. I lean over my crossed legs and kiss her.

She pulls away. "Do you honestly think you can make me abandon this by—"

I press my lips to hers, stopping her words. My stomach flips over because I cannot believe I could be bold enough to do such a thing without asking her, but being around Evangeline makes me feel as though I could do anything.

I can feel her smile against the kiss. Her hand has begun snaking through my tangled hair when a knock on the door startles me so badly that I nearly tumble off the side of the bed.

"Francesca?" It is Miles again. "Are you ready?"

Evangeline covers her mouth to stifle a giggle. So much warmth rises to my face that it's a miracle my skin does not melt off.

"Er, yes," I call to Miles. "I will come out in one minute."

In exactly one minute or perhaps a couple of seconds more, Evangeline and I emerge into the parking lot, illuminated only by a couple of dim streetlamps above. Miles stands beside his beige sedan wearing a baseball cap, a pair of khakis, and a form-fitting green sweater that is not dissimilar to the one that he used to wear to school. Although it is five o'clock in the morning and the sun has still not risen, he looks wide awake and ready to depart. He carries himself so much like a grown-up. I suppose he is a grown-up.

He swings a pair of car keys around his finger and catches them. "I checked us all out. You ready to go home?"

Home. I have not considered Bethany as my home in a long time. It was the place where I lived, but I never felt connected to it the same way I felt I should to a place I considered home. My mother used to tell me that home is not a place and instead is the people who love you. I stopped being particularly attached to Bethany after she died, and I am fairly convinced my father stopped loving me on the day I set George R. Haggarty's corpse on fire, but Shiloh came to my rescue when nobody else cared where I had gone. Miles came to the hospital every day to ensure I was all right, and Jonah accepted me into his group as if I had always been his friend. The three of them are the people who love me, and as long as I am with them, it does not matter where I am. I will be home.

Jonah comes out of his room with a duffel bag slung over his shoulder. The dark circles under his eyes make him look like he was just woken up from a deep sleep, but he does not look angry anymore, only sad. He drops the bag on the ground beside me, offering a nod in greeting.

The long-haired woman Fiona comes to say goodbye, along with the man who had been caring for Max. She is wearing pajamas, and he is in a wheelchair and looks much less annoyed than he did yesterday. Fiona pulls each of us into hugs. The man shakes Miles's hand, but he does not appear to want anything to do with Jonah for reasons that I am unaware of.

Fiona reaches up to hold Miles's face in both of her hands. "If you need anything—and I mean *anything*—you call me, okay?"

Miles promises her that he will call as soon as we have freed Shiloh. "Do you still have those magnets?"

The man holds up a red and white horseshoe magnet stuck to a chain on his neck.

"We ain't afraid of no ghosts," he says, with a toothy grin. "No siree!"

Fiona and the man both wave to us as we get into Miles's car, and he drives us away from the motel.

I sit beside Jonah in the backseat, and Evangeline goes up front with Miles because she wants to push the buttons and play with the radio. Jonah looks out the window, biting his nails and pulling at his cuticles. He looks as though he is feeling rather ill. His skin is a greyish color, and his hands are trembling. Perhaps the foolery is still exiting his body. I want to say something to him, but I am not entirely sure how to speak to Jonah anymore. I also know I cannot avoid speaking to him at all.

"How are you feeling?" I ask.

He shrugs. "Physically, mentally, or spiritually?"

"In your head."

"I'm not actively daydreaming about killing you, if that's what you're asking, so I'd say that's a win."

I was never concerned about Jonah wanting to kill me. "Are you dreaming about killing Shiloh?"

In the rearview mirror, Miles glares at me, but his glare is not very scary. Jonah releases a short exhale.

"I can remember her trying to kill me," he says. "Miles says the memory's not real, but it feels real, so it's confusing."

"Do you remember anything about her?" I ask.

"Oh, yeah. For sure." He pauses. "I mean, yesterday was pretty rough, but things are coming back to me in pieces."

He does not seem to be very happy about this news, which is strange because I would think it is a good thing that he is starting to remember Shiloh. I give him an encouraging smile.

"Shiloh loves you," I say. "You love her as well."

Jonah runs a hand down his face. "I don't think so."

"You do," I say. "You simply do not remember."

"I don't want to talk about this, okay?"

Nothing about what happened to him is all right, but I do not ask him a single question for the remainder of the drive. By the time we arrive in Bethany, the sun has risen. Miles drops Jonah off at his house first. Jonah appears more than happy to exit the car.

"Would you like us to come in with you?" I ask.

"And have Aunt Moe ask why my favorite cop is babysitting me before work? I don't think so. This'll be enough of a bloodbath as it is."

Jonah goes in. I do hope he will be all right. Even though he has had a hard life, his foster mother cares for him and she will ensure his safety, even if she is upset that he ran away.

Miles drives Evangeline and me to the trailer next. He gives me a big bag of magnets to put all around it, and I climb out of the car and behold the familiar surroundings. I had been expecting to feel something upon my return—perhaps relief, or like I have finally returned to where I belong—but I feel nothing of the sort when I step into the trailer.

The lights are off. It is quite chilly in here. I expected that because the heater would have been off, but what I did not expect is the foul odor that hits me right in the face. The jug of milk on the counter has expanded and turned black from the rot that has consumed it during the week.

Plugging my nose, I go to throw the milk away and find flies buzzing around the garbage can under the sink. Evangeline opens every window and, together, we drown the odor with cleaning spray.

Because I want to ensure that the trailer is as protected from ghosts as possible, I place all the magnets around it. One goes under the bed. Two go inside our pillowcases. One goes in the kitchen. The trailer is quite old, and I realize the entire floor is held in place by a metal foundation, so I crawl underneath it from the outside and put two magnets where the metal struts join each other to make an X shape. Evangeline tapes the cabinets closed and puts all the knives and other sharp objects into a plastic bin underneath the bench I used to sleep on. The only thing we cannot secure is the ceiling fan. I am unsure of how to remove the blades, and they look sharp and potentially dangerous.

Evangeline is concerned about this. "Do you think the fan could kill us?"

I press my thumb into the crease between her eyebrows. "The magnets will stop Leonard from getting close to the fan."

"What if he does?"

"Well, if he does, I can see souls and move them with my mind, so I will stop him from getting to it."

"You can't see when you're sleeping."

I giggle. It is such a silly comment and shouldn't make me laugh, yet it does.

"Do you promise to protect me from the ceiling fan when I'm sleeping?" she asks.

I nod. "I promise to protect you from the ceiling fan."

Her smile widens. She is looking at me in a way that is unfamiliar, in a way nobody has ever looked at me before.

But maintaining eye contact with her floods my body with too many feelings, so I look away. Mrs. Oleson gave me clear instructions to clean up before our meeting with the district attorney, so I shower and pull out my plastic container of clothes from under the bed, sorting through it to find my best lavender dress with black polka dots on the skirt. I braid my hair down my back to draw less attention to the fact that so much of it has fallen out, and I buckle real shoes onto my feet for the first time in days. Once I am finished, I turn around to show Evangeline.

"Do I look all right?" I ask.

She smiles, pointing at the skirt. "The color is a good match for your cane."

As much as I dislike that I need to use a cane, I do admit, hearing her say that makes me feel quite fashionable.

Evangeline says she will lie low and not venture out of the trailer while I am gone on the promise that I will bring her back something to eat. She has only ever come back from the dead once, after all, and intends to spend her entire second life consuming as many yummy foods as possible.

I am sitting on the front steps when Mrs. Oleson arrives three hours later in a gray car I have never seen before.

The driver's side window rolls down. Mrs. Oleson's hair is pinned up. She has changed into a baby pink suit jacket and looks the picture of a professional businesswoman and not at all like somebody who died and came back to life twelve hours ago.

"The insurance company gave me a rental," Mrs. Oleson explains, gesturing for me to get inside.

The car has an odor that is like gasoline combined with something sweet. The odor churns my stomach and makes me realize how little I have eaten today. I once heard that leather in cars is preserved using chemicals similar to those morticians use to preserve bodies for funerals. I do not recall how the bodies in the hospital mortuary smelled. All I remember is that they did not smell pleasant.

On the way, Mrs. Oleson tells me that the district attorney's office is located inside the courthouse. The building is rather ugly and almost exactly rectangular, as if the builder intended to create a giant shoe box made of red bricks. Mrs. Oleson parks right in front.

"Ernest is good friends with the DA," she says, applying lipstick in the sun visor mirror. "He plays golf with him, and I'm on the PTA with his wife. If I had to spend six years of my life listening to that insufferable woman go on about brownie recipes and how *wonderful* it is that she and her husband are hosting the annual cookout again this year, so help me God it had better count for something."

She helps Max out of his booster seat and takes the boy's hand. He is all dressed up as well, wearing a collared shirt with his blond hair combed out of his face. A piece springs free, as though even all the hair gel in the world could not conquer it.

I join them. Mrs. Oleson appears nervous. The wind pulls strands out of her hairdo. She is tugging at her clothes and biting her fingernail. She has scrubbed all the dirt and grime from her body. The only sign that the events of last night happened is the small lesion on her cheek from when she fell into the dirt. After I struck her. And just before I ended her life.

I close my eyes and do my best to banish the negative thoughts from my mind. I had to do it. I killed Leonard's mother to save Mrs. Oleson's life. In the same way I helped Miles die when he was not overdosing fast enough, but that felt different because he had been trying to die.

Mrs. Oleson smooths down the front of Max's shirt. "Are you sure you want to do this?" she asks him.

He nods. A look of concentration wrinkles his small face.

Mrs. Oleson squeezes my shoulder a little too hard for it to be a comforting gesture, and we march up to the building. Before we reach the doors, they open, and two men come storming out of them.

Mrs. Oleson stops. Her hand grips mine so hard I am afraid she might pull it off my body.

One of the men is very angry. He is broad and quite strong-looking, with short hair and a face that is burning red. He whirls on his companion, a silver-haired man wearing a nice suit. He is not talking loudly enough for me to hear him, but it does not matter. So much anger has been bottled up inside of him that his body resembles a pressure cooker, as though he is seconds away from exploding and spewing pieces of bone and flesh and brain matter all over the parking lot and ruining our nice clothes. He jabs a finger into the old man's face. The older man shakes his head, and the angry man throws his arms into the air, turning around and noticing us all standing there watching him.

His face goes slack. Mrs. Oleson draws in a sharp breath, and I suddenly recognize him.

He is Shiloh's father.

I have never met him before, but now that he is facing us, I can see Shiloh's face in his features. Her wide nose. Her thick jaw. There is something delicate about Mrs. Oleson that Shiloh does not share. Shiloh is not delicate. But her father had more to do with that than simply giving her his nose.

He simply gapes at us for a couple of seconds before saying, "Heidi?"

The angry color that had filled his cheeks moments ago drains from his face. It happens so quickly that it almost makes me wonder if I had been imagining him being angry at all, but the older man still looks shaken.

"Oh my God, Heidi." Shiloh's father walks toward us. "Are you okay? Where the hell were you?"

Mrs. Oleson drops my hand and shoots her arms out in front of herself. He stops walking, perhaps six feet from us.

"Are you serious?" He presses a fist to his lips, then gestures at her. "I can't be happy to see my wife?"

"Stay away from me," Mrs. Oleson says. He steps closer, and Mrs. Oleson waves her arm at him. "I'm serious!"

"Okay." He holds his hands up, resembling the picture of sadness and confusion that almost makes me feel sorry for him. He does not look like somebody who would hurt his family. Not like the angry man he had been a couple of seconds ago. "What happened to you?"

"I'm fine." She does not sound fine. Her voice trembles.

"Your face." He reaches for her, but she swats him away. "You haven't returned my calls."

"I went out of town."

"With Max?"

"That's none of your business."

His jaw bulges. "Damn right it's my business. Do you have any idea how worried I've been?"

He sounds so honest. I find myself wanting to believe him, and I suspect I would if I had not seen Shiloh in the bathroom at school, lifting her shirt to reveal the horrible swollen stripes he had made across her back. I have trouble believing that any person who does that to their daughter can care for them deeply or worry if they are gone. How can you worry about their safety if it was you who made them unsafe in the first place?

Max stands so still. I can only imagine what Shiloh would do in this situation. Perhaps scoop him in her arms or put herself between her father and Max, but I am not Shiloh, and I am afraid that if I move, I could push the man back into his angry place.

"What are you doing here anyway?" Shiloh's father asks.

"I'm going to talk to Harold about Shiloh," she says.

"Don't bother. I just did. They're pushing it through to the grand jury."

The color drains from Mrs. Oleson's face. "That quickly?"

"That idiot is going to have an ADA present the evidence to them, and the damn jury's going to decide whether to indict her. Bunch of morons. Giving themselves a layer of insulation from deciding themselves."

"I can talk to Harold," Mrs. Oleson says. "Maybe there is evidence he didn't consider—"

"I'm handling it."

"But—"

"They're assembling the jury as we speak," he says. "It's done. Do you really think you and two kids can change his mind?" Shiloh's father looks at me for the first time since coming over. Under his gaze, I feel a whole foot shorter. "If you think that, you're as dumb as your daughter."

I wince. Mrs. Oleson does not react. She stands there, her chest rising and falling as she appears to weigh her options. I want to tell her not to give up. Shiloh would not listen to her father if she were here. She would march right into the office and demand to be listened to regardless of whether her father thought it was a good idea or not, but Mrs. Oleson is not Shiloh. This man does not have as tight a hold on Shiloh as he does on Mrs. Oleson. Shiloh would find no greater pleasure than to tell her father to jump in the community pond, but Mrs. Oleson would likely be on the edge holding a towel for him. She might be trying to help Shiloh now, but up until a couple of weeks ago, she was making excuses for a man who hit her daughter with a belt so hard that it made red stripes on her skin.

Shiloh's father reaches a hand to her. "Come on, Heids. Can I drive you home?"

I silently beg her not to listen to him. The DA may have already decided to present Shiloh's case to a grand jury, but we need to at least try to help her. Mrs. Oleson stares at his hand for a couple of seconds before shaking her head and brushing past him without a word.

I hurry after her, a smile spreading over my mouth as he calls her name. He says she is making a mistake. She does not slow down until we are all inside the courthouse. Once the glass doors close, I steal a glance over my shoulder to see Shiloh's father glaring after us, looking as though he needs to use all of his self-control not to follow us in here and yell at us some more. I sure hope he does not. I do not know why he is so upset. He is the one who hurt Shiloh and his family. They have done nothing to him except tell people the truth about him, and still he is watching us like it would be a great pleasure to come in and pull our heads off our necks. I am quite glad when he decides against it and goes back to his car.

Shiloh's mother's entire body is shaking as she pushes the elevator button. She blinks back tears as we step inside.

"Are you okay, Mommy?" Max asks.

She nods and wipes her nose with the back of her hand. The elevator stops on the third floor. She holds Max's hand up and smiles at him, before squeezing my shoulder.

"Okay, kids," she says. "Let's go get our girl."

26

FrANCesCA

The district attorney is a rather portly man with white hair on the sides of his head and glasses that are too big for his face. He is not particularly intimidating on his own, but every piece of furniture inside his office feels bigger than normal furniture. There is a gold coat of arms mounted to the wall behind him, as well as two flags: one belonging to America and a striped one with a fancy symbol in the middle.

He lowers himself into his tall chair and gestures for us to sit. I perch on the edge of an armchair beside Mrs. Oleson. She pulls Max onto her lap because there is nowhere else for him to go.

She leans over his shoulder to talk. "I appreciate you taking the time to meet with us. How's Patty?"

The district attorney releases a long sigh. "I am a busy man, Heidi, and you coming here is inappropriate."

"I'm not here to influence your decision," she says, which is confusing because I thought that is exactly what we had come here to do. "I came to bring my son and Shiloh's friend, Francesca, to speak with you. See, they were there on the day the man died."

He lifts a file off his desk. Licking his finger, he opens the folder and thumbs through the pages.

"I don't know what's been going on with your daughter's case," he says. "Just this morning, I've had three people call and say they're dropping charges. It's hard to know who is telling the truth about any of this."

Something blooms in the middle of my chest. Richie must have listened to me. The district attorney readjusts his blue spotted tie. "To be honest, Heidi, there's a lot of evidence suggesting Shiloh shot this man. The gun was Ernest's. Her fingerprints were all over it, and all over the casings found on the floor."

"She shot him to save my son's life," Mrs. Oleson says. "This was the man who kidnapped my son—"

"I understand that," says the district attorney, "but I also need you to understand that this man was shot nine times, once in the back. Does that look like self-defense to you?"

"He was going to kill my son," she says. "Max was in danger, and Shiloh saved his life."

The district attorney releases a heavy sigh. He clasps his hands together and leans over the desk.

"Max," he says. "Is that true?"

Max nods. The man presses his lips together.

"What, exactly, did this man do to you?"

"He ..." Max glances at me, his eyes appearing somehow sadder and bigger than usual. I give him an encouraging nod. "He put me in a cage. I was hungry and scared in the cage all by myself."

"And what was the man doing when your sister shot him?" asks the attorney.

Max gulps. Shiloh would be so angry if she knew what we were getting Max to do. Reliving these memories must be hard for him, and his brain protected him from them for a reason, but if this can get her to go free, it will be worth it.

"He was going to kill me," Max says, glancing at me. "He was really going to do it, right?"

All eyes go to me. Straightening my spine, I nod.

"Yes." I turn to the district attorney. "He was moving toward Max and away from where Shiloh and I were standing." I am painfully aware of every lie, but is it really a lie if this man would not believe the truth if I told him? "Shiloh shot him in the back, and then when he tried to run toward her, that is when Shiloh shot him again."

"Shiloh was clearly not thinking straight," Mrs. Oleson says. "She was distraught, and she loves her brother."

The district attorney gives a thoughtful nod. There is an eddy of silence when nobody breathes except for him, where every passing second is unbearable because he appears to be considering it. Close to a minute goes by before he finally leans back into his chair.

"Listen," he says. "I'm not saying your daughter is a bad person, or that I believe what she did was wrong, but what I believe is right or wrong doesn't matter in this situation. If this was self-defense, that's one thing, but to be honest, it's not looking like that, and killing an old man in retaliation is not something that flies under the law. The grand jury will convene tomorrow. They will deliberate, and if what you say is true, then I'm sure they'll come to the same conclusion and not bill the case, but in the meantime, there's nothing else I can do."

My stomach drops. Mrs. Oleson leans forward in her chair.

"Please," she says. "Max can go before the jury. So can Francesca. Both of them saw it all happen. They can tell the jury what happened. That has to count for something, doesn't it?"

The attorney pushes up from his chair and walks across the room, holding open the door. "Thank you for coming in."

The walls of the office creep in toward me. Mrs. Oleson tries again, but he shuts her down and gestures at the door. My heart drops as I follow her from the room, dragging my feet on the floor. It is as though each of my ribs is pushing in and making it hard for me to breathe. He dismissed us so easily. He did not listen to us. My fingers curl around my cane because after all of our trying and planning and scheming, everything we did was for nothing, and Shiloh's fate will be in the hands of a group of strangers who know nothing about ghosts or the fact that Leonard is not really dead even after Shiloh shot him, and that the real Patrick De Beauvoir died a long time ago. Keeping her locked in prison would be the same as sentencing her to death because no matter how many magnets we try to get into her, Leonard will get to her eventually, and there is nothing anybody can do to stop it.

Please, angels. Please have the jury take pity on her and see the situation from her eyes.

But the only answer is the rustle of leafless trees outside, and I am afraid my angels may not be around to hear me.

27

JONAh

Coming home was either a good idea or a shit idea. It doesn't really matter because I have nowhere else to go.

I undo the fence latch. A heavy bark comes from inside. In seconds, Bessie is perched in the window with her paws braced against the sill. She's got her cloudy eyes trained on me, but I don't know if she sees me or just thinks she sees something. I'm not convinced she can see anything at all these days.

"*Bessie,*" Moe yells from inside. "For God's sake, you stupid animal. What's gotten into you now?"

I'd expect Moe's voice to make me want to run and hide. Especially since it's been over a week since I was here, and I never told her where I was going. But it just makes me feel small, like I'm eleven again, standing on this doorstep for the first time, hoping she'll like me enough to let me stay.

I hope she still likes me. Or at least doesn't kick me out. I'm feeling too queasy to go anywhere else, so I force myself to open the door.

The smell is the first thing to hit me—citrus and covered-up smoke. Moe doesn't smoke in the house. She'd cut off my head if

I ever did. Still, the smell finds its way in, and nothing she does ever gets rid of it. Especially not the fruity perfume she sprays on everything.

Aunt Moe has her cell phone pressed against her ear. She sees me. Stops walking.

"I'm going to have to call you back," she says.

She drops the phone on the carpet and runs to me. I brace myself for a slap across the face, or for that high-pitched scream she does when she's pissed. I'm not expecting a hug.

"Oh, Jonah." She's much shorter than I am, but stronger than she looks. She holds me so tight that my arms are pinned against my sides. "Oh, my boy, what happened to you?"

Bessie licks my fingers. I scratch the top of her head.

Moe lets me go. I guess that happy-family shit can't last forever because she smacks me on the shoulder.

"What the hell happened to you?" she asks. "Where in holy hell did you go?"

I open my mouth to reply when she hugs me again, holding the back of my head and squeezing me. A fresh wave of nausea washes over me. That drive didn't do me any good. I need something to eat.

"Seven days you're gone. You leave with no note. No word."

"I'm sorry." And I mean it.

She looks me in both eyes, holding onto my arms and touching my face. "Are you okay?"

A shrill baby scream sounds from the kitchen. I almost want to smile. Oh, I did not miss that. Moe lets me go for real this time, wiping her eyes with the back of her hand and gesturing for me to follow her into the house.

"Are you hungry?" she asks. "I'm making enchiladas for dinner, but there's food in the fridge. I can make you a sandwich."

I drop my backpack on the couch. "A sandwich would be awesome."

She nods, a worried crease lingering between her eyebrows like she doesn't know what to do with herself. She blows past a red-faced, crying Kaylee who's sitting in a highchair and goes straight into the kitchen. Kaylee looks the same, with her chubby cheeks and a small tuft of hair sticking up from her head. Not that I was expecting anything different. I've only been gone a week. It's not like I went off to war. Or, at least, not any normal war.

I rest my hand on Kaylee's head, but I'm no good at comforting babies, so she keeps crying.

Aunt Moe opens the fridge. "Roast beef or turkey?" she asks.

"Beef." I pull up a chair at the kitchen table. "Thanks."

This is weird. Her hugging me and making me a sandwich. She's spent most of my childhood busting my ass for every stupid thing so it feels weird for her not to be chewing me out right now. But I'll take it.

I shrug off my jacket and immediately regret it, because even though the lighting is orange and all the plants and bright colors in here scream warm, Moe doesn't let this place get over sixty-three in the winter. She rarely turns on the heat before November, so it's not even on yet even though it's blowing like crazy outside.

Still. This feels like home. Or at least the closest thing to home I've ever known. More than the apartment I lived in with Mom and Catherine, and definitely more than that stupid tent. Maybe it's because of the foolery, or because I'm really struggling right now to tell the difference between what's real and what's not, but I'm surprised by how good it feels to be back here. Like my entire body is letting out a sigh. This is familiar. I understand this place. It's not confusing.

Moe untwists the bag of bread and drops a piece onto a plate. Her movements are jerky.

I'm starting to feel like I should say something. Tell her I'm sorry again because honest to God, I didn't think she'd be this worried about me. Aunt Moe acts like she's annoyed with me most of the time, so I didn't think it would be any sweat off her back if I left. Actually, I didn't think about her at all when I left, but as she slaps the roast beef onto the bread and drops the plate down in front of me, I realize I probably should have.

She gets me a glass of water, sits down across from me, and braces her arms on the table. I chug the water in the hopes that it will stop me from having to puke.

"I've had the cops round here," she says. "I've had your probation officer threaten me. I even got a visit from the goddamn sheriff because his entire goddam family went missing, and he thought you might have something to do with it. You want to tell me what's going on?"

I take a bite of the sandwich to buy myself a couple of seconds as I think of what to say.

Moe has no problem filling the silence. "I mean, you disappear without saying a word. Break the terms of your probation—you need to call Marcie, and she won't be pleased."

I remember the look on Officer Groves' face that day she came to the house to remind me of the terms of my probation. It wasn't even disappointed. She looked pissed as hell, but she's the least of my problems right now.

"You must have had a good reason to run off like that," Aunt Moe says. "I trust it's a reason Marcie will find compelling?"

I swallow a bite of the sandwich. "Totally."

She narrows her eyes at me. "You on something?"

"What?" My voice comes out sounding like a squeak. I guess, technically, I was on foolery, but that wasn't my choice and I don't think Moe wants to hear about that right now. "No."

"Don't lie to me. Where were you this week?"

Let's see. Definitely not holed up in a motel trying to defeat an evil ghost while recovering from a major dose of some sketchy circus drug no one's ever heard of. Moe never talks to me about feelings or anything like that, but she knows when I'm in a bad way. I can see it in her eyes. I don't think she knows how to talk about it. Or maybe she just knows I won't tell her.

"I saw on the news that they found Miles's body in the woods out by the park," she says. "And I heard the police got your friend. The girl. They say she killed somebody. Then you go missing."

My heart pounds. Every beat sounds louder than the last, and I dig my fingernails into my palm.

Shiloh killed somebody. In the car, Miles and Francesca promised she wasn't dangerous, but here Moe is, claiming she killed somebody.

Just like she tried to kill me.

No. She didn't try to kill me.

At least that's what Miles said. So why did she kill someone else?

"Who did she kill?" I ask.

"Some man," Moe says. "The one who kidnapped her brother."

Oh. I heard the gunshots ringing out in the woods. But that was before Leonard got to her, before he …

"Your best friend is dead," Aunt Moe says. "This girl gets arrested for murder. It doesn't take a genius to see the connection. Did she do something to him? Or to you?"

I don't fucking know. Moe needs to stop talking about Shiloh. I need to stop thinking about Shiloh, but everything I do, every conversation I have, it all goes back to her.

"You need to get yourself together." Moe says this like it's some big come-to-Jesus moment and not something she'd been saying since I came to live with her. "If Marcie doesn't recommend you go to a detention center—and that's a big, fat 'if', because last time I talked to her she seemed pretty sold on the idea—she's going to want you to clean up your act. That means no more skipping school, no more disappearing, no more mouthing off to Marcie, and no more mouthing off to me."

"I know."

"You're turning eighteen in a couple of months," she says. "I believe you can clean up your act, but you need to start meeting me halfway, got it?"

Every time Moe has ever given me this speech, I've always rolled my eyes and made her empty promises just to make her shut up, but now … I've got no fight left in me. Maybe it's because I'm tired. Or maybe it's because I messed up my brain so much that I can't tell what's real or what I need to be scared of, but I don't have to be scared of this. I'm done with making empty promises. I've spent so much time ignoring what Moe wants for me, but as much as I hate to admit it, she's right. If I keep going the way I was going before all of this happened, I'd probably end up behind bars. I believed that deep down. That's why I never tried.

But all Moe wants is for me to do better for myself than my mom or sister did. Which shouldn't be that hard. Come to think of it, she's the only person who believes I can be more than they were.

So I say, "Okay."

Moe raises her eyebrow. "Okay? Just like that?" I nod. Moe blinks at me. "You better be serious."

"I am. I'll do it."

Aunt Moe laughs. Actually laughs, before picking up Kaylee and planting a huge kiss on the girl's face.

"Don't you be messing with me, boy," she tells me. "I need to give Marcie a call and tell her you're back, and then the three of us can sit down and figure out how you're going to move forward from here, okay?"

I nod. She goes to put Kaylee back into her playpen, and I finish my sandwich before going to my room. It still feels like my room. So much has changed, but some things have stayed the same.

A memory comes to me. Washing Shiloh's hand in a bathroom. Running my thumb over her broken skin. She looked up at me like … what?

Like she wanted to kiss me.

I feel like the memory should make me feel more than it does. But as hard as I try to push her out of my head, her face stays with me for the rest of the day.

28

Shiloh

I hug my knees to my chest and press my back against the damp wall, forcing myself to keep breathing while I still can.

The officer believed me when I said I'd been attacked. She had to. My voice sounded hoarse as hell. I could barely breathe without coughing, and there were red marks around my throat. In the medical wing, the nurse ruled out damage to my airway or major arteries. There was some minor bruising so my throat will be tender for a couple of days, but Leonard didn't choke me too hard or too long to cause any serious damage. I got lucky. The only thing the nurse did for me was give me Tylenol for the pain and promise they'd find out who did this.

I doubt it would have taken them long. They caught the whole thing on camera. But if they sent officers to the man's house, I know enough about Leonard to know what they would find: the man would be dead, and Leonard's ghost would be long gone. It's only a matter of time before Leonard finds a new host and comes for me again. The magnet isn't strong enough to stop him—no magnet would be when he's in human form—but I don't even have it anymore because the officers took it away when they came in to bring me to the nurse. I'm going to die in here, and there's nothing I can do to stop it.

I pull the sleeves of my undershirt over my hands. The coarse fabric scratches my skin. I know I can't give up. I need to keep fighting for Max. But I've been fighting for Max for so long that I don't know how much longer I can keep going.

Someone knocks on my cell door. My stomach drops.

"Put your hands against the wall and turn your back to the door," a female voice says. Cold and authoritative. It echoes in the cell.

Is this Leonard back already to finish me off? I have never seen him use a woman's body before, but maybe he thinks it will take me off guard and make me easier to kill.

I will not go quietly. If I'm going to die, I'm going to give him the fight of his never-ending life.

The hand bangs on the door again. "Now."

Choking down on my tears, I stand up and brace my hands against the wall. The door opens behind me. Rough hands pull my wrists behind my back and lock them into handcuffs.

Leonard's not taking any chances. He's handcuffing me before he can kill me. Of course he is.

I brace myself for hands to wrap around my bruised throat, but they don't. The woman turns me around and leads me out of the holding wing.

I glance over at the expressionless woman on my left. It's the same woman who came in here after my attack, the same one who took away my blanket and pillow and who thinks I've lost my mind. She might not be wrong. A young man grips my other arm. His grip is firm, his hand a little rough. I try to read his expression to see if there is any hint of malice or any sign that Leonard could be possessing him, but he stares ahead.

"Where are you taking me?" The question comes out as a painful croak, like the voice I'd make telling Max a story about a grumpy bullfrog. When the man doesn't respond, I glance back at the woman. "Where are we going?"

She opens another door. I try to remember if this was the

same hallway I saw when I was first brought into this place. It's hard to tell. Every door and hallway look the same in here. They smell the same, too. A staleness mixed with cleaning products and something devoid of hope.

Panic curls around my throat. Am I in trouble for keeping the magnet in my cell?

The woman leads me through an unmarked door, and I step into what looks to be an office, not unlike the one belonging to my school principal. There's a framed diploma. Two flags. They flutter in the breeze of a fan I can't see. Like in Principal Orr's office, there's an overwhelming sense that I'm going to be punished for something. I stare out the window and into the parking lot, where the browning leaves are rustling on the trees. I haven't been outside in days, but right now I don't think I could ever want to go outside more.

An older guy in a navy polo sits behind the desk with an envelope in his hand. His nameplate says he's a warden. I don't know if that means he's *the* warden or one of many. How many wardens does this place have?

"Shiloh Oleson." He takes off his reading glasses and runs his eyes over me, making me feel extremely small. One officer takes off my handcuffs. Using the envelope, the man gestures at the chair. "Take a seat."

I do as I'm told. Both officers stay standing behind me.

"You're going to need to give a statement at your local sheriff's department," the man says. "You can have a lawyer present."

The man passes me the envelope. The paper crinkles as I open it, pulling out a copy of my mugshot and some other stamped forms.

I glance back up at the guy. "I'm sorry, sir. I don't understand."

"The grand jury no-billed your case," the man says. "The charges against you have been dropped. You're going home."

The words hang in the air, almost tangible. I stare at him. Did

I hear him correctly? I glance back at both officers. The man looks serious, but the woman smiles at me.

Oh my God.

A long breath slips through my lips. I press my hands to my stomach as warmth fills my body.

I'm not going to die in here. I'm going home.

Why am I going home? From the way Babin talked about it, I thought I'd be in here for the rest of my life or strapped to the electric chair for what I did. "What happened?"

"The jury reviewed the evidence and chose not to indict," he explains. "Your mom is here to bring you home."

His words take a second to sink in. "My mom is here?"

He nods again. A throaty laugh flies out of me. The last time I saw Mom, she was trying to kill me, and Leonard's mom had taken over her body. Which could only have meant that she was dead. Francesca must have put her soul back. My powerful kick-ass superhero of a friend saved her life.

The door re-opens. The blonde officer who strip-searched me on my first night here hands me a plastic bag of my old clothes and tells me to come with her. I glance back over my shoulder at the warden.

"Go on, kid," he says. "What are you waiting for? You're free to go."

The officers step out of the way of the door. They don't put handcuffs on me. I practically skip down the hall as the officer brings me to an unmarked room to change. Ripping the jumpsuit off my head, I put on my T-shirt and pull the neckline over my nose to smell it. Sure, it smells like smoke and sweat and blood from the night of the fire, but it also smells like the laundry detergent Mom uses, Jonah's boyish deodorant, and home.

I'm going *home*.

The officer tells me to put my jumpsuit on the bench, and she scans her ID on another door. The light flashes green.

I see her immediately. I'm back in the main entrance where I did all the intake paperwork, and Mom is standing at the desk, dressed in a pair of yoga pants and a soft beige coat, talking with the woman at the computer. She sees me. A hand wraps around my heart and squeezes.

I don't know if she moves toward me, or I run at her first. In seconds, I'm crashing into her, flinging my arms around her and making her stumble back to catch me. I bury my face in her clean hair, clinging to her harder than I have ever clung to anything.

She holds the back of my head. "Oh, my angel, it's all right."

That's all it takes. Hearing her say that, a sob gurgles out of me.

"Honey, don't cry," she says. "You're okay."

I cry harder. It's not until I lean my chin on her shoulder that I see Max standing behind her with huge brown eyes looking up at me. His blond cowlick pushes the hair out of his head.

"Are you okay?" he asks. "Is something wrong?"

I stop crying and let go of Mom. Wiping my eyes with the back of my hand, I crash to my knees in front of Max and pull him to me. He melts into me. I sink back onto my ankles, hearing my tears fall onto his puffy jacket. I smell his blond hair. I squeeze his arms and smooth out the front of his familiar green shirt. He's okay. After all of it, he's here, and he's okay.

There are so many things I could say to him at this moment, and so many things I could ask, but the only thing that comes to mind is: "Did you take good care of the lizard?"

"I fed it crickets," he says. "It was gross."

I laugh and kiss the top of his head. A hand falls on my shoulder, and Mom smiles down at us.

"Are you ready to go?" she asks.

It hits me. "Home?"

She nods. "We're going back to Bethany, Shiloh. I'm taking you home."

As excited as I am to go home, I'm so hungry for some real food that I can barely think about anything else, so Mom stops at a diner outside the city and I order the biggest stack of pancakes they have. It's the middle of the afternoon, between the lunch and dinner rushes, so our food comes fast, and I eat my pancakes as fast as possible without bothering with table manners. Max is impressed. He tries to keep up with me for a couple of minutes before giving up.

Because, according to Mom, this is a special occasion, she orders a piece of chocolate cake. I smile as the waitress puts the slice in front of her. Before all of this happened, Mom would have never ordered cake, but before all this happened, I also never thought I'd be in jail, so it's not the craziest thing that's happened to us this month.

She takes some ibuprofen out of her purse and takes a pill with water. I pause eating.

I don't know how I'm supposed to phrase this question in a sensitive way, but I need to talk to her about it.

"Did Francesca bring you back?" I ask, side-eyeing Max, who's paying more attention to the picture he's drawing on his menu than anything I'm saying. "How … uh … did you … are you okay?"

She doesn't appear to know how to answer it either, but she knows what I'm talking about because she stares at me for a couple of seconds before nodding. Slowly.

"I had no idea any of this was possible," she says. "You should have told me about all this."

"I did," I say. "Remember? You didn't believe me."

"Can you blame me?"

I guess not. Max drags his red crayon over his menu, then reaches over to draw on mine.

"I'm sorry," I tell Mom. "For all of it."

She waves her hand. I cut a piece of pancake with the edge of my fork and dip it into the puddle of table syrup that's pooling in the corner of the plate. There are so many things I want to ask her, but one of them seems more important than all the others.

"Is Francesca okay?"

Mom nods. She tells me she had been staying in the motel in

Dayton until this morning with Francesca, Miles, and Jonah. Hearing their names coming out of her mouth tightens something in my chest. Her memories from when she was a ghost are hazy. She can barely remember anything that happened before she came back into her body last night, and what she does remember is vague. She imagines it was like being in a coma and having some vivid dreams, but she's never been in a coma before, so I don't know how accurate that is.

"Those friends of yours care about you," she says. "They were all so worried about you."

"Can I go see them on our way home?"

"Yes, but Miles …" She looks at Max, then leans over the table and lowers her voice. "Miles is very different from how I remember him."

I snort with laughter. "I know."

Mom goes to say something else but stops. She reaches out and touches Max, as if he is some kind of anchor to reality. I get the feeling we're going to be doing a lot of talking soon.

Once we're done eating, we drive back to Bethany. I have never been so excited about going home in my entire life. I hated that town. Or, at least, I hated it once Dad started having his episodes. The angrier and drunker Dad got, the less the cornfields made me feel like they were protecting me and the more they trapped me. I used to love how nice everybody was, but that changed when Dad did because everyone was nice to him and I couldn't understand why. Surely they knew what was happening at home. As more time went on, it became clear that nobody did, and no one was coming to help me, but that wasn't anyone's fault.

When we pull off Route 13, my stomach flutters. I roll down the window and stick my head outside like an excited dog. Air blasts into my face. Wind runs through my hair. It thumps in my ears and then pours down the neckline of my shirt, but I don't feel cold. I feel completely and utterly alive.

Mom yanks me back into the car, but she is smiling. I slump against the passenger seat but keep my eyes trained out the window. Mom turns onto Main Street and passes the sidewalk corner where I fell off my bike when I was ten and scraped my chin. I can see Ethel through the front window of Simply Sweet. I wonder if she's still selling those dinosaur cookies. Miles came to give me cookies on the day he first asked me out, back before any of this happened, and he was just a boy with floppy hair and kind eyes who liked me.

I glance over at Mom. "Is Miles at his place in Mount Keenan?"

Mom's eyebrows pull together. "Are you talking about the police officer's apartment?"

"He is Miles, Mom." I glance in the back seat, but Max has his headphones on and he's playing a game on Mom's phone.

"Don't you think it's a little weird that he is pretending to be your ex-boyfriend, when he is most certainly—"

Did Miles not explain to Mom what happened? "His soul is Miles, Mom, just in another body."

Mom shakes her head like all of this is too impossible to believe, but then her eyes widen. "Oh, God, honey, please don't tell me you are seeing him. You're sixteen. He is a grown man, and a police officer—"

"*Mom.*"

"I'm just saying there are much more respectable and age-appropriate choices for you."

"Like who, Mom?"

Mom launches into the whole "one day, you will meet a nice boy who brings you flowers and has you home at a reasonable hour and isn't a twenty-six-year-old man pretending to be your ex" conversation, but I'm not really paying attention because she's driving by Duncan's. I glance down the alley behind the restaurant where Jonah brought me that one time to clean out my hands.

Oh my God. Jonah. I can see Jonah again. I could even go see him now.

His house is only a couple of minutes from here. I'd given up on ever seeing him again. I thought I was going to die, so thinking about him only ever made me sad, but knowing that he's in his house right now a couple of minutes away is enough to make my throat feel clogged and it hard for me to breathe.

I glance at Mom. "Could we stop and see Jonah on our way home?"

"Shiloh. When I said an age-appropriate choice, Jonah Weatherby was certainly not the boy I was thinking of."

My face gets hot. Dad told me once he knew Jonah on a professional basis. He must have complained about him to Mom. I don't want to make excuses for him. Selling drugs is unnecessary, and he does mouth off to authority figures too much, but that doesn't mean he's a bad person.

"You don't know him," I say.

"Oh, believe me, I know him."

"You're judging him from the things you've heard about him," I say. "He's had a hard life. His mom left when he was a kid, and he's been on his own with no one to look out for him. I promise, he has a really good side to him."

"I don't know, Shiloh, from the things I've seen and heard—"

"Like what things?"

She lowers her voice. "Skipping school, getting into fights with other kids, underage … you know what, and selling … bad things."

"He's not like that."

"He was very rude to your father."

I scoff. "Oh, what a crime."

"I understand what it's like to be your age," she says, and I roll my eyes so high that it sends a stab of pain through my head. "But you have only just gotten out of jail, honey. The last thing you need right now is to spend time with a boy like Jonah, who can get you into trouble."

I'm about to say something else about how she doesn't even know him, but then I remember … last time I saw Jonah, he was trying to kill me. Foolery was controlling his brain. It's possible that's the reason she has a negative perception of him. "Did he do something wrong in the past couple of days?"

"He has done a number of things wrong in his life, but to my knowledge, he spent most of the past couple of days sleeping."

Okay, so I guess my first instinct was right. I'm glad he's sleeping. Sleep is good. If he got to sleep, he's probably over the foolery. I want to find out how badly the foolery affected him without telling Mom about it. She has had to come to terms with enough crazy stuff and telling her that Jonah was brainwashed to kill me will not make her want to drive me to his house. I try to phrase this question in a way that won't raise alarm bells in her head. "Did he seem … normal to you?"

Mom shoots me a look. Behind us, I see Max has taken his headphones off. He smiles at me.

"Is Jonah your boyfriend?" he asks, in a sing-song voice.

If I thought I was red before, it's nothing compared to how red I am now. I'm like a tomato in the side mirror. I open my mouth to say something, but quickly close it because I don't know the answer to that question. Jonah said nothing about being my boyfriend. I never asked because it didn't feel important. I know what he is to me. He knows what I am to him. We have been through so much together that boyfriend doesn't feel like a strong enough word to describe what I feel for him. But now that I'm out of jail and there is a chance for us to have a future, the question doesn't seem so ridiculous.

"Can you please drive me to his house?" I ask.

Mom sighs, but doesn't say no, which I take as a good sign. I feel like if Jonah were dangerous and had been running around hopped up on foolery talking about how much he wanted to kill me, she'd say no.

I tell her where he lives. In two minutes, she's on his street and pulling up to the curb. His front yard looks neat. All the toys have been picked up and organized on the lawn, the grass has been mowed, and the leaves have been raked into a pile on a blue tarp.

Seeing the house makes me clam up. I shouldn't have come here. My hair is a mess. Because I gave up my toothbrush in case Leonard could use it as a shiv, I haven't brushed my teeth in days. I'd been so excited to see Jonah that I hadn't thought of how gross I am.

Oh well. I'm here. I will not go home now.

I steal two breath mints from Mom's purse and tell her I'll be right back, going up to the house. My heart is pounding so hard that my fingers fumble with the latch. Jonah's big white dog Bessie has her paws braced on the windowsill. She's barking her head off. Because I can't contain my excitement, I run to the front door and knock on it hard.

The door opens. Jonah's blue eyes meet mine, and the air is knocked out of my lungs.

He looks exactly as I remembered him. He's wearing a blue Nirvana T-shirt and red flannel PJ pants, and his wet black hair falls over his forehead in limp strands. Even from here, I can smell the soap on him. He doesn't smell like smoke like he usually does. Probably because he used soap to cover it up. His black eye has all but disappeared. The only sign that he ever had one is the faint green tint to his skin.

The corner of his mouth twitches. For a second, he looks like he's about to smile, but then his eyebrows pull together. There's no time to register what's happening before he grabs an umbrella from the basket next to the door and drives it at my face.

PART 3
Possessed

29

Shiloh

Of all the things to get attacked by, an umbrella is not the most intimidating. But it's definitely more intimidating when it's being stabbed at my head.

I grab the closed umbrella and yank it toward me, throwing Jonah off balance and driving my knee into his groin. He doubles over with a yell.

He's not the only one yelling. Mom is out of the car in a second, charging through the gate and screaming at Jonah to stop. He hears her and looks up from the ground, first at Mom and then at me. The crease disappears from between his eyebrows. He looks down at the umbrella, then back up at me as if realizing what he just did.

"I'm sorry," he says. "I didn't mean to—"

"The charges were dropped," I say, but I don't have time to add anything else before Mom reaches me.

She drags me away from Jonah, glaring at him. More ferocity burns in her eyes than I have ever seen from her before. It's more than she ever looked at Dad with, which is so messed up and unfair, but my heart is pounding too hard to get angry about it right now. I let her lead me back to the car. She stands behind me as I get into the passenger seat, then drives off so fast.

I turn to look through the back window and see Jonah standing in the doorway, his expression filled with so much self-loathing that I need to look away.

Jonah didn't get better. He still wants to kill me.

I should have known. It was so stupid to think he'd get better after a couple of days and a good night's sleep.

"I can't believe this," Mom says, glancing in the rearview mirror like she's expecting Jonah to chase after the car. She stops at the end of the road and places her fingers under my chin, turning my head from side to side. "Are you all right? Did he hurt you?"

"I'm fine." At least, physically. "He didn't touch me." Thanks to Phil's Krav Maga lesson.

She runs a hand down her face. So many expletives tumble from her mouth that even Max doesn't laugh.

"I always said he was bad news," she says. "But this … he has to be on drugs. You will not see him again, you hear me?"

I clench and unclench my fist. "Can we go home?"

My voice shakes a little on the words. Mom notices, and her face softens as she touches my hand.

I move away from her. "Please, can we just go home?"

She turns her attention back to the road, her concern changing to anger as she drives. I stare at the passing storefronts: the bakery, the post office, the Rite Aid where I used to work, where Miles came in looking for an excuse to buy something just so he could see me what seems like an entire lifetime ago. I remember the day Jonah and I woke up together in the motel, when he had wrapped me in his arms and looked at me like I was the only thing in the world that mattered to him.

You really are the best thing that ever happened to me, he mumbled against my hair, pressing his lips to my forehead and filling my entire body with warmth. *I meant every word.*

I didn't think any amount of foolery could make Jonah forget me, but I guess I was wrong.

Mom parks in our driveway. I go straight to my room, slamming the door behind me and plugging my dead burner phone in. As soon as the screen turns white, I dial Miles's number.

He picks up after the first ring. "Shiloh?"

Even though his deep voice isn't his, it sounds familiar. Hearing my name laced with so much desperation and warmth makes me temporarily forget all about Jonah. I smile. "Hi."

"Oh my God." Miles laughs. "They let you out? Obviously. You wouldn't be calling me on this phone if they hadn't released you. Did they drop the charges?"

"Every single one," I say. "The grand jury ruled there wasn't enough evidence to prosecute—which I might have you to thank for."

He laughs again, as if confirming it. I want to reach through the phone and hug him.

"Are you okay?" he asks. "Did Leonard hurt you?"

I flop down onto my bed, touching the tender skin around my neck. Telling Miles about either attack would only worry him, and I don't want to do that over the phone. It's a conversation better had in person. "Can you come over?"

He says he'll come as soon as he gets off work. I can't wait to see him, but I don't exactly have a choice, so I focus on making myself look more like a person, showering and washing my hair and brushing my teeth for the first time in days, which makes my gums burn. I change into the softest pair of sweatpants I own and a T-shirt I got years ago at some police department fundraiser before parking myself in front of the TV and eating ice cream right out of the tub for dinner. In an hour and a half, I hear a knock on the door.

"Who is it?" Mom asks as I jump up from the couch, ignoring her. "Shiloh, who is it?"

I open the door to find Miles standing there. I run my eyes over his new body: six-two with short brown hair gelled out of his face, a square jaw, and wearing a police uniform that hugs his giant arms. He must have come straight from work. Unlike with

Jonah, I can read the emotion on his face—complete and utter relief.

He walks toward me. I step into his arms, feeling all the breath leave my lungs as he gathers me up. When he first came back in this body, I didn't want him touching me because he didn't feel like Miles, all big and muscular and smelling like AXE body spray, but he feels like Miles now. I don't know when it changed. I guess it happened slowly. He wraps a hand around the back of my head and holds me like he used to, all gentle like he's telling me I'm safe and no bad things can happen to me as long as I'm in his arms.

He lets go of me and steps aside, revealing the girl standing on the steps behind him.

Oh my God. In the dim light of Leonard's creepy cellar, I could see that Francesca had changed, but those physical changes are unmissable right now. Her dense black curls have turned white. Her once brown eyes have drained of color. Her olive skin looks all papery and wrinkled. A bandage is wrapped around her left hand. She is wearing an old painter's shirt with tiny purple flowers embroidered on the front and is leaning on a purple cane you'd buy for an old lady who wanted to look hip. But she smiles at me like not a single thing is different, like she's completely fine and really happy to see me.

I brush past Miles and hug her, too. She wobbles on her feet and holds onto me for balance, which makes me hold her tighter.

"Thank you," I say. "For everything you did for me."

"You should thank Miles, as well," she says, letting me go. "He was the one who discovered how magnets work."

"You did that?" I turn to Miles, who is looking pretty happy with himself. "How?"

He shrugs. "I'm just that good."

Both of them come inside and say hi to Mom and Max. Mom side-eyes Miles like she's waiting to see if he does anything to suggest I was lying and the two of us are still together, but I bring him into my room before she can say anything embarrassing. Francesca sits on the edge of my bed. Miles stares at the empty walls like he did the first time he came in here, like he's wondering why I have no posters and thinking it's kind of depressing and sad. Maybe one day I'll put decorations up. This room doesn't need to be such a sad place now that Dad doesn't live here anymore. I need to put my Justin Bieber poster back up. It's still in the duffel bag, all crinkled and ripped from being in with all my stuff, but now is not the time to think about that because the sad and scary things happening in my life aren't over yet.

Crossing my arms, I lean against the door. "I went to go see Jonah," I say. "On my way home."

Miles whips his head around, his jaw dropping. His expression gives me all the confirmation I need.

Francesca pulls one of my pillows onto her lap and hugs it as she tells me about the foolery and everything they've done for Jonah to help him get over the foolery. He's not completely gone. He remembers who Miles and Francesca are, but when it comes to me, everything is messed up.

"He was acting normal this morning," Miles says. "But seeing you in person must have made him snap."

I remember the guilt that crossed Jonah's face after he heard my mom scream. She had pulled me away so quickly that he had no time to say anything to me, and he looked like he wanted to.

"So ... what, he's totally fine until he gets an intrusive thought about killing me?" I ask.

"He remembers you," Francesca says. "But the foolery is still working its way out of his body, so he is still under its influence."

"Is he ever going to go back to normal?"

Francesca and Miles exchange a glance that makes me sick to my stomach.

"I am honestly not sure," Francesca says. "But he is not very happy with himself and is trying very hard to be like he was."

Like that makes it better. Who cares what he remembers if being around me makes him snap and try to kill me? I want to hit something. To grab something and rip it apart. Anything to loosen this knot in my stomach and quiet the screaming in my head. But doing that will not get the old Jonah back. I picture Leonard's smug face. I want to pluck his eyeballs out and rip his ears off until he screams with agony for what he has done to Jonah ... to Max ... to *Mom*. To me.

Something on Miles's face changes. He points to his own neck and then points at me. "Did Jonah do that to you?"

"No." I'm surprised Miles noticed. I didn't think the bruising was bad because Mom didn't say anything about it, but I guess Miles is more in tune with that stuff after Officer Zweering got strangled with that rope and he had to cover it up. "Leonard did."

Miles goes pale. So does Francesca, and I sit down on the carpet and keep my voice down.

"Leonard possessed an officer last night," I say.

Miles blinks at me. "He tried to kill you?"

I nod. "He came into my cell and tried to strangle me. It would have worked too if I hadn't made enough noise for someone to come and stop him. I'm guessing he figured out that magnets only work on ghosts."

"Well, that's just fantastic," Miles says.

"Has Leonard attacked you guys yet?" I ask. Francesca and Miles shake their heads. "Cool. So he's starting with me. Makes sense. I'm the one who bashed his head in with a police baton."

"I would have thought he would be most angry with me," Francesca says. "I escaped his cellar, brought him to the other side, turned his old friend against him, killed his mother ... the list is quite long, actually."

"He doesn't like me," Miles says. "Because he keeps killing me and I keep coming back."

I guess it doesn't matter who he hates the most. None of us are his favorite people ever.

"He will not stop until he kills all of us, and now that he's started possessing people, it's only a matter of time until he gets us," I say. "We need to kill him before he kills us."

Nobody says anything to that. I was hoping someone would

have an idea about how we can track down his ghost or set a trap for him or something, but Miles yawns into his elbow and, a couple of seconds later, so do I. Getting out of jail had been so exciting that I didn't even stop to think about how tired I was, or how much I want to sleep in a real bed again.

"Should we get some sleep and make a plan in the morning?" I ask.

Miles and Francesca nod. In case Leonard tries to come into my house as a ghost, Miles gives me a bunch of magnets to put under my bed, as well as Mom's and Max's. We all work together to ghost-proof the bedrooms, getting rid of a bunch of objects that could be used as weapons. Since Mom is now a believer in ghosts, she gets on board quickly, helping us carry nightstands, dressers full of clothes, and lamps out into the hall. Mom takes off the blades of the ceiling fan. Max puts his plastic dinosaurs in the hall. All of us debate what to do with the gecko for a long time. He's inside a glass terrarium, and I don't like the idea of keeping any glass in Max's room, so we put the lizard in the living room. I take Dad's old belts and clothes from the closet and shove them in a garbage bag, more because I want them out of here than because I think Leonard's ghost will use them. By the time we're done, there's not much inside each bedroom except for our beds. The only way Leonard could get to us now is by using a possessed body.

Mom holds Max's shoulder. "I want you in with me tonight, honey." She looks at me. "Both of you."

I turn to Miles and Francesca. "Do you guys want to stay over?"

Francesca shakes her head. So does Miles.

"I want to go give my parents some magnets," Miles says. "In case Leonard tries to kill them."

I give him a look. "Are you sure that's such a good idea? You going back there?"

"They're defenseless," Miles says, "and Leonard could kill them just to get back at me."

This plan still sounds risky. "How are you even going to get into their room?"

"I could always …" His voice trails off.

I raise my eyebrows. "You could always do what? Do you know someone else who can help?"

"You," he says, and my stomach sinks. "Would you come with me and distract them?"

"Uh …" The last time I saw Miles's parents, I was in the hospital wearing a dress covered in his blood like some kind of Stephen King character, when he was fighting for his life after having just been shot. "Your parents kind of hate me."

"Which is why you'll make such a good distraction," he says, not denying it. "Come on, please?"

I sigh. After everything I've put Miles through, I will owe him for the rest of my life, so I nod.

Miles and I will go to his old house after we drop Francesca off at her trailer. We're putting on our shoes when something occurs to me. I stop walking.

"What about Jonah?" I ask.

"I was planning to give him some magnets after we're done," Miles says. "And tell him what's going on."

I sigh. "Can I do it?"

Miles winces, but I keep talking before he can say anything.

"I need to see him again," I say, even though part of me can't believe those words are coming out of my mouth. "He's not going to get over this if he never sees me in person."

Miles still looks unsure. "What if he attacks you again?"

"I'll fight him off," I say. "Or scream so his mom can come help me. It's really not that complicated."

Miles looks like he can think of a hundred reasons why this is a bad idea. He opens his mouth to tell me all of them when Francesca says, "I think that is a good idea."

So it's settled. Except for one sort of big thing—I need to figure out what to tell Mom. I consider leaving the whole Jonah part out and saying I'm going to help Miles with something, but she's been through enough with me to deserve the truth about where I'm going, and it's not like I can leave the house without telling her. I end up saying Miles will be there the whole time, and that I'm going quickly and coming home. To say she's not happy about me going to see Jonah would be the understatement of the year, but I beg her to trust me. Begrudgingly, she does.

On the way to Jonah's house, I start to feel like I'm going to throw up. But I need to do this. Jonah might never get back to being the person he used to be, but if I never talk to him again, there's no chance at all.

I unbuckle my seatbelt and step out of the car. It's dark out, now. Cold, too. But it's not a long walk up to Jonah's house, so I don't put on my coat.

Miles rolls down the window and leans over the center console, bracing a hand on the steering wheel. "I'll be right out here. If anything happens, and I mean anything at all, call me and I'll come in."

"Okay," I say. "Thanks."

He nods. I stare into his eyes. There is just enough light in the dark car to see them. They're multiple shades lighter than his old ones, but I swear, every time I look at him, those eyes look more like his.

He gives me a sad smile. "You really care about him, don't you?"

His question takes me by surprise. It also makes me feel bad. Part of me wants to downplay what I'm feeling but, like with Mom, Miles and I have been through enough together for him to deserve the truth, so I nod.

But I don't stick around to talk about it any longer. I grab the bag of magnets from the trunk and go up to Jonah's door.

30

JONAh

My probation officer rips me a new one, but I deserve it. Running away last week violated so many terms of my probation that Officer Groves has the grounds to throw me back in front of a judge. But I guess the whole dead best friend thing makes her feel sorry for me because she ends up giving me a long talk and telling me it's my last chance. If I had a nickel for every time someone has told me that … well, I wouldn't have much, but I'd have too many nickels.

I'm going back to school on Monday. I will not skip class. I will turn in my homework. I will answer questions and stop being, in Moe's words, rude and hostile to everyone who gives a damn about me.

She wants me to send in my application to the Career Center so I can get a job once I finish school. I tell her I'm useless at fixing cars and no one would want to live in a house I've had a hand in building, but she says I'll learn. She has me sit at the kitchen table and doesn't let me get up until I write the entire application essay, which makes me want to stick my pen through my eyeball but at least it gives me something to think about other than Shiloh. Once I'm done with that, I crash on the couch and put on my music, but not even blowing my eardrums out with Metallica gets Shiloh's face out of my head.

I can't believe I did that. Just lost it on her like that. One second I was staring at her, and the next I was on the ground, and she was looking at me like I'd ripped her heart out, which is not the way she'd look at me if she'd come to kill me. I can't keep doing this. Blacking out and going on rampages I don't remember. There's something wrong with me, and it's so damn shitty and exhausting that I just want to sink into a hole of nothingness where I don't have to talk to anyone or pretend to get better or do what everyone expects of me.

I wring my hands together, staring up at the popcorn ceiling until it gets blurry. Maybe if I get high enough or turn my music loud enough, I can pretend I'm in that void, but no matter how hard I try, Shiloh's stupid face stays there, tethering me to this crappy reality.

Some time goes by. I start to feel sicker—more nauseated—and I start sweating like the weird kid at the prom. This damn foolery withdrawal is kicking my ass. Aunt Moe puts Kaylee down and retreats into her room for her nightly "me" time, leaving me alone with my music. I should go to bed. Try to sleep off the foolery because it's seriously kicking my ass. I'm about to turn in when there's a knock on the door.

I pull my headphones down around my neck and get up. Bessie's at the door, her tail thumping like she already knows who it is. I tell her to quit because Moe already put Kaylee down and she's going to be pissed as hell if I wake the baby up.

Gripping Bessie's collar, I open the door, and immediately wish I hadn't.

Shiloh stands on the porch. Alone. She's in different clothes than she was when she came here earlier. They're too big on her. Her hair is tied up in a ponytail, and the skin around her eyes is the same greenish-yellow color as mine. The corners of my vision blur.

Get her.

Kill her before she kills you.

I close my eyes and focus on breathing. No. I'm not going to lose it again. Bessie's tail hits my leg as she wags it, and I grip the buckle on her collar to the point of pain.

Shiloh's not possessed. She's not dangerous to you.

But even though I logically know that, I can still see her in the dim light of that basement, swinging a Bowie knife around with an evil grin on her face. The memory is so clear. The blood on the front of her camo hoodie. The baby hairs glued to her temples. The gleam in her eyes that said she was going to enjoy every second of what she had planned for me.

I force myself to open my eyes and look at Shiloh again.

"You shouldn't be here," I manage.

"Why not?" she asks, the smallest hint of sarcasm in her voice. "You going to try to kill me again?"

I grit my teeth. It's not like last time was a conscious thing. I just saw her and something … came over me. I was so sure she was trying to kill me in Leonard's basement that I thought she was here to finish the job, but she says it like it's casual. Like me waltzing around blacking out and trying to kill people is a normal thing for me now.

So I can't help but bite back, "I'm not making any promises."

"I brought you some magnets," she says. "Can I come in?"

I'm surprised she wants to come anywhere near me. I wonder if she has a death wish. Or maybe I'm so bad at fighting that she knows she could beat me if I tried anything. She's done it before.

I let her in, releasing my hold on Bessie and watching as she runs up to Shiloh, licking her fingers. Shiloh pats her on the head. I listen for Moe getting up or coming through to see what's going on, but she doesn't, and by some miracle, Kaylee doesn't wake up.

"You need to be quiet," I say. "Moe can't know you're here."

Shiloh nods and turns her back to me, dropping the duffel bag on the couch.

Go get her.

She's not watching.

You can take her by surprise.

I turn away from her. Where are these thoughts coming from? Not even Bessie thinks she's a threat.

Because Shiloh's not a threat. If she wanted me dead, she would've killed me already. She'd have bought her dad's gun, or that Bowie knife. I don't know how to get that through my head.

"You should lock your doors," she says. "In case Leonard possesses someone and tries to break in the old-fashioned way."

She double checks the locks on the living room windows. In that baggy shirt and with her hair up like that, she looks so young.

She's just a kid. She isn't capable of killing anyone.

But I know better. It's like looking at a spider and thinking, oh, it's just a spider, it wouldn't hurt a fly.

No. *She's here to help me.*

The pressure builds in my chest. She needs to leave. I'm on the verge of either puking or passing out, and I can't handle this right now. Shiloh goes through the kitchen and locks the back door, sliding a chair under the knob to barricade it. To stop Leonard from getting to me. And to Moe and Kaylee. Because she's here to *help me.* I release my breath and glance at the hallway, hoping Moe has her headphones on or has fallen asleep and will not hear Shiloh in the house. She still thinks Shiloh is a murderer and killed a bunch of people, and I didn't do much to change her mind.

Shiloh comes back. I expect her to leave, but she sits on the couch across from me. Bessie goes over and nudges her hand, begging for some more attention. Dogs are supposed to be good judges of character. I guess that should count for something.

I wait for her to say something, but she doesn't, so I stare at her. Really study her to see if I can find any hint of anger on her face, but there's nothing.

Close to a minute goes by before she talks. "Can I ask you a question?"

"Shoot."

"What do you remember about me?"

I don't want to talk about this, but I owe it to her to at least be honest. "A lot. Some of it might even be true." I risk a smile.

She doesn't return it. Eventually, she asks: "Is everything … about us … gone?"

I pause. I can remember more about her than I could yesterday. As the drug works its way out of my body, it's lifting the fog clouding my memories and I'm getting her back in pieces. How she likes Broadway musicals. *Les Mis*. The yellow of her homecoming dress. Hooking up at the motel. Her standing under the Upside-Down Tree questioning her entire life and lighting a cigarette she looks scared of. But honestly, I don't know much that matters when, right now, it's all I can do not to bash her head in with the magnet on the table.

When I say nothing, she gets up from the couch.

"I'm going to go," she says. "It's getting late."

I need to say something. I tried to kill her twice this week. The least I can do is not be a jerk to her.

"Shiloh," I say. "I remember going to the abandoned house with you."

This makes her stop. She turns around. "Yeah?"

I nod. "We saw your dad. You punched the wall and got your hand all messed up, so I took you to Duncan's and helped you wash it out. You asked me to tell you something funny, and I told you about me pissing in my sister's humidifier."

I don't know why I'm telling her this. It sounds stupid to say out loud, but I just don't want her to look so sad.

Shiloh nods. "That happened."

I remember how close she was to me. How I had to use every ounce of my self-control not to touch her face or run my thumb over the soft bend of her cupid's bow.

"I wanted to kiss you," I say. "Bad. But I didn't."

Shiloh nods. "Because of Miles."

Oh yeah. Miles was dying, and I was in the bathroom at Duncan's, trying not to kiss his ex-girlfriend. Some best friend I am.

"Frankie keeps saying I loved you, which is weird because I've never loved anyone." I get an uneasy feeling in my stomach like what I'm saying is stupid or too much, but I want to know. "Did I?"

Shiloh drops her eyes to the floor. "Only you can answer that question."

A memory comes to me. It rushes to me all at once, and it's like the bottom of my stomach drops out.

"You said you loved me," I say. "That night. In the basement, after I got the foolery."

Shiloh swallows, then nods.

I don't know if I should say this next thing, but I want to know. "Did you mean it?"

Shiloh says nothing. She's quiet for such a long time that I'm starting to think she won't reply, when she finally says:

"No." The word catches in her throat, and she tries to cover it up with a cough. "I don't think so."

I press my lips together. I look away from her because what am I supposed to do with that? Why did I even ask her that? It doesn't fucking matter. She's practically a stranger to me. I may remember some of the things we did together, but they don't make me feel anything other than frustrated and confused. I just want her to leave. But at the same time, there's still a part of me that doesn't like seeing her sad, and she looks really sad right now.

I can't do this. It's late, and I feel like crap and can't think straight. I need to get her out of here in case I snap again.

So I try to kill the moment. "Good."

She closes off. Her eyes get steely. This is the reaction I wanted, but getting it doesn't feel good. I open my mouth to say sorry, but she walks out the door before I get the chance.

31

Miles

Drumming my fingers on the steering wheel, I glance out the window at Jonah's house. Shiloh has been in there for ten minutes. In the grand scheme of things, ten minutes isn't all that long, but I don't know how much time is too long when she's in the house alone with Jonah.

I told her to call me if something goes wrong, but will she be able to call me if something does? I get a horrible image of her phone flying out of her pocket and sliding under the couch as Jonah backhands her across the face or brings a vase down onto the side of her head.

I peer back at Francesca through the rear mirror. "Should I go in and check on her?"

Francesca shakes her head. "I am very confident in Shiloh's hand-to-hand fighting capabilities."

I nod. She's right. As always. I'm worrying too much.

A couple of seconds go by before Francesca pokes me in the shoulder to get my attention.

"Shiloh loves you very much," she says.

I don't know how I'm supposed to react to that, so I just

laugh uncomfortably. "No, she doesn't. She told me so. On multiple occasions."

"There are different types of love," Francesca says, her voice getting airy the way it does when she's offering one of her strangely worded insights into the meaning of life. "Simply because she does not love you in the way you expected her to does not mean she does not love you at all."

My eyes go back to Jonah's front door. I mean, I'd be lying if I said I didn't still love Shiloh. I think I always will, but not in the way I used to. Part of me wonders what would have happened between us if Max had never gone missing. If I'd taken her to the homecoming dance, and we'd dated for another couple of months until her inability to talk about her feelings became too frustrating for me to take anymore. I wonder if we'd have broken up and barely acknowledged each other at school until I went to college and chalked her up as nothing more than my first girlfriend. Don't get me wrong, I'd never choose what happened to me over the alternative, but it does mean Shiloh is going to stay in my life. She's become as much a part of my family as any sibling I could have ever had, like Jonah has been and Francesca has become. Every cloud has a silver lining, I guess.

The door opens. Shiloh storms out, getting back into the passenger seat and yanking the seatbelt across her body.

"What happened?" I ask. "Did he try to hurt you?"

She shakes her head and points at the road in front of us, like she's asking me to drive. I may not have known Shiloh for long, and I wouldn't call myself an expert in reading her feelings, but I recognize the look she has on her face. It's the same one she had that day on the bus when I pushed her to share how she was feeling about Max being missing. It's a look that says, "Good luck getting me to share anything about myself with you. Now, get lost."

Shiloh closes off when she feels something that's too intense to put into words. It's not her fault. She never had a safe environment to feel and process her emotions. I used to think I could help her change that, but at times like this, her defenses are impenetrable. I can only imagine what Jonah said to her.

"It's not personal," I say. "Whatever he said to you, he didn't mean it. He's not himself right now."

"Can you please just drive?" she asks, rubbing her nose and looking out the window.

I know better than to keep pushing. Not even Francesca says anything as I pull away from the curb. Shiloh keeps her eyes out the window. Passing headlights and streetlamps light up her face enough for me to see the tears glistening on her cheeks, but she wipes them away fast. I want to do something to show her I'm here for her, like touch her hand or her shoulder or something, but she'd flinch away if I tried. Besides, she already knows I'm here for her. I don't need to touch her hand for her to know that.

Because I'm unsure of whether Francesca has anything to eat at her trailer, I stop at Domino's on our way. She doesn't eat a slice from the box during the drive because she wants to save it and eat it with Evangeline. From the sounds of it, the two of them got pretty close when they were in the cage. It sounds kind of Stockholm Syndrome-y to me, but Francesca seems happy, and Evangeline seems harmless—at least for a girl who's been dead close to seventy years and then brought back to life in someone else's body—so I don't say anything about it.

It feels wrong to drop her off at the trailer alone, but she'll be with Evangeline, and I gave her enough magnets to stop any ghost from getting within a five-foot radius of that tiny trailer. Not to mention she's better equipped than anyone to handle a ghost attack because she can see ghosts and move them with her mind like some kind of superhero. But she's in pretty rough shape for a superhero.

Before she gets out of the car, I ask her: "Could you have Evangeline come out here for a second?"

She nods. A couple of seconds after she goes into the trailer, Evangeline runs over to the car with her shoulders slumped and a hood over her head which must be Richie's because it's way too big on her.

I roll down my window. She pokes her head into it.

"Is something the matter?" she asks.

Reaching over Shiloh to open the glove box, I give her the test tube of benmjöl.

"In case of emergency," I say, and she takes it. "Just don't tell her you have it because she might … want some."

Evangeline nods. I don't know what her personal experience with benmjöl is, but she knows enough about how bad it is for me to feel safe giving it to her.

Once she goes back into the trailer, I don't make any move to start driving. I know where I need to go next, but I'd rather keep sitting in this car all night surrounded by magnets than go back to my house. In fact, I'd rather pull all my fingernails out one by one than go back to my house, which is saying something because I have a low pain threshold and there's no way I could stomach that.

Shiloh looks over at me. She doesn't look like she's been crying anymore. "You ready for this?"

"Not at all."

"You don't have to do this if you don't want to."

"I do. I've put them through enough. If Leonard kills or possesses them, I will never forgive myself."

She hangs her head and nods. I know she still blames herself for what happened to me. To be honest, I blamed her, too, but it's not her fault. I'm the one who chose to help her look for Max. I didn't have to. We'd only been dating for three weeks. I could have said, no, thank you, that sounds dangerous, but I didn't. Blaming Shiloh for what happened won't change anything, and I'm tired of being mad at one of the last people I have who knows me for who I am.

But I don't feel like opening that can of worms with her, so I put the car in gear and drive to my old house on the other side of town.

I park on the curb and cut the engine, leaning my forearms against the steering wheel and staring up at the gray house with the picket fence and the ivy climbing the sides. My family always had dinner at 6 o'clock, so they'd be done eating and cleaning up by now. Even though the curtain in the living room is mostly drawn, I can still catch a blue glow coming from the TV. I wonder what they're watching. They were almost done with the last season of *Community* when I died the first time. I bet they've finished it by now and have moved on to something new. Or maybe they couldn't bear to watch it because it would make them think of me.

Focus. I need to focus.

"So what's the plan here, officer?" Shiloh asks. I know she's trying to keep the mood light, and I appreciate her for that. "Dress in drag and do the hula?"

Her reference to *The Lion King* doesn't go over my head, but I still don't feel like laughing.

"You're going to go in and distract them," I say. "Tell them you have something to share about me and give them this."

I pull the poem I wrote on the back of that receipt and hand it to her. She holds it up to the window to read it.

"What's this?" she asks.

"It's a poem I wrote," I say. "Give it to my parents and say something about how it's the last poem I wrote you before I died."

"Your handwriting is different."

For some idiotic reason, my stomach flutters, like her remembering what my handwriting looks like is something to swoon over. I wrote her my fair share of poems when we started dating. On pieces of notebook paper when I got bored in class. She was very distracting.

"It doesn't matter," I say. "It'll still work as a distraction."

Shiloh nods. Closing her hand over the poem, she gets out of the car and walks up to the front door with more confidence than I had when this was literally my house and I lived here.

A jolt of adrenaline shoots through me. Oh my God. She just got up and left. I'm not ready.

But am I ever going to be ready? Not for this. So I get out and run around the side of the house, just in time for me to hear her ring the doorbell. It's a couple of seconds before the door opens.

"Hi," Shiloh says, in that awkward and uncomfortable tone she gets when talking to adults. "I'm sorry to bother you so late, but—"

"Get out." My mom's voice drips poison. I have never heard her sound like that, and it chills me to the bone. "Get away from my house."

"Wait!" Shiloh exclaims. "Please, I have something for you from Miles that he wanted you to have. He asked me to give it to you. Can I come in? It will only take a minute."

There's a pause. I know I should keep walking, and that every second I spend standing out in the open is a second I'm daring a neighbor to peer out and notice me, but I can't move. I strain to hear my mom's reply. Any sound coming from her at all. I can't hear anything. I do hear the door closing though, which leaves me in silence.

Cold wind billows against my back. They let her in. Good. Keeping one hand pressed against the bag of magnets so they don't clink too loud, I walk around the side of the house to my bedroom window.

I hope Shiloh remembers what I told her. She knows where my room is. She has snuck through this window before. As much as I know what I gave her will stir up terrible emotions for both of my parents, I had to do it so that they would be distracted enough not to hear my giant new body stomping around in their house.

Listen to me. I sound like Shiloh. All scheming and planning and believing that the end always justifies the means. Is it bad to scheme if the scheming could save someone's life?

I lean against the side of the house and glance over at the rocking chair on the back porch I used to have my morning coffee on. The bird seed is running low in the feeder. Refilling that used to be my job. Each passing second feels slower than the last. A chill cuts through the fibers of my uniform. I should have changed after work before going to Shiloh's house. I was just too excited to see her. I shove my hands in my pockets to protect them, but it's no use. Not even jumping up and down would keep me warm.

Inside, a door opens. Faint light shines against the back of the curtain and my heart soars as Shiloh appears, unlocking the top of the window and shimmying it up.

"Go," she whispers. "I need to get back in there right now."

"Is it going badly?"

She gives me a glare that says, *what do you think?*

I hate thinking about my parents being in pain. But if I had to choose between thinking about them in pain, and thinking about them possessed by Leonard, I would choose a couple of tears.

Shiloh hurries away back through my bedroom door. I do my best to lift myself through the window. It's an awkward angle—too high off the ground for me to get in without jumping, and I'm too big to fit through it in this new body, so I bash my head against the frame on my way in. My heart is thumping so hard that I barely feel the impact. The smell of my room hits my nose. Lavender and cooking spices. Detergent and my dad's sleeping shirts.

I hear crying coming from down the hall. It's my mom. Forget everything I said about necessary scheming. I feel like the biggest loser in the world doing this to my parents.

"I'm so sorry," I hear Shiloh say. "I just … knew he would have wanted you to have it."

"It's his voice," my mom says. I cup my hand over my mouth because I may be in a different body and have a different brain, but my mom still recognizes my voice as being the same.

Not eavesdropping on them is maybe one of the hardest things I've ever had to do, and maybe if I weren't a total stranger standing in their dead son's room, I'd be less afraid of being caught, but not today. I glance around my room. The lights are off, but they don't need to be on for me to know that the debate trophy I won freshman year of high school still sits above my desk, or that my copy of *Lyrical Ballads* is still sitting on my nightstand right next to *The Iliad* which is going to be due at the library soon. Oh God. Are my parents going to remember to return that? Probably not. I don't want them to have to pay any fines because of me, so I drop the book into the bag with the magnets. I will return it in the morning.

I close my eyes and breathe in deeply, savoring the smell of books and my old cologne that has always hung in my bedroom but smells unfamiliar now that I haven't smelled it in a while. A creepy sensation come over my skin. Being here, smelling the smell, makes me feel almost like I'm being hugged.

The sound of Shiloh's voice forces my eyes open. This is not my room. This is not my home, and I have to get out of here before my parents see me.

Blinking away tears, I open the door. The lights are off in the hallway. Because it's a straight hallway, it's possible to see into the living room, but I told Shiloh to make sure my parents were sitting in front of the fireplace where they couldn't see me if I walked out of the room.

One glance into the kitchen tells me she did. I press the tote bag against my chest as I hurry down the hallway. The first time I woke up in this body, I was shocked at how hard it was to walk with these giant feet and boots, but I've gotten used to it apparently because the floorboards are quiet under my weight.

I hope my dad fixed their bedroom doorknob. It used to make this loud popping sound like it was coming out of its socket, which would be inconvenient right now. Pulling it against the frame, I turn it. I guess the universe decided it was time to cut me a break because it doesn't make a sound.

I step into their bedroom. My heart is beating so fast I can feel it in my head, which is making me dizzy, but I force myself to keep breathing. Trespassing in your own house is weird. Being here doesn't make me feel nervous. In fact, I feel more at home than I have in weeks, but it won't look like I'm at home to my parents, and if I get caught in this house, it will have consequences I can't even think far ahead enough to comprehend.

I don't remember the last time I stood in my parents' bedroom. I might've run in here to grab something. To get a Band-Aid or something that they keep in their cabinet. I wish I'd known it was the last time. I remember all the other times I came in here when I was younger when I had a bad dream or was too scared to sleep in my room for a week after seeing *Flushed Away*. (The evil rat got mud on all the white furniture. It was. stressful, okay?). My parents' room is not as familiar to me as my room, but in a way, it's even more familiar because it makes me feel close to them.

I can feel the tears beginning to well in my eyes again. I need to get in and out of here fast or else I'm going to cry.

I hurry around the bed to my mom's side. She always insists on sleeping on the left side of the bed and is so particular about the blankets and sheets that she'll notice if anything is put under her pillow. Peeling back a piece of tape so slowly that it can't possibly make a noise my parents can hear, I tape a magnet to the headboard. I lift the mattress with one hand like it's easy and fit another magnet between the slats in the frame.

My dad is not as fussy with his space and will never think to look behind or under the bed for magnets, so I tape them as close to the head of the bed as I can.

It's not perfect, but it doesn't have to be. All it has to do is protect them for the next couple of days until we can figure out how to set a trap for Leonard and kill his ghost for real.

As I reach under the bed to place the final magnet, the memory hits me too late—there's an iron strut bisecting my parents' bed frame. The magnet surges forward and clangs against it. The sound rings out like a gong.

I cup my hand over my mouth and listen for any sign that anyone heard anything. My mom is still talking. That's a good sign because it means she didn't stop to listen.

But it still means I have to get out of here. I throw the tape back in the bag and run to the door. I'm about to grab the handle when I hear footsteps coming toward me.

My heart jumps into my throat. I press my ear against the door to make sure that footsteps really are coming closer and it's not just my brain playing tricks on me the way it likes to do because it enjoys torturing me, but those are definitely footsteps, and they're definitely coming my way.

Before the door opens, I drop to my stomach and drag myself under the bed.

This body is too big for me to do this. My shoulder blades press up against the bed frame, and I hope my feet aren't hanging out the other side because that would be a pretty obvious sign that someone is hiding under here. The door opens. I cover my mouth with my hand to stop myself from breathing so loudly. I see my mom's small feet and the black liner socks she likes to wear that make her look like a ballet dancer. She opens her dresser drawer, rummages through it for a couple of seconds, and walks back out of the room.

A long exhale slips through my lips. I'm not a religious person by any stretch of the imagination, but I feel like some higher power deserves thanks for this moment.

Only when I hear my mom's voice coming from the living room do I crawl out from under the bed and climb out of the house through my parents' window. My boots land on the grass with a heavy thump. I do my best to close the window all the way from the outside. I'm about to go back out into the parking lot when the door to my parents' room opens again.

Every muscle in my body freezes. My mom's eyes lock with mine. I stare at her. I want to open the window and run to her. Wave my hands over my head and tell her it's me. But I force myself to duck under the window and run away before she has a chance to react.

Oh my God oh my God oh my God.

I run down the street to my car as fast as I can and jump into the back of it, pressing myself down in the backseat and pulling both Shiloh's and my coats over me. This body is too big. I don't fit, and the seats dig into my shins and hips so hard they hurt, but I don't care.

I wait for the door to open. Or for my mom to bang on the car window and demand to know who I am and what I was doing in her house. Nothing happens.

She didn't scream when she saw me. Why didn't she scream? Could it be because a tiny part of her knows I'm not really gone? Did she recognize the expression that was on my face like Shiloh once said she did? Is that a stupid thing to hope?

I don't know how much time passes before the passenger door opens, and Shiloh gets in. I can't see her, but I know it's her from the way she breathes.

"Miles?" she asks. "Is that you back there?"

"Yes," I say, but it comes out sounding more like a sound a surprised goat would make.

"Your parents didn't murder me," she says. "Did you get all the magnets secured?"

I say yes this time, and it comes out sounding like a word.

"Good."

It is good, but my hands and legs still haven't stopped shaking. My whole body is shaking. I can't get it to stop.

When I've been quiet for around a minute, she asks, "Are you okay?"

"I just ..." I try to find the words. "Being there was hard."

The coat lifts off my face. Shiloh peers down at me, then reaches down and touches my cheek. I'm immediately transported back to the time she came over to my house for the first time and we watched *The Empire Strikes Back*. She listened to me talk about how much I loved that movie until I was blue in the face, and when I was done, I asked how badly I had bored her, and she had touched my face like she is right now and smiled in a way that made me feel I couldn't have bored her that badly. So much has changed since then, but in some ways, nothing has.

Cupping my hand over hers, I let out a shaky breath. She offers me a small smile.

"I liked your poem," she says. "Especially the part about the acorns."

"The whole thing was about acorns."

"Well, I liked the whole thing." She pulls her hand out of mine. I wish I could stay holding it a little longer. It's the only thing about this night that feels even a little bit normal. "Are you going to drive me home, or should I?"

"You behind the wheel?" I ask. "No, thanks. I choose life."

"Says the guy who used to go twenty miles under the speed limit with a death grip on the wheel."

"I was safe."

"Going slow is not always safer," she says. "Someone should have pulled you over and told you that."

Because I'm too scared to be seen by my parents, I climb into the driver's seat over the center console, accidentally elbowing Shiloh in the head and kicking her in the stomach. She yells at me to get a hold of my limbs, but she's laughing, so I couldn't have kicked her that hard. On the drive home, she puts on an ABBA song, and even though she doesn't listen to ABBA and it's an obvious and over-the-top attempt to cheer me up, it helps, and she gets me bobbing my head by the time we reach her house. Shiloh might not be great at talking about feelings, and I used to think that meant she didn't care, but I was wrong about that. She does care. She shows it differently than I do, but that doesn't mean it's not as real.

She grabs her coat from the back. "Are you going to be okay by yourself tonight? You can sleep here."

I shake my head. If anyone finds my car parked here overnight… especially Lindsey …

"I'll be fine," I say. "I promise."

She tells me to call her if I need anything before going inside. It only takes me ten minutes to ghost-proof my apartment, but I still have a hard time going to sleep. Not because I'm scared of Leonard, but because I keep thinking of my mom, and the way she looked at me when she saw my face through that window. That expression. Was it fearful or knowing?

32

FrANCeSCA

Once Evangeline and I lock every door and window in the trailer, we sit on the floor to eat our pizza.

"I ordered plain because I did not know which toppings you liked," I say, lifting a slice from the pie.

Evangeline's eyes go wide as the cheese stretches. "Will I need a fork and knife for this?"

"You can use your hands, if you like." I bite into the end of a slice. Evangeline still does not make a move to pick it up. Something occurs to me, and I swallow before speaking. "Have you eaten pizza before?"

Evangeline shakes her head. "I've only heard tell of it."

"Oh, it's delicious," I say. "If you like macaroni and cheese, you will like this."

I give her my slice. Evangeline takes a tentative bite and moves the morsel around in her mouth as though to draw every drop of taste out of it. She licks a string of melted cheese from her fingers, and her tongue runs over her skin. Watching her makes me feel funny inside. Like my insides are all flipping over.

After we are finished eating, we change into sleeping clothes. I open the plastic bin underneath the bench, taking out some of my matching pajama sets that I have not worn in quite a long time. I choose a pair of purple fleece pants and a long-sleeved cotton shirt that feels like silk on my skin. Evangeline pulls out a pair of shorts that I have not worn since I was much younger. And smaller.

She holds them up. "Are these really nightclothes?"

I nod. "They are shorts."

Evangeline presses them to her hips and laughs. "My behind would peek out of these."

I try to picture what she describes. Heat rushes into my cheeks and I look away, embarrassed by the strength of my reaction. "You could wear something else if you would prefer."

An unreadable expression comes over Evangeline. Glancing at me from the corner of her eye, she pulls down her pants.

The air catches in the back of my throat. Evangeline lifts her shirt over her head and drops it on the ground, not turning away from me, and it is all I can do to remain standing. Evangeline and I have seen each other in compromising positions before. We were stuck in a cage together for days, and even though I turned my back or closed my eyes when she went to the bathroom in the corner on the bed of straw, seeing her with no clothes on feels more revealing than anything we have been through until now. I run my eyes over her shoulders. The soft bulge of her hips around the seam of her underwear. I feel funny again. Sort of tingly and warm. She looks so soft and pretty that I want to touch her, but my body refuses to move. She puts on the tie dye T-shirt that my father mailed me for the holidays last winter and it covers up her back and stomach. She wiggles the tiny shorts onto her hips. Her upper thighs bulge out of them.

She turns around and glances at me over her shoulder, a coy smile playing on her lips. "So? Does my behind peek out?"

I open my mouth to respond, but all that comes out is a hoarse whispering sound. "Yes."

Evangeline smiles. "Is it dreadful?"

I do not answer. She raises her eyebrows at me, and I realize that my eyes are still glued to her shorts.

Oh, goodness. I turn away from her because I simply cannot look her in the eye, but when I turn around again, she is looking at me in the places I was just looking at her. She steps toward me. A moment ago, the trailer felt spacious enough, but now, it feels as though it is the size of a can of soup.

Evangeline brushes her thumb across my lips. She is very close to me. So close that I could count the freckles on her nose if I wanted to.

I lean closer to her. Her nose brushes against mine. I can hardly remember what it feels like to breathe when she kisses me.

Her lips are soft and warm. She pulls back and I gasp, pulse racing, until she kisses me again. Her hands thread through my curls, drawing me closer as her lips move against mine. She touches my face. The tip of her tongue strokes my bottom lip. Her breath is hot against my skin. Am I supposed to open my mouth?

It is too much. I pull away, breathless and more than a tiny bit dizzy.

Her eyebrows knit together. "Are you all right?"

"Yes," I say. "I am simply … embarrassed."

Evangeline presses her lips together, as though doing her best not to laugh. "How come?"

"Because I am not sure how to do this properly," I say. "I have never kissed anybody before. I am afraid that ..." My voice trails off. I cannot tell her that. It is too humiliating.

Evangeline does not drop it. "Afraid of what?"

I press my hands to my cheeks to cool them down. "That maybe you will not think much of me afterwards."

Evangeline presses her lips together. I want to bury a hole in the bottom of the trailer and hide inside it.

"That could happen," she says.

My eyebrows jump up. "Really?"

"Oh, sure," she says. "But don't worry. You'll get better. With the proper tutoring and many hours of practice, I reckon we'll make you quite good."

My stomach drops. That is, until the corner of her mouth twitches, and I get the feeling that she may be making a joke.

"I am being serious!" I say.

"So am I." Her grin grows like she is not being serious. "So quit yammering and practice."

She kisses me before I can say another word. Her hands grip my shoulders, guiding me backward until my knees meet the bedframe and I sit heavily on the mattress. She bends over me, tangling her hands in my hair and holding the back of my head. Her tongue flicks my lip again. Because I think it is what she would like me to do, I open my mouth to meet hers. She smiles against me, making me so giddy I am glad I am sitting down.

She gently guides me down until my head rests on the pillow. Her body presses against my side, kissing me as though she means something by it. As if there is nothing else she would like to do. Her hand travels from my head down my neck and along my side to my hips, and it is as though something cool and effervescent is filling my entire body with tiny bubbles that tickle and feel good at the same time.

She plants quick kisses on my neck, going up toward my ear. Her teeth close around my earlobe.

I yelp in surprise. She scrunches up her freckled nose.

"I'm sorry," she says. "Was that too much?"

She looks so worried that I cannot help but smile. "It surprised me a little."

"I promise not to do that again."

She plants a quick kiss on my lips. Then another. And another. Each one is light and playful. I giggle. She appears to enjoy this, and she kisses me more, causing my giggle to grow into a laugh.

Somebody else laughs outside. The laugh is familiar, and it makes baby hairs rise on the back of my neck.

Evangeline does not notice and continues kissing me. I worm away from her, holding a finger to my lips.

She stops. "What is it?"

I listen hard, straining to hear more of that same laugh I have heard before, the one I hoped I would never hear again after that night in the cornfield.

Perhaps I imagined it. This would not be the first time I have imagined something that frightened me.

I am ready to go back to kissing Evangeline when I hear it again. Clear and unmissable.

"Oh, Francesca," Leonard's mother sings from some place above the roof. "Step out and play, little miss."

All the blood drains from my cheeks. Evangeline sits back and examines my face, unable to hear the ghostly voice.

"What's the matter?" she asks. "Do you hear something?"

Outside, there is a thunderous crash. Evangeline's head whips around, signaling she heard the sound as well.

I crawl across the bed to peer through the small window. It is completely dark outside, but that does not mean that the trailer park is asleep. The faint glow of television screens shines through the night like flickering stars. A couple of children from my school are sitting at a picnic table, passing a cigarette between each other. The orange ember glows in the night. An old man and woman drink tea while sitting beside each other in lawn chairs. A cat with silvery-blue fur prowls along the road. Everybody, including the cat, is staring in the direction of the sound.

Somebody screams. I try to figure out where the sound came from, but I do not need to guess for long. Leonard's mother's soul rises from the old couple's trailer. She is so bright that looking at her makes my eyes sting, shining like a lantern and casting a harsh shadow across the old couple's faces.

There is something in her hands. Before I can see what it is, she drops it, and a glass vase smashes between the couple.

Broken glass shatters over the pavement. The man and woman leap up from their seats, scrambling away, as Leonard's mother barrels into one of the lawn chairs, sending it flying into the old man's legs. He falls forward onto the broken glass. The old lady screams. She looks around wide-eyed, trying to find what could cause objects to fall from the sky and rush toward her all by themselves.

I yell at Leonard's mother to stop. In response, she soars at me, getting a couple of feet away before the magnets hold her back. She pushes against the barrier and moves away with a frustrated scream.

"You tell me where to find my son, and maybe I'll let 'em be."

The old woman is doing her best to help the man to his feet. He has a large piece of glass in his cheek. Blood flows down his face. In the light cast by the soul, the blood appears black.

I ball my hands into fists. "Please, you must not hurt anybody."

"I want back what you took from me." She throws herself at me again. Her soul flickers and dims with the effort. "You took my life from me. You harmed my sweet little boy, and I'll see to it you pay."

I raise my palms and hold them out to her. "I have ways of making you go."

A smile grows on her lips. "And I have ways of making these folks die."

She gathers herself into a ball of energy, flying at the teenagers at the picnic table who have stopped what they're doing to watch the old couple. The table splinters and they scream and run away.

I cover my mouth with my hand. Leonard's mother knocks into the legs of one of the girls, sending her falling onto the pavement. The girl cradles her ankle and rolls onto her side. Slowly, Leonard's mother regains her human form. She drifts over to the picnic table and picks up a splinter as though she were a real person and not simply a soul. The girl on the ground looks at Leonard's mother with terrified eyes. I realize that from her point of view, she is not looking at a ghost, but at a sharp piece of wood hovering in the air all by itself.

I cannot watch this girl get hurt. Before I consider the consequences of my actions, I grab my cane, put on my shoes, and run down the steps.

"Stop!" I cry. "Please, stop!"

Both the girl and Leonard's mother look at me. One looks horrified. The other is simply amused.

"Ready to meet your endin', little miss?"

"You cannot touch me."

"Oh, yes, sure 'nough I can."

She hurls the shard of wood at me. It whips past by ear, so close that the wind tickles my neck and makes goosebumps break out over my skin before clattering into the trailer door.

Leonard's mother rushes at me in a flash. Gathering all my strength, I stand my ground, using my mind to push back on her with every ounce of my will.

She stops in the air. I narrow my eyes, my temples throbbing with the effort.

"What you plannin' to do?" Her face knits with the effort of getting the words out. "You reckon you can end me? How many tries do you think it'll take? How many rounds we gotta go through?"

I push against her harder. I can feel the weight of her gossamer shape on my palms as every ounce of energy in my body pushes against her. She is slipping through my fingers. I have not taken any benmjöl. I did not even think about taking anything before running out here. I cannot let her go, but I also cannot fall unconscious, or I will be defenseless.

I narrow my eyes at Leonard's mother. I will not allow her to hurt me or Evangeline. She will stop tormenting my friends.

And she will do so tonight.

A surge of power runs through me. I raise Leonard's mother's soul in the air and smash her down into the ground as hard as I can.

There is a deafening scream. The world turns white, and I am catapulted backward to the ground. I raise my limp arms to rub my eyes, blinking a couple of times before I see a small hole hardly the size of a quarter hidden between blades of grass. There is something on the other side of it. Cold pricks at the base of my skull. I crawl closer, careful not to put any weight on my bandaged hand, and flatten onto my stomach to peer inside the hole.

Uh oh.

I can see through to the other side. The undead dimension is colorless and gray, with small particles lingering in the air. I am looking at the other side as if peering upward from below the ground. Energy runs across the opening like parts of a spider's web, obscuring the view of the white shingles peeling off the sides of the mobile homes, and the underside of a cat with two tails that flick independently of one another as it steps over the hole.

On the other side of the opening, I see Leonard's mother regain her shape. She peers around as if trying to understand how she was forced through to this dimension, then looks down at the hole from her side like I am looking down from mine. Our eyes meet. Her eyebrows knit together. With a guttural yell, she surges up toward me, but before she can get to me, I place my hand over the opening. Her energy pushes against my palm. Only when I stop feeling her there do I lift my hand to find that the hole has disappeared.

I go to sit up, glancing around for Evangeline, but the world surges away from me and I collapse on the grass. In a couple of seconds, I feel hands on me, on my arms and shoulders, guiding me into a sitting position. I cannot see anything, but I can make out the familiar smell of my laundry detergent and the shampoo that smells like tea tree oil Richie buys at the store. I slump against Evangeline because as long as she is holding me, I am safe.

Until a foul liquid reaches my lips, and I do not feel as safe anymore. I know Evangeline does not want me to take benmjöl. I must be very weak for her to think I need it, so I gulp it down, trying to think of anything else except for how bitter the taste is.

Every one of my taste buds begs me to spit it out, but Evangeline rests a finger under my chin, forcing me to swallow.

I feel nothing at first. But after nearly a minute, a warm sensation floods through my veins, chasing away the cold.

I open my eyes. The world blurs at the edges, but I can now see Evangeline staring down at me, her red hair hanging into her face and tickling my cheeks. My heart slows. I can feel every beat as it reverberates through my chest. It is as though I am being wrapped in a thick blanket. Everything around me dims and fades. Everything except for her.

"Are you okay?" she asks. "Did you stop the spirit?"

I nod. Behind her, the girl Leonard's mother knocked down glares at me.

"Did you make that table explode?" she demands.

Of all the things she could have said, this is not what I had been expecting. I grip Evangeline's hand and pull myself into a sitting position. Spots flood in through the corners of my vision. I squeeze my eyes closed to allow them to settle.

"That is not what happened," I try to say, but each word comes out slow and slurred like my tongue is swollen.

Evangeline grips my shoulder. "She was trying to help you, you blockhead."

"Freaky Frankie?" The girl scoffs. "Oh yeah, sure."

A pain stabs through my heart. Nobody has called me Freaky Frankie in weeks. I have never seen this girl before, but she clearly knows who I am, like every other person at my school. Other children have called me names for most of my life. This is not the first time it has happened, but it feels wrong to be reduced to such a small name after everything I have been through, and after everything I have learned I can do.

I am more powerful than any of them could ever believe. I saved this girl's life. The least she can do is call me by my real name.

"Francesca," I say. "My name … is Francesca."

The girl is not paying attention to me anymore. She is staring at Evangeline with her mouth hanging open.

"Oh my God," she says. "You're Talulah Monroe."

Evangeline's eyes go wide. She looks at me. I try to think of something to say.

But the girl does not give me very much time. "Oh my God, Talulah, are you okay? What happened to you? You've been missing for a week. Nobody knew where you were. Did this freak kidnap you?" She points at me. "We thought ... we all thought you were ..." The girl shrugs, not wanting to say the word.

Evangeline says nothing. The girl turns to her friends and yells at one of them to call the police. An old woman appears, crouching down in front of us. She looks at Evangeline as if she knows her quite well.

"Talulah," she says, tears welling in. her eyes. "Oh, sweetheart, your parents have been worried sick. Where were you, honey? What were you doing running away like that?"

Evangeline tells her to go away. She tells them all to go away and stays holding onto me and does not let me go. I do not know what to say. I cannot tell any of these people that the girl in front of them is not Talulah Monroe, because none of them will believe me. Certainly not the girl who believed I was the one who destroyed the picnic table and called me Freaky Frankie. More people gather around us. Evangeline screams at everyone to get away. There is something wild about her, and utterly fierce. In that moment, I can see through Talulah's face and picture the girl I met on the other side, kicking and screaming and cursing everybody's names as they dragged her through the circus to her death.

I am not sure how much time passes before red and blue lights flash across her face. There are hands on Evangeline. Hands on me. They peel my fingers from around Evangeline's arms. I hear her call my name. I try to find her, but I cannot see her through the blurring of my vision and the people pressing toward us from all angles. Digging my fingernails into the grass, I try to pull myself after her and see where she has gone, but I am not strong enough.

A police officer appears in front of me, blocking my path. She is very pretty, with warm brown skin and her hair pleated into many tiny braids pulled into a bun at the base of her skull.

"Francesca Russo?" she says. "My name is Officer Owens, and I'm going to need you to come with me."

33

JONAh

I need to stop thinking about Shiloh. I know that, so I don't know why I find it so hard.

I just need to go to bed. I'll feel better in the morning. But I can't go to bed until I put the magnets under Moe's and Kaylee's beds, which is going to be hard now that the baby is sleeping and Moe has turned in. Moe usually doesn't crash right away. She has her "me" time, reading nasty shit on her Kindle and breathing in the essential oils she puts in her diffuser. I've known Moe long enough to know not to disturb her during this time, which will make it hard to sneak a magnet under her pillow. I need a reason to get her out of her room.

I fling open Kaylee's door and throw on the lights. The baby starts crying, because of course she does. That's all she ever seems to do.

I stick the magnet to the metal bar under her crib. It connects with a *bong*, but it's fine because I need Moe to wake up.

A door opens and closes down the hallway. In a couple of seconds, Moe appears. She's in her pajamas. Her hair's all messed up like she's been sleeping for hours, but her eyes are awake.

And she doesn't look happy. "What're you doing with my baby?"

"She woke up," I say, which technically isn't a lie. "I came to check on her."

Moe blinks at me. She shakes her arms and legs out at her sides like she's trying to wake them up, then takes Kaylee from the crib. This gives me the opening I need to slip out the door and into Moe's room, where I dump the rest of the magnets in a pile under her bed. When I open the door to leave, she's standing on the other side of it.

I stop. She frowns, glancing down at the bag in my hands. I try to think of a way to explain what I was doing, but she just sighs and walks back toward the kitchen.

"I'm hungry," she says. "Want something to eat?"

"Uh ..." I had dinner already. So did Moe. I honestly don't know if my stomach can handle eating again, but who knows, maybe it'll make me feel better. So I nod.

Kaylee screams on the other side of her closed bedroom door. I pause outside it. Moe isn't into any of that tough love parenting crap. Not when it comes to Kaylee, anyway. She never leaves the baby crying.

I jerk my thumb at the door. "You're just going to leave her like that?"

"She'll stop on her own," she says, and keeps walking.

I feel bad for the kid. She's really screaming. But Moe's a good mom. If she says Kaylee's fine, then Kaylee's fine. So I follow her and pull up a chair at the kitchen table.

Aunt Moe gets two plates out of the cupboard. The tuna casserole she made for dinner is still sitting out on the stove. She knows I'm not one to turn down a late night second dinner, so I'm usually the one who puts stuff in the fridge before going to bed. She never joins in.

But she's joining in now. She scoops a good helping of tuna onto her plate with a satisfying splat.

She points at the dish with a spoon. "You good for some?"

I nod. She cuts a square and lifts it onto the other plate, sliding it across the counter at me and tossing me a spoon.

The cold pasta holds its shape, but it tastes fine. Moe sits down across from me and shovels a heaped spoonful into her mouth.

"Mm-hm." Closing her eyes, she licks her lips. "I sure outdid myself with this one, yes, sir."

I hold back a laugh. I've never seen Moe like this before. Maybe it's because of the conversation we had this afternoon. I told her I wanted to be better and did a real good job of sucking up to Officer Groves, so maybe she believes me now. When Catherine got older, before she met that dirtbag, Moe started treating her less like a parent and more like a friend. Could that be what's happening here?

She pulls a face. "It's chewy. Don't you find it chewy?"

"Uh … no. I like it. Tastes good cold."

Aunt Moe puts the plate down. She pulls a chef's knife out of the block and uses it to cut the end of her wad of casserole. The knife is big. Too big for what she's using it for. Once she's finished, she wipes her mouth with the back of her hand and puts the knife on the table.

"So," she says. "I saw you had yourself a visitor tonight."

Oh. I didn't think Moe was awake when Shiloh was here. Moe can get pretty sensitive about me bringing girls around the house. I don't think she'd have her panties in such a twist about it if it hadn't happened so much, and I hadn't pulled crap like hooked up with Rachael in my room when everyone was home or stashed girls in closets when Moe came in to check on me. Moe would always bust my ass, but that's why I did it. Giving her a reason to chew me out made me feel like a loser, so I guess it was a sort of way to beat myself up. Even though Shiloh isn't exactly a girl I'm bringing back, Aunt Moe wouldn't see it like that.

"She was just here ten minutes," I say. "She came over to drop off some stuff."

Aunt Moe grins. "Like those magnets?"

My stomach drops. "You know about the magnets?"

"Oh please. I could hear the two of you out here yapping." She picks up the knife, licking the clumps of tuna off the blade. "You know, it's a real shame."

A clammy feeling comes over me. "What do you mean?"

"You went to so much effort," she says. "But those magnets ain't gonna help you much."

She lunges across the table at me. I jump back, sending the chair crashing to the floor.

"What the hell are you doing?"

Aunt Moe jumps off the table. I run to the other side of it. In middle school, Catherine used to chase me around this table every time I did something stupid like piss in her humidifier or steal weed from her loose floorboard. I used to get so out of breath. She wasn't that in shape or anything, but she was mad at me, and I was so scared of her catching me—especially when Rachael was around—so I'd run around this counter like I was running for my life. But that's nothing compared to how I'm running now.

I slip and careen into a chair. Aunt Moe catches up with me, but I throw the chair at her and keep running.

Bessie barks. Why she's not attacking, I don't know. Useless dog. Before I have time to register what is happening, Aunt Moe vaults over the table and pounces on me, knocking me to the ground with the force of an NFL linebacker.

I slam into the floor. She digs her fingernails into my bad shoulder, and a strangled sound comes out of me. Her weight pins me under her. I struggle for breath, my pulse pounding in my ears, but her grip only tightens as she leans in close to my ear.

"You didn't think you'd shake me off that easy, did you?" Her lips curl into a grin, and everything inside me dies. "Just cos you got them magnets don't mean I can't reach you."

Understanding of what Leonard has done hits me. It slams into me like a punch in the gut. It knocks the air out of my lungs.

But I don't get a lot of time to process it because Aunt Moe reaches over my head and grabs the kitchen knife.

She yanks my shirt up, laughing as she jabs the tip of the knife into one of my scars.

"Looks like you started 'fore I got here," she says, bearing down harder while I grit my teeth in agony. "Ease up some. It'll go in smoother if you ease up."

Before she can push the knife in, I summon every ounce of strength and I thrust my hips upward, throwing us sideways.

The knife clatters to the floor. I claw myself onto my feet and bolt down the hall. Aunt Moe chases me. Leonard's rage fuels her, making her fast, but she's old. Her joints aren't what they used to be. I can outrun her. I have to.

I burst into Kaylee's room, scooping the baby into my arms. Her cries pierce the air. Cradling her doesn't calm her down, but I really don't care about that now.

Bessie barks again. I hope that means she's gotten off her ass and is doing something to help, but that hope is crushed when Moe appears, blocking the door and trapping us in. She reaches for the knob, but she's not going to lay a single hand on this kid. Not if I have anything to do with it.

I lay Kaylee in the crib and seize the lamp, swinging it into Aunt Moe's chest. She stumbles back with a grunt.

"You want to fight?" I readjust my grip. I know I can't kill her. If I do, then Francesca won't be able to put the real Aunt Moe's ghost back inside this body. But the whole 'do no harm' thing is hard when all this bastard is trying to do is kill me. "Go ahead and kill me then, you sick son of a bitch!"

I swing at her legs, but she kicks the lamp away. She runs at me. Her hand closes around my shoulder, drawing back the knife. I kick her shin as hard as I can. She howls in pain.

I don't wait around to see how bad she's hurt. Snatching Kaylee up, I sprint past her.

My fingers fumble with the deadbolt. I jiggle the front doorknob. No. *No!*

The damn thing is locked.

It can't be locked. Not from the inside. Bessie runs up to the door next to me, barking her fucking face off. I want to yell at her to stop barking. Scream at Kaylee to stop crying.

I whirl around, pressing my back against the door as Moe walks toward us, murder in her eyes. There's nowhere to run. Nowhere to hide. She has us cornered.

In one last ditch effort, I try the door again. By some miracle, it opens.

I run out of the house. The wind beats against my face as I leap off the steps. Kaylee shrieks at the top of her lungs. I throw open the gate and let Bessie onto the street with us.

"Help!" I scream, hoping the neighbors are still awake and won't leave us alone here to die. I turn to Ella Ruggles's house. I doubt the old broad will want to help me do anything after I stole her monocle, but desperation makes my voice raw. "Someone. Please, call the police!"

The neighbor's door opens, silhouetting a woman against warm light. Another door opens across the street—a man, with his phone already pressed against his ear.

The woman comes over. She asks me something. If I'm okay. Where's Pamela?

I can't say anything. I can't even form words. I'm breathing so hard to catch my breath, but the air isn't there and I can't get any, and I'm hyperventilating. "She …"

Moe comes out through the door, knife still gripped in her bloody hand. Our eyes meet. I crush Kaylee closer like that could protect her more, which makes the girl scream louder.

Everyone else sees her, too. In the distance, I hear police sirens ring out and, for the first time in my life, I wish they'd just get here already.

Aunt Moe smiles. It's not her smile. This one is cruel and amused, like life is all some big joke. She turns the knife toward herself. Before I can do anything, she plunges the blade into her own throat, then rips it across her artery. Blood sprays from her neck. Aunt Moe sways on her feet for a second before falling to her knees, then tipping face-first down the steps.

34

JONAh

There's the crunch of bone. Behind me, a woman screams.

I shove Kaylee into the arms of the nearest stranger and run to Aunt Moe. She's lying face-down on the front path. I roll her over. Red swims before my eyes. Blood. So much blood. It spurts out of her neck. Pools on the concrete. Squirts onto me like a bad special effect from a horror movie. Except it's real.

I press my hand against her neck, but blood rushes through my fingers. "*No!*"

Aunt Moe grins up at me. Her front teeth are gone. The rest are covered in blood. She tries to say something, but the effort makes fresh blood bubble from her neck.

The angry gleam disappears from her eyes. She goes back to being herself again, but she's not moving.

I slap both of her cheeks, my own hands smearing blood all over her pajamas. "No. *Please.*"

But her eyes are empty. There's no soul in her body.

She's gone.

The blood coming from her neck slows to a steady stream. Bessie runs up and nudges Moe's shoulder, letting out a low whimper. I glance around for any sign of a ghost, but I can't see one. Of course I can't. I can't see ghosts. I need Francesca. She can see ghosts. She's the only one who can fix this. I turn to the crowd assembled on the street. Some of the faces are familiar, but most are strangers and none of them are Francesca.

My phone. I need to find my phone so I can call Francesca. I dig around in my pocket, but the phone is too slippery to grab. There's blood on my hands. So much blood. I sit next to Aunt Moe until the ambulance comes. The paramedics run up the path, but when they see her, they stop running. Even from that far away, they can tell. There's too much blood for a soul to go back into her body.

I let them lead me to the ambulance. They check to see if any of the blood is mine. They ask me questions, but I can't bring myself to talk. I don't know how long it is until the police come. Red and blue lights flash across the side of my face as a cop asks me more questions.

Can you walk me through what happened?

Has Pamela ever shown signs of suicidal behavior?

Has she ever done anything to hurt you or her daughter?

It doesn't take long for the cop to give up on me. I'm in shock. Or, at least, that's what the paramedics tell me.

It's my fault. All of this … my fault.

Cops tape up the place. They snap pictures of Moe and get statements from neighbors. Seeing the coroners cover Moe's body with a sheet should make me scream or cry or want to punch something. None of this feels real.

Until a familiar gray car pulls up. It parks behind the cops, and a woman I know climbs out of it.

She goes up to the closest cop. The guy glances around for a second before pointing at Kaylee, who's still in the arms of the woman I handed her to. Then he points at me.

And suddenly, I'm eleven again, sitting in the hospital on the day my mom OD'd, watching that purple dinosaur dance on TV because it was better than looking at the social worker crouched in front of me, doing her best to balance on her brand-new stilettos.

"Can you come with me for a couple of minutes?" she'd asked, wrapping the flaps of her cardigan around her body. "I need to tell you something about your mom."

I knew what she was going to tell me. Sure, I was just eleven, but I'd found enough of Mom's needles to know that whatever was in them made her ugly. As the social worker led me into a private room, I felt so empty that I thought I was going to die.

I'm not about to put myself through that again.

Before my social worker can reach me, I slide off the side of the ambulance and sprint down the street. Someone yells at me to stop, but their voice barely registers through the pounding in my head. I run past the animal control officers taking Bessie away, past the stranger clutching Kaylee. I run until I reach the woods, then run harder still, away from Aunt Moe, away from the social worker, and away from all this bullshit that won't ever let me catch a fucking break.

I run until I collapse, pounding my fists into the cold, damp earth. A scream rips from my throat as I drag my nails down my face. I kick and claw and scream until I have no fight left. I lie on the ground. I'm so empty. Empty enough that Leonard could probably possess me if he tried.

Aunt Moe is dead. Kaylee has no mother. Bessie's at animal control.

Because of me. All of this is because of me.

My teeth start to chatter. It serves me right for wearing a T-shirt. I wonder if this is normal cold, or a ghost kind of cold. I honestly don't care either way. Come and get me, Leonard. I just want this to end. I want the ground to open up so I can sink into a hole of nothing, where no one can make me face the fact that Kaylee is out there somewhere, and Bessie has no home. Where I don't have to make things right because I'm in a literal hole in the ground and won't be making it out of it alive. But the ground doesn't open up. I'm still here.

With a pang, I realize I've never hated anyone before. Not my dad for not being there. Not my mom for preferring her habit over her kids. Not Catherine for leaving me with Aunt Moe to go live with her dipshit boyfriend. Not my social worker who couldn't understand me. Not even the cops who had it in for me, or the teachers who wrote me off. I hated myself for not being enough for any of them, even if it sounds dumb, but even I don't hate myself as much as I hate Leonard. The image of the light leaving Aunt Moe's eyes fills me with rage. I can't give up yet. Not until I watch that asshole die beyond the grave, once and for all.

My body starts shaking with cold. Somehow, I drag myself to my feet and stumble out of the woods. I can't go home. I don't want to see the police lights flashing down my street, or face my damn social worker.

So I shuffle down the sidewalk in the opposite direction from home, eyes lowered. I pass the police station but don't look up, not wanting to draw attention even though it looks pretty dead to me, what with all that's happening out here in the big wide world keeping the cops from their patrols tonight. The roads are empty. Bethany is always dead this late at night. Unlike the city, this is a place that sleeps, but I kind of wish there were other people around because being the only one out here is starting to feel a little too much like being in the abyss I wished for. It feels just a little too good, and it scares me.

So I focus on putting one foot in front of the other until I get to Shiloh's house.

I stare up at the house. This was probably a bad idea, but I've got nowhere else to go. A light shines through a downstairs window. I cross the grass and peer between the curtains. Shiloh is sitting on her bed. Her sandy hair spills down the back of her white T-shirt. I guess she couldn't sleep either.

I tap on the glass. She whirls around, body tense, like she was expecting someone else. Her shoulders relax when she sees it's me, like I didn't just try to kill her today.

She opens the window. "What are you doing here?" she asks. "Are you okay?"

I shake my head. Her eyes drop to the rest of me. She registers the blood.

Her mouth presses into an angry line, but I don't think she's angry with me. "What happened?"

"He found us," I say, my voice cracking as I talk for the first time. "Can I come in?"

35

Shiloh

Jonah is waiting for me when I open the front door. He's covered in blood that he says is not his, which makes me feel relieved for half a second until my brain catches up and I start wondering whose it is.

I should be worried about bringing him into my house, because he literally tried to kill me a couple of hours ago, but the way he's looking right now—all pale, puffy-eyed, and covered in blood—none of that other stuff matters. I can see the old Jonah under all this.

I wave him inside, bolting the door behind him and leading him into my room. His muddy shoes leave a trail across the floor that Mom won't be happy about when she wakes up, but I don't care. He steps over all the ceiling fan blades, furniture, and other random stuff we pushed out into the hallway when ghost-proofing the place, and he doesn't say a word. In my room, I sit him down on the edge of my bed and lean against my closed door across from him, wrapping my arms around my stomach.

"Whose blood is it?" I ask, keeping my voice low. I'm almost positive Mom is asleep, but I don't want to risk waking her up to find Jonah in my room.

He opens his mouth to reply, but his chin quivers. Oh my God. I've never seen him like this before.

"Aunt Moe," he finally says, his voice raw. "Leonard ... he killed her."

His words knock the breath from my lungs. "What?"

"He possessed her, and he killed her." Jonah's voice is deep and rough, like each word is a struggle. "I couldn't stop him."

"Did you call Francesca? Can she bring her back?"

Jonah shakes his head. "There's too much blood. Her body ... she's gone."

A chill seeps through me. Jonah remains rigid on the bed like he can't stand up or lie down, like he's trapped inside his head, forced to replay the memory over and over again like a YouTube clip on loop. I can feel his pain like a blow to the chest. It's suddenly hard to breathe.

But one of us has to. I steady myself and offer him my hand. He stares at it.

"What are you doing?" he asks.

"Get up," I say. "You need to wash this blood off."

He continues looking at it. Is he going to say no? Or try to wring my neck again? A couple of hours ago, Jonah saw me as an enemy. But now he came here, to me, which has to mean something.

Close to a minute passes. I'm about to pull my hand away when he curls his fingers around mine.

He lets me pull him to his unsteady feet, smearing blood and mud on my comforter. I lead him across the hall into the bathroom and close the door behind us. His blue eyes dart around at the bottles of shaving cream and shampoo strewn over the floor like he's wondering if I'm about to use one to bash him over the head. As if that makes any sense. This is not a big bathroom. We're standing close to each other. I can feel the warmth coming from his body, and I remember the last time we were standing in a bathroom together like this, the time he cleaned out the grime and pieces of brick embedded in my knuckles. Even though I don't know how much he remembers about us, he said he remembers that day, but I don't think he's thinking about that right now.

His breathing is ragged. I grip the hem of his Nirvana T-shirt, tacky with blood, and raise my eyebrows, asking permission. Jonah doesn't resist as I peel his T-shirt up over his head, tossing it onto the floor with a wet slap. He draws in a jagged breath at the loss of that barrier. There's blood on his chest and stomach. Patches and streaks. Mostly dry. Aunt Moe must have bled a lot. Picturing it makes bile burn my throat, and I push my feelings down. I barely knew her, but she was nice to me every time I saw her. She was serious and a little scary, like a mom needs to be if they have Jonah to take care of. Jonah never said it, but I know she's the only grown-up who ever told him she believed in him, and that he could be more than he thought he was destined to be. She was more his mother than his real mother. And now she's dead.

But I can't be sad, and I can't panic. I need to be there for Jonah.

Carefully, I kneel and remove his sneakers and socks. All that's left to take off are his pants.

He glances down at them, arching a brow. "You going to take these off, too?"

"Uh ..." I was going to, but I wasn't thinking about how that would be weird. I wasn't thinking at all.

Heat flushes my face. I step away from him.

"You shower," I say. "I'll get a towel and wait outside."

I go to leave, but Jonah catches my wrist. Our eyes meet. For a second, I wonder if he'll try to break it, but he just holds it.

"Shiloh," he says. "Please. Stay."

My heart is hammering so hard I can hear it. All I do is stare at him. *Stay.* How can he go from not wanting me near him at all to wanting me to stay and watch him shower? That makes no sense. But then again, he's going through one of the worst moments of his life right now. He needs me too much for me to get caught up thinking about it.

Because Aunt Moe is dead. It's too much to process, so I need to focus on the one thing I can actually do to help right now, which is making sure Jonah is clean.

I turn on the shower. Jonah unbuttons his jeans with shaking hands and steps under the spray in his boxers, letting the water wash over his face and his black hair. I stand there, unsure if he wants me to get in with him, but he looks so beaten up and broken and he needs somebody right now. Plus, it doesn't look like he's making any move to wash himself.

So I step in fully clothed. The water is hot. It scalds my exposed skin, so I reach behind him and turn the temperature down to protect both of us from getting third-degree burns. Steam fills the shower stall. The steady stream of water glues my hair and shirt to my body. I was expecting to go to bed. He was the last person I expected to show up on my doorstep tonight. I'm also painfully aware that I'm not wearing a bra.

Jonah doesn't seem to notice what I'm wearing or not wearing. He's standing under the shower, unmoving, with his eyes closed. The blood clumping his hair melts away, turning the water a pale crimson as it runs into the drain.

Moe's blood. Leonard killed Moe.

Aunt Moe is dead.

Picking a hair out of the bar of soap, I lather it up in my hands. I'm as gentle as possible when I press my soapy hands to his bare chest. He freezes at my touch, but doesn't pull away.

I rub the soap into his skin. The blood is dry and hard to get out, so I scrape the stubborn parts with my fingernail. I'm careful not to get much soap on the healing cut on his shoulder, but it has scabbed over now. Jonah stands there, moving under my hands, turning around when I ask him to. His body feels achingly familiar. Sinewy and hard. Not exactly muscular, but strong. The only time I ever saw him without his shirt on was when we were tangled in covers at the motel in the early morning light, and I was too busy kissing him to look at him for long.

I can see all of him, now. I rub soap over the veins in his forearms, the curve of his shoulders, down to his hips just above his boxers. I press my palms to his pale scars as if to tell him I got him, that I know he's trusting me and I will not let him down.

There's a speck of blood that doesn't come out with the soap. I go to scrub it with my nail, but Jonah winces.

"Sorry," I say, wiping my thumb over the spot and realizing that it's not a bloodstain.

Jonah shakes his head as if saying he's fine. Except he's not fine. Because Leonard just killed his mom.

I push the thought from my mind as I rinse my hands, and put some shampoo in my palm. The citrusy smell fills the stall. Jonah ducks his head, and I work the suds into his black hair, careful not to make any sudden movements that could set him off or somehow break this delicate peace between us. There's a sharp ache in the center of my chest. I want to gather him up in my arms, run my hands over him, and press my lips to every part of his body. I missed him. More than I thought was possible to miss someone. I didn't realize how much I missed him until he was standing right here in front of me, and I still could not have him the way I used to.

I rinse the shampoo from Jonah's hair. Should I put conditioner in? No. This is not a conditioner moment.

I climb out of the shower before he does, wrapping myself in a dirty towel before getting him a clean one. I put his clothes in the washing machine on cold and add extra detergent so the blood will hopefully wash out, and then I go back to my room to get him something else to wear. Pressing my hand to my forehead, I try to think of which clothes to give him. Some of Dad's clothes are on the floor in the hallway, but even though this is a weird situation, I don't think I could handle Jonah smelling like him, so I choose my biggest pair of PJ pants and the only T-shirt of mine that I think will fit him, which is by some cruel joke is an XL Care Bears tee I used to wear as a nightgown.

I'm waiting for Jonah in my room when he walks in, toweling his hair dry and wearing the Care Bears shirt. If this were any other night, he'd be giving me crap for making him wear a shirt like that, but he doesn't even look like he's noticed the dancing bears. The blood might be gone, but he still looks as empty as he did when he got here.

He stands there. I stand up from the bed and gesture to it.

"Do you want to sleep here?" I ask.

He stares at me, examining me. Heat rushes to my face. Is it okay that I said that?

He nods. I'd be lying if I said my heart doesn't double-thump when he crawls under my blanket.

I'm about to flip the light switch when I pause. I'm about to sleep in the same bed as a boy who tried to kill me a couple of hours ago. Maybe sleeping in the dark is not the best idea. None of this is the best idea. There is no best idea.

Oh my God, if Mom were awake right now … I can only imagine the words she'd have for me. But I'm not going to ask Jonah to go.

I will keep the lights on. Neither of us will get any sleep, but something tells me we wouldn't be sleeping much tonight either way.

Getting into bed, I lie facing Jonah's back as he curls away from me. His shoulder blades jut out from under his shirt. I want to reach out and touch him so badly, but I'm still scared that if I touch him, something in his head will snap.

His breath comes fast. I can only imagine the terrible images playing in his head. He blames himself for what happened. I know him well enough to know that, but none of this is his fault. I want to tell him that. I want to do *something*. Because lying here watching him in pain is too painful.

Screw it. So what if he snaps? I can't lie here watching him like this.

Rolling over, I scoot back until my back presses against his.

It's not a hug. Or me grabbing him. But I can still feel his body against mine, and that's as close to me saying I'm here as I'm going to get. He says nothing, but he doesn't pull away. He lets out a shaky breath that sounds an awful lot like a sob, and it's all I can do not to cry myself.

36

FrANCeSCA

The police officer drives me to the station. On the way there, I hear sirens ringing, and two police cars race around us. Seeing them makes my stomach uneasy. I hope nothing terrible has happened to Shiloh, Jonah, or Miles.

I do not understand why I have to go to the police station. Simply because the police found Talulah Monroe in front of my trailer does not mean I have done anything to harm her, but they still will not allow me to see her. Officer Owens brings me to a small room containing a wooden table and three chairs that are much more comfortable than I had been expecting. The chairs are plastic, but they are padded and have wheels on them so I can spin around on the floor.

"May I see Evangeline?" I ask, then curse myself for being so foolish. "I mean Talulah. Could I see her?"

Officer Owens frowns. "I'll come back in a couple of minutes. Hang tight."

She leaves me alone. I scoot the wheely chair across the door and turn the doorknob. The door opens, which is peculiar. If the door is unlocked, it means I am not being held here against my will, but I still suspect I will get in trouble if I try to leave, so I close the door and wrap my arms around my stomach to help myself feel less jittery.

Officer Owens returns with a bottle of water and a bag of chips. She even brings me a blanket, which is nice of her, but I do not need it. The benmjöl is warming me from the inside out. The drug has not worn off yet, so it is as though my entire body is one of those hand warming packets I put in my mittens in the winter, burning for hours before going back to normal. I know becoming dependent on such a thing is a bad idea, but it makes me feel as though I am trapped inside a mitten, bundled in warmth and protected by any of the pain the cold can bring.

Officer Owens sits down at the table across from me. "Francesca, are you aware that Talulah has been missing for seven days?"

I nibble on the end of a chip and do my best to ignore the memory of the real Talulah on the day she died. Her arms had been tied behind her back. There had been silver tape over her mouth. She had kicked and screamed and fought as Leonard pushed her face into the mud, and when he turned her over, the rain washed the soil from her teeth and her open eyes.

I cannot tell Officer Owens any of that. I dislike lying, but what good would the truth do?

"Talulah did not run away," I say. "Her parents banished her from the home for kissing another girl."

Officer Owens examines my face as though she can tell I am hiding something. I hope it is not the benmjöl. "Francesca, what exactly is the nature of your relationship with Talulah?"

I suspect she would like to know if I was the one who Talulah was caught kissing. I did not know Talulah at all. She attended my school, so I saw her from time to time, but she never called me names, or laughed at me when the other children did.

But I do know Evangeline. She loves twirling around in pretty dresses so the fabric floats up like a cloud around her. On the days her mother used to bake pies for dessert, she used to always sneak a slice as soon as it came out of the oven, even though dessert before dinner was forbidden in her household. Her favorite candy was saltwater taffy. She loved hiding whoopee cushions under her brother's chairs at the dinner table and wearing mismatched gloves to church service despite her father's pleas for civility. Her over-the-top impressions of Leonard in the cage were the only thing that made me laugh, and I have never felt closer to a person in my entire life.

There is no word that encompasses what Evangeline is to me. She was my enemy at the beginning, but then she became my friend. She is also somebody who I like to kiss.

I am not sure if I should tell Officer Owens about the kissing. There is something pointed in her gaze, as though she suspects I have been kissing her, and that if I were, it would not be a good thing. I do not understand why. Kissing Evangeline fills me with such a bubbly feeling. How could something so good ever be seen as a bad thing?

"Talulah is my friend," I say.

Officer Owens leans back in her chair, pulling a face as though she suspects me of not telling her the truth. Or at least not the whole truth.

"May I see her?" I ask. "Please?"

"Talulah's parents have arrived and are reuniting with her now," Officer Owens says.

My stomach lurches. "No."

"Francesca …"

"No!" I exclaim. "You cannot send her back to them."

"We've been in touch with Social Services, and they're going to schedule a welfare check to look into Talulah's living situation."

I wrap my arms around my stomach and bend over, doing my best to continue breathing. Officer Owens seems a kind person, and even though her words should reassure me, they do not. Talulah left home because her parents caught her kissing another girl. She did not run away. Her family cast her out. Will the narrow-minded people who inspect her living situation find that home to be unsafe, or will they reach the conclusion that Evangeline is troubled?

I am tired of all these grown-ups acting as though they know every single thing in the world. They say they want to protect children, but the rules they uphold have never protected me.

Officer Owens stands. "Your father is on his way. He will bring you home."

I did not know that this conversation could get any worse, but I was wrong. "No."

"You're a minor," she says. "We can only release you into the custody of a legal guardian. Try to make yourself comfortable, okay? I'll bring him in to see you when he gets here."

She leaves. The door closes, and I am alone again.

All I want to do is run out of that door, brush past the officers in the police station, and run all the way to the Monroe family farm where those terrible parents have taken Evangeline, but I will not get all the way across town on my wobbly feet.

I close my eyes and try to reach out to Evangeline with my mind, but I cannot feel her at all, presumably because she is no longer a soul. Is she all right? I would assume that Talulah's parents would be relieved to be reunited with their daughter because they thought she was dead, but these people threw her out of their home before she disappeared. Will they punish her for running away? Will Evangeline tell them she is not really Talulah Monroe? I shudder to think of her spitting in their faces and demanding they release her. Although I do not know much about Talulah's parents, I do not believe they would take kindly to this sort of perceived disrespect.

Close to an hour goes by before the door opens, and Officer Owens brings my father into the room. He has put on a collared shirt for the occasion. It does not look as though it has been ironed.

His face has not been ironed either. Big angry wrinkles cut into the skin around his eyes.

"Francesca." He says my name as though it were a bad word, as though I am a terrible inconvenience to him. *"Vieni con me."*

Dropping the blanket onto the chair, I follow him out of the police station. He takes hold of my upper arm as if he's worried I will run away again like I did at the hospital.

The chilly night air hits my face and jars my senses to attention. I had been getting quite sleepy waiting in that small room, but I am not even a tiny bit sleepy anymore.

"Francesca," my father says again, puffing from the speed at which he is walking. He clutches his chest, as though marching me out here was difficult for him, as though his body is the one degenerating, not mine. He is moving too quickly for me to use my cane. It hangs from the tie around my wrist, slapping against the asphalt. *"Scapperai di nuovo?"*

His voice is filled with disdain. I understand he is not happy with having to drive down to Bethany in the middle of the night, but I did not ask him to come here. I asked nothing of him. I never have.

"Verrai a casa con me," he says.

This, I understand. "I am not going anywhere with you!"

"Ti ho cercato all'ospedale," he says. *"Sei appena scappata. Ero preoccupato."*

He could not have been that worried about me after I ran from the hospital, because he did not come looking for me. I have been at our trailer for two days and he did not come to find me.

My father's face turns an angry red. *"Ti chiuderò in una stanza se è necessario."*

"You can lock me up in any room you want, but I will escape from it," I say.

"Cosa stavi facendo con quella ragazza?" he demands, talking so quickly that I can hardly understand his Italian. *"Chi è?"*

I understand the last question. *Who is she?*

He means Evangeline.

He knows nothing about her. I have always done my best to let go of anger and not allow it to bury into my heart, but I have had enough of my father's lies and pretending.

I stop walking. He tries to pull me forward, and I stumble to catch my balance.

"Basta!" He rolls his eyes. "*Smettila di essere così difficile!*"

"I am afraid I will not be going anywhere with you," I say, my voice trembling.

My father's eyes wrinkle. I know he is trying to play the role of being my father, but he never has been, and it is time I told him that.

"I wish things could have been different between us," I say. "But I am not the daughter you wanted. I have come to accept that, even if it makes me sad."

My father's face falls. He opens his mouth to protest, but I hold up a hand to stop him.

"Please, allow me to finish," I say. "You have always seen me as odd, or troubled, but the trouble was never mine. It was your unwillingness to understand me or treat me with compassion. I have been alone for so long that I do not need you to be my father anymore. If you ever cared about me at all, please drive me to my friend Shiloh's house, and do not make me go with you."

He stares at me. A frosty wind whistles through the trees, ripping leaves off branches and carrying them away. In the bandage, my four exposed fingertips burn from the cold. I try to fit my bandaged hand in my pocket, but it is too large.

Enough seconds go by for it to be uncomfortable. Ultimately, my father nods and opens the car door for me. His quiet acceptance somehow pains me more than if he had fought me, but I do not go back on my words. I dislike hurting people's feelings. I have spent so much of my life attempting to make myself as small as possible so that people could like me more, or at least ignore me if they could not bring themselves to do that, but I am tired of allowing my father to hurt me. If this had happened even one month ago and my father had come and asked me to live with him, I would have jumped at the opportunity, but that is not what he wants. He is not my family. In the same way that home is the people who love you, your family are the people who come for you, every time, when you need them. The only reason he came for me now is because somebody in charge told him to.

He is selfish, and he is a coward. He is many things, but he is not my father. Not anymore.

I say nothing on the drive. My father has gotten a different car from the one he had when I was a little girl. The seats are smelly and stiff, and the floors have no crumbs or garbage on them. There is nothing out of place in my father's life anymore. Except for me.

In the corner of my eye, I glimpse a booster seat behind me, but I do not want to turn round and look at it because it will cause an overwhelming bucket full of sadness to pour over me and I do not want to show any amount of emotion in front of my father.

He drops me off at Shiloh's house. I raise my hand to wave at him as he drives away, but he does not look back. I wonder if he ever cared for me at all. Or perhaps he does care about me, and his allowing me to go is his way of showing that.

I must put quite a bit more weight on my cane as I go up the front path and knock on the front door. Even though it is the middle of the night, Shiloh appears in seconds, her blonde hair damp and sticking up in haphazard directions.

She stares out behind me. "Did you walk all the way here? Did something happen?"

I tell her about the soul of Leonard's mother coming to attack me, and about Evangeline being taken away. I do not tell her about my father because my mouth still feels dry, and my hands are still shaking and I do not want to continue thinking about him.

Shiloh's eyes widen. There is something the matter with her. Something more than concern for me.

"Did a soul come to attack you as well?" I ask.

Shiloh shakes her head. "We have a situation."

Before I can ask what it is, she takes my hand and pulls me inside the house, locking the door behind us.

37

Shiloh

Inside I tell Francesca about Aunt Moe, and she goes deathly pale. She asks me question after question, and I can't answer any of them because I don't know what happened myself.

It's been long enough that there could be something online about it. I wake up the computer in the living room with a jiggle of the mouse, and it comes to life with its usual labored whir. I feel weird doing this. Like I'm betraying Jonah by looking it up. But I don't want to ask him to tell me more about it, so I type in "woman dead Bethany Ohio October 10" and hit enter.

And immediately wish I hadn't. Francesca gasps over my shoulder. I dig my teeth into my knuckles as I play the clip taken on somebody's phone of Aunt Moe slashing the knife across her throat. The video is grainy and far away, but the mean look in her eyes is unmistakable.

Oh, Jonah.

No wonder he couldn't talk about it. What kind of asshole films something like this and posts it on the internet? People are sick.

I close the link and turn away from the computer, breathing

hard. Francesca lets out a strangled sob. One thing about her that always surprises me is how she makes everyone else's pain her own. It's like she doesn't just feel bad for you—her heart actually breaks when yours does.

"Where is Jonah right now?" she asks.

"In my room," I say. "Sleeping. Or at least pretending to."

She goes over to the couch, pulling a knitted blanket off the back and wrapping it around her shoulders.

"I am so sorry," she says. "I should have been there to save her."

I sit next to her. "You couldn't have saved her even if you were."

"I could find Aunt Moe's soul for him," Francesca says. "So he could explain to her what happened. Perhaps the two of them could find a bit of peace."

"Jonah won't want that."

"Should I ask him?"

I shake my head. Even though I haven't known Jonah long, I know him really well because of everything we've been through, and I know that he wouldn't see that as an opportunity to fix things with Aunt Moe. He'd see it as having to look Aunt Moe's ghost in the eye and admit that he's the reason she's dead, and the crushing guilt of that might actually kill him.

Francesca frowns. "I hope he knows she is still here. She is not gone. She will be with him again."

I glance around at the empty living room. "You mean literally here?"

"Not at the moment," she says. "But the first thing many souls do is try to find their families, so unless she has faded to the other side, I am sure she will come for him."

I lean my head against the back of the couch. My chest is so empty it aches, like it needs something to fill it.

Francesca looks sad, too. Something occurs to me. I'm shocked it took me this long to think about this.

"Hold on," I say. "Why are you here? Why did you come here in the middle of the night?"

"Somebody recognized Evangeline as Talulah Monroe and the police came," she says. "Her family took her away."

Oh. "That's probably okay, right? I mean, if I had a daughter and she went missing, I'd just be happy she's alive."

My words sink in a couple of seconds too late. Their daughter is dead, and Francesca knows that.

I try to think of something else to say. "Talulah's family owns the farm across from the cemetery, right? The one with the abandoned farmhouse?" Francesca nods. "Aren't they kind of … Mennonite or something? Like full-on horse and buggy stuff?"

Francesca gives me a disappointed look, like that was an insensitive way to phrase the question.

"I do not believe they drive a horse and carriage, and they are not Mennonite, but yes, they are deeply religious," Francesca says. "They found Talulah kissing another girl and banished her from the house, all because they believe in a story more than they care for their daughter."

That must have been the excuse Leonard used to kill her. He killed Max because Dad hit us. He said he was doing Max a favor. Putting him out of his misery, or whatever. I bet it was the same deal for Talulah.

Talulah died because she kissed a girl. Even thinking about it makes me want to hit something. "That's so messed up."

"I know what the religions say is not real," Francesca says. "I know it, Shiloh, because I have seen what is real."

Oh, yeah. I guess she has. There is no heaven or hell waiting for us after we die. Just the other side, in all its bleak and depressing glory.

I don't know if it's because life gets a lot scarier when you know that this is all there is, or because everything I thought I believed about religion was just proven wrong in one fell swoop, but I feel the need to wrap a blanket around my shoulders, too. "Did you ever believe in God?"

Francesca nods, which makes sense. Bethany sure loves its religion. "Did you?"

"Not after everything started happening with my dad." I

glance over Francesca's shoulder at Dad's old La-Z-Boy recliner. It sits empty now, but it's impossible to look at it without thinking about him and the way he used to lounge in it, drinking scotch and listening to that country station on the radio. "I had a hard time believing in a God who could sit by and watch what my dad did and still reward him, you know?"

"I do," Francesca says. "My mother did not go to church, but she believed, and she told me stories from the Bible, especially about heaven and hell and what was waiting for us after we die. I had always been very worried about death because I saw souls. She told me not to worry when they faded away because there was heaven waiting for them on the other side. I always thought of her there. In heaven. But I suppose she must be someplace on the other side."

Francesca's face falls. Oh my God, this night is getting even more depressing, which is saying something because it was already really freaking depressing.

"Maybe there are some better places on the other side you haven't seen yet," I say. "It can't all be bad."

"I hope so." Francesca pulls the blanket tighter around her shoulders. "I wish angels were real, because I would want them looking over Evangeline right now."

"You know, maybe this isn't the worst thing in the world," I say, trying really hard to find the silver lining in this whole situation. "If Evangeline is going to stay in Bethany in Talulah's body, she's technically a minor, so she needs to live with her parents and do things like go to school. Even though Talulah's parents are homophobic assholes, they might not be criminally bad to live with at least until she turns eighteen, and the two of you can be friends after all this is over. You can go over to her house and hang out at school, and you guys can just be normal, which would be kind of nice for a change."

Francesca looks up at me. "Normal?"

"It's a good thing," I say. "I'd take normal over running around fighting ghosts."

Francesca doesn't look convinced. There's something wrong.

I know she and Evangeline got close, but it's not like Evangeline died. She just got reunited with a family who thinks she's their daughter.

"What's going on?" I ask. "Why are you worried?"

"Because Talulah's parents were very angry with her for kissing another girl," Francesca says, her voice barely a whisper. "So I do not believe they will be happy about her kissing me."

Understanding of what she said settles in my stomach. A smile spreads across my lips.

"Wait, you and Evangeline are a thing?" I ask. Francesca nods, eyebrows furrowed like this is bad news, but I grip her hand. "Oh my God, *Francesca*. That's awesome!"

She shakes her head. I've never heard Francesca talk about anything like this before. I mean, admittedly, not a whole lot of our conversations were normal, and we became friends under some pretty weird circumstances, but she never mentioned ever liking anyone or having a crush on someone. I didn't even know she liked girls. I also didn't know if she liked boys, or liked anyone, really. She'd never mentioned it, so I guess I kind of assumed she wasn't interested in anyone. Judging by the terrified look in her eyes, I'd guess she doesn't talk about her feelings much, but now I can understand her anger.

I also understand why it's not good for Evangeline to go back to that family. Crap. Talulah's parents might not let her see Francesca ever again, but it's not like we can just go back in there and rescue her because then where is she going to go after all of this is over?

"We'll figure something out," I promise her. "We always do."

"Leonard could hurt Evangeline now because I cannot protect her," Francesca says. "She is in a lot of danger."

A sinking feeling settles in my stomach. What will Talulah's parents do if Leonard's ghost shows up at the Monroe house? Pray?

This is not good. None of it is, but I don't know what to do about it.

After a minute or two of silence, Francesca asks if she can

sleep here. I tell her of course and bring her to the guest room, giving her some of my old clothes and one of the magnets I have under my bed. When I open the door to go back to my room, someone is waiting for me.

I jump in surprise, a spike of adrenaline coursing through my body, but then I realize it's just Mom. Her eyes are bloodshot, but wide awake.

She points behind me. "Who's that in there?"

"Francesca," I say. "She's sleeping over, if that's okay."

Mom nods, but she doesn't look like it's okay. "Do you care to explain why there is mud all over the carpet and blood in our bathroom?"

I'd rather not explain, but it's not like I have much of a choice, so I tell her it's Jonah. Her eyes widen.

"It's not like that," I say, and by that, I mean: "He didn't do anything to me. His foster mom was just murdered in front of him."

Her eyebrows shoot up. "Jonah's mother *died*?" I nod. "Did … was it …?" I nod again. Mom pinches the bridge of her nose like this is all too much to wrap her mind around. "Shiloh, he shouldn't be here right now. The state will want to put him in emergency care. They will be looking for him, and it won't be long before they check his friends' houses."

A chill runs through me. I didn't think of that, which is dumb. That should have been the first thing I thought of.

"Can he at least stay here for tonight?" I ask. Mom opens her mouth to protest, but I cut her off. "Please? He's really scared, and he's got nowhere else to go."

Mom sighs. "I know Jonah means a lot to you, honey, and I'm so sorry he is going through this—"

I already know where this is going. This is not the tone she uses when she's telling me something I want to hear. *"Please."*

"I think the best thing you can do for Jonah right now is to call Child Protective Services and have them come get him," she says. "They can put him somewhere safe, someplace with good counselors who can help him get through this."

"He doesn't want a counselor."

"I can't in good conscience hide him from CPS, or the police if they call," Mom says. "They must be looking for him."

"To take him away—"

"To put him somewhere safe as he works through this."

"There's nowhere safer than this house right now," I say. "Please, Mom. Just let him stay for tonight?"

She lets out an exasperated sigh. The air catches in the back of my throat as I wait for her to respond. When she gives me a small nod, I throw my arms around her.

She pushes me off and jabs a finger at my face. "You are sleeping in the guest room with Francesca, and will not go in there with him. Do you understand me?"

I nod. She raises her eyebrows. I guess she's going to watch me go back into the guest room, so I do, and make a big to-do of telling Francesca that I'm going to stay in there with her, making sure I talk loudly enough that Mom will hear me. Francesca gives me a tired smile, like she knows exactly what's going on. Mom takes way too long to go back into her room. I wait until I hear her door close before sliding out of the bed and tiptoeing back across the hallway into my room.

Jonah raises his head to look at me. I say nothing as I slide under the covers, wrap one arm around him, and rest my cheek against the space between his shoulder blades. He shudders but doesn't move away from me, and somehow, I manage to sleep.

Jonah, on the other hand, doesn't sleep. I'm hugging him from behind so I can't see his face, but his breathing doesn't even out like it usually does when he's sleeping. It's shallow and forced. Like every breath is something he has to remind himself to do.

I fall in and out of sleep, not dreaming, but groggy enough to feel like having Jonah sleep in the same bed as me is a dream. I give up trying when the sun comes up. The curtain gets brighter.

Gray light seeps through and brightens the room so slowly that I can't see it happening, but after half an hour, the room is light enough for me to make out the floral pattern sewn into my carpet and all the chips in the paint on my walls.

I keep my arm around Jonah and feel his ribcage expanding and contracting. I want to say something to him, but there's nothing to say. I guess I want him to know that I'm here for him, but I don't know how much that matters right now. Being here isn't making things any better. It's not reversing what happened. It's not bringing back Aunt Moe. Nothing I do or say can bring back Aunt Moe, and nothing I can do or say is going to make Jonah feel okay.

The image of her from the video, standing in the front yard with that knife, is burned into my memory. The clip was shaky and out-of-focus, but I can still make out the flash of her smile as she plunged the knife into her neck.

When the clock hand hits seven, a quiet knock sounds on the door. I let go of Jonah, slide out from under the sheets, and open the door to find Francesca standing there. She looks kind of sick, with dark circles under her eyes and a sort of pallor on her face. I wonder if she caught a cold last night. Or maybe she's just not sleeping enough. She can join the club.

"How is he doing?" she whispers.

I step out of the room and lean against the closed door. "About as good as you'd expect. You?" It's her turn to shake her head. I scoff. "Some depressing group we are," I say.

"I called Miles on the phone," Francesca says. "He is on his way here, and he sounded quite anxious."

Of course he did. Miles gets worried about everything, but I guess if there is something to be worried about, it's this.

I'm standing by the front window when Miles gets here. He parks in the driveway, right out in the open, and gets out of the car holding a grease-spotted paper bag. Nothing about him is put together. His shirt is wrinkled. So are his sweatpants. He looks like he rolled out of bed and got in the car, because I bet that's exactly what happened.

He doesn't have to knock before I open the front door and usher him inside. He puts the bag on the table and the smell of muffins hits my nose—sweet and warm and exactly what I need right now.

Miles points down the hallway. "Is Jonah asleep?"

"He's pretending to be."

Miles follows me to the crowded hallway outside my room. It's full of all the furniture and other random crap that Mom and I moved into it yesterday when ghost-proofing the house, so we step over the bags of clothes and the ceiling fan blades covering the floor. I sit against the wall. Francesca is already across from me. Miles sits next to me with a heavy thud. His hair looks dry and stands up almost straight. I reach over and tug on one strand.

"Did you forget your gel?" I ask, and he pushes my hand away. "You look like a mess."

Miles tries to flatten his hair. "I missed out on some beauty sleep last night."

"I think we have some molasses you could use," I say. "Or some motor oil in the garage."

Miles smiles, but the smile doesn't reach his eyes. He drops his gaze down to his lap.

"This isn't fair," he says. "Jonah doesn't deserve this. Aunt Moe definitely didn't."

"Most of the people who die do not deserve to," Francesca says. "Death is not something you deserve or do not deserve. It is simply something that happens."

"Do you think Jonah will like the muffins?" Miles asks. "Because I could get McDonalds. Do you think he'll eat?"

I shrug. The wall moves behind me. I glance up to see my door opening, revealing Jonah standing behind us in the Care Bears T-shirt looking just as broken as he did yesterday.

Francesca stands up and throws her arms around him. He lifts his eyes to me, and a stab of pain goes through my heart. I hug him from the other side. In seconds, Miles's enormous arms wrap around all of us.

Jonah's ribcage begins to shake. He cries into my shoulder, and all of us stand there with our arms around each other, protecting each other, and safe. At least for the minute.

"I want to kill him," Jonah says, clearing his throat. "Leonard. I want to watch him die."

I've never heard Jonah sound so mad. Even though we're talking about Leonard and I want him to die too, it makes goosebumps rise on my arms. Miles and Francesca both nod.

"Okay," I say. "I guess we all agree. Let's kill the son of a bitch, and let's do it today."

38

JONAh

I can't believe I just cried in front of my friends. I swore I'd never do that. But I swore I'd never do a lot of things that I've done in the past couple of weeks, so I guess nothing means anything anymore.

I slump down in a chair at the kitchen table. Miles drops a bag of muffins in front of me like he's doing me a favor. Francesca's in the kitchen, brewing tea for herself because she's looking pretty rough. Shiloh rips open a family-size bag of Goldfish and starts shoveling them in her mouth.

Nobody wants to be the first one to talk. I sure don't. But there's a roar in my head, like feedback screeching through an amp after some band's trashed their equipment at the end of a show, and I just want to make it stop.

So I cross my arms and say, "What do we know about killing ghosts?"

As a surprise to no one, it's Francesca who answers. "I am not sure it is possible to kill souls. You see, souls are made of energy ..."

"And energy can neither be created nor destroyed," Miles

cuts in, sounding like a science book. Where's Aunt Moe's energy, then? Where did all that energy go?

"I spoke to the Soothsayer," Francesca says. "She has never heard of anybody destroying a soul before, but if somebody were to find a way, she said it would be very bad."

Shiloh pauses, eating her Goldfish. "You went to see the Soothsayer?"

"Yes, when I was on the other side," Francesca says, all casual, like visiting other dimensions is no big deal. To us, I guess it's not.

"How's she doing over there?" Shiloh asks. "I mean, all things considered?"

"She did not appear to be suffering very much," Francesca says. "She was listening to a peculiar sort of musical performance, which she appeared to be enjoying."

"They've got concerts on the other side?" I ask, and Francesca nods. "Damn. That's metal as hell."

Francesca shrugs. "Ms. Wilma said our best option would be to trap Leonard."

"Like with the ghost handcuffs?" Shiloh asks.

"Possibly," Francesca says, "although I am sure he could break free from those."

"Sending him to the other side won't work," Shiloh says. "Since we tried that already."

And it killed Aunt Moe.

"So what else traps ghosts?" I ask. "It's not like we can run to the store for ghost traps, or …"

It hits me like a slap. What we have to do. When I say it, I can barely hear my voice.

"The orb," I say.

Francesca makes a confused noise. "What?"

"That creepy glass ball the Soothsayer's got," I say. "We could put Leonard in there."

I just look at Francesca, avoiding Shiloh's eyes. I may not remember much about her, but I remember enough to know that she knows me. She'd see something's up if I made eye contact. Can't risk that.

"Isn't that thing made of glass?" Shiloh asks. "What if it breaks? I've seen Leonard break tougher things."

Yeah, Shiloh. So have I.

But I just shrug. "Bubble wrap that sucker. Bury it. Wrap it in magnets until they shred his ghost to pieces. I don't care."

"I could build a box for it," Miles says, leaning across the table and grabbing some Goldfish from Shiloh's bag like what we're talking about isn't life or death. "Engineer something to make sure it doesn't break. Put magnets in it, or encase it in concrete and bury it deep underground."

Shiloh smiles, kind of sad. "Like those egg drop projects we did in school?"

Miles nods. "Except a weirder version."

"Is it possible to trap a soul in that glass ball?" Francesca asks, twirling a white curl around her finger.

I nod, instinctively touching the pink scar on my thumb where I bled on the Soothsayer's orb. That's how I bound my soul to the damn thing.

Francesca tilts her head at me. "Do you know how she does it, Jonah?"

"Nah." The lie is easy, but my pulse is racing. Shiloh's eyes narrow at me. "But she must've had a way."

"Oh!" Francesca exclaims. "Ms. Wilma has a book. She showed it to me when I was on the other side. It has every one of her soothsaying rituals in it."

Oh, yeah. I remember that thing. The Soothsayer read the freaky chant from it when she trapped my soul.

Can't let on that I know that, though. I have to sound casual.

"I bet the chant thing's in there," I say.

Everybody digests this information. I bounce my knee. Shoving Leonard in that orb means spending eternity stuck with him in Miles's stupid ghost trap egg contraption, but we're out of options. If we can't kill ghosts, this is our best plan, and if I say anything about my deal with the Soothsayer, they won't do it, and we'd be back to square one. That stupid glass ball's our only shot at getting Leonard as close to dead as possible, and if being stuck with him is what it takes, so be it. I deserve it, after what I did to Aunt Moe and everything I put Shiloh through. Being trapped in there is as close to my hole of nothingness as I can get, anyway.

"Ms. Wilma told me I could have been a natural student of hers," Francesca says. "If I can find the book, I may be able to trap Leonard in the glass ball."

Shiloh nods. "Where's the book now?"

"On the other side, it was in the circus trailer," Francesca says. "So on this side of the veil, that lady Fiona may have it. It must be with the rest of the Soothsayer's belongings."

"What about this orb?" Miles asks. "Is that with her things, too?"

I shake my head. That much I remember—I was quick to ask that. "Fiona shipped it to some chick down in Florida."

"*Florida?*" Miles squeaks. "How are we going to get it if it's in Florida?"

"Drive?" suggests Shiloh. "You have a car."

"Yeah, and a job," Miles says. "I just took half the week off. I can't just skip town to go to Florida."

Shiloh pours some Goldfish into her mouth. "Why don't you just quit?"

Miles blinks. "Quit the police force?"

"Yeah," she says. "You don't want to be a cop, anyway. You wanted to write poems. Be a journalist. Travel."

"I also didn't want to die at sixteen and have my entire family not know who I am," Miles says. "I wouldn't say things went according to plan, would you?"

Shiloh goes pale. I feel a rush of protectiveness toward her, even though I'm fuzzy on why. Miles's words cut her deep.

Miles notices, too. He shakes his head at her, like he knows what she's thinking, and tells us to pump the brakes on this whole Florida thing. We don't even know if the orb's in Florida, or if the chick Fiona sent it to still has it, so Miles calls Fiona and puts her on speaker. She sounds hoarse. I don't blame her. It's ass o'clock in the morning, and we definitely woke her up. Phil only came back from the hospital yesterday so the two of them are back in their apartment in Columbus, but she can drive to Bethany this afternoon and pick us up so that we can go through more of the Soothsayer's old things. She says she sent the orb to a woman named Gayle Winters, some hippie psychic in Tallahassee who looks like the kind of freak who eats tofu for fun and aligns chakras for a living. I twist the beads on my bracelet. According to my mom, this thing is supposed to heal my chakras, too, but I don't know why I still wear it. The whole chakra thing is dumb. Healing Moe's chakras won't bring her back.

Because she's dead. You saw to that.

Miles leaves Gayle a message saying it's an urgent matter of life and death and begs her to call him back.

"Could we see if Gayle could overnight it to us?" Miles asks. "Then nobody has to drive down there."

Shiloh shakes her head. "Too risky. It could break."

"What if she doesn't want to give it to us?" Miles asks. "Am I supposed to steal it?"

"Uh … well, stealing is bad, but maybe you could offer her a lot of money?" Shiloh shakes her head. "I don't know, Miles, but I think you should just tell her our problem, and if she doesn't want to help us, we can figure out what to do about it then."

Miles sighs, clearly not loving any of this but doing it anyway because, as I said, we're out of options. "How long is the drive to Florida?"

Using Miles's iPhone, Shiloh looks it up, and finds that it's about thirteen hours, which makes Miles groan and drop his head into his hands.

"I guess if I leave now, I could get there late tonight, grab the orb in the morning, and drive back," Miles says. "It's, like, 900 miles, so it will take me a long time."

"The rest of us can get the book from Fiona," Shiloh says.

"And rescue Evangeline," Francesca adds.

Shiloh nods. "Yes. And rescue Evangeline."

I don't know what's up with Evangeline, but Shiloh and Francesca are quick to fill me in. All in all, this plan sounds workable. It's not a great plan, but it's better than no plan, and it's the only one we've got. I just have to keep my head down for the next day and a half so that the cops or my social worker doesn't find me.

"Okay, well, I should hit the road," Miles says.

Shiloh bites her lip. "Be careful, Miles, okay? Don't talk to strangers."

"Don't worry," he says. "If anyone offers me candy from a van, I will say no, thank you."

Shiloh rolls her eyes. He gives her a reassuring smile.

I guess we should get moving, too. Go rescue Evangeline, so we're not just sitting around with our thumbs up our asses waiting for Fiona to finish her skincare routine. I push up from the chair, shrugging and shoving my hands into my pockets. For the first time, I notice the shirt I'm wearing. Oh, Jesus. I just needed a clean shirt last night. I wasn't paying attention to the happy dancing bears on it.

I find Shiloh's eyes. It's like that girl can read my mind because she fights back a grin.

"Do you think you're funny?" I ask.

She smiles innocently. "Maybe a little."

I shake my head, but feel the knot loosening in my chest. Even with everything going on, she still finds a way to smile. To find good things in all the bad. I wish I was better at that. But I'm pretty sure ghosts stay in the clothes they die in so, if I'm going to be trapped for eternity, there's no way in hell I'm doing it in a goddamn Care Bears tee.

I tug at the fabric. "Can I please have a different fucking T-shirt?"

39

Miles

Driving for thirteen hours alone sounds like torture. Driving for thirteen hours in any circumstances sounds like torture, but I kind of sort of have to. We need the orb for this insane plan to work, and because I'm the only one with the car, I'm the one who gets punished.

It'll be fine. I'll alternate between music and podcasts to keep my brain busy. There is no way I'll make it through the round trip without sleeping, but I'll find a good hotel to stay at to lessen my chances of, I don't know, say, being murdered, although I guess I'm now a six-two white cop, so I'm pretty much invincible.

The one tiny problem with all of this is that I need to figure out what to tell Chief Schnebly.

I'm supposed to show up for work today. I've been telling the chief I'm not feeling well for days now, but I don't know how many stomach bugs one guy can get. Shiloh's words keep ringing in my head.

Why don't you just quit?

Could I? Quit? Is that how easy it would be?

I never planned on being a police officer forever. I never planned on being a police officer at all, and I didn't exactly have much time to do any planning in the past couple of weeks, but being a police officer is stressful and hard. Not to mention I'm terrible at it. I guess I could get better. Once I figure out what I'm doing, I could have a good job giving people speeding tickets or helping old ladies cross the street. Is that what I want? Does it matter what I want?

Randall Zweering kept one picture in his wallet. It's of him—which, I know, narcissistic, much?—and in it, he's wearing a police uniform, but he's a lot younger than he is now. Maybe ten or eleven. And the uniform is not the uniform he wore on the job. It's a Halloween costume.

Officer Zweering always wanted to be a police officer, even when he was a kid, and he grew up to be what he wanted to be. It might be a costume, but in that photo, he's dressed like what he's supposed to be. Am I dressed like the thing I'm supposed to be, too, or am I the one who's in a costume now?

Quitting the police force feels wrong. Or maybe it's just scary. I've never been that good at telling the difference.

But one thing I know—I am not Randall Zweering. I am still Miles Barot-Renaud, and even if I have to spend the rest of my life masquerading as someone else, there's more to me than being a cop.

So instead of turning onto Route 13, I pull onto the road leading to the police station and try to swallow the bile rising in my throat.

Showing up at the police station in the clothes I slept in the night before is not exactly professional, but neither is what I'm about to do, so I guess it doesn't matter.

The woman behind the main desk does a double take when she sees me. I doubt she's ever seen Officer Zweering in normal clothes before. He probably never showed up here in a uniform that hadn't been ironed to within an inch of its life.

I give her a tense smile and let myself through the door into the back of the building. Even thinking about doing this on the drive here was making my stomach ache, but that's nothing compared to how much it's aching now.

The door to Chief Schnebly's office is open. I knock once, then open it all the way.

"Hello?" I poke my head in. "Chief?"

Chief Schnebly is in his leather-backed chair, looking pretty depressed. He doesn't look like he has slept at all. The hair on his mustache is flattened on one side, and the skin under his eyes is ashen. I wonder if he was up all night because of Aunt Moe dying. Or if he responded when someone found Evangeline. Probably both.

He blinks at me, then rubs his eyes under his glasses. "You didn't come to roll call."

"I know," I say. "I'm sorry."

Chief Schnebly sighs. Oh God. I feel so bad. The chief has been nothing but good to me, and I have not been good to him in return. It's not fair for me to keep taking unexplained absences, saying I'm not feeling well and not showing up when he needs me to, especially when Bethany has been having a bunch of weird stuff happen in the past couple of weeks that demands a more intense police presence. To make matters worse, I like Chief Schnebly and don't want to disappoint him. It's like letting your grandfather down.

He seems to notice my clothes for the first time. The wrinkled shirt and sweatpants. I doubt he's seen Officer Zweering in clothes like this before, either. "You all right, Randy?"

Oh, boy. Here we go. Telling authority figures things they don't want to hear is a nightmare for me. Literally. I have literally had nightmares about doing this kind of thing.

Clearing my throat, I'm sure to keep my voice low. "I'm so sorry to tell you like this, but I can't do this anymore."

I sound like I'm breaking up with him. I guess I kind of am.

Chief Schnebly drops his hands from his face. "Can't do what?"

"Be a police officer," I say. "Any of it. I'm … resigning."

Chief Schnebly doesn't seem like he knows what to do. He asks if I'm sure. He asks me why, and I make up some stuff about personal issues. The blood drops from his face as he realizes I'm serious. He's known Randall Zweering for a long time. He was his mentor. His teacher. They must have been close for the chief to call him Randy. But I'm not Randall.

"Randy," Chief Schnebly says. "Are you sure you want to do this?"

I nod, my entire body buzzing with a feeling that could be either excitement or mind-numbing nerves.

Chief Schnebly curses under his breath. "When are you planning to quit?"

"Today," I say. "Right now, actually."

This isn't the right thing to say. It's not the right thing to do. People have to put in two-week notices for regular jobs. I'd assume it's even more for police officers because so many people rely on there being enough people in the force, but I'm tired of worrying about other people for once.

"You're going to leave the rest of us busting our asses," he says. "I guess you realize that."

I say I'm sorry again. He asks me for my resignation papers. I don't have any, so write a perfunctory letter explaining that I'm going to quit, print it in the bullpen, and give it to him. He tells me to turn in my badge and gun. I don't have them on me, so he tells me I can return them in the next couple of days. I have never been so excited about anything in my life.

"I will say that I'm surprised," he says. "You had a long and promising career ahead of you."

I hold back the apology burning on the tip of my tongue. Even though I feel bad about disappointing him, with every passing second, there's fresh energy creeping into my body. "Things change, sir."

"Right."

Chief Schnebly nods at me. It occurs to me that I don't need to stand here anymore. There's nothing more he needs from me.

It still feels wrong to leave without saying anything. "Thank you for … everything."

He says nothing, but he stands and holds out his hand. For a moment I panic, thinking he might be arresting me for something, but that's stupid, so I come back to reality and shake with him. I walk away before he can see the smile fighting its way onto my face. I say goodbye to the woman behind the counter and push through the doors into the outdoor air. The sun has come out. It warms my skin and makes me smile like it came out just for me.

Oh my God. I'm not a police officer anymore.

I did it.

I've almost reached my car when I hear a voice call from behind me:

"Randall!"

Great. Not this again. I turn to find Lindsey walking out of the station, her eyebrows knit in an angry expression that I'm starting to think is permanently etched onto her face.

I take a deep breath. "Yes, Lindsey?"

"What are you doing?" she asks. "The chief just told me you quit."

"I did."

She sputters, like she's at a loss for words. I guess I should feel pretty good about myself that I rendered her speechless, but I don't.

"I'm sorry, Lindsey," I say. "It's been good working with you, and nice knowing you."

Her shoulders slump. She strains to keep her face straight, like she doesn't know whether to scream or laugh or cry. I don't know which, so I give her a close-lipped smile and get in the car because I have a lot of driving to do today and I might as well get started.

As I pull out of the parking lot, I notice Lindsey still standing where I left her, squinting as she stares at me inside the car. She doesn't look angry with me. Which is a surprise. There is an unreadable and cutting expression on her face, like she can see right through me. It's not the look of someone who is sad that their friend is no longer a police officer. It's the look of someone who is going to take a former friend down. A friend who has abandoned her and did the one thing so out-of-character for him that she just might doubt his sanity.

But Lindsey can't do anything to me. Not anymore.

Or at least that's what I keep telling myself as I get on the highway and start my super fun thirty-hour round trip to get the Soothsayer's orb.

40

FrANCeSCA

Jonah finds a different shirt to change into, although his options are quite limited because although he is quite thin, he is much broader than Shiloh. He ends up wearing a pair of her father's old jeans which sag around his hips, along with a faded plaid shirt. I think the blue color suits him nicely, bringing out his eyes, but Shiloh seems uneasy. Presumably because it reminds her too much of her father.

I tap on her shoulder and lean in to whisper: "Imagine how much your father would dislike seeing Jonah in his clothes."

A hint of a smile flickers across Shiloh's face. "He'd really hate it."

I wear the same clothes as yesterday because they are not too dirty to reuse. Shiloh changes from her pajamas into loose, comfortable things that could still pass for sleepwear. I recall her telling me once she likes the coziness of sweatpants. They are more comfortable than regular clothes, but still acceptable to wear outside. It made sense. So many uncomfortable things have happened to her in her life that if she had the choice, of course she would choose this small comfort. I told her I stopped caring about what was acceptable when everybody stopped accepting me.

All three of us bundle up against the bitter cold in jackets and heavy shirts from Shiloh's family's coat closet. Jonah tugs a cap low, concealing his face. I am not sure he is right to assume the police will be looking for him. He has done nothing wrong, although I suppose they will be worried about his welfare.

Shiloh does not live far from the Monroe farm, so it will not take us very long to walk. It is chilly today. So chilly that I can see each frosted breath I exhale. The wind nips at my nose and ears, making me wish I could hide completely within the soft material of my coat, but I continue walking.

I allow my gaze to drift over to the cemetery as we walk past. Ghostly figures hover among the headstones, pale and shimmering like the opposite of shadows. I scan their faces, seeking those I know, but I do not recognize any of them. Both Mr. and Mrs. Lewis have faded away. Reverend Guessford is absent as well, though I had not been very pleased to see him after he betrayed me to Leonard. I cannot spot Poppy, Esther, Gus, or Charlie, either. Perhaps they have all crossed to the other side. The thought wraps around my heart and squeezes. It is not quite grief, but the aching is its distant cousin.

My eyes catch a familiar face in the crowd. Never have I been so pleased to see Jeremy in my life.

He swoops over to the iron gate, beaming at me with crooked teeth. "Howdy there, Kika. Haven't seen you 'round here in ages."

I am surprised he says nothing of my white hair or wrinkled skin. In the past, Jeremy had no shortage of comments on my appearance that made me uncomfortable.

"It has only been eleven days," I say, prompting a confused glance from Shiloh and an amused one from Jonah.

"That's ages," Jeremy insists. "You going to come hang out today?"

I shake my head. "Perhaps soon."

Jeremy's face falls. "Well, don't be a stranger, m'kay?"

I promise I will not be, then continue walking along the sidewalk toward the farm. It feels strange. The cemetery used to be more my home than any house I ever lived in, but I suppose houses stop feeling like homes once the people you love are gone. Perhaps it is the same with cemeteries.

Shiloh loops an arm through mine as though she can sense the sadness inside me. I lean my head onto her shoulder.

To avoid being seen, we decide to approach the farmhouse through the cornfield. It is fortunate that the Monroes have yet to harvest because the tall stalks shelter us from curious onlookers. The dry stalks tower over me. They rustle as I push through them and threaten to snatch my cane out from under me every couple of steps. The morning sun washes over the land. A couple of brave birds chirp, but most keep quiet. I suppose it is becoming too cold for them to feel much like singing in the morning. A distant moo echoes across the field. The air is fresh with the earthy scent of tilled soil and the unmistakable aroma of livestock. I use the tall silo ahead as a guide. Its faded paint and peeling metal stand out against the gloomy sky.

Once we get close enough to see the house through the corn, we stop walking. I drop to my belly on the soil. Shiloh and Jonah do the same, one on either side of me.

"What's the plan here?" Jonah asks, inhaling from his JUUL and blowing out the vapor. He used to refrain from smoking in front of Shiloh. Perhaps the foolery has made him forget how much she dislikes it, or perhaps he does not care anymore. "Barge in guns a-blazing and grab her?"

"No guns will be needed," I say.

"Yeah, obviously," Jonah says. "Just a figure of speech."

I do not think it was obvious, since Shiloh has used a gun before, but I focus on surveying the house. It has a nice wraparound porch, and a rocking chair in front. In a pen beside the house, a cluster of chickens peck at the dirt. Occasionally, a curious chicken clucks, but none of them appear to be bothered by our presence, if they notice us at all.

I examine each window, trying to peer through the curtains for any sign that Evangeline is hiding within, but I see nothing.

"I do not believe there is a good way to do this," I say. "Perhaps some sort of distraction is needed?"

Shiloh and Jonah both appear to be thinking of ideas when I hear gravel crunching down the driveway and a black sedan comes into view.

Jonah curses under his breath. "Looks like we got company."

I flatten myself lower to the ground. Shiloh and Jonah do as well, and the sound of their breathing is loud.

The car parks in front of the house. A man steps out. I have seen him before, although I am not entirely sure where. He is of average height and build, and dressed in that classic black robe worn by priests. His face is lined with age. The only thing that is not average about him is his facial hair. His beard is concentrated right on the point of his chin.

He walks up to the front steps. Before he reaches them, the door swings open and a woman steps onto the porch.

Oh my goodness, this woman looks almost exactly like Evangeline. I never paid much attention to Talulah at school, but I have spent a lot of time looking at Evangeline. In my mind, all of Talulah's features—the plumpness of her lips, her smattering of freckles, her sea-green eyes—belong to Evangeline, and so it is strange to see another person who looks so much like her. This woman is much frailer than Evangeline. She is wearing a tattered apron that Evangeline would never be caught in, yet she has the same orange hair and soft skin free of any blemishes or worry lines.

She says something too quiet for me to hear, reaching to take his hand. Opening the door, she gestures for him to come inside and closes it behind them.

Everything is quiet again—except for the clucking of the chickens and my pounding heart.

Shiloh glances at me. "Who was that guy?"

"I am not sure," I say, "but there was something about his energy that I did not like."

"Don't ask me how," Jonah says, "but I know him. He's a priest at that ugly church with the spire thing on it. You know, the one by that preschool?"

I do not know which one he is talking about. Bethany has many churches and more than one preschool.

Jonah shrugs. "He preaches there. Gives sermons and shit."

Shiloh side-eyes Jonah. "How do you know him?"

"I just told you, don't ask," he says.

A cold and sort of clammy chill runs through me. "Could he be here for Evangeline?"

Jonah swears. "You don't think he's here to go full-on Exorcist on her ass, do you?"

Shiloh glares at him. My stomach drops.

"An exorcism?" I ask.

"Think about it," Jonah says. "Of all people, the ultra-religious types are most likely to believe that someone was being possessed by someone else. To them, demonic possession is, like, a thing, you know?"

A creepy sensation crawls over my skin. I am not entirely familiar with the process of exorcism. Richie used to enjoy horror films, and I used to pretend not to be scared because he would turn up the volume if he knew it was getting to me. People bound to chairs. Screaming. Hands in manacles. Vomiting green liquid. Strange symbols painted on walls. Holy water thrown on people's faces as men hold crosses out in front of themselves as though they were weapons. I can picture Evangeline, screaming at the top of her lungs for them to leave her alone, and that she is not possessed by anyone.

Shiloh's hand touches my arm. "They wouldn't perform an exorcism on her. She's only been home for one night."

"Maybe he's come to help pray the gay away," Jonah says.

Shiloh glares at him as if to tell him he is not helping. He certainly is not.

Would an exorcism work on Evangeline? Could it cast her soul out of Talulah's body? If it did, it would leave Talulah's body empty, and she would be dead.

I need to rescue her. I will not sit here and do nothing while Evangeline is in danger.

In hushed voices, the three of us make a plan. Once we have finished, Jonah sneaks off into the corn. Shiloh and I wait for his signal. A couple of minutes go by before he makes a loud hooting sound. The chickens pick their heads up, seeking the source of the disturbance, but quickly return to eating.

Shiloh looks worried. "You don't think he'd be dumb enough to actually mess with a cow or something, do you?"

I peer behind her at the field filled with cows. A black clad figure is streaking through the pasture being chased by what appears to be a very angry cow.

I turn Shiloh's chin before she spots him. "I would certainly hope not."

She nods and squeezes my hand. Silently, she rises and goes to knock on the door.

I hold my breath as it swings open, revealing Talulah's mother. Her eyes narrow.

"Can I help you?" she asks. She does not appear to recognize Shiloh, which is good.

"Hi," Shiloh says. "I was passing by and saw some kids bothering your cows."

On cue, a distant yell rings out.

The woman gasps. "What on Earth …?"

The woman slips on a pair of boots and rushes toward the field. Shiloh waves me over and I slip into the house.

The house smells like fresh bread and something warm that makes my mouth water. Being in a stranger's house feels terribly intrusive, but I try to breathe through the discomfort.

A man's voice drifts from deeper within. It must be the religious man. He appears to be reciting scripture. The prayer is not one I know. Perhaps this is a different religion than the one my mother shared with me, or perhaps I am not well versed in all the different prayers because my mother did not teach them all to me. Moving swiftly before I lose my nerve, I turn the corner into the living room.

Evangeline is sitting on an armchair with her orange hair tied back off her neck. She is all I see, but she does not see me, because she is facing the opposite direction.

The religious man does not notice me for a moment. When he does, he closes the book on his finger.

"Can I help you?" he asks gently, with no hint of malice in his voice.

Evangeline turns, and the air appears to vanish from the room. She is wearing brand-new clothes. A modest blue dress hangs over her frame, with sleeves that are puffy on the shoulders. The dress is plain. It has no chiffon or lace or flowers. I doubt Evangeline would have chosen it for herself, but it does not matter, because she seems unharmed.

Her face lights up. She leaps from the armchair, bouncing over to me and grabbing my hand in hers.

"Please get me away from here," she says. "These people are very strange."

A tingly feeling spreads over me. "I will."

The priest does not appear to like this at all. "Excuse me, Talulah, but we were in the middle of—"

Evangeline pulls me along, rushing for the door. She runs out in front of me, pulling me behind her. "Goodbye, Father What's-Your-Name. And thank you!"

She releases a giddy laugh as she pulls her shoes on, hopping from one foot to another. She drags me from the house, which feels strange because it was me who came to rescue her, but as soon as I step onto the porch, something slaps my forehead. I glance up to see a flimsy arrow suction-cupped to my skin. A young girl with fiery red hair stands at the bottom of the porch steps, bow poised.

"Get away from my sister," she warns, nocking another arrow and aiming it at me. "Right now."

I am not sure how to react, but Evangeline is. She rushes over and kneels before the little girl, redirecting the arrow and planting a single kiss on the girl's forehead. I am too stunned to say anything. So is the little girl, because she stands there, staring at the girl she thinks is her older sister.

"It's okay," she says. "This is my friend."

The girl eyes me. Evangeline takes the girl's hand in hers.

"I have to go, now," Evangeline says. "Please tell everybody that I love them very much, and no matter what happens, I will never stop loving them. Can you do that?"

A moment goes by before the girl lowers her bow. Evangeline kisses her cheek, then takes my hand. She pulls me along toward the cornfield.

"Talulah!"

I glance over my shoulder to see Talulah's mother standing in the mouth of the driveway. Her features are scrunched together like she has eaten something sour. There is something broken in her expression that wraps around my heart. Evangeline does not stop running, and I grip her fingers tightly as I stumble to catch my balance.

"Talulah, get back here!" The woman screams, quickening her pace to a run.

Evangeline goes even faster. "Don't come looking for me!" she calls. "I'm sorry!"

"Talulah!"

Evangeline tightens her grip on my hand as we crash into the corn. I run much too quickly for my cane. I am amazed my legs are able to carry me at all. She weaves between the stalks, and I hobble after her like a drunken gnome, but we do not slow down. Soon, Talulah's mother's cries fade away behind us. I can hear nothing over the crunching leaves under our feet and my ragged breaths as I struggle in vain to control my breathing.

Once I am sure we have put a safe distance between us and the farmhouse, I tug on Evangeline's arm.

"Please slow down," I say between gasps. "Evangeline, stop!"

Evangeline stops, her hair falling loose from its knot and blowing across her face. There is mud on the hem of her dress and on her socks, but an exhilarated smile lights up her face, as though she is coming undone at the seams, shedding her polished exterior until the girl that is underneath shines through.

"You doing okay?" she asks, gripping my hand so tightly I find myself hoping she will never let it go.

I step toward her and gently press my lips to hers. The entire world seems to drop away from us. I cannot help but smile against her mouth as my pulse thrums in my ears, and we stand there, hidden in the softly waving corn in our own little universe where nobody can ever touch us, my stomach swooping as if I am falling from a cloud in the most pleasurable way.

41

Shiloh

When I get to the abandoned house, Jonah is there, swinging around on that stupid tire swing like he doesn't have a care in the world.

"*That* was your big distraction?" I say, slowing down to a walk. "Chasing a few cows?"

Jonah shrugs. "I don't recommend almost getting trampled by a cow. On the scale of one to fun, I'd give it a zero."

"How did you even get them so worked up?"

"A magician never reveals his secrets."

"What are you still doing out here?" I ask. The plan was that we were all supposed to rendezvous inside the house, not sit outside it on the tire swing waiting for someone to see us.

"I'm not going in there alone," he says. "That place is haunted as hell."

"You have a magnet."

"So what? This was that house from *The Conjuring,* all creaky doors and whispering and whatever."

I almost want to laugh. After everything we've been through with Leonard and the ghosts, Jonah is freaked out by some rundown old house? But at least he's sounding like the old Jonah. He's looking like it too, and I'd be lying if I said it wasn't doing something to me.

"I promise I'll protect you," I say. "Now, get in there."

Jonah leads the way around to the back of the house. I've only been in here once before, that time Francesca astral projected to the other side with her head in a cooking pot and Dad caught us, which made me so mad I tried to punch a hole through a fireplace. Good times. It's just as cold in here as it was outside, not to mention it smells like mouse crap and old wood, and it's even darker than I remember. No natural light gets through the boarded-up windows, and I can barely see two feet in front of me. This place gives me the creeps, too, but no way am I going to let Jonah know that.

I glance at him. "You didn't bring a flashlight like last time, did you?"

He shakes his head. Oh, right. He probably doesn't remember the last time we were here, or the flashlight he gave me.

"It's cool," I say, rubbing my nose to restore circulation to it and make it less numb. "Our eyes will adjust."

My eyes don't adjust. I can see the vague outline of a table, and some old solo cups on the ground. Not being able to see what's lurking in the shadows doesn't make me want to go explore the place, so we stand by the window until I hear footsteps on the porch. The splintering board swings back to reveal Francesca and Evangeline.

I lend Francesca a hand and help her through the window. Even in the harsh shadows, I can tell her lips are rosy and her cheeks are flushed, like she was doing more than just running through those cornfields.

I don't want to embarrass her, so I stop myself from smiling. "Everything go good?"

She doesn't even try to hold back her smile, tucking her hair behind her ears. "Yes, very good."

Evangeline climbs in after her. She's wearing a ridiculous

floor length dress that looks like it belongs on an American Girl Doll or that girl from *Little House on the Prairie.* It doesn't look easy to run in. I wonder if that's why her parents dressed her in it. I guess it didn't work that well.

Because we need to lie low until Fiona comes to pick us up, we do our best to get comfortable, which is hard to do because it's so cold that it's impossible to feel comfortable, and none of us can see anything in here. At least, none of us except for Francesca, who says ghosts act like lanterns and even cast shadows on the floor, which would freak me out more if Jonah didn't look like he was about to pee his pants.

I have nothing better to do, so I go in search of snacks left over from any of the parties thrown in here, using my flip phone screen to light my way. It casts a pale and grainy light onto the uneven floorboards and the dead flies on the floor, but it's better than nothing. Jonah follows me. Probably because he doesn't want to be left alone.

Once we're out of earshot of Francesca, Jonah leans in and whispers, "Are the two of them, like, a thing?"

"Yep."

"Cool." He glances over his shoulder back at Francesca, and I wish he wouldn't so that she doesn't know we're talking about her, but it's so dark she probably couldn't see him anyway, even by ghost light. "Go, Frankie."

I find an open bag of tortilla chips on top of an old piano in the living room. The top of the bag has been curled over, but the bag isn't exactly sealed, and it expired two months ago. Two months isn't that bad. There's an old lantern on top of the piano. It doesn't work, because of course it doesn't, so I shine the light from my phone screen into the bag to check for mice or worms or any bugs that could have gotten into it.

Jonah makes a face. "You're not seriously about to eat those, are you?"

"I'm hungry."

Placing my open phone on top of the piano keys, I pop a chip into my mouth and bite down. There's not a lot of crunch anymore, but all things considered, it could be worse. Nothing wriggles, at least.

Jonah gapes at me. The light from my phone casts harsh shadows under his cheekbones. He looks gaunt, and much thinner than he used to be. I am, too. Both of us have lost weight in the past couple of weeks. All of us have. Except for Miles, I guess, but he cheated.

I offer Jonah the bag. He sighs before taking a chip and sinking onto the dusty piano bench. The bench creaks under his weight, and the light gleaming under his chin makes him look like he's about to tell a ghost story around a campfire and is trying to make himself look like a monster. Except he doesn't look like a monster. He just looks like Jonah.

My Jonah.

Is he my Jonah? Was he ever my Jonah?

He seemed like my Jonah that night in the motel. It felt like he wanted to be my Jonah when he made me feel things I'd never felt before and told me I was the best thing that ever happened to him.

Remembering makes my chest ache. I wonder if he remembers that night. Or the morning after. Even if he doesn't, he did sleep in my bed last night. He came to me when everything in his life fell apart, and he didn't try to kill me, so that has to count for something. It's not lost on me that the standard I'm holding him up to is that he did not try to kill me. Mom would tell me I could do better. Anyone would. But I don't want to do better. I want the old Jonah back, and last night was the first time it felt like maybe he wasn't completely gone.

Jonah plays a note on the piano. It rings out for a couple of seconds, discordant and ugly.

I slide onto the bench next to him, breathing on my hands to warm my fingers. He looks at me like he's trying to figure me out.

"Do you know how to play?" I ask.

He hits another note. "I dabble."

I said it as a joke. I didn't think he knew how to play piano, and I'd be lying if I said I wasn't a little impressed.

"Play me something," I say.

"What do you think I am, a jukebox?" I glare at him, and he flexes his fingers. "Fine, whatever."

He places his fingers on the keys. I'm so surprised to learn that Jonah plays the piano that I have no idea what to expect, but when he jabs his pointer finger into one key at a time and bangs out the melody to *Mary Had a Little Lamb*, I roll my eyes.

"You're an idiot," I say.

"You don't like the song?" he asks, finishing the verse. "That sucks because I only know the one."

He looks over at me, and it gets a little hard to breathe. He's sitting so close to me. Our shoulders are inches apart, not exactly touching, but we might as well be because I can feel the space between us like it's tangible.

"I'm sorry everything got so messed up, Scooby," he says quietly.

Oh my God. It's like he reached into my ribcage and wrapped his hand around my heart. Hearing his nickname for me lights up something in the pit of my stomach.

And makes me go crazy, apparently, because one second, I'm staring at him, and the next, I'm pressing my lips to his.

He sucks in a breath. Even though neither one of us is moving, I'm dizzy from how fast my heart is beating, and so much adrenaline is coursing through me that I can't think straight. I can't be thinking straight if I thought kissing him less than a day after he tried to kill me was a good idea, but I'm doing it, anyway.

He doesn't move. I go to kiss him deeper.

But he shoots up from the bench and walks away from the piano. He runs a hand down his face, shaking his head.

"I'm sorry," I say.

He says nothing. I go toward him. He's still turned away from me. The muscles in his shoulders and back are tight, and his chest is rising and falling fast. The logical part of my brain is telling me to leave him alone, to give him space, and most of all, not to push this, because I just kissed Jonah and I never thought I'd kiss him again, but it's not enough.

"Are you okay?" I ask, my voice hoarse with how much I want to kiss him again.

When he says nothing, I lay a hand on his shoulder.

He spins around to face me. Even in the dark, I can see the angry gleam in his eyes.

"Why did you do that?" he snaps.

A lump forms in my throat. I do my best to swallow it down. "Uh …"

"I tried to kill you," he says. "Twice. Why didn't you run away?"

Blood rushes to my cheeks. I hope it's too dark for him to see. "Because I miss you."

He shakes his head again. I reach for his hand, but he yanks it up, clenching it into a fist.

"You really want to know what I was going through my head just now? That lantern on the piano was looking pretty good for bashing your brains in when you weren't expecting it. I had to stop myself from grabbing it and going to town on your head."

His words hang in the air. It takes a couple of seconds for them to really hit me. My eyes travel to the old-fashioned kerosene lantern sitting on the piano. While I was thinking about how good it felt to be kissing him again, he was thinking about bashing my head in.

I can hear myself breathing. He searches my face as if looking for some kind of reaction. I wish I could say it doesn't matter. That I don't care what he thinks about me. But that's not normal.

"Shiloh … something's not right with me," Jonah says. "I keep getting these twisted thoughts, and if I stop fighting them … I'm scaring myself. I'm not the person you used to know."

A sharp pain pierces my heart. It overwhelms me, so I shove it down.

"Yes," I say. "You are."

"Shiloh."

He says my name like an ending. Like it's that easy, and he gets to decide what ends and when, but he doesn't.

He may not think he's the same person I remember, but he is. I saw it today. In the way he was joking around with Francesca, and the way he thought he could just run into a field of cows and rile them up as a distraction. Jonah is funny and reckless, but the world has let him down, so he's also guarded. When things get too much for him, he pushes people away, and that's all he's doing right now. He blames himself for Aunt Moe's death, so he's punishing himself by pushing me away. He might not think that he's the same person, but that is literally the most Jonah move in the book, and I'm not going to let him do it.

I need him to be the person I remember because the thought of losing him is more painful than any threat about lanterns he can throw my way. It's worse than watching a video of Aunt Moe slitting her own throat. It's worse than Leonard. Worse than Miles not being Miles anymore. Worse than anything my dad ever did.

All at once, it hits me. Why I can't let him go.

I love him.

I never thought I'd be able to love another person except for Max. I didn't even think I'd know what love would feel like when it wasn't for Max, but I recognize the feeling like an old friend.

And I can't help it. Despite everything, I smile.

Jonah doesn't look like he knows what to make of this, which makes me smile wider.

"Why are you smiling?" he asks.

"Because I love you," I say, my stomach flipping over because as I say the words, I know I mean them.

He's not smiling. "Shiloh—"

"I love you," I say it again. "And I'm not giving up on this."

He stares at me. My heart is pounding so hard I don't understand how it hasn't crapped out yet. A long enough silence goes by for me to think he won't say anything in response, but I don't care. He needs to know how I feel, and I want to tell him regardless of whether he feels the same way.

He walks toward me. I raise my hands to defend myself, but he closes the space between us, pulls my wrists out of the way, and kisses me.

His lips crash into mine. His hands grip my arms. He kisses me harder, hungrier, and more desperately than he ever has before. I clutch at his shoulders, the only thing keeping me from crumpling to the ground.

Oh my God.

Oh my *God*.

He walks me backward and pins me against the wall, grasping my wrists and pinning them on either side of my head. His body presses against mine until there is no space between us at all. He kisses me with a bruising pressure that borders on frantic. He runs his hands over me like he's trying to feel me and hold me everywhere at once, digging his fingernails into my skin.

I cling to him. His strong hands release my wrists and span my waist, then roam upward, under my shirt. His fingertips press into the tender skin at the small of my back, causing me to gasp into his mouth. He knots his hands in my hair, angling my head back as his mouth plunders mine. I trace my fingers over his jaw, relearning its contours, reassuring myself that this is really happening. Because it is. I want him so badly that it hurts, but I kiss him through the pain, like just one more kiss will make it go away.

He pulls away from me to catch his breath. Our eyes meet. I expect a grin, or that sort of mischievous look he gets in his eye when he's kissing me, but he doesn't smile. Actually, I can't read his expression at all. A finger of worry trails up my spine. Is he thinking about the lantern again? Or something worse?

I stand no chance against him if he goes for it right now. I'm too dizzy from the kiss. So I try to deflect.

"If you try to kill me again, I'll stop you," I say. "Because let's face it. You're crap at hand-to-hand combat."

I don't know how that's going to go over. I'm still not thinking clearly. But in seconds, Jonah's pulling me into his arms and kissing me again. His breath is the only warm thing in this room. His weight presses into mine. He whispers my name into my ear, his lips sending shivers down my spine. I run my hands around the back of his head and pull him down to me and his guttural groan is followed by a kiss that says that he wants me and needs me and has to have me so much that he can't stand it. My hands slip under his shirt. He pushes his hipbones into my palms. His hands are in my hair and his lips are everywhere and all I ever want to do is stand here in this room kissing him until I run out of air or pass out from the sheer ecstasy of it all. I did not know it was possible to feel so much of everything all at once.

Because I love him.

This is the boy I love.

When Jonah breaks away from me, I hold on to his arms to make sure I stay upright, smiling so widely that my face hurts. He finally manages a smile, stumbling to the side to catch his balance and gripping me even tighter.

"Promise me you won't give up on yourself," I say. "Because I'm not going to give up on you."

Jonah nods, but his lips purse. His throat rolls as he swallows, and he glances at the door behind me.

I go to ask him what he's thinking about, but I feel his phone vibrate in his pocket. He lets me go and checks his texts.

"Fiona just left," he says. "She'll be here in around an hour."

I glance up at the clock on the wall. It's stopped. So is the one on top of the piano, and it's stopped at the exact same time. Creepy haunted house crap.

I lean against the wall and wrap my arms around my stomach, smiling at him a little. "Sounds like we've got time."

He grabs the bag of chips. "I'm going to go see if Francesca and Evangeline want any of these."

"Stale chips?" I ask. "I don't think Francesca will be all that interested."

I expect a smile, but Jonah is already leaving the room. He hurries through the kitchen and back into the dining room, leaving me with a weird feeling in my stomach that I can't exactly place.

42

Shiloh

One hour later, Fiona gets here. The four of us trudge through cornstalks to get to her, and her old green dented Subaru is parked on the side of the road. I see her mouth drop open through the windshield when we all emerge like teenagers of the corn.

The last time I saw Fiona was the night I got arrested. She's unironically the most beautiful person I have ever seen, even though she's wearing some kind of Y2K velvet tracksuit the same color as her car. Jonah looks happy to see her, too. His smile is genuine when she leaps out of the car and runs over to us.

She gives me a big hug that I'm not expecting or prepared for. She hugs me so hard that I'm honestly surprised my eyeballs don't pop out of my head like a cartoon.

"Oh, hon, I'm so happy you're okay," she says. "Come on, get in the car. You need to tell me all about jail."

She says it like I just got back from a one-in-a-lifetime trip to the Bahamas, but it's sort of funny, so I roll with it.

"The food was to die for," I tell her from the passenger seat. "Soggy waffles, half soaked with baked beans."

"Delicious," Fiona says.

"I had my very own private suite," I say, smiling. "All the natural light made it so … cozy."

Fiona makes me call Mom as soon as we get on Route 13 to tell her where I'm going. She has spent enough time with us to know that Mom would be wondering where we are, and sure enough, she is. It's a good thing Mom knows Fiona. I guess the whole idea of me disappearing for half a day is less unacceptable when Mom knows the person driving us to the city, and we aren't actively on our way to fight an evil ghost. Who knew?

In an hour and a half, we arrive in Columbus and pull into the parking lot of a condo complex. She leads us up a battered wooden staircase to a door marked 1733B, and punches in a code on the keypad. The door beeps, and she gestures for us to go inside.

This is not where I pictured Fiona living. Come to think of it, I don't know where I pictured Fiona living. I guess in my head she lived in the motel or in the circus bus surrounded by pieces of canvas and beds of nails, but this is an odd mix of eclectic and modern and … ordinary. The walls are white. Her gray couches look comfortable, and her trendy carpet is plushy and soft under my socks. The entire back wall is taken up by a painting of a tiger in flaming orange and red, and plants of all different shapes and sizes are crowded into a patch of sun coming in through the window.

Fiona drops her keys into a bowl held up by a bronze statue of a monkey. She gestures at the condo.

"This is the place," she says. "Home sweet home when we're not on the road, which is pretty much all winter. You caught us at a busy time of year. Does anyone want water or something to drink?"

She gets some bottles of water from the fridge and calls in a pizza because none of us have eaten a real meal all day and I guess she's putting her mom hat on. I'm sitting on the couch when a slender hairless cat comes slinking into the living room, followed by Phil, who is leaning on the wall for support. His face is still paler than usual. It has that stereotypical hospital glow, but I guess he got discharged yesterday, so that's understandable. Apparently, his stab wound wasn't that deep and missed all his major organs, so he ended up being mostly fine. I can see the bandage obscuring his stomach tattoos through his white V-neck.

Jonah gets to his feet as soon as Phil walks in. I didn't know he was that close to Phil, but Jonah looks just about ready to hug him.

Phil sits in a red armchair, and we all eat pizza together in the living room, trying to keep our slices away from the cat. Once we've finished eating, the cat jumps up on the counter and nibbles at a few crusts we left while Fiona brings us to a room at the end of the hallway and flips on the lights.

It's a bedroom jam-packed with cardboard boxes. The air smells different in here than in the rest of the place. Sort of elderly. Stuffy, and a little like mothballs. There's a walker in the corner with tennis balls covering the ends, and a basket filled with yarn in all different colors.

"She was living with us full-time toward the end," Fiona says, gesturing. "I put her things in here. Every diary you guys read, and everything else she collected over the years."

I peel back the flap of the closest box to find it full of glass jars plugged with corks. I wonder what she has in those. Probably more circus drugs. Or potions that do weird things like turn you into a llama or make you grow a tail.

Fiona picks up a clump of knitting that must have been some half-finished project. "Is there something in particular you're looking for?"

"A book," Francesca says.

Fiona laughs. "There are a bunch of those."

"It is quite a comprehensive book," Francesca says. "It contains all the instructions for her soothsaying rituals. Ms. Wilma showed it to me when I saw her on the other side."

Fiona's mouth drops open. I keep forgetting that seeing someone on the other side is not a normal thing to other people like it's becoming to us.

"You saw her?" Fiona asks. Phil appears in the doorway. "Is she ... I mean, how is she?"

Francesca hesitates, which is not the reaction anyone wants to get when asking how their dead loved one is doing, so I nudge her with my elbow. But Francesca doesn't lie to people.

"She was at peace with what happened to her," Francesca says. "And when I met her, she was attending a peculiar musical, which she seemed to find quite enjoyable."

Fiona laughs, and Phil rests a hand on her shoulder. I wish I could add something else to comfort her, but anything I might say would be a lie and everyone here would know it.

Fiona wipes her eyes, then makes an exasperated sound. "Sorry. I need to pull myself together. Well, you guys have at it. Let me know if you need help finding anything."

She goes to walk back to the kitchen, but Phil lingers for a second.

"I, on the other hand, will be no help at all," he says, in his smooth British accent. "So don't bother asking."

With that, they leave four of us alone.

My hands hang at my sides as I glance around the room. It feels weird, standing in the Soothsayer's bedroom all made up like it was when she was living in it. I know we have permission to snoop. We also don't have a choice. People's lives depend on it.

Jonah is the first one to dive in. "We doing this or what?"

I don't know what this giant leather-bound book containing all the deepest, darkest secrets of soothsaying looks like. It's probably not going to have *Soothsaying for Dummies* written on the cover, so I poke around for anything big and crusty and old. The first thing I see that looks promising is a leather-bound photo album, but when I show it to Francesca, she frowns.

"On the other side, the book appeared more battered," she says. "As though the covers were peeling off."

That's not very helpful, but I keep looking anyway. Around ten minutes go by before I hear Jonah clear his throat.

"I got it," he says, holding up a deep brown book that looks pretty much exactly how I'd expect a spell book in some sort of high fantasy TV show about elves and dragons and wizards to look, except for the fact that it's not chained shut and doesn't have monsters writhing on the cover. It looks a million years old. Brass buckles hold it closed. Each stitch in the leather looks like it's the last one holding the old thing together. Even though it doesn't look rotten, I can see why Francesca used that word. I don't need to see what's inside to know it's what we're looking for.

Jonah still asks, "Is this it?" to confirm, but the tightness in his jaw tells me he knows it's the right one too.

With trembling hands, Francesca takes the book from him and sinks onto the edge of the bed. She peels back the cover. The pages come apart with a loud crunch. I sit next to her. So do Jonah and Evangeline, and we all lean over Francesca's shoulder as she flips through the pages.

I'm not an expert in soothsaying, nor do I understand what exactly it is that soothsayers do, but let's just say I'm glad my experience with the Soothsayer was limited. Everything in here looks like it was written by hand with a quill in a loopy script. I never learned to read cursive, so I don't know what the words say, but if the words are anything like the drawings, I'm glad I can't read them. There's a picture of a knife with blood dripping from the tip. A white rabbit with scarlet eyes. A crescent moon, so yellow it looks like an old man's toenail. There are a lot of different interpretations of the orb—some clear, some filled with white smoke, and some filled with a bunch of small human faces, mouths open and screaming.

I glance up at Jonah, who is sitting on the other side of Francesca. "Is this creeping you out, too?"

Jonah says nothing, but all the blood has drained from his face. He must have a weaker stomach than I thought.

"This is quite alarming," Francesca says. "The seers, as this tome calls soothsayers, do quite horrible things to the souls in the glass balls."

Jonah side-eyes her. "What kind of things?"

"Being trapped inside prevents souls from ever taking their proper form, which causes extreme discomfort," Francesca says. "I feel bad doing this, even to Leonard."

"He put you through agony and nearly did us in," Evangeline says. "That swine has it coming."

Francesca purses her lips, but nods. She pauses on a page and points at the title.

"Binding ritual," Evangeline reads. "Does that mean tethering someone's soul to the orb?"

Francesca nods. She runs her eyes down the page, and I have never wished I'd learned cursive more.

"What does it say?" I ask. "Does it tell us what we have to do?"

"Erm …" Francesca keeps reading. "There appear to be two separate rituals. One for binding a soul to the orb when a person is alive, and another for when they are dead."

That's good. We don't know if Leonard will possess someone or be a ghost when we do this, so we need to be prepared for both. "How do the rituals work?"

"To bind a soul when somebody is alive, they must bleed on the glass ball, and then certain words must be recited." Francesca points at the knife drawing.

Jonah runs his finger over the pale pink scar on the fleshy part of his thumb. I don't remember when he got it, but it can't be that old because it looks like it's still healing, so it has to be in the last couple of weeks. Jonah catches me staring and tucks his hands in his pockets.

I point at a creepy drawing of a woman who looks like she's glowing, with her eyes rolled back into her head. "Uh, is that supposed to be you in this whole equation?"

"When binding a soul to the glass ball who is already dead, the seer becomes a sort of passageway," Francesca says. "The energy will pass through me and go into the orb, but I will need to be careful to resist possession or something else called … cauterization."

I don't even want to ask what that could be. "Do you think Leonard is possessing someone right now?"

"He could be," Francesca says, "but I do not think he would enter somebody else's body so quickly. Possessing a person must take a significant amount of energy, so Leonard may need some time to recover before he does it again, and because he possessed somebody last night …" She glances at Jonah, who's looking at his shoes. "I would surmise he is rebuilding his strength."

"That doesn't take him long," I say. "He's been possessing a different person every day."

"He could be ready to possess somebody else this afternoon or evening?" Francesca suggests.

"Miles won't get back until tomorrow," Jonah says, "so we can't let him do that."

We sit in silence for a couple of seconds while we think of what to do.

"I mean, who's he going to possess?" I ask. "Everyone we know has magnets all over their houses. If he wants to get in, he'll need to get in as a ghost, and even that will be hard if we all stay over at my house tonight and lock the doors and alternate watches."

"Like a slumber party?" Francesca asks.

Jonah rolls his eyes. "Not a fun one."

"We'll lie low tonight," I say, "and then set a trap for him tomorrow once Miles gets back."

"A trap?" Francesca asks.

"I'm the one Leonard has been trying to kill since this started. If we give him an opportunity he can't refuse, he wants to kill me so bad that I think he'll walk right into a trap." I take a deep breath before dropping the bombshell. "And I'm going to be the bait."

43

Miles

Growing up loving reading as much as I did, I used to dream of traveling. Even though my parents have been to every corner of the globe, I have barely left home, and I used to want to travel the world or at least see more of the country I live in. I'd make detailed itineraries on my computer. My plan was to do a road trip, but a slow one, driving no more than eight hours a day so I'd have plenty of time to check out museums or weird roadside attractions like giant rubber band balls or the world's biggest pistachio. I used to dream about all the things I was going to see. In general, I thought I'd see fewer trees.

Because that's pretty much all I see. Trees. Some cornfields. Double highway lines and exit signs. I've never been more excited to see a herd of cows in my entire life for no other reason except they're not trees.

I try to pass time by listening to a history podcast I used to like, but after a couple of hours, I get tired of that, and switch to ELO and Lady Gaga. Because it's just me in the car, I sing along. My singing voice sounds so deep in this body. I guess I have never tried singing in Officer Zweering's body until now. but it's not terrible, so I smile and just go for it because there's no one around to hear me.

I'm not loving all this fast driving, but I need to keep moving if I have any chance of making 1,800 miles before tomorrow night. I push the car to 80. 85 if a good song comes on. When I start going so fast that the car starts feeling less like a car and more like a metal deathtrap on wheels, I slow down. For someone who was terrified of driving just a few weeks ago, I sure have been having to do a lot of it. Exposure therapy at its finest.

Around four hours in, after crossing into Kentucky, an unknown Florida number calls me.

I pick up so fast. "Hello?"

"Is this Miles?" a breathy and kind of chirpy woman's voice comes through the car speaker.

Using my real name throws me off guard. I guess I had a momentary lapse and used it when I called Gayle Winters this morning. Or maybe it's not a momentary lapse. I had no reason to tell her I was Randall Zweering. I don't know when lying started feeling more comfortable than telling the truth, but it's not good.

"Uh … yes," I say. "Is this Gayle Winters?"

It is. She tells me she was surprised to get my message and seems pretty anxious about the whole thing, which makes me think I should have told her what I was calling earlier. But I tell her now.

She unleashes a torrent of swear words so over the top that I turn down the volume.

"I know about this man," Gayle says. "I mean, I don't *know him* know him, but I know *of* him. You kids have enough to worry about. I'll bring the orb to you. I just have my 11:30 yoga class and my 3 o'clock palm reading …" She hisses in a breath through her teeth. "Oh, I couldn't cancel that. The woman's son has a terrible case of the *measles*."

She whispers the word "measles" like she's telling me a secret. There's a loud clang, like a cooking pot falling on the kitchen floor. I sure hope that wasn't the orb. Oh God, was it the orb?

"Where are you right now?" she asks, more casually than I'd assume she'd be if she smashed the orb.

I tell her I'm already driving to her. She offers to meet me at a rest stop just north of Atlanta, which is still four hours away from her, but cuts my drive down by over 300 miles.

"I'll send you the address over text," Gayle says. "We'll meet at nine tonight." I hear the jingle of something sounding a lot like a wind chime, and she gasps. "Oh golly, yoga time! Ta-ta!"

She hangs up before I can thank her. What a kooky lady. At least I don't need to go all the way to Florida. I'll have the orb before I go to bed tonight. If I have time to sleep. I'm going to have to. I've been driving for what feels like forever, but is only a quarter of how far I'm going to drive in total, which is just flipping fantastic.

I hit traffic near Atlanta. Because of that, it's 8 PM when I pull into the rest stop where Gayle said she would meet me. I've never been so thrilled to see a fast-food court in my entire life.

I get out of the car, bending my stiff knees like I'm the Tin Man taking his first steps. Oh man, that was awful. Nothing about that was remotely enjoyable. Not the leg cramps. Not the gas station snacks. Not the way I listened to so many podcast hours in a row that the English language stopped being something that I could understand, but it's over. At least for today.

The cool evening air soothes my driving headache. The white overhead lights from the gas station blend with the colored ones from the fast-food places, casting an array of different hues across the front of the car. It looks like the sort of rest stop you'd find much closer to home, which is more than a little discombobulating, but I guess highway rest stops all look the same.

I scan the parking lot for any sign of Gayle. I have no idea what a sign would even look like, but I'm hoping it's a know-it-when-I-see-it sort of thing. The only cars I can see look ordinary, so if she's here, I don't know it when I see it. Guess I have time to get some dinner.

I get a footlong from Subway and eat at a picnic table. As I'm finishing around 8:45, this van pulls in, and I instantly know it when I see it. Yep. This has to be her.

The van looks like it's been plucked from the traffic jam outside some psychedelic-fueled music festival from the 70s. It's bright purple with pink flower decals on the sides, and loops of beads hanging from the front mirror. The paint is so glossy it's obvious that it's well taken care of, or at least suggests that Gayle has a subscription to a car wash.

Gayle drives into the parking lot. I place the end of my sandwich on the yellow paper and wave, prompting the van to pull up in front of me. In seconds, a tiny middle-aged woman runs around the back of the car.

She's so much smaller than the van that it's comical. I mean, every person is smaller than their car, but this woman looks like she'd need help to reach the pedals. She's one of the smallest people I've ever seen. Maybe four feet tall and thinner than Fiona, which is saying something, with frizzy blonde curls and wearing a knit multicolored sweater with moth holes in it. Her beaded necklace is so chunky it must weigh ten pounds.

"Are you Miles?" she asks. I nod and open my mouth to respond, but she doesn't give me the option and extends her hand to me. "Gayle Winters. Pleased to meet you. I have the orb, like you asked." A stunned look comes over her face as though she's trying to remember if she really did put it in the van. My stomach drops because oh my God if she forgot the orb—but she shakes her head, and her smile reappears. "I'll get it for you."

She goes around the back of the van. In a couple of seconds, she reappears with a FedEx box.

"I was so surprised when Wilma left the old thing to me." She talks too fast. She's almost tripping over the words. "I won't use it. Those things are so outdated, you know? Like am I really going to torture a bunch of dead people who know nothing about the future so I can make guesses about what's coming?" Her tone tells me the answer is no.

She holds the box out to me. I take it eagerly, peeling back all the layers of green bubble wrap until I can see the smooth and unbroken glass surface.

"You're frowning," she says, and I glance up at her. "Why are you frowning? Is that not what you wanted?"

"No, it's exactly what I wanted," I say. "Thank you so much for coming to meet me. This is going to be so helpful."

She sniffs the air. "Something's not right." She reaches out and pokes me in the cheek, and I flinch. "You. You are not right."

"Um …" How am I supposed to respond to that?

"Put the box on the ground," Gayle says, and I hesitantly do what I'm told. "Let me have a look at you."

Gayle grabs my face and pulls me down toward her. I bend over at the waist and stumble forward to catch my balance.

"Open your mouth," she says.

I'm not sure I heard her right. "My m—?"

She yanks my jaw open, and the word turns into a strange sound resembling something I'd make at the dentist. Gayle peers inside my mouth, peels back my eyelids, and traces the lines in my palms.

"Your soul," she says. "It does not match this body."

I stare at her. All at once, the blood rushes from Gayle's face and she goes ghostly pale. "You are going to want to come with me," she says. "Into my van. Right now."

She climbs into the back of her van, but I just stand there, my feet rooted to the asphalt. I was always taught not to go anywhere with strangers and especially not to get in their cars. Getting into a stranger's car allows them to take you to a secondary location, and once you're at a secondary location, your chances of death go up tenfold. But I got that advice when I was a scrawny teenager incapable of winning a fight against my shadow. Even though this woman is weird, she is also small, and I feel pretty confident in my ability to take her in a fight if it comes down to it.

Besides, she looks so freaked out. I can't just leave without figuring out why.

So I put the orb into the back of my car and lock it, then climb through the open van door.

The smell of incense and cinnamon hits my nostrils. Both things are supposed to smell good, but most good things smell bad when they're super intense, and that's what's happening right now. There are no lights in here except for a lantern on top of one of those low tables which everyone sits cross-legged on cushions around. Decorative tapestries hang from the walls, and long strings of multicolored beads dangle from the ceiling. The lantern flickers like the bulb is struggling with the effort to stay alive.

Gayle sits on a cushion, shuffling a deck of cards. She gestures at me, not looking up.

"Oh, don't worry about the beads," she says. "I'll clean them up when we're done."

I barely have time to be confused before I feel something snag on my arm, and a string of beads rips off from the ceiling. I stare at the beads crumpled on the ground, then back up at Gayle. Did she just predict that?

There's no way Gayle could have known. She must have seen my arm reaching for it, and then said that. Or at least that's what I feel most comfortable telling myself.

Gayle beckons to the cushions. I sit. I'm expecting the pillow to be thick, but it's not, and my butt sinks through to the hard van floor.

In one swooping motion, Gayle fans the cards out across the table. She jabs a finger at me.

"You," she says. "Choose three cards."

I blink at her. "They all look the same."

"Choose the ones that compel you," Gayle says, her eyes

wide. Whatever she's afraid of, she really believes it. "You will find the way."

I pick the card closest to me. Gayle urges me to take another. This seems pretty dumb. If there is something urgent Gayle needs to warn me about, she already knows what it is, so she doesn't need tarot cards to tell me. Time is of the essence here, but if there is one thing I've learned since all this started, it's that even if things seem unbelievable on the surface, there might well be something to them if the person saying them believes in them with all their heart. I wonder if things would have turned out differently if I'd believed Shiloh when she first came to me about the whole ghost thing.

I choose two more cards and arrange them in a straight line in front of me.

Gayle looks me in the eye. "The three-card reading is blunt, but it can be effective if we know what we have to deal with. Sometimes, I do a four-card cross, sometimes I put a fifth card in the middle of the cross and four more cards to the right."

Uh … okay. I wasn't expecting a lesson in tarot reading, and I don't foresee it becoming a hobby of mine.

Gayle flips over the first card. She covers her mouth with her hand. I stare at the picture. I wouldn't call myself an expert in tarot card readings, but I can say right off the bat that this one doesn't look great. In the illustration, two people are falling through the windows of a burning building.

Gayle extends a shaking finger to the vaguely concerning card. "The Tower."

"What does it mean?" I ask.

"Destruction," she says. "Upheaval. There is something in your life that needs to be destroyed, or will be destroyed. You will experience a sudden and devastating change in your life."

Before I have time to process this information, Gayle turns over the second card, revealing another showing a woman, blindfolded, bound with rope and surrounded by sharp swords. Call me crazy, but this doesn't look like the promise of a good omen, either.

"The Eight of Swords." Gayle shakes her head, not liking what she's seeing. "You will be trapped. Powerless. You are not powerful enough to fight this dreadful thing that's coming into your life, or to stop it."

Why did I have to pick all the bad ones? Gayle flips over the next card. While the first two had pretty intimidating images, there's no mistaking the skeleton holding the sword or the word under it:

Death.

Gayle gapes at it, then looks up at me. "Do you know what this means?"

My heart is beating faster than I'd like to admit. I glance over my shoulder at the van door, but it's closed. "I'd guess it's probably nothing good?"

"Something is about to go terribly wrong," she says. "I felt it as soon as I met you. The cards just confirmed it."

"What's going to happen?" I ask. "I mean, if you could feel something, you have to know what it is, right?"

Gayle shakes her head. "I can feel things … your energy … and the cards … they do not lie."

I cringe at how stupid this is going to sound. "What else is my energy saying?"

"Are you sure you want to hear it?"

Obviously I want to hear it. But I'm too nervous to hear what she has to say that I can barely speak, so I nod.

"This evil specter will not stop until he has killed you and every one of your friends, not only in this world but beyond the grave," she says, and my stomach drops. I told her about Leonard already, but I didn't tell her about Shiloh, Francesca, or Jonah. "So you have to stop him, but you are going to have to make a choice. One of you will die—and if you choose to bring them back, you will unleash a terror upon your town unlike anything you have ever seen."

A powerful chill runs through my body. "Which one of my friends?"

She closes her eyes. "I'm … sorry. I don't know."

"Can you look a little harder?" I'm breathing so hard I'm almost hyperventilating. "Or describe what the person looks like?"

Do I really want to know? Do I really want to carry this information around in my head until it comes true? Shiloh only just got out of jail, and the two of us are finally feeling like friends again. Could I bear seeing our plan succeed only to lose her? Francesca was friendless and alone when I first met her, but now, she's sure of herself, and unafraid to stand up for what's right. And Jonah. He just lost the closest thing to a mother he's ever had. He doesn't deserve to die. None of them deserve to die. Which leaves ...

Me.

Gayle's pupils dart around behind her closed eyelids. I try to keep breathing as I think of my friends. I knew defeating Leonard wouldn't be easy, but I had no idea it would cost so much.

"What kind of thing will happen to the town?" I ask. "Do you know anything else?"

Gayle shakes her head. Her mouth opens and closes, like she's doing her best to form the words.

"If you move forward with this," she finally says, "you will have to choose between the death of one person you love, and every other person in your town."

PART 4
Requiem

44

Shiloh

If we're going to set a good trap for Leonard, I'll need to be the bait.

It makes the most sense. He's been trying to kill me since the beginning, so I'm the one he wants dead the most. If I give him the opportunity to kill me, he's not going to resist.

Jonah is the first to protest. "No. It's too dangerous."

"It's the only way," I say.

Francesca glances between us, conflicted. Evangeline just sits there. Jonah opens his mouth to argue, but I cut him off.

"I won't let him kill me," I say. "I just need him to think he has a chance, so he shows up."

Jonah still doesn't like it. Even though it's a weird situation, the fact that he's worrying about me makes me feel a little warm. I wonder if the foolery is slowly clearing from his system, or if kissing him got through enough of it to make him worry about me again. Either way, it's a good thing. I tell him I'll be fine because Francesca will be there and can step in when Leonard arrives. He goes to protest, but I tell him it's happening, and there's nothing he can say to stop it.

So he changes his approach. "What happens if he doesn't go for you? He could try to kill the rest of us, and there are not enough Francescas to go around."

"You'll have magnets." I stand up. "And maybe there are some ghost weapons in these boxes. I mean, Ella Ruggles got the monocle from the Soothsayer, right? The Soothsayer could have picked up some other random stuff from her circus days that could be useful."

Francesca and Jonah shrug. We rummage through the boxes and crates piled in the corners. Sure enough, there are some weird things under all the books and diaries. Corked vials of unidentifiable liquids. A cigar box filled with dehydrated chicken feet. Francesca uncoils what looks like a whip or a lasso. She runs her fingers along the length of it.

"Do you think this could work against souls?" she asks.

I point at the ghost figure carved into the handle. "Looks promising to me."

Francesca flicks it out in front of her. The rope loops around a lamp, pulling it onto the rocking chair and knocking over the basket of yarn.

Jonah snorts with laughter. "Let me see that for a second."

Francesca gives it to him. Jonah shakes the rope out in front of him, holding the loop in one hand before swinging it over his head and throwing it my way. I raise my arms to cover my head. The loop wraps around me, and Jonah pulls it tighter, grinning like he thinks he's so funny.

"Gotcha," he says.

I roll my eyes and pull the rope off from over my head, fighting the smile creeping onto my face because this is not the time to get all giddy about how normal that just felt.

Jonah finds some kind of powder that's all clumped together in a small glass bottle, and when he takes out the stopper, it makes the entire room smell like rotten eggs. Evangeline has to run out. Francesca opens the window. Even though the smell makes my eyes water, I keep searching through the discomfort, and eventually find what looks like a pair of old-fashioned round safety glasses so thin they can barely hold themselves together.

I put the glasses to my eyes and peer through them at Jonah and Francesca. The lenses are scratched and warp the corners of my field of vision so that the floor looks like a fun mirror, but they don't seem to do anything else to the room.

Are they … could the lenses work the same way as the monocle?

Maybe they do, and there are just no ghosts in here for me to see. In case that's true, I add the glasses to the pile of things that we're taking.

Nobody says much on the drive back to Bethany. I'm preoccupied with trying to figure out the best way to plan our trap for Leonard. By the time Fiona pulls into my driveway, my heart is pounding so hard it's making me feel like I have to throw up.

"I'm sorry I won't be able to be there for you kids tomorrow," Fiona says. "Phil needs me at home, and he won't be happy if I go and get myself stabbed as well. He'll say I'm making it all about me."

I tell her it's fine. She winks at me before driving away, leaving us all standing in the driveway.

Because some of my neighbors have prying eyes and I don't want any of them to see Evangeline, we go inside. Mom is waiting for us. She's standing on the other side of the door like she was waiting for me to open it, and she does not look happy.

"Shiloh," she says. "Can I talk to you for a second?"

Something in her tone tells me that the others shouldn't be here for this conversation, so I tell them to bring all our ghost-hunting stuff to my room and follow Mom into the kitchen.

I pull up a stool. She pours a glass of water from the sink and slides it across the counter over to me.

"Social services came," she says, and I catch the glass of water. "They wanted to know where Jonah is."

I swallow the lump in my throat. "What did you say?"

"That I didn't know," she says, and I sigh in relief. "Which is technically true because God only knows where you went today, but I did not appreciate having to cover for you. They're worried about him, and I can't really blame them, considering all that's happened. Is he okay?"

"He's a long way from being okay, but he's more okay than he would be letting Social Services bring him to a stranger's house," I say.

She frowns. "Was that Talulah Monroe who just walked in here? The police found her yesterday. It's all over the news. Do her parents know where she is right now?"

"No," I say. "And you can't tell them."

"*Shiloh.*"

"No, Mom, I'm serious. Please, give me one more day. Thirty hours. Tops. I have a plan to stop Leonard, but I need to do it tomorrow night, and I need everyone's help to pull it off."

The color drops from Mom's face. "What is this plan, exactly?"

I go to answer her, but she holds up a hand.

"You know what? Don't tell me." She pulls her bottom lip between her teeth, thinking. "I don't like that you're doing this."

"Neither do I," I say. "But trust me, we're the only ones who can, and I'm going to need you to let me do it."

Mom hangs her head. I can see her digesting this information and trying to sort through what she's going to say. I wish I could have kept this a secret from her, but I stopped being able to do that when Leonard killed her.

"I understand what it takes to stop this man," she says, "but I don't want you to go back to jail. I don't want you killing anyone, or dragging any bodies around. I'm serious, Shiloh. Do you hear me?"

The ridiculousness of this conversation is not lost on me.

"I should help you," she says.

"Stay with Max," I say. "He can't be on his own when all of this goes down."

"I know."

"Please," I tell her. "Let me do this."

"I'm your mother." She draws in a pained breath. I know she's my mother, but she left me alone to deal with hard things my entire life. I know we've been bonding lately, but nothing she does can erase our history. "I know nothing I'm going to say is going to stop you, but promise me you will be careful."

"I'll be as careful as I can."

"That's as good as I'm going to get, isn't it?"

I give her a glum nod. Anything I could say would feel like a lie. How can I promise her I'll be careful when our entire plan hinges on me literally offering myself up to Leonard like some kind of human sacrifice? She doesn't need to know that.

A small voice behind me interrupts my thoughts. "Shiloh?"

I turn around and find Francesca standing in the opening of the hallway, her hand resting against the wainscoting like she's using it to balance. "I have discovered something that you must see."

I give Mom a close-lipped smile because I guess our talk is over, and I follow Francesca back to my room, where Jonah is wearing the wire glasses I found. He offers them to me. Side-eyeing him, I hold the glasses up to my eyes.

And jump in surprise because, hovering right in front of me, are two ghosts. One is a boy in an old-fashioned newsboy cap, and the other is a girl with … four legs?

The glasses are not as good as the monocle, but at least they cover both eyes, and the picture is pretty clear. The lenses give everything a sepia tone and bounce and when I move is going to give me motion sickness if I walk around wearing them, but it's better than having nothing.

"Shiloh," Francesca says, and I turn my head to look at her through the lenses. "Meet Patrick and Maude. I brought them here from the other side when Leonard had me locked in the cellar."

The girl raises her hand in a wave. The boy—Patrick—says something to Francesca.

"What's he saying?" I ask.

"That he and Maude have had quite the adventure, exploring our world," she says. "They were able to find and terrorize her ex-husbands new wife in her old age. They cut off all her hair and made holes in her clothes, which Maude says was great fun, but now, Patrick would like me to help him return to the other side."

I pull off the glasses, squinting against the bright light. "Right now?"

Francesca nods. "Patrick would like to be reunited with his elephant."

He has an elephant. Of course he does. But just because this guy wants to be reunited with his pet doesn't change the fact that Francesca is too weak to be making any trips to the other side right now.

"I'd like Leonard to drop dead and spend tomorrow stuffing my face with frozen custard instead, but that's not going to happen," I say.

Francesca shifts between her feet. "I promised I would bring him back."

"I don't care."

"Shiloh." Francesca rests a gentle hand on mine. Her skin is so papery that I can see the blue color of her veins through it. "I would like to do it."

"Are you sure?" I ask. "Because you don't owe this guy anything."

"Actually, I do," she says. "I do not have the helmet to use to cross over, so could you draw me a bath?"

I still don't think it's a good idea, but Francesca has decided and nothing I say will talk her out of it, so I do as I'm told. In the bathroom, I plug the drain and turn on the faucet. I'm adjusting the temperature when Max appears next to me, peering into the empty tub. He's already in his pajamas. He smells like shampoo. I bet Mom gave him a bath before we got home.

I toss his semi-dry blond hair and smile over at him. "Can you go get a clean towel for me?"

He nods and comes back in a couple of seconds with a folded bath towel. He watches as Jonah and Evangeline half carry Francesca into the bathroom. Once the water has filled the entire tub, she steps into it, fully clothed.

Max wrinkles his nose. "Why are you taking a bath with your clothes on?"

"Because the clothes keep me warm." Francesca offers him a smile.

Max doesn't smile back. "That makes no sense."

Francesca sits in the water, bracing her wrist on the ledge of the bath to lower herself down. I wrap a Ziploc bag around her bandaged hand and secure it with some hair ties. It won't hold well, but I have a feeling we're going to have to change the bandage after this anyway, so who cares? The warm water laps up over Francesca's torso, soaking her shirt and making it cling to her body. Max drops a yellow rubber duck into the water. Francesca smiles down at it, then up at him like she's glad to have the company.

"You don't have to do this," I tell her, like saying it one more time is going to make a difference.

She unfurls her hand, revealing a coarse silver hair that's easily three inches long.

She lifts her eyes to Evangeline. "May I please have some benmjöl?"

"It's back at your place," Evangeline says. "I didn't have time to snag it before those lugs found us."

"Oh," Francesca says. "All right."

"You shouldn't do this without benmjöl," I say. "You could …" I side-eye Max, not wanting to say the word.

But I don't need to because Francesca understands. "I feel quite strong at the moment."

I don't know if she's saying this because she really does feel fine, or because she doesn't want to disappoint this ghost. Francesca has always cared too much about what people think of her. She is the best person I've ever met. Way too good to worry about what idiots say about her.

I open my mouth to protest, but Francesca holds up her hand and looks at a space above my head. "Are you ready?"

I don't hear the ghost's response because, obviously, he's a ghost, but he must have said yes because Francesca nods.

She turns to me. "Will you please turn off the lights?"

Jonah hits the switch. Shadows fall over the bathroom, but enough light comes through the window on the back wall that it doesn't get dark in here. Francesca frowns. I tell Max to go and get a pair of sunglasses from my room. He comes back with the fluorescent orange ones I got from a trampoline park when I was nine or ten and gives them to Francesca. She considers them for a second before putting them on her face.

"How do I look?" she asks, a crease between her eyebrows like she really is concerned.

"Like the cat's meow," Evangeline replies.

Francesca seems to appreciate this. I have never heard anyone call someone else the cat's meow before, and neither has Jonah, apparently, because he looks like he's doing his best to hold back a laugh.

Francesca reaches out a hand. Her fingers curl. She's probably holding the hand of her ghost friend, but Evangeline is using the glasses to see, so to me it looks like she's holding the air.

"Shiloh," she says. "If I do not come out, please, will you pour cold water on my face to wake me up?"

I wish she would listen to me and not do this, but I still promise her I will. Inhaling a deep breath, she lowers herself into the tub. Because this is not a sensory deprivation tank, her body rests against the bottom and doesn't float. Only her face and bagged hand break the surface. Her white curls fan out around her head, and, in a horrible way, she looks like a corpse staged in a coffin. I force myself not to think of her like that.

Max taps on my shoulder and leans close to whisper in my ear. "Is she going to drown?"

I shake my head. He asks if he can stay to watch. I guess he can. There's nothing bad or scary about what's happening. So I wrap my arms around him and he sits on my knee.

No one says anything. Francesca lies in the tub, limp. Her chest rises and falls. Her eyes flicker behind her lids. It's almost like she's looking for something. I wonder what it is.

Jonah sits next to me on the damp bathmat, bracing his elbows on the side of the tub. Evangeline stands over us, chewing on her fingernail. I guess she's seen Francesca do this before.

I nudge her ankle. "How long does this usually take?" I ask.

"Usually, no more than a minute," Evangeline says. "Cause Leonard dunked her head so she couldn't breathe."

"Gee, he's a nice one, that Leonard," I say.

Jonah jerks his thumb at the tub. "She can do all this in a minute?"

"Time moves differently on the other side," Evangeline says. "One minute here can be way longer over there."

Jonah grunts. "Trippy."

In the tub, Francesca's mouth twitches. I lean closer to her. I can see the lines in her skin deepening, like they're being carved into it with a chisel. A clump of her hair springs free from her head, floating away from her skull and sticking to the side of the tub. Her eyes dart back and forth. She's looking for something. Whatever it is, she can't find it.

She kicks her feet. Her back arches.

I glance up at Evangeline. "Is this normal?"

Evangeline says nothing. Just stares.

Francesca's mouth opens. She makes a choking sound, like she's trying to form a word.

Help.

I lift Max off my lap and point him at the door. "Go." He runs out of the bathroom but doesn't go away, standing in the doorway watching me.

There's no time for me to make sure he doesn't see this. I yell at Jonah and Evangeline to help me, and together we lift

Francesca's twitching body out of the bathtub. Her mouth stretches open into an O like she's screaming, but no sound is coming out.

"Cold water," I say. "She said cold water, right?"

Evangeline disappears and is back in seconds with a bowl from the kitchen. Jonah fills it in the sink, and I dump it on Francesca's face. She doesn't wake up. Evangeline refills it.

I grab Francesca's shoulders. "Come on. Come on!"

Jonah pours more water on her. My heart pounds like a fist against my ribcage. This can't be happening. I knew she shouldn't have done this. Why didn't she listen to me?

I shake her harder. "*Francesca!*"

Jonah fills the water again and dumps it onto Francesca's face. Her eyes fly open.

Francesca coughs hard, buckling over and gasping for breath. I help her sit up. She spits a glob of saliva onto the front of her pants, and I narrow my eyes at it. There's something in her spit. A clump of gray plant material that looks sort of like … moss?

Francesca whimpers. Her bottom lip is trembling so much it's hard for her to form words.

I pull her to her feet. Evangeline wraps the towel around her shoulders and the two of us carry her back into the guest room and get her changed into dry clothes. I try not to let the shock register on my face when she takes her shirt off. Before all of this happened, Francesca wasn't overweight, but she wasn't exactly what I'd call skinny either. Now, it looks like all the fat and muscle under her skin has disappeared, leaving behind sagging pouches hanging down from her back and arms.

Francesca searches my eyes, her chin trembling. I thread her arms through a clean hoodie of mine and help her into bed, pulling the blanket over her legs and propping the pillow behind her back.

She slides down the pillow until she's lying flat. "Evangeline, could you leave Shiloh and me alone for a moment?"

She can barely get the words out through her chattering

teeth. Evangeline's eyebrows knit, but not like she's hurt. More like she's dying to know what Francesca wants to say to me.

"I'll go fix you some tea," she says, and leaves us alone.

I get onto the bed and lie down next to Francesca, pulling up the blanket over her more so it covers her ears. She still doesn't stop shivering. If anything, she's shivering even more than before. Seeing her like this is like a punch to the stomach. I didn't know crossing over would hurt her this much. I told her not to do it. I told her.

"I need to ask you," she says, struggling to form each word like her body isn't cooperating, "something serious."

I brace my hand underneath the side of my head. "What's going on?"

Francesca draws in a shaky breath. "I fear putting Leonard's soul into the glass ball might kill me."

"Then you don't do it," I say. "You can't die."

Francesca presses a finger to my lips. Her skin is ice cold. "You need to promise that you will let me die."

"No."

"I am already dying," she says, "and if I am going to die, then you have to promise to let me take Leonard with me."

A lump forms in my throat. With her face this close to mine, she's almost unrecognizable. All the brown has drained from her irises and turned them gray. Up close, she doesn't look much like Francesca anymore. She looks like a much older woman.

Pressure builds behind my eyeballs like I'm about to cry. Francesca has given so much to other people. To us. She has sacrificed so much of her body that she can barely stay in it anymore. I remember how angry I was the first time she told me she knew where Max was. She'd been telling me the truth, and I was horrible to her, shoving her and screaming at her and calling her names. All she has ever tried to do was help people, and now she's willing to sacrifice herself to save us.

I swallow hard. I can't cry right now. If Francesca's not crying about what's happening right now, I sure can't.

So as much as I wish there was another way, I nod against the pillow. "I promise," I say, and her face relaxes.

I stay with Francesca until she falls asleep, then turn off the lights on my way out of her room. Evangeline is waiting outside with a mug of tea that has gotten cold. She goes inside without saying a word. I guess she's allowed to sleep in the same room as Francesca because Mom doesn't know the two of them are together.

Jonah, on the other hand, is not allowed to stay in my room. He's already unfolding a blanket and pillow on the couch when I go into the living room.

"How is she?" he asks.

I shrug and sit on the La-Z-Boy, kicking the footrest up and sinking back into the soft leather cushions. My dad never let me sit in it, and sitting in it now feels like I'm giving him the finger, which makes me feel pretty good.

Jonah sits on the couch across from me. "Want me to take the first watch?"

"I can do it."

"Okay."

Jonah rubs his eyes. The dark circles under them are heavy, like they're threatening to form craters in his face. In the dim living room light, he looks overwhelmingly sad.

I can't believe it's been less than twenty-four hours since Aunt Moe died. He's held it together pretty well today, and I'm not sure how he did it. If Mom were the one who died … or Max … I'd be way more of a mess than he is. But just because he's not showing how sad he is, doesn't mean he's not feeling it.

I walk over and sit next to him on the couch. He glances at me, and there's a second of stillness where the breath catches in my throat, and I don't really know what to do or say.

So I fill it with the first thing that comes to mind. "You know, my mom made this blanket out of a bunch of my old baby clothes."

Jonah pulls up the corner of the quilt. "Yeah?"

I take it from his hands and turn it until I find the sewn-together rip across the front. "I tore it one day when I used it as a magic carpet for Max. He sat on it, and I dragged him all around the house, but then it snagged on a nail. My mom was so mad when she found out."

I don't know why I'm telling him this story. I guess I just want to tell him something so we don't sit here in silence and maybe so he can think of something other than Aunt Moe.

Jonah keeps smiling, but the sadness is still there in his eyes. "Sounds like fun."

"I'd offer to take you for a spin," I say, "but I think my mom might actually kill me if I ripped it again."

Jonah nods. The smile fades from his face, and his shoulders slump. I want to make some kind of joke about how I didn't know he'd be that broken up about missing out on a magic carpet ride, but it doesn't seem like the right time. Maybe I could share another anecdote or embarrassing story about me. Say something to bring the light back into his eyes. But I don't have time to think of anything before he leans forward and drops his forehead onto my shoulder.

My stomach lurches. He's bending over at an unnatural angle, but he doesn't seem uncomfortable. I wrap my arms around his shoulders and press my lips to the side of his head. His breathing slows. His body is heavy against mine. I guess there's nothing I could say that would get Jonah out of his dark place right now, but at least I can be here for him when he surfaces. He seems to want me to be there when he comes out of it, and maybe that can be where we start. Maybe that will be enough.

At nine o'clock the next morning, my phone wakes me up. I'm half-asleep, slumped in the La-Z-Boy with a blanket pulled over my legs. I rummage through the folds of the blanket for a couple of seconds before finding the vibrating phone, flipping it open, and pressing it to my ear.

"Hello?" I ask, my voice hoarse from sleep.

"I got the orb," Miles says, with way more energy than is normal to have after so little sleep. "The GPS says I'll be there in around nine hours, but after adding one or two more for traffic and gas and food, I'll probably end up getting in around nine."

"Is the orb intact?" I ask. "Did everything go okay?"

"Everything's fine," he says. "Can you get everything else together to do this thing as soon as I get back?"

I tell him to drive safe, and I hang up. When Jonah and Francesca wake up, I update them on the progress with the orb and tell them everything we have to get set up. If all goes according to plan, Leonard will spend the rest of eternity screaming in agony like those pictures in the creepy book, and he's going to start screaming tonight.

45

Shiloh

Of all the places to do this, the abandoned house is our best option. It's far enough from the main house that nobody will hear us. It's also haunted in the most literal sense of the word, so it's the perfect place to go to war against an evil ghost, which is good because that's exactly what we're about to do.

We spend most of the day lying low, eating cereal and pasta and other things we find around the house. It feels weird just hanging out with Jonah and Francesca. All of us have been so busy trying to survive this past month that we haven't had time to do normal stuff, like hang out or watch movies. I haven't watched that many movies. Most of the movies I've seen are ones that Max would also like, so I'm well versed in *How to Train Your Dragon* and *The Lego Movie* but not so much in anything not made for kids.

Jonah puts on *Almost Famous*, and I sit next to him on the couch, my heart flipping over when he puts an arm around me. Francesca sits on the floor while Evangeline plays with her hair, and at some point, I fall asleep. Another movie is playing when I wake up. Jonah sleeps through that one, and after it's done, I pour myself some more cereal.

So it's pretty much the perfect morning, and in the afternoon, I go to Francesca's trailer alone to get the rest of the benmjöl. I'm expecting the place to have some police officers milling around, but it's dead, and I find the benmjöl where Evangeline said it would be.

We order pizza for dinner. Once we're done eating, Jonah, Francesca, Evangeline, and I get ready, changing into black clothes and borrowing extra jackets from the coat closet because it's so cold out. I end up wearing Dad's dark-brown Carhartt jacket. Unfortunately, it smells like him, but it's also one of the warmest options and the sleeves go right down over my hands. Evangeline has to wear a gray sweatshirt because it's the only thing of mine that will fit her. She and I change the bandage on Francesca's hand because it got sort of soggy and gross in the bath yesterday, and because it has to be changed daily anyway.

I hug Mom and promise her I'll be careful. She looks like she's barely holding it together, like it's taking every ounce of her self-control not to forbid me from stepping out of this house. On pretty much every level, I know it's not normal for a parent to let their child do what I'm about to do. But it's also not normal for her to sit by and watch her husband backhand her twelve-year-old daughter for not cleaning her room, so I guess we've always had an atypical relationship.

Our relationship is getting better. It's still not great, but I doubt it ever will be after everything we've been through, so I will settle for better.

I still have the rubber Freddy Krueger mask I wore that time I broke into Francesca's dad's house. There's also an old hockey mask with the holes in it and a box of orange and green smoke bombs that I never got to use. I'm trying to decide whether or not to bring them when Francesca walks into the room, dressed in some of my black clothes with her white hair braided down her back.

She points at the masks. "Are we wearing disguises?"

I shrug and pick up the floppy Freddy Krueger mask. It has a smear of dried blood on the inside, probably from my broken nose rubbing up against it. "I wore this when I broke into your dad's house while I was looking for you," I say. "He chased us out of there with a shotgun."

Francesca's eyes widen. I guess the boys didn't tell her about our failed rescue mission. I'm expecting her to ask why we thought her dad would be keeping her prisoner, or how we figured out where he lived, but after a couple of seconds, she asks, "My father owns a shotgun?"

"He's got terrible aim," I say. "Couldn't hit us when we were, like, three feet away."

Francesca hums. "Well, I am glad he missed."

"You and me both."

I leave the rubber masks behind. Our trap relies on Leonard recognizing us, so the masks will be pretty useless, but I put the smoke bombs in my backpack because you never know what's going to come in handy. Francesca insists on carrying the Soothsayer's book in her arms. In case Leonard has possessed someone and shows up in their body and not as a ghost, I pack my Swiss Army Knife. I'm not going to mess around with guns anymore. There's no way I'm going back to jail. I learned my lesson last time. Everything else we need is at Miles's apartment, so I text him a list of what to bring, and he says he'll grab it on his way to meet us.

Everyone goes to wait for me outside. I stop walking in front of Max's closed door. No light shines under it. Mom must have already put him to sleep. I want to go give him a hug before I leave, but he doesn't need to know where I'm going tonight. He's been through enough without me getting his hopes up about killing the bad man again.

Except this time, it's going to happen.

Sort of. He won't be dead, but he'll be trapped. I can only imagine explaining that to Max.

Guess what, buddy? I trapped the bad man in a glass ball I will bury under concrete or drop in a lake or keep in a box like the Annabelle doll in a case. Don't worry. He can't hurt you anymore. Unless he gets out.

Probably better to say nothing.

Besides, it's different this time. Last time, I knew I was going to go to jail, but this time I'm coming home, and I'll see him when he wakes up in the morning.

On our walk to the abandoned house, the night sky gets super dark. Thunder rumbles in the distance, and I hope it's not going to start raining. Not many things could make what we're about to do suck more, but doing it in the rain is one of them. Fog hangs over the cornfield like a haze. It's cold on my face as we trudge through the corn, stepping over ears that are near the ground and weaving around the stalks to cause the least amount of disturbance. The police have to be out there looking for Talulah. Ideally, we don't want to leave them a trail to follow. I didn't see any cars or flashing lights around the farmhouse, so they must be looking somewhere else—maybe back around the trailer park where they found Evangeline with Francesca. I don't know what Evangeline is going to do after all this is over. Talulah was only fifteen, so it's not like Evangeline can just strike out on her own and not live with her parents. If she stays in Bethany, she will have to go to school and deal with the Monroes one way or another.

Will Evangeline want to stay in Bethany if Francesca dies tonight?

I glance over at Francesca walking next to me. The clouds haven't covered the moon yet, and its light reflects off her braid and pallid skin, making it look even whiter. I clench my jaw. Francesca is not dying tonight. Over my dead body is Leonard getting his hands on her again.

The moonlight glints off the metal NO TRESPASSING sign nailed to a tree. Thunder rolls. Lightning flickers in the distance. Jonah pulls back the loose board for all of us to climb through, muttering something about how this is crap and how much he hates this house, but following us anyway. Because there's no electricity, it's still impossible to see anything, but we came prepared this time and all turn on our flashlights and place them around the main room. Only being able to see things in the narrow cones of light from the flashlights is unnerving to say the least, but it's better than seeing nothing like yesterday. Pieces of broken glass cover the floor where a window has been smashed. Cobwebs hang on the interiors of the panes, and where there are cobwebs, there are spiders. I'm cool with spiders. I try to set a good example for Max and catch them under cups, sliding paper under and throwing them out the door, but Dad used to smash them, leaving their broken little bodies like scrunched-up balls of black cotton for Mom to clean up. There are probably some big ones in this house. I imagine them spinning webs and hiding, waiting for their prey. Kind of like we're about to wait for Leonard.

Come get trapped in our cobweb, Lenny, old pal.

Francesca wipes a bunch of mouse poop off the table to make room for the book. Enough dust billows up from around the pages that she coughs into her elbow.

Jonah leans over her shoulder to look at the pages. His eyes are trained on the same drawing of the ghosts inside the orb screaming in. He looks bothered by it. I don't know why. Personally, I'm not bothered by the idea that Leonard will spend eternity in pain.

I nudge his shoulder. "You okay?"

He flinches at my question like I'm a jump scare at one of those haunted houses with the actors, then gulps. "I'm fine."

He does not sound fine, but if he's using that tone, he's not about to tell me what's going on with him in front of everyone else. So I drop it.

Francesca rests her palms on top of the pages and looks at me.

"I would like to practice the words," she says. "To ensure that I do not mess them up when I am performing the ritual on Leonard."

"Good idea," I say. "Can I help?"

She nods and turns the book around, handing it to me carefully, like she's scared I'm going to drop it.

"I want to memorize them." She sits down in one of the rickety chairs. "In case something happens to the book and I cannot read from it."

Also a good idea. Especially since we have nothing else to do while we wait for Miles.

So I do my best to read out the words to her, and she repeats them after me. Jonah loops an arm around my shoulders as I read, and it's such a quiet moment that it's easy to pretend I'm helping her learn lines for the school play and not an ancient chant that will be the difference between life and death for us and every member of our families.

I'm not sure what this language is, but it sure is hard to pronounce. All my pronunciations are just guesses that I'm sure are butcherings of what they're supposed to sound like, which stresses Francesca out.

I read every word phonetically. "Chavo drome, a marrow shoono, soono tay …" I screw my face up around this next word because I know it won't be right. "A-veevee?"

Francesca points at the accent on the E. "How does this change the sound?"

"How should I know? I'm not fluent in ancient soothsaying. I skipped that class in school."

"Could it be Latin?" Francesca asks.

I wish Miles were here. He would know. But I don't, so I shrug.

"This is not Latin," Evangeline chimes in. "My daddy used to make me take lessons. I paid no attention to the tutor. The old man was such a bore, but I remember enough to recognize the language, and this isn't it."

"What if the ritual does not work because I do not say it correctly?" Francesca asks. "Can you read the entire thing to me again?"

The whole chant sounds so dumb when I read it that I can't help it. I burst out laughing.

Francesca's frown deepens. "Shiloh, please, this is serious."

"I'm trying!"

"Can you search it on the internet?"

Even Google Translate can't help us with this one. At first, it thinks it's Gujarati, which would be super convenient because Miles could give us proper pronunciation, that is if he still knows how to speak it now that he has a different brain and all, but when I ask Google to translate it from Gujarati, the words stay the same.

I laugh at how ridiculous this whole situation is, but Francesca looks like she's about to throw up, so I stop acting like it's funny. By the time the board slides back at 9:30, Francesca is able to recite the phrase in a way that sounds serious enough to be right without stumbling on any of the words.

I glance up from the book to see Miles climbing in through the window, carrying a FedEx box with a backpack slung over his shoulders. In the harsh glow of the flashlight, he looks exhausted. There's a dead look in his eyes, like he's struggling to keep them open, which is probably pretty normal for someone who drove 1,800 miles in a day and a half.

I put down the book and run over to him. I want to hug him, but he has a backpack on and is holding a box so a hug would be awkward, so I settle for touching his shoulder, which is not at all the same.

"How was the drive?" I ask.

"Oh, you know," he says. "It was the most fun I have ever had in my life. I'll be writing a memoir about my journey—it will be called *Miles from Home.*"

"Have I told you that you're the best?" I say.

Miles smiles. "You might have mentioned it once or twice."

"Because you're the reason we're all here tonight," I say. "You're the reason all of this is possible."

"Okay," Miles says, as if to tell me to stop.

But I'm not done. "You're the wind beneath my wings."

Miles rolls his eyes, but he doesn't look mad which I'll take as a win. I point at the box. "Is that the orb?"

"The one and only."

He pulls the glass ball out of the box and holds it up for me to see. I don't know if it's because it's dark in here or maybe because everything was more intimidating when I was up on stage with the Soothsayer, but I remember it being a lot bigger and the glass being … well … thicker. The idea that the only thing stopping Leonard from escaping and coming back to haunt and kill us is a thin piece of glass is unnerving in more ways than one.

"That drive lasted so long I started contemplating mortality," Miles says. "It had me considering the general sanity of people who go on drives that long for fun."

"Did you bring the rest of the stuff?"

In reply, he takes off his backpack and removes the horseshoe magnets, cameras, and radios. I don't know how any of it works, but I remember watching videos on YouTube about paranormal investigators who would go into houses they thought were haunted with radios and cameras like these to see if they could detect ghost activity. None of that activity seemed at all real to me at the time. Knowing what I know now, I'm rethinking that.

He dumps a bunch of magnets in the middle of the table.

"This will be the ghost-free zone," he says. "Or at least, the relatively ghost-free zone. No zone will be safe because ghosts can still throw stuff at us or do stuff to hurt us even when we're in here."

He points up at the iron light fixture hanging above our heads. Each of the bulb covers looks like the bowl of a bell. Having that dropped on my head would give me more than just another concussion.

I open my mouth to say something else when the sound of a little girl's laughter comes from somewhere upstairs.

Everyone goes quiet. The laugh stops, but I exchange a glance with Francesca across the room. She gives a small nod.

There are ghosts in here.

I already knew that, but for some reason hearing that giggle made it way more real.

Nobody says anything for close to a minute, until Jonah breaks the silence: "Well, this is going to be a Baja Blast."

Miles ignores him and stays looking serious. "So, uh, what is our plan here?" he asks.

Miles wasn't here when I came up with the plan, so I update him on what we're doing. A gust of wind hits the side of the house, causing the boards and walls to creak and groan.

I do my best to ignore the rising unease in my stomach and glance at my watch. It's getting close to ten. I can't put this off any longer.

We need to get moving.

I tell everyone to get something to defend themselves with and stand there watching as Miles turns on the thermal camera. Evangeline takes a horseshoe magnet. Jonah picks up the ghost goggles and the ghost lasso. I can't stop the corner of my mouth from curving up.

He side-eyes me. "What are you looking at?"

"Can you please use a magnet or something?" I ask. "If you're attacked by a ghost, I don't want you to die because you can't lasso it."

"I'm not going to die," he says. "Because I'm not going to miss. And if I do miss, you still don't have to worry, because I'll have these handy-dandy smoke bombs to protect me. I will kill the ghosts with color."

"Go ahead. Mock the smoke bombs." I grin like an idiot. "You'll eat your words when they save your ass."

Jonah pockets a smoke bomb. I want to wish him good luck, or kiss him one last time, but last time I did that, I ended up in jail and he ended up getting injected with foolery, so I don't want to jinx anything. I could tell him I love him, but he already knows that. I don't need to say anything or wish him anything because we're going to be fine. He will be fine, and I will be fine, and this will not be an ending to anything except for Leonard.

Miles carries a thermal camera to the back of the house. Evangeline uncorks the vial of benmjöl and mixes it into a water bottle before giving it to Francesca, who drinks about half of it.

It's not a lot, but it's more than Francesca has ever taken at once. I hope it will be enough.

Francesca leans on Evangeline as the drug takes effect. Her spine straightens. She inhales and rests the cane on the table because I guess she doesn't need it anymore.

"Shiloh?" Francesca's voice is even, and her eyes are wide awake. She picks up the book from the table, clutching the leather monstrosity to her chest. "Are you ready?"

As I'll ever be. Taking deep breaths in the hopes my hands will stop shaking, I loop my flashlight around my wrist, pick up the orb, and carry it up the rickety stairs.

46

Shiloh

I'd been so focused on designing a plan that could work that I'd underestimated how utterly terrifying it would be. Because I'm about to pee my pants lying here on this dusty mattress with my eyes closed, pretending to be asleep.

Somewhere down the hall, a hinge creaks. There is a second of silence before the door slams shut.

It's probably nothing, I tell myself. *Just the wind.*

Except it's not just the wind. I saw for myself how many ghosts were in here when I came with Francesca for the first time. I gulp down air so I stay quiet and don't do something stupid like run away, which is all I want to do right now. Jonah, Miles, and Evangeline are outside keeping watch, but Francesca is hiding in a wardrobe ready to come out and surprise Leonard as soon as he gets here. She won't let him kill me. But for some reason, knowing she won't let him kill me doesn't make it any easier to breathe, especially since I need to pretend to be asleep.

This is fine. I am fine. I'm not alone in here.

The door to the room creaks open. The roof of my mouth goes dry. Could that be Leonard? Is he here?

Keep. Your. Eyes. Closed.

Opening my eyes won't help me. I can't see ghosts. Still. I strain to hear any sign of movement, but my heart is pounding too loud in my ears for me to hear anything. The temperature has dropped ten degrees. Is it colder than other parts of the house because there's a ghost in here, or is the entire house cold because there are ghosts everywhere?

A hand grabs my foot and yanks me to the foot of the bed. I scream. My eyes open and search the shadows for my attacker, but no one is there.

I scramble back up onto the bed, pulling my knees tight against my chest. Oh my God. Was that a ghost pulling on my legs?

Was it Leonard?

The wardrobe doors creak open. Francesca peeks her head out.

"Are you all right?" she whispers.

I wish I could nod. "Is L-Leonard here?"

She scans the room and shakes her head. "There are no spirits in here … for the moment."

"Then what the hell just grabbed my leg?"

Francesca shrugs and closes the wardrobe. Somewhere deeper in the house, I hear a little girl's laugh. Goosebumps prickle my skin. Why are the ghosts of kids so much scarier than the ghosts of adults? Probably because of how they got to be ghosts, so much sooner than they should have.

The ghostly girl must have been the one pulling my leg. She must have done it as a joke. Because she's having fun. Not because she's trying to kill me. But she must be strong to move me.

I press my face into the dusty, moth-eaten pillow. Something slithers and crawls under the fabric, which is so insanely gross, but I force my eyes closed, pretending to be asleep when my heart tries to jump out of my chest.

Come on, Leonard. Come and get me, you bastard.

Hands wrap around my leg and drag me to the end of the

bed again. My sneaker comes off my foot and crashes into the wardrobe.

Cursing under my breath, I kick the air in front of me.

"Go away." I grab my shoe and wrestle it back onto my foot, hopping back over to the mattress. "Seriously, leave me alone."

Only a heavy silence answers me. In a couple of seconds, the door slams shut on its own.

I hope I didn't piss off the ghost too much. That's all I need. Another angry ghost. As much as I have learned about ghosts and now know that most of them aren't mean, it freaks me out that other people can see and touch me when I can't see them. It's fine. After tonight, I'll never have to set foot in this creepy house again, and I can go back to pretending ghosts don't exist— even though I'll sleep with a magnet under my bed for the rest of my life.

Outside, there is a crack of thunder. Each rumble sounds closer than the one before. The storm will be on top of us soon. This rotting house won't protect me much. With each gust of wind, the house groans and bends. Lightning flashes against the boarded-up windows. I half expect to see the ghostly girl hovering over me, her hair and nightgown tattered, lit up by those brief flashes of light, but only shadows dance across the peeling walls.

I close my eyes. My eyelids flash pink, but no sound comes. Hold on. That's not lightning. My hands curl around the musty blanket. I didn't even know the electricity in here worked.

I peek open one eye to find my phone, the screen flashing and vibrating on the nightstand. My blood runs cold.

It's the signal.

Leonard is here.

Oh my God. This is happening. Jonah or Miles must have seen him with the ghost glasses. The timing has to be perfect. If I open my eyes too fast and he sees that I'm faking being asleep, he'll soar out of the room before Francesca can catch him, and if he sees Francesca before she sees him, the same thing could happen. I need to sell it. He has to think he could get me. I have to be such an easy target that he won't even question what I'm doing napping in this abandoned house alone at night. I roll onto my back and pretend my eyelids are glued shut. I remember reading something once about how when you lose one sense, all the other ones are amplified. I wish that were the case now so I could hear him gliding up the stairs … or whispering my name under his breath.

A solitary note plays on the piano downstairs. It rings out for a couple of seconds before it goes quiet.

I have never wanted to open my eyes so much in my entire life, but I'm determined not to mess this up. I hear a faint rustle from the other side of the room and lose my ability to breathe. Maybe I can take a quick peek. Just to give myself a clue what's going on. Cracking my eyes open the tiniest bit, I can see a blur of faded magenta. Flowers. Big green leaves. I open them more—just in time to see a pillow dropping down onto my face.

The pillow smothers me, muffling my senses. I try to scream, but the sound is trapped. Rough fabric scratches my skin. I kick out at the air. I claw at the pillow to dislodge the hands, but there are no hands there. Because Leonard is the one pushing down on it.

A weight crashes onto my chest, knocking the wind from my lungs. Leonard is strong. Unnaturally so. Stronger than he was that time in jail. The pillow presses into my face with so much force that it drowns out everything except for the rush of blood in my ears and the pounding of my own heart.

I scream for help, but the pillow melds to my face and stops the sound.

Why isn't Francesca stopping this? Can she not hear me?

I scream harder than I ever have before. I scream against the pounding of my heart and my burning lungs. I slap my hands on the bed and kick at the bedposts to make as much noise as I can. I'm getting sluggish. I need air. I drive my knee up, and tear at the pillow with weakening fingers.

Just as blackness creeps into my vision, the weight lifts. I rip the pillow away, gulping down breath after breath. There's not enough air in this world for me, let alone in this room.

Francesca stands in front of the wardrobe. Her arms are extended. Her feet are planted.

"This is over, Leonard," she says. "You will not hurt any more people."

I push myself into a sitting position, but my vision swims and I collapse back onto the mattress. I reach out for my flashlight and shine it on the wall next to Francesca. It's enough for me to see the frown on her face. The line between her eyebrows.

She takes another careful step, arms extended as if to hold back an invisible force. The tips of her fingers curl in. Her eyes are fixed on me. Or on the space in front of me.

One of her curls falls out, drifting to the floor. I wish I had the goggles to see what's going on, but I don't need to see Leonard to know what Francesca is doing. Every one of her movements is deliberate. Gone is the girl who was afraid to forget the words of that dumb chant. She knows exactly what she's saying.

Her hand clasps around something in the air. She cries out in surprise and pain, knuckles flashing white.

"Shiloh," she says. "The glass ball, please."

Gripping the bedframe, I slide the cardboard box out from under the bed. The world pulls away from me for a second before coming back. The joys of being suffocated. I guess my body is still catching up. Peeling the bubble wrap out of the way, I bring the box to Francesca with unsteady steps. She keeps her eyes trained ahead, not breaking concentration as she presses her palm to the smooth surface. I stagger to catch my balance under the sudden pressure.

She chants the words we rehearsed. Her voice is so low that I barely recognize it. Like she's possessed.

On the second repeat of the phrase, her voice gets louder. The room warms up. The air pressure changes. The hair on my arms stands straight up. A gust of wind swirls through the room, extinguishing what little light my flashlight gave off. So subtly that I almost don't notice it happening, her body glows. I close my eyes for a second and reopen them because a human being literally glowing is not something I ever thought I'd see, but she is. She outshines my flashlight and lights up the corners of the room. Her skin and eyes and teeth gleam like she's been dipped in glow stick fluid. Her hair isn't white anymore. Her skin is not sallow. Francesca is radiant, like a vision, and I swear, her feet are hovering a few inches off the floor.

Oh my God, this is happening. She's doing it.

The chanting speeds up. Her words are so fast that they blend together. They sound less like words and more like a scream. My heart pounds. Do I need to stop her? Plenty of soothsayers have done this before, and they've been fine. They wouldn't have written the instructions in their book if this hurt them. So maybe this is normal.

But the sound she's making is not normal. Her eyes roll back into her head. She's glowing so bright I have to look away. I hold on to the cardboard box with all my strength as she screams.

Until she stops. All at once. An eerie silence comes over the room, and the glow drops away from her like she's been pulled out of water. Her eyes open. She glances around for a second before crumpling to the floor.

I catch her limp body one-handed and brush the sweat-dampened hair from her face with a shaking hand. Her head lolls to the side, knocking into mine. Oh no. Her eyes are closed.

"Francesca?" I ask, tapping her on the cheek. "Francesca, are you okay?"

Her eyelashes flutter. She opens her eyes, gazing blearily past me for a second before focusing on me. A weak laugh slips out of me. She's alive.

"Did I do it?" she whispers.

I glance around the room. "Is Leonard still here?"

She surveys the room and shakes her head.

"The orb?" she asks. I check the box—it's still there. Untouched.

I set Francesca on the edge of the bed and bring the box over to her. She peels away the bubble wrap and picks up the orb, holding it up and examining the sphere from all angles. To me, the thing looks empty. Like some kind of decoration. An empty snow globe. But I can see Francesca's smile through the glass.

"He is in there." She glances up at me, eyes brimming with tears. "I can hear him."

She can hear him. Her words sink in, and I'm flooded with warmth.

Leonard is trapped in the orb.

We did it.

A laugh bubbles out of me. I have never been much of a jump-for-joy person, but I jump right now, clasping my hands together because otherwise I'd throw them around Francesca, and I won't risk breaking the orb. Or Francesca.

"How about you put that back in the bubble wrap?" I ask.

Francesca wraps the orb in the box. I help her stand on still-wobbly legs and fling my arms around her. She giggles.

"You did it!" I say, leaping around while still holding onto her. She taps my shoulder. I probably shouldn't be moving her too fast. "That was insane. You're a superhero."

"I am certainly not a superhero," she says.

This doesn't feel real. Leonard will never hurt any one of us ever again. Francesca is alive. So are the rest of us, and apart from the pyrotechnics and the fact that he almost killed me, it was easy.

If this creepy house had functioning windows, I'd open one and scream the news to the others, but everything is boarded up, so I pick up the box containing the orb and wave at Francesca to follow me back down the stairs. Both of us go down slowly, me going first so that we aren't standing on them at the same time to decrease our odds of crashing through them. Once she's sitting on one of the wooden chairs in the kitchen, I climb through the loose board.

"Guys!" I call, unable to keep the smile from creeping into my voice.

Jonah's eyes widen through the glasses. "You got him?" I

nod. He grins. "I knew I saw the punk. He was younger than I thought he'd be. All of us have been getting our asses kicked by a literal child."

"Not anymore," I say.

Jonah crosses the overgrown lawn in a few strides, crashing up the steps and sweeping me into his arms. My toes lift off the ground. I hug him tight, pressing my chin into his shoulder, laughing because even though Leonard tried to take him away from me, we managed to find a way back to each other.

As Jonah sets me down, his gaze lifts over my shoulder. "Frankie, you did it! You're the coolest person I have ever met."

I turn to see Francesca standing in the gap in the window. He goes to high-five with her, and she claps her hand to his.

Evangeline runs up to the broken window to hug Francesca. She hugs her the way Jonah hugged me, like it's all over and nobody died and they have each other now and can face whatever comes with a combined strength that's greater than the sum of its parts. Miles runs around the outside of the house. He raises his eyebrows, like he's asking if he's thinking what we're thinking. When I nod, he bends over his knees, gasping and laughing.

All of this is so surreal that I'm scared to believe it. Miles looks like he is, too, because he asks, "Can I see him in there?"

Jonah gives Miles the glasses and I press the orb to my stomach as we climb back through the broken glass, interrupting Evangeline and Francesca, who are making out by the window. Francesca's face turns all kinds of pink. I smile at her because there's nothing to be embarrassed about.

We crowd around the dining table as Francesca lifts the orb out of the bubble wrap and explains how you can't see each individual soul in there, but sometimes, you can see glimpses of their faces.

Miles puts on the glasses. Because he's on the other side of the table from me, I can see his eyes widen through the lenses.

"How many souls are in there?" he asks, and Francesca shrugs.

"I hope it's crowded," I say. "So Leonard really suffers."

Jonah winces. I glance at him because that's a weird thing to wince about. "You okay?"

"Peachy." He grabs my hand and squeezes it.

Miles gives me the glasses. I peer through them at the orb. Pale smoke swirls and swishes inside it, moving fast and angrily. Every couple of seconds, small faces appear. Some look bored. Some look numb. Some look like they're screaming, or saying things. I'm glad I can't hear ghosts because I'd imagine being around something like this would get old really fast.

I gesture at the orb. "So, what are we going to do with this thing?"

"Bury it in concrete and throw it in water," Jonah says, "so nobody can ever get to it."

"Burying it in concrete could actually break it," Miles says. "Concrete heats up when it cures, so this rapid change in temperature could cause stress to the glass and break it, especially if the orb is cold."

Jonah rolls his eyes. "Okay, nerd. Anyone else got anything?"

"Build a box packed with bubble wrap and magnets and store it in the back of a closet?" I suggest.

Jonah snorts. "Who's going to volunteer to store it?"

I will. I honestly don't care, but nobody likes that idea either. All of us are too busy trying to figure out the logistics of the whole thing that I don't notice Evangeline trying to get our attention until she clears her throat for the second time.

Everyone stops speaking. Looks at her.

She points over her shoulder. "I was about to lug the gear inside when I saw something is off with your camera."

Miles's brow knits. "What do you mean, off?"

He goes out to where he had the thermal camera set up to look for ghosts, and all of us follow him. It's on the front porch, pointing at the cornfield. The screen is tiny. With everyone crowding around, it's hard to see what we're looking at. The camera has turned the cornfield into a strange picture of green and turquoise, but there's a dark blue haze hovering over the stalks. In the distance, lightning flickers. I wonder if the haze is a curtain of rain blowing in over the corn.

I glance over my shoulder at Francesca, but she's staring at the rustling stalks with her mouth dropped open into a small O.

My stomach sinks. I already know the answer to this because she looks like she's staring down the barrel of a gun, but I ask it anyway: "Those are ghosts, aren't they?"

She nods. I try to press down the tide of fear rising in my body. "How many are there?"

"I ..." She glances around the field, like she's trying to count.

"Five," Jonah says. I turn around to find him using the ghost glasses to look out at the field. "And they look pissed as hell."

I put on the glasses to see for myself. All the relief and happiness I had been feeling a couple seconds ago dies.

Pale figures glide through the cornstalks, glowing like pale will-o'-the-wisps. They're all ... young. One boy can't be older than twelve. His ripped denim overalls hang over his bony frame, and a pair of broken glasses is perched on his crooked nose. An older teen hovers farther back, wild tangles of hair falling around his gaunt face. He catches my gaze and smiles, gripping his head with both hands and twisting it until it comes free, dangling from his fingertips like a gory lantern. There's a girl in modern clothing with a bullet hole going through her skull. The exit wound is massive, and half of the back of her head is missing. Another specter, closer to my age, wears a long shimmering dress, and looks put together despite the flap of skin hanging from her cheek. She looks pissed, but not as angry as the youngest girl with little blonde pigtails, who has blood smearing her chin and the area around her mouth. She picks up a rock from the ground and tosses it up in the air.

"Who the hell are these creepy kids?" Jonah hisses.

One ghost leads the group. His arms and legs look like twigs. He's so skinny and small that, at first glance, he doesn't look all that intimidating, at least until I see the murderous way he's looking at us, like he wants to rip the skin from our bones.

I point at him and glance up at Francesca. "Do you know who that is?"

"Guilherme," Francesca says. "He is one of Leonard's friends."

Jonah swears under his breath. "How many friends did this guy have?"

"I am not sure who the children are," Francesca says. "Or why they appear to be helping Leonard."

"Maybe he brought them back to this side in exchange for their help?" I guess, but Francesca shakes her head. She's right. That wouldn't explain the murderous gleam in their eyes, like they're about to kill us and enjoy doing it when we've never even met them before.

Something else occurs to me. Something that makes goosebumps break out all over my skin.

"Oh my God," I say. "Maybe Leonard promised to bring them back to life in our bodies if they helped him kill us."

"There's five of them and five of us," Jonah says. "Even I can do the math on that one."

I'm going to be sick. "What kind of person would agree to that?"

"Someone who passed before their time," Evangeline says. "Or thinks they got the short end of the stick and kicked the bucket too early."

Something whizzes past my ear. A rock crashes into the side of the house and drops onto the porch.

The girl with the pigtails chooses another rock and hurls it at us. It smashes into the porch with so much force that it splinters one of the railings. Oh God. I can't imagine what it would do to the orb.

The orb.

I glance around at everyone on the porch. All five of us are here.

"Guys?" I ask. "Where is the orb?"

Francesca's eyes widen. She looks back at the house just as a loud crash comes from inside.

47

JONAh

I jump through the broken window and run to the table. The orb is where we left it, in a box and wrapped in half the postal industry's supply of bubble wrap.

Shiloh clutches the box to her stomach. "Oh, thank God."

"Don't thank anyone yet." I pocket a smoke bomb. "Especially not that guy."

Miles pulls a magnet off the giant pile on the table, holding it out in front of himself like a weapon.

"Remember," he says, breathless and sounding all panicky. "Ghosts probably can't touch you as long as you stay close to the table, but they can still throw things at you."

Probably. Well, that's comforting.

All five of us stand with our backs to the table. I face the loose board and side-eye Shiloh.

"So, what's our plan, Scoob?" I ask.

"We need to get out of here," she says, holding one of those horseshoe magnets out in front of her.

"I'm with you there," I say, "but how are we supposed to do that?"

"We fight our way out and run."

"Run where?" I ask. "Back to your house and lead those ghosts to your mom and Max?"

"You got a better idea?" she snaps. "I didn't exactly plan for an entire army of ghosts to come steal our bodies."

"Five."

"What?"

"There are five ghosts," I say. "One each."

She glares at me so hard that she almost looks like Miles.

"I'm not trying to be a jerk," I say. "I'm just trying to figure out how to get out of here because I don't do creepy murderous ghost children any more than I do needles."

"Let's go to my house," Shiloh says. "Maybe we can lose them."

"Go to my car," Miles says somewhere behind me. "So we can drive there."

Okay. Miles's car. It's parked right outside. We just got to get there. Which we can do because we're, like, professional ghost hunters now.

A door slams upstairs. We all look up.

I grab the lasso and shake it out in my hand. This is so dumb. I'd only been messing around with it before because it made Shiloh laugh. I didn't think I'd have to use it, but I guess the world hates me. Winding the loop around over my head, I throw it at a chair to practice. It lands four feet to the left and catches nothing but air. I'm going to die.

Miles picks up a magnet. So does Evangeline, and Shiloh hands the orb to Francesca because it's safest in her hands. The room's real quiet, except for the wind beating against the house. I tighten my grip on what, in my hands, is the world's most useless weapon.

A couple of seconds go by before the loose board creaks open. The screech of that rusty screw makes me wince. It drills into my ears until it stops.

The board stays open by itself. I can see my breath. Shiloh's nose and cheeks have turned pink, like she's standing outside in the winter on some early morning. She's got her lips pressed in a determined line. In her hands, that magnet is a weapon.

A weapon she could use to bash my head in.

Where the hell did that come from? No, she will not bash my head in. She loves me.

Shiloh loves me.

Remembering her saying those words is making me want to smile, but I force myself to focus. Ghosts are coming in here to kill us. That's what I need to pay attention to right now.

The board slams down. I search the shadows for any sign of ghosts, but everything's still.

"Okay, Franks," I say, hoping I don't sound as terrified as I feel. "You gotta be our eyes. Where are they?"

"Everywhere," she says. "There are so many of them ... I do not know how to—"

"*Try.*"

In the corner of my eye, a lampshade lifts into the air across from Miles. I point at it.

"*Incoming!*"

The lamp flies at Miles. He smacks it away. Pieces of broken ceramic hit my legs.

Something hard smashes into my shoulder. I yell.

Shiloh turns to me. "You okay?"

I nod. A rock drops next to my sneaker. I bet it was thrown by that creepy little ghost girl.

Francesca's doing a crap job at being our eyes. Who has the ghost glasses? The things are sitting on the table. The scratched lenses warp reality like a funhouse mirror, but it's better than being blind. I hold the heavy things up to my eyes in time to see the little pigtailed girl with blood around her mouth hovering not two feet from my face.

I yell and stagger backward into the table, snapping the lasso up at the girl. It cuts through her. Wisps of ghost energy billow around the slice for a couple of seconds before she puts herself back together.

I slice the girl again. I feel bad for beating up on a kid, but this kid wants to wear my body like a skin suit, so my guilt doesn't last long. Why does she have blood all around her mouth, anyway? Did she, like, eat someone before she died or something?

She grabs a shard of ceramic on the floor. Her hands pass right through it. All this lassoing must be weakening her.

I swipe her with the lasso again. She rushes away from me, disappearing through the wall.

Shiloh cries out. I glance over to find her rubbing her arm. A warped version of the headless ghost rushes at her through the open kitchen door. Something glints in his hand. I don't need the goggles to know what it is.

The ghost raises the knife, eyes trained on Shiloh. She doesn't see him.

But I do. I tackle her to the ground just as the knife lets loose from the guy's hand. I roll over so my back hits the wood first, and she crashes onto me.

The knife sticks into the chair behind us. Shiloh glances down at me, her blonde hair hanging down and brushing against my cheeks.

You should have let him stab her.

I force the thought from my mind. I can feel the foolery there, trying to get control of me again, but I won't let it. This is my girl. Nothing's going to take her away from me again.

Shiloh rolls off me and helps me to my feet. She grabs the lampshade and holds it out in front of her like a shield, deflecting the shards of glass, bricks, and pieces of broken furniture coming our way. Knowing she's behind me fuels me. I won't let any of these creepy fucks lay a hand on her.

"We need to get to the window," Shiloh says. Her shoulder blades are sharp against mine.

Going to the window means stepping out of the range of the magnets. "You want to make a run for it?"

"Clear a path for the others." She grunts as she shoves the lampshade to deflect something.

Okay. I pass her the ghost glasses and the lasso. "Will you cover me?"

She nods. I take a deep breath. Here goes nothing.

I sprint across the room, dropping to my knees in front of the loose board. My fingers tear at the wood. It's jammed. Of course it is. With a yell, I wrench up on it. The board comes free with a crack.

"Jonah, look out!" Shiloh screams.

I turn around. I'm not wearing the glasses, so I don't know what I'm looking out for. Not until I notice the wooden dresser tipping down onto me. Plates slide out and crash to the floor. I hurl myself sideways as it comes down, smashing into the floor where I was kneeling just seconds ago. Splinters spray outward like shrapnel. I raise my arms to cover my face. Once the noise quiets down, I glance up to see the wooden monstrosity blocking the window and trapping us inside.

Ears ringing, I run back to Shiloh and the others, vaulting over smashed furniture, and skidding through shattered glass.

"Okay," I say, taking the ghost lasso back. "So there goes that plan."

"Wh-what are we g-going to do now?" Miles asks. He sounds a lot like his old self, all squeaky, even though his voice is still deeper than before.

There's a deep crunching sound above our heads. A jagged crack slices across the ceiling. Dust and flakes of paint rain down.

Before any of us have time to react, the light fixture plunges toward the table, stopped only by a wire. Understanding of what's about to happen hits me just in time. I yank Shiloh forward as the fixture smashes onto the table.

Screams pierce through the air. Still clutching Shiloh, I back away from the table, eyes darting around. There's so much dust. The flashlights are all over the place. I can't see a thing.

Something whizzes past my ear. Another rock. Shiloh coughs into her elbow. We need to get out of here.

I tell the others to follow me. More debris comes down as I push Shiloh in front of me, doing my best to shield her as we stumble toward the basement. I can barely see through the choking dust.

But I can see enough to make it to the creepy wooden door. I shove the rickety thing open and urge Shiloh through. Behind me, Francesca screams as a piece of ceiling just misses her.

I start to follow Shiloh down when the door smashes into my face. I cry out, stumbling back and cupping my nose. My palm comes back red.

Stars flash in my vision, but enough adrenaline is pumping through my veins to keep me going. I jiggle the door handle. It won't budge.

I slam my palm against it. *"Shiloh!"*

No answer. I throw my shoulder into it. The door holds fast. Something's blocking it.

Francesca places the orb box in my hands and raises her bandaged hand to the door. Her eyebrows and nose scrunch up, and when I try the knob again, it opens.

I flash her a grin. I'm over being surprised by what Francesca can do. She can do anything. I give the orb back to her and take off down the steep concrete stairs, praying I don't trip on one but not slowing down because I can't see Shiloh and I need to make sure she's okay. Cobwebs stick to my face, but I pull them out of my eyes and don't slow down. I reach the bottom of the pitch-black cellar, scanning for Shiloh.

Something slams into my gut, forcing the air from my lungs. I double over with a cry. The snow shovel swings down again, but I grab it mid-arc and hurl it away.

The shovel lands at Shiloh's feet. She stares at it, breathing hard. Some weird expression comes over her face. Like she's not surprised the shovel hit me.

Like she's the one who hit me with it.

The corners of my vision blur. Shiloh stands there, all smug. My heart pounds in my ears. Shiloh did not hit me with the shovel. But the thoughts are louder, screaming in my head.

She's possessed.

She wants to kill you.

She is not who you think she is.

I cover my ears, but it does nothing to drown out the noise or stop the images flashing in my head. I can picture her with the knife, grinning as she shoved me back into the flames. She wants to kill me.

It's not real. It's the foolery. But it feels so real.

I push the images away, but more come at me. I'm seriously losing my shit here. I'm going to hurt her again.

"Jonah?" Shiloh asks. "Are you okay?"

I shake my head and dig my nails into my temples, wishing I could claw out my brain. I feel her hands on my wrists, yanking them away from my face.

"You're good," she says, her brown eyes boring into mine. "I'm good, you're good, and we really need to get out of here. Can you run?"

Run. Sure, yes, I can run. She hauls me to my feet. I entwine my fingers with hers, focusing on how strong her fingers feel between mine as she leads me across the room and through the cellar doors.

A piercing scream comes from behind me. I turn to see that an invisible force has grabbed Evangeline's hair. It yanks her backward and knocks her off her feet, dragging her across the concrete as she thrashes and kicks.

Before I can react, Shiloh hurls a magnet into the space behind her. Evangeline's hair is released, and she lies still.

Shiloh is so badass. She's got me. And it's good that she does, because my heart is still pounding too hard for me to pay attention to anything else. Shiloh pushes up on the bulkhead. I go to help her and pull back on the latch as hard as I can, but the damn thing has rusted.

I try two-handed. So does Shiloh. With a screech, it gives way, and we get the doors open.

Shiloh climbs through. She reaches down for my hand and helps me through the door. Gripping the rough stone, I pull myself up. Searing pain flares through my hand. I wince, turning it over to find blood streaming from a gash across my palm.

There's no time for pain. I crouch through the bulkhead and stumble out onto the grass. Shiloh holds the door for the others. I stand behind her. The steady sound of her breathing quiets the screaming in my head. I'm okay. She's okay.

Miles has slung Evangeline over his shoulder and has to almost bend in half to get out. He cracks his head hard on the frame.

"You okay?" I ask.

He nods, and gapes at the blood running from my hand. "What happened to you?"

"It looks worse than it is."

Miles lowers Evangeline onto the grass. Tears cut through the blood and dirt on her cheeks, but she's fine. Just scared.

Francesca is the only one still inside. She drags her feet across the uneven floor, each step looking like a painful effort as she tries to get to us. Her cane is nowhere to be seen. She's holding the orb box in both hands.

"Run!" I call to her. "You gotta get out of there!"

Something knocks into Francesca from behind. She flies forward. Her arms shoot out as she crashes to the floor, and the box flies from her grip. The orb rolls onto the concrete, snagging on every dip and bump in the floor, daring any of those ghosts to come and break it.

I'd be lying if I said part of me didn't want that to happen. I'm destined to spend eternity in that stupid thing with Leonard and who knows what other ghosts good ol' Wilma put in there, but at least we got Leonard trapped. We can all live the rest of our lives without needing to worry about him. What happened to Aunt Moe won't happen to anyone else. He won't be able to hurt Shiloh, Miles, or Francesca ever again. If the only person he'll hurt is me once I'm dead, I can live with that.

So I run down the stairs and scoop up the orb, getting blood all over the glass like the first time I touched it. Everyone screams at me to hurry. I shove the orb back into its box and scoop an arm under Francesca's shoulders, dragging her up the steps.

Outside, I give Shiloh the orb and pull the ring on one of the smoke bombs, tossing it into the cellar. I have no clue what the smoke will do to ghosts, but it seems better than nothing. Orange smoke pours out of the doors as I drop them closed, even though I know it won't hold the ghosts for long.

Shiloh runs down the driveway. I follow her around to the front of the house. I see two cars through the warped lenses. One I recognize as Officer Zweering's sedan. The other is a cop car. Before I have time to react, the barrel of a gun appears inches from my face.

48

Miles

In my old life, encountering a police officer who was mad at me could have easily been one of my recurring nightmares. I never broke the rules. I got a stomachache when an authority figure so much as offered me a gentle suggestion, so I'm surprised when now, staring down the barrel of Lindsey's gun, I don't feel like I'm about to throw up.

Lindsey has all five of us kneeling in a line like we're about to face a firing squad. All the weapons we once had are lying in front of us on the overgrown grass. Mud seeps through the fabric of my jeans and makes my knees numb. The box with the orb in it is lying upturned in front of Francesca. I hate it that the box is lying right here in the grass, and that a few pieces of bubble wrap are all that's protecting the orb from the elements. One angry ghost could pick it up and smash it. Or one really upset police officer. We could make a run for it. It's just her alone out here and there are five of us, including me, and I'm bigger than she is. We could get away from her pretty easily if we split up, but not all of us would get away, and it would send the message to her, an actual police officer, that we were doing something wrong, which could blow back on all of us when we're so close to this being over. So we can't run. I'm going to have to talk our way out of this.

Lindsey offers me a smug grin. "I knew it. Oh, I so totally knew it."

Panic rises in my body like a tide, but I push it down. "Lindsey, this is not what it looks like."

She scoffs. "Oh, yeah? Enlighten me, Randall. What does it look like? Because to me, it looks like you're trespassing with a bunch of teenagers—one of whom was just in jail for murder, another who you used to call the bane of your existence, and one who's been reported missing not once but twice in the span of a week. So tell me, Randall, what is happening here?"

Shiloh raises an eyebrow, as if asking who this person is and why she's calling me by my first name. Any display of friendship with Shiloh will not help me right now, so I keep my eyes on Lindsey. In the corner of my eye, a cornstalk bends too far to the left to be normal. It stays like that. A lump forms in my throat. The ghosts are still around us. A few seconds ago, they were trying to kill us, and now we can do nothing to fight back. It's only a matter of time before one of them makes a move. I need to get Lindsey to go away before that happens. I wish my AP Psychology class had spent less time teaching me about mice and more about how to navigate this particular emotional situation.

"Lindsey, please," I say. The corn stalk snaps back into an upright position. "This is the worst possible timing."

"I'm sorry if this is not *convenient* for you," she spits, "but I don't care. Do you want to tell me what's going on here, or should I just ask these guys?" She waves her gun at everyone but me.

I'd rather not go into any kind of detail about what's happening. Lindsey wouldn't believe me, anyway. If things had gone the way I wanted, I never would've seen her again. Now that Leonard is trapped in the orb, I could've moved away from Bethany and learned how to be this new person I've become without having to pretend to be someone I'm not. Everyone at the police department could still think I'm Randall Zweering, and nobody would have been the wiser, because who's going to believe the insane story that I'm the ghost of someone else possessing the body of the real Randall Zweering, who is actually dead?

A raindrop hits my cheek. I glance up to see that the storm clouds have covered the moon.

Another drop comes down. Then another. There's a dramatic clap of thunder and then, all at once, the sky opens up.

Rain pours onto us. So much of it comes down so suddenly that it takes my brain a couple of seconds to catch up to the fact that I'm kneeling in a torrential downpour that's colder and more powerful than the shower at my apartment. The rain gets under my jacket and glues the fabric to my skin. It sticks to my eyelashes and gets in my eyes, making it almost impossible to see anything.

Lindsey doesn't seem to like it either. I can see it register on her face that she doesn't stand a chance of keeping us all in line if it's raining and she can't see, so she tells us to stand up and keep our hands above our heads. Francesca goes to pick up the orb box. Lindsey turns her gun on her.

"Stop," she says. "Leave that there."

Oh no. Here comes a stomachache.

"She can't leave it there," I say, and immediately curse my big mouth. Now Lindsey knows how important it is to us. Even if she doesn't know why. So I might as well see it through. "Please, Lindsey, I'll do anything you want, but we can't leave that behind."

Lindsey seems to consider it for a second, but then shakes her head and angles the gun to the collapsed wooden barn behind the house. "I'm getting us out of the rain."

"No," I say. "Please, you don't understand, we can't leave that here—"

"Go."

Jonah glances at me as if asking if we should run. So does

Shiloh. Both of them are so impulsive and quick to run and will never trust authority figures for different reasons of their own, but they don't think things through, and they will go right to jail if they run now.

I remember the first day I met Lindsey, and how she joked around with Randall, like they were good pals. She'd called Randall her best friend. I doubt she would admit it, but that kind of feeling for a person doesn't go away overnight. Surely I can get her to believe me.

I just hope I can do it fast because leaving that orb unprotected in the grass is begging for one of those ghosts to come and smash it. Lindsey makes us all stand up and walk toward the barn in a single-file line. I scan the yellowed corn stalks for any sign of ghost activity. Do they know what the orb is? Can they hear Leonard in there, screaming to be let out? I sure hope not.

I also hope Lindsey will not make us go inside this barn, because it might very well be one of the most terrifying structures I've ever seen. It looks like it has been on its last legs since the day it was built. Or like something made by that pig from that children's story who builds a house of sticks. The roof is caving in. Pieces of the wall are missing. The structure is clearly no longer being used and I doubt it will provide us much shelter from the rain, but Lindsey marches us all in there anyway, through a hole in the wall from where the siding has literally fallen down.

In here, there's still rain coming through the roof, but not as much. The water worsens the smell of rotten wood and rusted metal, as well as the faint stench of livestock. Because it's pitch-black outside, it's hard for me to see anything through the shadows, but my eyes have adjusted enough that I can make out the vague shape of a tractor that looks a hundred years old, an old plow, and some scythes and other tools leaning against the walls. I'd guess this barn used to store hay because there's still some left on the floor. I can see the faint outline of an old-fashioned pulley system mounted to the ceiling beams. There are ropes threaded through a series of worn metal wheels and shafts, forming a complex network of pulleys. The main line is anchored to a massive iron hook near the peak of the roof. It's bigger than the biggest dumbbell Randall Zweering has in his home gym. I'd bet it's heavier, too. Seventy or eighty pounds, easy. This apparatus must have been used to haul bales of hay up to the loft. I imagine generations of farmers operating the system, heaving their body weight onto the ropes to lift hundreds of pounds of hay up to the second floor. The pulleys and gears creak and groan, barely hanging on to the overhead beams. I give the hook a wide berth, grateful my parents are academics and I wasn't born a farmer.

Lindsey turns on her flashlight. The beam of yellow light is blinding after the inside of the house. She has us kneel with our backs to the door. Pieces of hay dig into my shins.

My heart hammers in my chest. I need to get her to stop this, but telling her the truth about how I'm not really Randall Zweering is going to take a lot of explaining, and I don't have time for it. I need to focus on telling her something that I can back up with proof.

"Lindsey," I say. "What I'm about to tell you is going to sound crazy, but I need you to listen to me because right now, we're all in danger. Including you and anyone you might have called for backup."

She waits for me to talk. I picture the orb out in the rain, unguarded, and my throat closes as I imagine everything we've worked so hard for being destroyed while we're trapped in here. Our survival hinges on Lindsey deciding to do something completely uncharacteristic and believe me. I doubt I'd believe her if I were in her shoes.

"So, uh …" I start, even though I don't know how to start. This isn't something you can just start. Except that it is because that's what I'm about to do. "Ghosts are real."

Lindsey pauses. To her credit, her angry look cracks and is temporarily replaced by total bewilderment.

"Excuse me?" she asks.

"I know it sounds crazy," I say. "But it's true, and there are some super evil ghosts in this place who are trying to kill us right now."

Lindsey stares at me. So does everyone else. Shiloh's looking at me like I have lost my marbles, which I guess I must have if I think what I'm doing is a good idea.

"I got pulled into this a couple of weeks ago when a ghost tried to kill me," I continue, trying to spin a version of this story that doesn't involve the real Randall Zweering dying, because a big part of this plan relies on Lindsey's existing friendship with Randall, and I need to be careful not to cross the line between off-his-rocker and completely and utterly certifiable. "Shiloh and Jonah saved my life, and I found out there were some super evil things happening in our town. I needed to help stop them."

She continues staring at me. She doesn't seem to know how to process any of this information.

Behind her, I hear something creak like a door hinge squeaking in the wind. I glance at Francesca, who is focusing on something deep in the shadows. Her eyes are brimming with tears.

I try hard to stay focused on Lindsey. "There's so much I can tell you about all of this and I promise, I'll tell you anything you want to know, but right now, there are a bunch of ghosts around us who would be more than happy to see us all die, including you. So please, I'm begging you—let us go."

Lindsey finally finds her words. "You're telling me there are ghosts in here right now?" She looks like she's going to start laughing any second, but there's a part of her, a tiny part, that looks a little unsure of herself.

Cold air winds around my arms. My heart lodges itself in my throat and makes it hard for me to croak out the word, "Yes."

She scoffs. "Do you *seriously* think—"

"I can prove it," I blurt out, and she stops talking. "I will prove to you that ghosts are real."

"And how are you going to do that?" she asks.

"There's a pair of glasses on Shiloh's face," I say. "It will let you see them."

"Do you think I'm a moron?"

"I have a thermal camera," I say, as the rope to the pulley system trembles like someone has grabbed it and is waving it around. "Behind the house. Come on, Lindsey, you know me. I'm a rational person. I've never believed in anything supernatural, but I swear this is real."

I open my eyes more, hoping to show her I'm serious. She looks like she's considering it. Something flutters in my stomach like maybe—just maybe—this is going to work.

But then she reaches for her handheld radio to call for backup. I open my mouth to tell her not to when a scythe shoots out from the shadows.

It arcs through the air. I yell at everyone to drop to the ground and hit the floor so hard it knocks the wind out of me. There is a scream. I pick up my head to make out Evangeline in the shadows, all the way at the other end of the line. She stares down at her stomach. Blood is soaking through the front of her gray sweatshirt.

Evangeline cups the wound on her stomach. Her face doesn't knit like she's in pain. She just looks surprised. The scythe lies on the floor. The blade is covered in her blood.

Francesca screams, a bloodcurdling noise that sounds like it's being torn from her.

Lindsey gapes at the scythe that moved all on its own, and then at Evangeline as she falls to her knees.

Lindsey spins around and points her gun into the shadows where the scythe came from. "Who's out there?"

Francesca runs to Evangeline. So does Shiloh. There's blood on both their hands. Evangeline scrunches her face up as she holds her palms to the wound, as though she's trying to stem the flow of blood or hold the skin together. The blade must have gone in deep.

Lindsey changes the grip on her gun. She yells for them to keep their hands up, but they ignore her.

Jonah stands up, wiping his hands down the front of his pants.

"Call 911," I say. "Get them to come for Evangeline."

He flips open his phone, fumbling with the buttons, then holds the phone up over his head.

"No service," he says.

"Could you go outside and get a signal?" I ask. He nods and runs out of the barn.

Lindsey follows him with her gun, but it's not like she's going to shoot him, so she points the gun at me instead. I raise my arms, but she knows she's losing control of the situation.

"Lindsey, listen to me," I say, standing up slowly. "A ghost just threw that at us, and we need an ambulance. Can you radio for one?"

Her gun trembles. "Who threw that scythe?"

"A ghost," I say, and she rolls her eyes. "We were all standing right in front of you. You saw us. There's no way we could have thrown that. You need to call an ambulance. Call for help. Do *something*."

She looks paralyzed. I've seen Lindsey in action before. She's by far the smartest and most capable police officer in Bethany, which is why she was the one I was most scared of finding out I was a fraud, but she has to digest this insane reality in real-time, so it's more than understandable that she needs a second to process everything.

She lowers her gun. She presses a button on her radio and calls for an ambulance. My shoulders slump. I turn to see Jonah running through the barn doors.

"I got through to someone," he says, holding up the phone. "An ambulance is on its way."

A loud scraping sound comes from above us. I look up to see the corroded pulley hook ripping free from its anchor. The hook swings down on the rope in a sweeping arc, picking up speed as it goes the length of the barn. Jonah glances up just as the monstrous hook crashes into his torso.

49

Shiloh

The impact echoes through the barn. Jonah flies sideways, crashing into the tractor tire and crumpling to the floor. The pulley hook creaks back and forth on the rope, looming over his body.

"Jonah!"

I run to him and drop to my knees at his side. He grunts, his eyelids fluttering as he leans his head against the tire. I run my eyes over him, searching for any visible blood or injury. There's not a lot of light in here. Just the glow coming from Lindsey's flashlight, which is dim and not trained on us, but it's enough for me to see him. His left arm hangs wrong, like his shoulder has been torn out of its socket and is broken in more than one place.

"Oh God," I say. "How bad is it?"

I can tell from his grimace that it's not good. Being hit by an eighty-pound weight propelled by ghosts will do a lot of damage. He shakes his head. My ribs tighten.

"The ambulance is coming," I say. "I'll get you some help, okay?"

He jerks his chin down at his shoulder. "My … arm."

His voice is hoarse and gurgling, like every word is a struggle to get out. It's not his voice at all. I try not to let my worry show on my face.

"The doctors will fix it," I say. "They do that sort of thing all the time."

He gasps for air, but his breath is shallow. I hear a crash behind me, followed by a shout. It's only been a couple of minutes since he called 911. I listen for any sign of sirens, or any clue that the ambulance is on its way, but I can hear nothing over the sounds behind me.

Jonah coughs, a hard and painful sound. Blood bubbles on his lips.

I wipe the blood off his chin with a trembling hand. "You're going to be fine. Do you hear me?"

Even as I say the words, doubt creeps in. It's taking too long. He's not breathing right. But I need to convince myself that it's okay as much as I need to convince him, so I keep talking.

"You're not going to die. The doctors will give you a cast for your arm, and I'm going to sign it as Scooby."

Jonah coughs again. More blood.

I hold back the tears blurring my vision. "And even if you do die, it's okay, because Francesca will bring you back."

Jonah shakes his head. I don't know why.

"She can do it," I say, my voice breaking. "You know she can."

Jonah grabs my wrist with waning strength. His throat rolls as he swallows, like he has to prepare for the effort to speak. His mouth opens, face screwing up as he forces out more ragged words: "I … won't see you."

What is he talking about? Of course he's going to see me again.

"I actually have this cool pair of glasses that lets me see dead people," I say, wiping the tears from my cheeks and trying to make my tone lighthearted so that I don't panic. "So I won't even have time to miss you before Francesca brings you back."

He squeezes my hand, willing me to understand, but I don't. I glance up at the barn door. There are no sirens or flashing ambulance lights. What is taking them so long?

Some of the strength leaves Jonah's grip. I don't know where the blood is coming from. Or what I can do to save him.

Jonah wheezes for breath. The sound is gurgling. He brings his hand up to my face, brushing his thumb against my lips. He tries to take a breath, but all that comes out is a wheeze. Because he can't breathe.

The light disappears from his eyes. A sharp pain drives into my heart.

"Jonah?"

His head lolls forward. I catch it, holding it back up. His eyes stare forward at nothing. I feel for his pulse, for the steady rhythm of his heart pumping in his veins, but it's not there.

"Jonah?" His name is more of a sob than a sound. "No no no. Jonah. Please come back."

He doesn't answer. Because he's gone.

A scream rips from my body. It sounds far away and all-consuming at once, coming from some place deep inside the chasm inside me. I gather Jonah's body in my arms and press him against me as sobs course through me, breaking my ribcage and splitting me in half.

Francesca can fix this. She needs to fix this. I turn and look around for her, but I can't see her in the shadows. "Francesca, *help*!"

She hurries over to me.

"You can fix him," I say, snot and tears running from my nose and eyes. "Put his ghost back."

I know that doing that will be hard on her. Jonah would say it's not worth the risk, but it is. It *is*.

Francesca's eyes dart around the space above Jonah. "I'm sorry, Shiloh, but his soul is not here."

"What do you mean, it's not here?" I clutch him tighter, like holding onto him can stop him from going away from me. "Is it still in his body?"

"He must have already gone to the other side."

"You can go find him, though, right?" I ask, my voice breaking. Jonah can't die. I won't let him. But there's nothing I can do about it if Francesca can't find his soul.

Miles appears next to me, shouldering me out of the way and lying Jonah flat on the ground. He laces his hands together and pumps his chest. After almost a minute, he pinches Jonah's nose and breathes air into his mouth, resuming compressions. I shift back onto my ankles and wrap my arms around my stomach, rocking back and forth as sobs wrack my body. I replay Jonah's voice in my head, trying to remember what he sounded like so I can hold onto it.

Something occurs to me. The sob dies in my throat.

I won't see you again.

Jonah said that to me. Just a few minutes ago. Did he know his ghost wouldn't appear when he died?

How would he know something like that?

I glare at Jonah's dead eyes. It's not normal for Francesca to be unable to find his ghost. His ghost had to have gone somewhere.

"Is it normal for him to have already gone to the other side?" I ask Francesca.

"Not really," she says. "Usually, souls who have unfinished business or died in a traumatic fashion remain on earth for longer."

Jonah had unfinished business. He died when he was not supposed to.

I drop my eyes to the cardboard box sitting on the ground. There's an itching feeling at the base of my skull. I run into the rain and search through the grass to find the glasses in the mud. The lenses are covered in water. I do my best to dry them with my shirt as I rush back into the barn.

I lift the orb out of its wrapping. The glass is covered in blood. It's slick in my hands and even feels fragile. The raindrops on the glasses warp the image, but there's no mistaking the souls swooshing around in there.

"What are you doing?" Miles asks, glancing up at me but not stopping his compressions. "Shiloh, what are you thinking right now?"

"Is there something wrong with the glass ball?" Francesca asks.

I hold the orb closer to my face, almost pressing my nose against the smudged glass. I catch glimpses of fists pounding on the glass. Open-mouthed screams. They appear and disappear into the swirl of energy so fast that it almost feels like I'm imagining them until I catch a flash of an eye staring back at me. And not just any eye. A blue eye that I know. One I'd know anywhere.

I scream and smash the orb against the side of the tractor.

50

FrANCeSCA

The glass ball breaks against the rusted red tractor, showering Shiloh with a spray of tiny shards.

I whirl around, raising my hands to cover my face as pieces of glass graze my skin. Miles shouts at Shiloh. He sounds rather angry. He has every right to be, considering the long way he traveled to fetch the orb. I turn back to ask what could have made Shiloh do such a thing when a gust of wind blows into my face.

This is no ordinary wind. It is so cold that it turns the air into vaporous ice, searing my skin in every place it touches. The blast freezes the raindrops in mid-air. The leaks streaming through the broken roof transform into icicles poised to impale.

A blinding light pierces my eyes. I shield them with my hand and squint through my fingers at the ball of light hovering where the glass orb had just been. It shines against the dark. No sound comes from it. I would have assumed that the souls in the orb would jump at the opportunity to escape, but that does not seem to be the case, because the souls are as closely tied together as they had been when the glass had encased them.

The ball of light pulses like a tiny sun. The orb thrums with the energy of something living, writhing as though something—or somebody—is attempting to break free.

A wisp of smoke unfurls from it, curling up into the shadows. A small arm springs from the ball of light, bending at the elbow and pushing against it. I grip Shiloh's wrist, pulling her away from it because she cannot see what I see.

An entire person springs free of the tangle. She tumbles out, somersaulting and stopping in front of me. The soul is hardly bigger than a doll I would have played with when I was young. This woman appears to have died in her middle age and has unruly brown hair, a pointed nose, and bangs that curl over her eyes. Her high-waisted jeans and tweed coat look fairly recent.

She stretches her hand out to me. Her arm doubles in size. One by one, her limbs bend and stretch like she is connected to a balloon pump that is inflating her into a bigger version of herself.

Once she returns to normal size, a tearful smile grows on her face.

"Thank you," she whispers.

Throwing her head back in laughter, she shoots upward and disappears through the ceiling.

A groan comes from inside the pulsing light. More hands and feet emerge. All of the souls appear to have been trapped together for so long that they have lost their real shapes and have become a tangle of hands and feet and bodies, stretching, groaning, morphing, screaming, pulsing, and fighting to recover their original forms.

I yelp as another soul springs free—a bearded man wearing a hat in the shape of a cloche. A wide leather belt cinches around his flowing white blouse, which is decorated with delicate stitches made to look like flowers.

I imagine Jonah making a joke with me, telling me I had freed Santa Claus, but Jonah is gone. This man does not appear to be from our time. His eyes dart between Shiloh and me before he vanishes through the wall.

Another soul breaks free. Then another. Wisps of energy unwind from the orb-like tendrils snaking around Shiloh's arms. Goosebumps rise on her skin, and her breath comes out as fog.

A tendril of energy winds through the air across the barn, all the way to Evangeline, who is lying unmoving on the floor beside the police officer. I want to run back to her and tell her that help is coming, but Officer Owens is there, putting pressure on her abdomen. Officer Owens assured me she called an ambulance, but her lip was trembling when she did so, and I am not sure I have ever seen a grown-up look so afraid. I am not sure I have ever been so afraid, either.

But I cannot go over there right now. I cannot look at anything except for the ball of light.

Shiloh's teeth begin to chatter. "Do you see Jonah?" she asks. "Is he there?"

Miles stops doing CPR. "Why would Jonah be in there?"

"Because he sold his soul to the Soothsayer," Shiloh says, wiping at the tears that are still streaming down her face.

Miles says a bad word. I have never heard him use such language before.

In a flash, the pulsing ball of light explodes. The force blows me backward. Shiloh slams into me, and my sluggish feet tangle with one another underneath me and send me onto the hay. The jolt of the impact is disorienting. I rub my eyes and open them.

Souls soar away in all directions. They vanish through the walls too quickly for me to glimpse their faces. I try to find Leonard among the souls, but it is as though I am attempting to identify a person when all I can see is a flash of light. I search for him. Try to glimpse a tiny three-fingered hand. But one by one, every soul disappears until only one remains.

Jonah hovers above the pieces of broken glass. He is much paler than the other souls. I have spent so much time with the dead that they feel as alive to me as living people. Perhaps it is because I am accustomed to seeing Jonah in his body, but this version of him does not look alive at all. His soul has not fully taken shape yet. His feet are mere wisps of shapeless energy, and his once black hair is now a somber gray. Blood trails from his forehead down his temple. His forearm and upper arm both seem to have acquired extra elbows, causing his entire arm to bend much farther back than normal. If a person dies a traumatic death, the marks of it stay with them for a long time. Sometimes forever. I wonder how long Jonah's marks will stay with him.

A heavy feeling settles over me like a snake is wrapping around my body. I have never felt grief for anybody other than my mother. Grief comes when you will never see a person again, and usually I do see people after they die. But Jonah should still be alive.

He has lost so much. The gleam in his blue eyes when he smiles. The warmth in his skin. Certainly the fondness he used to have for me, judging by the anger wrinkling his face.

I tap Shiloh on the shoulder. "You should put on the soul glasses."

Shiloh's face lights up. "Is he here? Did you find him?"

I nod. Shiloh fumbles to put the glasses on her face.

Jonah points at the broken glass beneath him. "What the hell did you let Shiloh do?"

The ferocity in his tone makes me flinch. "Shiloh felt—"

"I don't care what Shiloh felt!" he snaps. "Leonard is gone. We *had* him, and now he's gone."

Pressure builds in my chest. I search the faces of the lingering souls, but none of them are Leonard.

"Does Shiloh have a death wish?" Jonah rages on. "What does she think will happen now? Leonard will not stop until we all look like this. Every single one of us is going to die because of what she just did."

Jonah's transparent figure blurs. Each of his words drives a needle into my heart.

"I died for *nothing*," he says, trying to kick his own body's arm but passing through it. Miles has not given up doing CPR, even though Jonah is dead.

Shiloh unleashes a torrent of accusations at Jonah. He snaps back at her, his voice rising to match her tone, until both of them are screaming at each other. I press my hands even tighter over my ears, wishing I could drown them out.

I cannot listen anymore. "Stop it."

"Just tell Shiloh—" Jonah begins.

"Stop it!" I exclaim. "Please, stop it!"

I crumple to the ground, my hands clasped over my ears as tears spill out of my eyes. I cry so hard my entire body trembles, tears falling on the front of my shirt and onto my pants as a series of hiccups runs through me. I had been so sure we had succeeded. That Leonard was gone for good. I am not sure if I can fight him any longer. Every part of my body hurts too much for me to even walk far on my own, let alone be the same person I used to be. I have given so much of myself to Leonard and even more to stop him, and none of it has been worth it, because he is still going to win. I turn to Evangeline, still lying on the hay with Officer Owens bent over her. Leonard will take her away from me. He will take Miles and Shiloh and everybody I have ever cared about.

A laugh sounds from above me. It is sinister and clear as day, echoing inside my head and raising all the baby hairs on my arms.

I glance up. Leonard's soul peers down at me from the rafters. There is a gleeful smile on his face.

"You don't oughta wear such a long face," he says in his lazy drawl, more high-pitched now that he is speaking in his real voice. "I always knew you weren't gonna come out on top."

I lower my hands from my ears. "This is not over!"

"Oh, but it is." Leonard drifts down to the ground with perfect control of his movements. He is young. My age. "What're you gonna do to me, now? You ain't gonna catch me. You ain't going to kill me. Face it, Cesca. You're beat. And soon enough, you'll be dead. Cause I'm gonna kill you, and there ain't nothin' you can do to stop me."

He moves toward Evangeline, whose breaths have grown ragged. I step toward her, but she is all the way across the barn from me, and my feet are sluggish.

"I thought Eveline was my pal," Leonard says, "but she ain't. An' if she ain't mine, then she don't belong to nobody."

The urgent voices around me fade to a dull throb in the background, as if my head is underwater. A clammy chill creeps up the back of my neck. My cheeks burn with scalding heat, contrasting with the cold sweat beading on my temples. The fingers on my unbandaged hand twitch, nails biting into my palm and providing momentary relief from the pressure building inside me. Something powerful builds in the core of my being. Every cell, nerve, and fiber of me cries out for release, but I will not let go.

Leonard laughs harder, clapping his hand to his stomach and pointing as though I am on display at the circus. As if I am somebody who deserves to be ridiculed.

Leonard's laughs stretch and deepen. My vision tunnels. There is a tug deep inside my chest, as though some long-buried part of me is rising to infuse my weary body with energy.

I am not something to be laughed at. I do not care what anybody says.

Raising my palms, I push them toward Leonard with seismic force. The laughter dies on his lips. I curl my fingers inward, twisting my hands away from each other as though turning two dials, and Leonard's back arches. His limbs splay out. He rises a couple of inches off the ground.

I am going to kill you, Leonard. Jonah will not have died for nothing. I do not care what the Soothsayer thinks is possible. I will show her what is possible. I will protect the people I love.

And I will kill you.

I concentrate harder than I ever have before. I focus every fiber of my being on Leonard's suspended form. He thrashes against my vise-like grip, but he cannot break free. I am too strong. I pull his arms and legs away from his torso. His scream grows louder. It hardly registers. I stretch his immortal body as far as it will go, straining his limbs, but it is not enough. I need more.

Even though I cannot see any of the other souls in the room, I can sense them. My mind snakes through the room, entwining with each soul, weaving their energy into mine with every furious beat of my heart.

Using my mind, I summon the closest soul and condense its essence into a ball of energy. With a guttural cry, I hurl it at Leonard.

The energy strikes his chest with thunderous force. He absorbs it, glowing brighter as the pale soul I flung bounces off of him. He grins, as though he has bested me.

He has not. I summon another soul, condensing its energy into a pulsating sphere and hurling it at Leonard. I summon another, and another, until there is a steady radiant beam of energy moving between the palms of my hands and Leonard's form.

His agonized wail shreds the air as his ghostly skin splits open in electric fissures. I push harder, visualizing the energy boring a smoldering hole through his abdomen. The ground shudders, heaving and buckling beneath me. Scorching heat buffets my face, licking at every bit of exposed skin. I had always thought souls were cold, but not a single thing about this is cold.

Every one of my nerve endings lights on fire. Soul after soul comes to me, channels itself through my body and rushes from my palms. They come so quickly, infusing my body with a strength I did not know I possessed.

Gritting my teeth, I push harder. So much heat courses through my veins that it feels as if my blood has turned to lava. I hear an otherworldly screech tearing out of my throat.

Wood splinters and cracks around me. Behind me, there is a booming crash. Somebody screams from what sounds like far away. My eyes search to identify who it was, but I cannot see anything except for Leonard. I am trapped in the channel of energy I created.

In the corner of my eye, Jonah's soul careens toward me, pulled into the stream of souls. My heart leaps into my throat. Oh no. I cannot do this to him. Using his energy may send him to the other side, but stopping means releasing Leonard, and I will not do that again.

Our eyes lock. His mouth forms words, but I cannot hear them over the noise in my head. He vanishes into the canal of souls, and I hurl his essence at Leonard with a gut-wrenching sob.

Leonard's chest glows white-hot. The smug superiority in his eyes is gone. He has always believed he could choose who lives and who dies, but he will not anymore. I would feel sad for him if he had not caused everybody I love so much pain.

The air fills with static. Something hums as the pressure inside of me reaches an unbearable intensity. With an earsplitting clap and a blinding flash of light, Leonard's soul explodes.

51

FrANCeSCA

The impact lifts me off my feet and flings me across the barn. I do my best to cover my head, but it is as though my arms are made of overcooked spaghetti, and they do not have time to move before my body hits the ground.

I curl into a ball, pressing my forehead into the floor and plunging my fingertips into my ears. There is the sound of wood splintering. A chorus of interwoven screams. So many noises come from all directions that there is no place for me to run to even if I could. The only thing I can do is cling to the thrumming ground and hope that nothing heavy falls on top of me.

Once a ringing noise replaces the sound of breaking and crashing, I lift my head. I try to open my eyes, but my lids are sluggish, and it takes much more than the usual effort to get them to move. The world swims. The splintered floor ... the broken beams ... I blink, struggling to clear my vision.

I am curled up in a ball on the barn floor. The waterlogged fabric of my shirt is glued to me like a second skin. What remains of my bandage is soaked as well and somehow singed as though it has been burned.

I call out to Evangeline, but no sound leaves my throat. Where are Shiloh and Miles? Jonah? The police officer? I try to find them, but I cannot see a thing through all of the ash lingering in the air. The small particles hover around me. The ash looks rather like snow, only it is falling upward instead of downward, which is not normal for either ash or snow to do.

The floor thrums beneath me. My stomach turning sour, I glance around for the cause of the noise.

Uh oh.

A yawning hole has torn through the floorboards in the middle of the barn. It oozes outward as though it is alive, devouring the wood with creeping black tendrils that crackle with energy. Even though I am lying quite a way away from it, I can still see through the twisting strands at the colorless dimension mirroring ours.

This is the largest opening I have ever seen. It runs nearly the entire length of the barn. I try to drag myself toward it, but my legs will not move. A gale blows out of the hole and into me, forcing me across the floor. I brace my palms on the wood, clawing for purchase, but it is no use.

My elbow snags on the metal arm of an old plow. I cling to it as hard as I can as souls pour through the opening.

There are so many of them. Perhaps hundreds, coming through all at once. The force stretches the skin on my face and makes it difficult for me to keep my eyes open, causing me to squint against the stinging air. The souls rush forth as if they are being sucked out by an enormous vacuum cleaner. They flash past me and vanish through the hole in the roof, flooding the rafters until the barn brims with spectral light.

There are too many. They should not all be coming here.

Did I cause this?

More souls come through. Their limbs flail as though they are trying to regain control of themselves. Some attempt to go back in through the hole, but the roaring wind forces them upward.

I crane my neck searching for Evangeline, but I can see nothing through the blur of light and motion.

I must stop this. Dragging my limp legs to the side and bracing them against the arm of the plow, I raise my palms to the hole, reaching out with my mind and trying to feel its edges. The edges of the passageway quiver. They creep inward. I push even harder.

Please, angels, help me be strong.

But I am not strong enough. I cling to my last shreds of power, feeling the strength slip from my hands. I need more benmjöl. More of something, because I have no more to give.

Forgive me, angels. I cannot do this any longer.

Sobs wrack my body. I succumb to the pressure in my temples and allow it to pull me away, but then—a gentle hand caresses my hair. There is a cooling sensation on my skin, resembling a kiss. I glance over my shoulder and gasp.

Mrs. Lewis shimmers beside me, blurred by the tears pooling in my eyes. Even though I have not seen her in weeks, she looks exactly as she does in my memory, with shoulder-length white hair, round cheeks, and a cardigan with roses knit into it.

In any other circumstance, seeing her would be enough to make me cry, but I am holding on so tightly to the plow that I cannot do anything else but gape at her and shout to be heard over the wind. "Did you come through the opening?"

She lays a hand on my shoulder. A shiver runs through me.

"You are stronger than you believe you are," she says, and I no longer feel so cold. Her voice is the same. I had not realized how much I missed hearing it, and it is all I can do not to cry.

"You can do this, baby girl," comes another voice from the other side of me. One I have not heard in so many years. One whose memory I clung to because I was afraid I would forget it. "You can do anything."

I turn. The corners of my vision fall away as I see my mother's soul beside me. Her body has turned to wisps in the powerful wind. A laugh slips through my lips and I really do start to cry.

"I did not think I would see you again until I joined you," I say, forcing the words out between sobs. "Is that what is happening right now?"

She touches a finger to my lips, shaking her head. I feel her there, cool to the touch but somehow still warm.

She points to the yawning opening. "Finish this."

I focus on the hole and the souls still pouring out of it. In my life, whenever I felt most alone in the world, I would always picture angels watching over me and protecting me. They looked like the angels in the stained-glass windows of the church my mother used to take me to, with golden halos and big wings that could shield me from the things that made me afraid. Those angels were just figments of my imagination. I never imagined they could be real, but perhaps they were this entire time.

My mother is right. I must finish this.

I scrape together the last dregs of my strength from the very depths of my soul. I push on through screaming muscles and rattling bones, through disbelieving joy and sobbing grief because I am the only one who can stop this. Even though this town has shown me very little kindness in my life, I am the only one capable of saving it.

Mrs. Lewis and my mother lay a hand on my shoulder. I can feel their energy running through me, giving me enough power to pull the opening closed with my mind as though I am using my muscles. They are with me. They are helping me. They will pull me through this. With a thin cry, I close the opening. The last tendril shrivels up. The howling wind stops. I slump onto my side and allow my eyes to close, waiting for my angels to carry me home.

That is not what happens. I feel hands on me, but they are not the chilled hands of Mrs. Lewis or my mother's. They are human and strong, turning me over and brushing the hair from my face.

"Francesca, what did you do?" Shiloh asks. I open my eyes, but she is blurry, so I close them again.

A sleepy smile forms on my lips. "I killed Leonard," I mumble.

Shiloh draws in a breath. "You killed his ghost?"

I nod, still smiling. "I exploded him."

"Oh my God," she says, and I can hear the smile in her voice.

"I exploded him and opened a passageway to the other side, but then I closed it." I shudder as fresh tears spill from my eyes, although I do not understand why. Perhaps it is because I am happy.

"It's okay," Shiloh says. "You'll be okay. Help is coming. Nothing bad is going to happen to you. Right, Miles?"

I peer up look up at their upside-down faces above me. All of the souls around us give off enough light that I can see them properly, as if this old barn has been lit up like the inside of a school or hospital. Shiloh and Miles are smiling through the rain running down their skin. They drag me out from under the plow and kneel in front of me so that I can look at them. They are both soaking wet from the rain. It has glued Shiloh's sandy hair to her forehead and turned it many shades darker, and the cold has given Miles's lips a sort of bluey tinge. I am so glad to see them that to me, they have never looked more beautiful.

I touch Shiloh's sodden cheek. She clasps her hand around my quivering fingers.

"Try not to move too m-much," Miles stammers through chattering teeth. "In case you're hurt."

I do not feel pain. Only lightness, as if I am floating. Leonard is dead. He is really, truly dead. Killing him should have been impossible, but it was not. Closing the opening should have killed me, but it did not. I can be happy again. I can breathe again.

I grab Shiloh's shoulders, dragging her down and wrapping my arms around her. She hugs me back, holding me in her bony arms. I rest my chin against her shoulder and glance over her shoulder at Miles.

"I would like it if you hugged me as well, Miles," I say.

He wraps his heavy arms around Shiloh and me. The warmth from their sopping-wet bodies chases away the chill inside of mine.

I release them and peer over to where Evangeline had been lying before the explosion. There were so many souls in this barn. I have never seen so many souls in one place, but there are not as many in here now as there were before, so I can see through the gaps in the moving figures. Evangeline is no longer on the floor.

My stomach plummets. "Where is Evangeline?"

"I don't know," Shiloh says. "There was so much wind. I'm not even kidding. It was like a hurricane in here."

I try to stand up, but my legs will not cooperate. I try to drag myself toward the place where she had been lying, but my arms will not stop shaking and I simply cannot move.

"Evangeline?" I call, peering around the blurred souls. I am not sure if my vision is blurry, or all of the souls blur together. "Are you there?"

I glimpse Evangeline's body crumpled in the corner. A lump forms in my throat. She is unusually still, blood smearing the floor around her and reflecting light from all the souls surrounding us.

"Evangeline!" I scream, dragging myself toward her. "I am coming!"

A spot of light pulses inside her chest like a heartbeat. I stop moving and watch as the light rises into the air, unfurling almost immediately into the shape of a girl.

Oh my goodness.

I have seen this girl before, but never like this. Not when I know her the way I do now. Not when she does what she does to my heart. Evangeline has traded her sea-green eyes for pale ones that I would imagine were blue when she was alive. A ribbon ties her pale ringlets out of her rosy cheeks. Her blouse is tucked into a long skirt that looks like something I would choose from a clothing store.

She smiles at me, and I suddenly cannot breathe. She was beautiful before, but now …

She weaves through the other souls and comes to a graceful stop in front of me.

"So?" she asks, gesturing at herself. "What do you think?"

Her voice is higher than it had been when she possessed Talulah Monroe's body. Every word she says sounds musical, but she uses the same intonation on every word as she did before.

She just died for a second time. Imagining what she just went through, gasping her final breaths when I was not there with her, makes me feel as though I had died with her.

"Did it hurt terribly?" I ask. This may be the wrong question to ask, but there are many confusing feelings moving through my body and I am not sure what I should say to her.

She gives me a gentle smile. "No, because I wasn't afraid. I knew I'd see you again."

Warmth rises to my face, despite the fact that I am still crying. She appears to enjoy seeing my face grow red because it only makes her smile grow wider.

She comes around behind me and curls her ghostly fingers around my shoulders, picking me up into a sitting position. I reach my hands out to catch myself on the wood, expecting her to vanish, but she does not disappear. I can lean on her. I can feel her. Her form is solid but cool, and touching her does not help me get warmer. I am losing all feeling in my fingers and toes.

Evangeline's face glimmers inches from mine, shimmering in the surrounding light. She may not resemble anybody I know, but she is not a stranger. The fluttering feeling she gives my stomach is the same one she used to give me when she was Talulah.

"One thing you already know about me," Evangeline says, "is that I've been dead for a very long time, which lets me pull tricks like this."

She presses her lips to mine. Liquid ice flares through my nerve endings. I gasp against her mouth. It is not exactly painful, but it is not something I am used to.

I pull back, breathing deeply to try and quiet the chattering of my teeth. "Perhaps we should wait until I am a bit warmer to do that."

Evangeline nods. Behind her, Shiloh clears her throat. I glance back to see her pointing at me, eyebrows raised.

"Uh, was that you just making out with a ghost?" she asks.

I do not believe one kiss constitutes making out, but Shiloh's words do not merit a correction, so I nod. She laughs.

"You looked like you were miming teaching someone how to whistle," Miles adds, but I am no longer paying attention to them because something on the other side of the room has caught my attention.

Jonah's soul hovers among the others who are dispersing from the barn. He is not paying attention to us. Instead, he hovers across from the soul of a rather stout middle-aged soul with a limp ponytail that hangs low against her neck. A long gash runs across her throat. As she speaks, Jonah shakes his head. He wipes his hands down the front of his face. She pulls him into her arms, holding him as his shoulders shake with quiet sobs. Even though I have never met her before, I know that she is Jonah's foster mother. She must have come up from the other side, along with all the other souls. Seeing them together, a drop of warmth blooms in my chest.

Jonah catches me looking at him. He lets go of his foster mother, then glides over to me.

"Hey, Frankie," he says. "How's it going?"

He floats beside Shiloh. She does not acknowledge him. She cannot see him, so why would she?

A sharp pain pierces my heart. Evangeline may be dead, but at least I can still see and touch her. There is no such reality for Shiloh. Jonah may be with her, but she does not know he is there.

Jonah smiles sadly, like he is thinking a similar thing. "You killed it, Franks. I'm so proud of you."

Shiloh searches my eyes, then turns her head to where Jonah is sitting. She looks back at me. "Is Jonah …?"

I nod. She glances around for where the glasses ended up, but they are not with her anymore. Perhaps she misplaced them during the explosion.

Jonah appears to want to avoid making Shiloh emotional, so

he flies up and around to Miles, winding around him so quickly that Miles's wet hair quivers.

Miles's fingers go to his hair. "Is Jonah touching me right now?"

"Tell him I'm going to haunt the shit out of him," Jonah says. "I'll hide his car keys. Pants him in public. My sole mission on Earth will be his public humiliation. He'll be begging me to go to the other side."

He laughs at his own joke, but I do not feel like laughing.

"I could bring you back," I say.

The smile drops off Jonah's face. "You're not strong enough."

"Yes, I am."

Even I know it is not true. I can hardly sit upright, and my legs will not cooperate anymore.

"Seriously, Frankie, no," Jonah says. "You just blew up the world and put it back together. You've done enough saving for one day."

"I am sorry," I say. Shiloh's expression goes blank as she realizes what is happening.

"Don't be," Jonah says. "Just ... don't let Miles and Shiloh be sad for too long, okay? They can both get kind of dark and twisty, and they're going to need you to pull them out of it."

I wipe my gummy nose. In the distance, sirens wail into the night. The ambulance is coming, but it will be too late for Jonah.

Unless ... perhaps it might not be.

I am not a believer in miracles, but they do happen, and when they do, they happen for a reason. Perhaps that reason is because somebody wants to be alive so badly they defy what is possible.

Jonah has not been dead for very long. No more than five or ten minutes, and Miles performed CPR, so re-entering his body may not be impossible. But he may not wake up, and even if he does, he will face a painful recovery. His broken arm is twisted nearly to the back of his body. Enough of his organs were destroyed for the impact to kill him, so he will need to fight for his life, but when I explain this to Jonah, he says he understands.

He promises to fight. For somebody who dislikes the world as much as he pretends to, he does not seem in any hurry to leave it.

His soul is waiting above his body when the ambulance arrives. Paramedics storm through the opening in the barn wall, shining flashlights through the lingering souls. I point at Jonah's body lying against the tractor. One paramedic checks his pulse. One begins CPR.

I hold my breath as a man uses scissors to cut Jonah's shirt off his chest, and a woman charges the paddles. Jonah's soul drops toward his body and flips over, aligning his arms and legs with his body like I told him to.

The paramedic places the paddles on Jonah's chest. His corpse jolts, but his soul does not disappear.

I clasp my hands together and utter a silent prayer. I am not entirely sure who this prayer is directed to, but I say it anyway.

Please, please, please work.

This will take a miracle. But miracles can happen if you want them to badly enough, can't they?

The paramedics recharge the paddles. They jolt him again. He still does not disappear.

"Try to go inside as soon as they shock you," I tell him. The paramedics raise their heads to look at me, but they find little value in what I have to say. Jonah gives me a thumbs-up.

I pull my lip in between my teeth. Beside me, Shiloh clasps her hands together.

The paddles charge. As soon as the paramedic yells, *"Clear,"* Jonah drops into his body.

The body's back arches under the shock. This time, Jonah's soul disappears.

I gasp. A paramedic checks Jonah's vitals, then calls for another to help. One of them intubates him. Another stabs a needle through his chest. They jolt to action, moving with the urgency of needing to save somebody who is alive, not with the lethargy of needing to conceal somebody who has died.

I laugh, covering my mouth with my hands to stop the sound from being too loud. He did it. He really did it!

Shiloh bends over, sobbing in gasps but smiling at the same time. I am sure the paramedics are wondering why we are laughing about our friend being in such critical condition, but injured is not dead. Jonah is not out of the woods yet, but at least he has a chance.

A paramedic bends over Talulah Monroe's body. He takes a pulse but shakes his head at his colleague, who radios for another ambulance. I feel a strange sort of sadness for her. I hardly knew her, but when Evangeline was possessing her body, I feel as though I did get to know her, memorizing the curve of her lips and the shape of her hips and the way her eyes crinkled when she laughed. She had the most beautiful laugh. I hear a guttural wail and glance up to find Talulah's mother crashing toward her daughter and raising trembling hands to cover her mouth. I hope that the real Talulah's soul came through the opening. I may not be able to put her back into her body, but perhaps I could help her give a message to her family.

Another paramedic runs over to me. She checks my vitals, removes my shoes, and asks me to move my feet. I can get my toes to twitch, but I cannot manage to move my entire foot. When she squeezes my big toe, I can hardly feel her fingers. I begin to worry, but I force myself to take deep breaths. I am only tired. Once I get some rest, the strength will return to my legs.

The paramedics lift me onto a stretcher and wheel me across the uneven barn floor. The boards are warped and black from where the opening had been. I am not sure if anybody else can see it, but they appear to have been burned by a fire or have rotted and collapsed in on themselves. I cannot stare at it for long because the stretcher wheels me past it.

Evangeline's soul glides above me, assuring me that things are going to be all right and promising that she will not leave my side. Given all the circumstances and people that have tried to come between us in the short time I have known her, the knowledge that nobody will ever force her from me again makes my stomach flutter. I wish I could kiss her again, but asking to kiss somebody who is not there in front of the paramedics who could very well be in charge of whether I am admitted to the hospital or some sort of mental institution may not be the smartest idea, so I smile up at her. We will grow accustomed to this. I have the rest of my life, and she has the rest of eternity to do so.

The paramedics wheel me outside over the withered grass. The rain is still coming down heavily, and everything smells rather damp and earthy. Something catches my eye. I know I am not supposed to move my head, but I still turn to look, and it is as if the world around me slows.

So many souls stretch over the cornfield that it looks as if the stars themselves have come down. They shine like beacons between the stalks, and blink like streetlights over the road. There are more souls here than I have seen in my entire life. More than I saw even on the other side.

Should they be here? Why are they here?

Did I do this?

The corn stalk closest to me withers. Rot consumes the leaves and ears, wrinkling the edges and turning the plant gray and black. I watch, wide-eyed, as the rot travels across the field, consuming stalk after stalk of corn like a hungry monster.

Bile presses against the back of my throat. Did that come from the opening? Why is it not stopping?

One paramedic above me gapes at the field. I suppose I am not the only one who sees the corn. But as strange as it is, I am still on a stretcher, and it is still raining, so the paramedic does not stare for long before pushing me through the back doors of the ambulance.

Evangeline passes through the doors and hovers beside me. I go to tell her that souls cannot ride in vehicles, but I am sure she already knows this, or will at least follow me if she loses me. Miles climbs in with me as well, ducking to get his head under the top of the door.

"I'm riding with you," he says.

I tell Miles that he should not be seen with me in Bethany, that people may not know what to think, and he replies he does not care. Shiloh has already left with Jonah, and he will not allow me to ride to the hospital by myself. I pull his face closer to mine, in the hope I can talk without the paramedic overhearing me.

"Did you see what happened to the cornfield?" I ask.

He nods. "It looks like it all died."

"Do you think that could be because of the opening to the other side?" I whisper. "Because of what I did?"

"You closed it," Miles assures me. "Maybe there was leftover energy looking for somewhere to go, and that's what killed the corn."

"I know, but … there were so many souls," I say. "More than I have ever seen."

"Just because there were a lot of them doesn't mean something bad is going to happen," Miles says. "This is over. You don't have to worry about any of it anymore, okay?"

The ambulance's engine rumbles to life beneath us. Because I am so sleepy, concentration is difficult, but I am mostly aware as we make for the hospital and I am able to answer every question that the nice paramedic lady asks me. I try to convince myself that Miles is right. Souls do not kill corn. There is a cemetery next door to this farm, and the corn has never withered like this before. Simply because many souls came through the opening does not mean anything bad is going to happen. I am merely afraid because so many bad things have happened to us in the past.

I grip Miles's hand, allowing a deep breath to slip through my lips before closing my eyes. He is right. The bad things are over. I wonder how long it will be until I believe it.

52

Shiloh

I drum my foot against the floor of the waiting room, wringing my hands together as I try to get warm.

The clock on the wall tells me it's just after eleven thirty. The TV in the corner is playing *How to Train Your Dragon*. Finally, they're playing a decent movie in this place. It's the least they could do given how many times I have been here in the past couple of weeks.

I haven't been here that long. Jonah and I got to the hospital maybe twenty minutes ago, and they rushed him to surgery and told me to stay in the waiting room. He stayed unconscious in the ambulance. I wasn't expecting him to wake up. He'd been dead five minutes before the paramedics brought him back and even though Miles did CPR, there's no telling how much damage was done to his brain. Plus, based on what I overhead in the ambulance, his arm is broken and his lung has collapsed. I don't need to be a medical professional to know he's barely hanging on. In the barn, I'd heard Francesca giving Jonah some instructions on how to re-enter his body, and as far as I could see, he went back in the old-fashioned way, with no supernatural help.

At least he's alive. At least he has a chance.

I raise my head and see Miles walking over to me. His clothes are dripping wet, just like mine. I wave at him to make sure he sees me, and he sinks into the chair next to me.

"Is Francesca okay?" I ask.

He nods. "The doctors wouldn't tell me anything, but she was awake in the ambulance and she didn't seem to be in any pain. They're running tests now. What about Jonah?"

"In surgery," I say.

None of the doctors would tell me anything, either. They said they couldn't release details to non-family members, but because Jonah has no surviving guardian, I don't know what rules apply to him right now. Is his social worker going to come?

I notice a red mark on Miles's forehead and point at it. "What happened to you?"

He says he hit his head when climbing out of the bulkhead at the abandoned house, but not hard enough to be concussed. By some miracle, both of us got through that with only minor scrapes and bruises. All four of us are alive. And Leonard is dead.

The enormity of what Francesca did hits me all over again. I can't believe Leonard is really dead. It feels unreal, but not in a bad way.

I lean my head on Miles's shoulder. I know this is the hospital in Mount Keenan, and I know Miles doesn't want me acting like I know him in public, but he doesn't push me away. His clothes are still wet and freezing, but nothing can make me colder than I already am at this point. A shuddering breath slips out of him. Something in my chest aches. Even though this is over, and Leonard is dead, Miles still hasn't gotten his old life back. His life has changed forever because of what he's gone through, and there's nothing I can do to fix that for him.

Except I can be there for him. At least he won't have to go through it alone.

In a couple of minutes, the glass doors slide open. Mom runs in, carrying a groggy Max in her arms.

A smile breaks out over my face. I stand up and run over, stopping right in front of her.

She touches my face with her one free hand, eyebrows drawing together. "Are you all right? Are you hurt?"

"Just cold," I say, and Mom utters some words of thanks. "We did it, Mom. Francesca … Francesca did it."

Mom gasps. Max rubs his eyes. He's still in his pajamas, and it's clear that Mom woke him up to bring him here.

He will want to hear this. Smiling, I take him from Mom's arms and put him on the ground, kneeling in front of him so I can look him in the eye. "Max. I helped kill the bad man."

This wakes him up. His eyes widen. "Really?"

"Yes," I say. "He's dead. He's never going to come and hurt you ever again."

Max smiles. I gather him into my arms and hug him, resting my head on his shoulder.

"You're wet," Max says.

I tell him to deal with it and hug him even tighter because Leonard will never hurt him again. Max went through being locked in that trailer with Leonard. He went through all the endless nights of being afraid that Leonard was going to come back for him, but he doesn't have to be scared anymore. He can live the rest of his life knowing that the monster who hurt him can never come back, and maybe—just maybe—he'll be able to heal.

Maybe we all will. I grin up at Mom, who lays a hand on my head, and for a second, I stop feeling so cold.

"You ready to go home?" Mom asks, raising her eyes to Miles, who must be standing behind me. "Both of you kids?"

I twist around to see Miles smile at being called a kid. He nods. If I were him, I wouldn't want to go back to an empty apartment all alone tonight, either. Mom gestures for me to lead the way, and I carry Max out of the hospital for what I hope is the last time in a very long time.

I sleep in Max's room. He wants me to put him to bed when we get home, and after I shower and change into more comfortable clothes, I only get through one chapter of his book before nodding off.

I wake up the next afternoon in his bed feeling so gross. My head feels like it's being crushed in some kind of garbage compactor, and my temples are throbbing with every beat of my heart. The curtains are closed, but the midday sun is powerful enough to cut right through them, making the room a cold gray. I don't get out of bed for over an hour until my headache gets pretty much unbearable and I need to get something to eat.

I drag myself into the kitchen like a zombie. Miles is already up, slumped on a stool with his hands wrapped around a mug. The welt on his head is red and slightly raised, and he seems to be nursing his own headache with coffee.

I do the same thing. The coffee was done brewing hours ago, so it's lukewarm, but I pour some for myself anyway and use it to wash down some Tylenol before sinking onto the stool next to him.

Mom got us bagels this morning. There are a bunch of them in a Panera bag on the counter and I slather one in butter and eat it in front of the TV. According to Miles, Mom and Max left to go grocery shopping twenty minutes before I got up. There's no update from the hospital, which is annoying and wrong. Jonah and Francesca are closer to us than they are to their actual families, so we should be the ones getting news on how they're doing. But it doesn't work like that.

Part way into our episode of some cooking show, the TV screen twitches, shaking the image just enough that looking at it starts making me motion sick. I look away at the magazines on the coffee table. A copy of *People* flips open by itself and fans through the pages before falling open on a random spread about the royal family.

I stare at the open magazine. A lump forms in my throat, but I try to push down my nerves. There has to be a breeze in here. Some way cold air is getting in from the outside.

I need to stop being so paranoid. This is the first day of the rest of my life without Leonard. I may spend the rest of my life knowing ghosts are real, but I need to try not to get too freaked out if something goes bump in the night or I will drive myself crazy.

Once our headaches subside enough for us to function, Miles and I walk back to the abandoned farmhouse to pick up his car. It's super cold out today. Way colder than it was even yesterday. Even the sun can't warm us up, and my breath comes out in puffs. I guess that's to be expected for the season. It's the middle of October. It's normal for it to be getting colder.

What's not normal is how dead the cornfield at the Monroe farm is. I could barely see it last night in the dark, but now it's impossible to ignore. Every stalk looks as though the life has been sucked out of it. The stalks are gray and ashen, and so withered that they are reduced to a fraction of their normal size.

Seeing them takes my breath away. The poor Monroes. Losing Talulah and their entire crop.

What the hell happened to it? Could this have come from the other side somehow?

At least Francesca closed that gate so no more strange things can get through.

Miles and I trudge through the dead corn. Each leaf is so brittle it turns to dust the second we brush against it. The stalks are shorter than we are now that they're all withered. I feel like we're super exposed, but I walk through the field anyway because it's the fastest way to the abandoned house.

The car is where Miles left it yesterday. Police tape flaps in the gentle wind, blocking off the barn. I'm surprised no one has questioned us about what happened yet. No one seems to suspect me of doing anything bad. I guess it helps to have a police officer witness the entire thing.

I nudge Miles on the arm. "Have you heard anything from the police officer from last night?"

"Lindsey?" he asks, and I nod. "Nope. Nothing. Which is surprising."

"Maybe she's trying to process everything she saw," I say. "Did you show her the ghosts through the glasses?"

He nods. "She did not like seeing that at all."

I wonder what she's telling the other cops. I wonder if they think she's crazy too now. It's hard to deny the existence of the supernatural when you see it for yourself, but maybe it's less hard to convince yourself that you're losing your mind. Some things just don't have logical explanations. I just hope she doesn't convince herself she's insane until all of this is behind us.

In the hospital, they refuse to give us any news about Jonah. I beg just to know if he's okay, but the nurse tells me sorry so many times that I want to bash my head against the desk.

"Can you at least tell us if he's alive?" I ask, my voice breaking as I grip the counter. "Please?"

"He's recovering in the ICU," she finally says, and I bend over as a long sigh runs out of my body.

He's alive. He's recovering. He made it through surgery.

She says that only immediate family is allowed in the ICU, but they usually move patients into recovery rooms between twenty-four and thirty-six hours after surgery, so after they move him, we could visit. I close my eyes and utter a silent prayer for him. I don't know who's listening to it, but saying it makes me feel better anyway.

Please, whoever is listening to this, protect Jonah, I pray, in case anyone is actually listening. *Give him the strength to pull through this.*

I wonder if he's going to wake up. He has to. I wonder if he's going to be okay after waking up. He was dead for five minutes, and not getting oxygen to his brain for that long could change him. I try to shove down the worry, because thinking about it is making me feel like I need to throw up.

The nurse also tells us that Francesca is here. Miles lies and says he's her brother, but the nurse gives his ID a funny look, so I don't know if she believes him. I wonder if that's because she's seen Francesca. She and Miles look nothing alike, and unfortunately for Miles, this nurse is probably fifty or sixty years old and she isn't impressed by his attempt to charm her. At least he doesn't call her gorgeous. Every time I remember him doing that, I get secondhand embarrassment.

"You sure are God's favorite in the family," she says, printing out visitor's passes for us.

Is that some kind of dig at Francesca? I get mad until we go up in the elevator and find the real reason she made that comment sitting in a chair in the waiting room.

Richie is bent over his knees, drumming his foot on the ground. He's wearing his snapback with the flames on it, the same one he always wore at school, and his meaty hands are clasped together. There's a patch over one of his eyes.

My knees jam up when I see him. So do Miles's. I guess, even though Miles is now leagues taller and more athletic than Richie. To him, Richie is still his childhood bully who pushed him around. Richie must be here for Francesca, which is surprising. I didn't think he cared much about what happened to her. At least, that's what he made it sound like when I was questioning him, but that was when he was under the influence of foolery, and I know from Jonah that foolery can do a number on someone's head. I guess that if Richie has a deep down, that's where he cares what happens to Francesca.

Richie sees me. His eye flies open like he's trying to decide which way to run, but he doesn't have to.

"Richie," I say, holding out a hand so he knows I won't hurt him. "I'm sorry about what happened with your eye. I wanted to find Francesca so bad that I wasn't thinking clearly, and I'm sorry."

Richie just stares at me through his one beady eye. He glances at Miles, then back at me, and for a second I wonder if I shouldn't have admitted to having anything to do with his eye, but then he just nods. I guess he remembers enough to know why we kept him hostage. Or maybe Francesca told him. Nothing I could ever do would bring back his eye, but being able to apologize feels like a weird kind of closure. Now that Leonard is dead, all of us can move on with our lives.

I point over his shoulder at the hallway. "Is Francesca …?"

He nods. "Second door on the right."

I give him an apologetic smile, and then go into the patient room. I brace myself for something bad, but when I see Francesca's smile from her hospital bed, her face warm and radiating light, I sigh in relief.

"Hello," she says, her voice sounding a little sleepy but not hoarse or in pain. She's not connected to any big machines. She's just lying in a gown with an IV pumping fluids into her hand. "How did you both sleep?"

I laugh. Considering what she's been through, it's such a weird question, but it's normal, and we need to get used to normal. I take her wrinkled hand in mine, smoothing her skin with my thumb.

"Pretty good," I say. "No nightmares. You?"

She shrugs. I guess hospitals would be loud for her, with all the people dying and all the ghosts in here.

But she'll be back in her own bed soon. "Are you going home today?"

"Possibly," she says. "My father and Richie are here. The hospital called them."

Oh crap. The last time I saw Francesca's dad, he was chasing me out of his house with a shotgun. I wonder if he's going to recognize me. Maybe not, because I was wearing a Freddy Krueger mask. But it wouldn't take a genius to put two and two together, especially if he sees Miles standing next to me.

He didn't press charges. I guess Richie ended up not pressing any, either. Francesca must have talked to them about what happened.

The rest of what Francesca said sinks in. Is her dad here to bring her back to Columbus? She shouldn't live in that trailer anymore, especially not on her own, but picturing her living an hour away makes my stomach feel heavy. I'm glad Leonard is dead, but that doesn't mean I want everything else to be over. Sometime in the past couple of weeks I've started to think of her as my best friend.

"I believe it is more likely that I will go home tomorrow," she says. "The doctors are waiting for the results of some tests. They are running several of them to figure out why I cannot move my legs."

My stomach drops. "You can't move your legs?"

Francesca shakes her head. "There does not appear to be any reason for it." Her voice quivers, like she's trying not to panic. "They are running tests."

"Maybe you're just tired," I say. "I bet your movements will come back once you get stronger again."

"I hope so," she says, but her tone tells me she doesn't believe it. She had been weak before she killed Leonard yesterday. Scared she was going to die. She didn't die, but doing what she did must have taken a lot out of her. What was that thing she told me before? Everything comes at a cost? Or for a price?

At least she's alive. She's alive, and she will never have to deal with Leonard again.

She squeezes my hand with waning strength. "Could you stay for the afternoon?"

I climb onto her bed next to her. Miles turns on the TV, and the three of us spend the afternoon mostly in silence, watching some nature documentary about migrating penguins that sends Francesca right to sleep. Her warm body presses against mine, and her curls tickle my cheeks. Even though my temples are throbbing and the angle of the bed is making my neck ache, I don't move.

When the credits roll, the room temperature drops. It's so sudden that I notice it immediately, and I have to tuck the tips of my fingers into the sleeves of my hoodie. The cold air presses closer to us. I wrap my arm around a sleeping Francesca because last time the temperature changed like this, it was when Leonard entered my jail cell, but this can't be Leonard because he's dead.

One of Francesca's curls moves out of her face all on its own. My eyes search the space above us. I hope that the ghosts watching over Francesca will also be watching out for her.

There is still no news about Jonah by the evening. The only thing the nurse tells us is that he's still in the ICU, but hopefully he'll be moved to a better room tomorrow, and then we can visit him.

Miles sleeps over at my house again. It's not even up for debate. He's so rattled after what happened that he needs a couple of days to recover before he goes back to living alone. I think it's slowly dawning on him that now this is over and Leonard is dead, what happened to him isn't just a big traumatic thing that will somehow be fixed. Being in Officer Zweering's body is his life, now. He has to figure out how he's going to be a person now that he doesn't need to be afraid for his life anymore, and that's not something that just happens overnight.

Mom makes a chicken and broccoli casserole for dinner, and we eat it all together around the kitchen table for the first time in weeks. For the first time ever without Dad. And Mom uses this opportunity to bring up my return to school.

"I had a call with your vice principal today, Shiloh," she says, swallowing a bite of broccoli. "He's excited to have you back."

I roll my eyes. "Call-Me-Bill gets excited about the socks he puts on in the morning. He gets excited about beige. It doesn't take a lot to get him excited."

Mom smiles and shrugs. I move my chicken around with my

fork. Going back to school is something I guess I'm going to have to do. It's not like I have any excuse not to. We found Max. Leonard is dead. I'm no longer in jail, and if I miss many more days, I'd have to repeat the year, which would suck. School has felt so unimportant these past couple of weeks. It was never all that important to me because the only thing I cared about was Max and keeping him safe from Dad, but now that Dad is gone and Max is safe, I guess school can become important.

"I set up a meeting for us on Monday," Mom says, "so we can go see how much you missed and figure out what we need to do to get you back on track."

"Okay," I say. "Thanks, Mom."

Miles gets up from the table. He puts his plate in the dishwasher and disappears down the hallway without saying a word, and I hear the door to the bathroom close. My stomach sinks. Oh. I shouldn't have talked about school in front of Miles. He always loved school so much more than I did, and now he's never going back.

I give Mom a close-lipped smile and follow Miles, knocking on the bathroom door. "It's Shiloh. Can I come in?"

He sniffles, like he's crying. A pain drives through my heart.

"Sorry," he says. "I'll be out in a second."

I let myself in. Miles is sitting on the bathmat, his knees tucked to his chest. He's so big he can barely fit in here. His feet are resting against the opposite wall.

I step over his leg and sit between his feet. He wipes his eyes, letting out an awkward, shaking laugh, but he doesn't look at me. I feel like I should say something, but I don't know what I'm supposed to say. Saying I'll always be there for him sounds too weak. Offering solutions to make it better will sound empty. I got through this whole thing with Max and Mom both alive, and I'm going back to a version of my life that's better than the one I had before.

Miles wasn't that lucky.

It's my fault. I know it is. If it weren't for me he never would have gotten into this mess in the first place, and I didn't even stay his girlfriend. I'm just a walking reminder of everything he's lost.

I try to meet his eyes, but he doesn't meet mine. "I'm really sorry, Miles, about everything I did."

He shakes his head. "You didn't shoot me."

"I pretty much did," I say. "Leonard told me to choose."

"It was an unfair choice—"

"I chose Max," I say. "I heard you scream my name, and I still ran with Max. If I had turned around, or done something … well, I don't know what would have happened, but I'm sorry."

Miles hangs his head. My heart is beating hard because I have never actually talked to him about this before.

"I'm sorry for the way I treated you before," I say, because now I'm on a roll and I have a lot to be sorry for when it comes to Miles. "When Max went missing. You were nice to me and kept trying to help me, and I was mean to you. I didn't mean to be. I just didn't know how to act or process what was happening. You were so good to me. And that night … when we …"

"I remember."

"You were kind to me," I say. "And I shouldn't have said all those things to you."

"It's okay that you don't love me," he says. "You feel what you feel."

"I really don't think it's that I didn't love you," I say, surprised at how easily the words come out. "It's just that when Max went missing, I stopped knowing how to be a person. I guess I thought by not saying any of my feelings out loud, I could stop myself from feeling them, but I learned it doesn't work like that. I don't know if I'm saying this right, but what I'm trying to say is that I'm sorry for everything, and even though my lame apology can't change what happened, I'm here for you, and I'm not going anywhere, and I want to help you figure all this out. You aren't going to go through it alone."

It's like all the air has left my body. Each of the words took the breath from me, but they don't leave me feeling empty. As I said them, I know that it's what I've wanted to tell Miles for a long time, and even though they make me nervous because I don't know what he's going to say, it feels good to have said them.

Miles lifts his eyes to mine. "I used to know who I was, but I don't know how to be this new person."

Yeah. That is the thing that Leonard never considered. He thought bringing kids back to life in another kid's body was going to give them a second chance at life, but your life is never the same as it was before when you're in a new body because it doesn't feel like yours. At least Miles doesn't have to pretend to be someone else anymore. He just needs to find a new way to be who he is.

"Do you think you'll ever tell your parents who you are?" I ask.

Miles presses his lips into a line. I know how close he used to be with his parents. There aren't many sixteen-year-old boys who would choose to spend time with their parents over anyone else their age, so getting cut off from them must be the most painful part about this entire thing. I'd imagine being rejected by them after telling them who he really is would hurt just as much as never telling them at all.

"I don't know," he says. "Do you think this is ever going to feel better?"

"If anyone can figure out a way, you can." I scoot forward and poke my finger into his forehead. "*The everlasting universe of things flows through your mind, young Padawan.*"

I hope I got the quote right. Miles used to be a stickler for the accuracy of quotes, especially when it came to Star Wars.

He smiles. "You do realize that quote is not from Star Wars, right?"

My stomach drops. "But you said it to me that day at the cemetery."

"I never said it was from Star Wars," he says. "You said it was, and I was too shy to correct you. The quote is from Mont Blanc. The Percy Shelley poem."

Oh. "Well, you get my point."

He leans his head back against the wall. I nudge his ankle with mine, and even though it's going to take a long time to adjust to this new normal, and he's in a different body and so many crazy things have happened to us that nobody else would ever believe, right now I feel like things might eventually find a way to be okay.

53

Shiloh

I sleep in my bed that night but I am woken up first thing in the morning by Max leaping onto my mattress.

"Scooter!" he exclaims, pulling on my arm to wake me up. "Come on, wake up. It's snowing!"

What? I rub my eyes, coming back to the world of the living. Max crouches on my blanket, his blond hair sticking up in all directions. His breath is sour, and his Tonka Truck PJs are wrinkled.

"Snowing?" I ask.

He stands to look out the window above my bed. I rise onto my knees and join him. Sure enough, it is snowing. A couple of inches have covered our front lawn and the road in front of our house, smoothing out all the texture and turning everything white. Big fluffy flakes fall past the window.

My breath fogs up the glass. Huh. It's weird to get snow so early in the season. Usually, we get our first snow in early December, which is still around two months away. I can't remember the last time it snowed before Halloween. Probably never in my life.

But that's definitely snow. I guess it explains why it's so cold in here. It's cold enough outside for it to snow, and the heat in here isn't turned high enough to hold up in such cold temperatures.

Max points at it. "Can we go outside?"

I nod and slide off the side of the bed, taking Max's hand and letting him drag me through the house. He has always gotten excited about the first snow of the season. I get excited because he gets excited. Maybe it's because my radar for weird things is extra sensitive now, but I can't shake the uneasy feeling in my stomach as I put a coat on Max and slide on some boots. Max crashes down the front steps and onto the lawn. His sneakers leave small imprints in the snow. He jumps and spins around, but I stand there with my arms wrapped around my stomach because oh my God, it's so cold out here. In the silence, I can almost hear the snow falling. The flakes conceal all the ugliness in the world.

But I don't feel like jumping. Call me paranoid. Maybe I'm still reeling from the fight with Leonard and everything still has to be about ghosts, but there's something not right about this. It shouldn't be snowing in October. And it shouldn't be snowing this much.

Max grabs a handful and holds it up, the dusty flakes slipping through his pink fingers. He frowns. "It's not sticky."

"Sorry, buddy," I force through chattering teeth. "I guess our annual first snowman of the season will have to wait. Can we go inside?"

Max throws his handful of snow at me. He's smiling so much that, even though it's cold as all get out, I can't help but smile back, because I haven't seen Max this happy in a long time.

I grab a bigger coat and wrestle a hat onto Max's head because his ears are getting pink, and I don't want him to get cold. The snow is too dry to make anything out of it—we'll have to wait for a warmer day or for the sun to come out to get it to melt—so I end up shoveling our walkway and driveway while Max makes snow angels and runs around.

I'm just putting the shovel away when the front door opens and Mom sticks her head out. Her breath comes out as a puff of fog.

"Shiloh, honey," she says, holding up her phone. "I just got a call from Jonah's social worker. Jonah's awake, and he's asking for you."

The world around me gets quiet. Suddenly, it doesn't feel so cold out here. "Really?"

Even Mom can't hold back a smile as she nods. "Would you like me to bring you to the hospital?"

Is she kidding? I drop the shovel in the garage and run back into the house, flinging my arms around her before going to change out of my pajamas. Jonah has seen me in many uncompromising and unattractive outfits and positions, so I shouldn't feel any pressure to dress up or make myself look better for him, but I still brush my teeth because I feel like that's the bare minimum and change into actual jeans and a warm sweatshirt so I look at least one step away from being in pajamas. Miles gets up from the couch and changes too before we all pile into the back of Mom's rental car.

It's snowing all over Bethany. The snow looks like it's picked up, and it's coming down so hard that the car doesn't get all the way warm even though the heater is going, and it takes the snowflakes a few extra seconds to melt when they touch the windshield. The wipers are struggling, and Mom has to go way under the speed limit to give them enough time to clear the snow off. The only sign that another car is coming in the opposite direction is their headlights flashing against the snow.

Mom goes so slow that an ordinarily twenty-minute drive takes over half an hour. Every extra second is killing me. I bite my fingernails down to the quick. My fingers drum against my knee like they're playing one of those ambitious classical songs on the piano.

The second Mom pulls into a parking spot, I'm out of the car and running through the hospital doors. It's freezing in here. Just as cold as it is outside, if not more. Miles catches up to me, and I breathe into my hands as the woman behind the main desk prints us visitor's passes. It's probably cold because of the unexpected snowstorm, but I shouldn't be able to see my breath inside.

A nurse jogs past me, and a visible puff of air comes from her on each exhale.

I glance around at the other people milling around the waiting room. Their breaths are all coming out as fog too.

Someone needs to turn the heat up in here. This can't be good for anyone who is coming here because they're sick.

The woman tells us Jonah's room number, and then Miles and I are running to the elevator. We go up one level and scan the walls for signs pointing us toward his room. His door is open. I step inside.

And my heart stops.

Jonah is lying on a patient bed, propped up by some pillows. He's covered in bandages. They're everywhere. Wrapped around his torso and taped to his shoulder, partly hiding the cuts and bruises and all the sensors taped to his bare chest. An oxygen mask is secured over his nose and mouth. An IV line drips fluid into his arm. His skin has an unnatural pallor, probably a product of the anesthesia, and big machines monitor his heart rate and other vital signs, their gentle beeping the only sound in the otherwise silent room. There's a tube sticking out of his ribcage, and a cast has encased his entire left arm, which is bent at the elbow and lying across his body.

His eyelashes flutter. His blue eyes meet mine.

Every part of me wants to rush forward and fling my arms around him, but I don't want to hurt him. I can see how weak he is from here. I worry that if I even breathe the wrong way, his eyes will close and not open again.

He uses his good arm to pull up the oxygen mask, his eyes drooping as he gives me a tired smile.

"Hey, Scooby."

Tears spring into my eyes at the sound of his voice, and I can't stop myself. I run to him and lean over his body to wrap my arms around him, pressing my forehead against his. My hands tremble as they find their way to his neck, his jaw, his face, as if touching him proves that he's real, and he's okay. I hear the sobs before I realize I'm crying.

I hold on to him until he taps on my shoulder for me to let him go, and I pull up a chair next to his bed. Wiping my tears with the back of my hand, I glance over to see Miles coming up next to me.

"How are you feeling, buddy?" Miles asks.

"About as good as I look," Jonah says, his voice thick from sleep. "So, you know, great."

Someone behind us clears her throat. I turn around to find a woman in a cardigan and stilettos sitting by the window. I didn't even notice her in here. I don't need to be a detective to know she must be Jonah's social worker. She reminds him he's supposed to keep his oxygen mask on, and Jonah rolls his eyes and holds the mask up to his mouth.

I ask him about his injuries. He doesn't know much because he only woke up an hour ago, but the doctor already gave him the briefing. Three broken ribs. A collapsed lung. His arm is broken in two places and was almost ripped off his body from the impact, so he's going to need to do a lot of physical therapy to get it moving properly again. He said the doctors told him his recovery would be long and painful, but that's okay, because at least he's alive.

The talking wears him out pretty fast, so Miles and I take over. Miles tells him about what we did over the past couple of days. He talks about the dead corn. The snowstorm. The reality TV show I made him watch last night because it was the only thing on. I barely pay attention to anything he's saying because all I can feel is Jonah's hand in mine as I stare up at him. His eyes are drooping but he's smiling as he listens.

Jonah asks how Francesca is doing. Miles goes to see if he can bring her up here because she's in a room on the floor below us and should still be there, while I get a marker from the nurse's station and wave to Mom and Max who are in the waiting room.

I sign Jonah's cast as Scooby, just like I said I would. He looks at me with so much emotion that it makes my stomach flip over. I don't care that his social worker is right behind us. It feels like we're the only two people who exist, and I have to stop myself from pulling his oxygen mask down and kissing him right here.

He pulls the mask away from his face. "So tell me what's been going on," he says, weakly. "I just want to listen to your voice."

He presses the mask back over his nose and mouth and rests his head back on the pillow, closing his eyes. I lean on the side of his bed and prop my chin on my arm. I can't tell him everything because his social worker is here, and if I started talking about killing ghosts, then pretty soon she'd be my social worker, too.

"Well," I say, "my mom wants me to go back to school. Apparently, Call-Me-Bill is very excited to have me back."

Jonah smiles through the plastic mask, then lifts it. "I bet Call-Me-Bill gets excited by his bowel movements."

I laugh a little. "That's pretty much what I told her."

The door opens, revealing Miles pushing Francesca in a wheelchair. As happy as I am to see her, my stomach sinks at the sight of her. I guess she's still not strong enough to walk on her own, or the doctors haven't found the reason she lost control of her legs. But just because she can't walk now, doesn't mean she never will again, right?

She smiles when she sees Jonah, and she and Miles come to sit around his bed. The social worker steps out to take a call, leaving the four of us alone in here, just like it was when this all started, and now just the way it should end. I look at each of them. At Francesca, whose face hasn't lost its innocence despite all the bad things she's seen, at Miles, whose body may look different than it did when I met him but whose eyes still hold the same kindness, and at Jonah, who looks like it's taking all the bandages and tubes in the world to hold him together but he's still going to get better.

Who knows where we are all going to go from here, or what we're going to do, but I'm really going to miss them.

I open my mouth to tell them that when a bloodcurdling scream comes from outside. A car alarm goes off.

I exchange a confused glance with Francesca and walk over to the window. The snow is still coming down hard. One car below flashes its headlights and taillights in time with the alarm.

Francesca wheels her chair over, gasping when she sees the scene below. She covers her mouth with her hand.

I've seen that look before. It's not good. "What is it?"

"Souls," she says. "There are so many souls. I … I have never seen so many in one place before."

I see nothing, but that's no surprise. "Miles, do you still have those glasses?"

He pulls the delicate things out of a case in his pocket and passes them over. I raise them to my eyes.

Oh my God.

Francesca was right. There are ghosts in the parking lot. So many of them, and they're almost invisible against the snow. They slide between and through the parked cars. One passes by the EMERGENCY sign, making the lights flicker and one bulb die. Another passes through cars, stopping at each one like it's searching for something. Or someone. Peering down the road, I can see spectral silhouettes at the bus stop. Other ghosts meander in front of the corner store and the closed pet shop, browsing like patrons. Some stand and watch the other souls around them with confused eyes. One angry-looking dead guy stands still in the middle of the road, not even flinching as cars pass through him.

My heart thumps hard as I glance down at Francesca. "This is not normal, right?" I ask.

She shakes her head. "Usually, I only see the occasional soul in town. Perhaps a few more in the hospital, but no, this is not normal."

"How did they get here?" I ask.

Francesca is pale. "They must have all come through the passageway to the other side I opened when I killed Leonard. I was hoping they would all fade away."

"Well, they clearly didn't," I say. Then something occurs to me. I know what makes things cold. In my jail cell, the temperature dropped by multiple degrees, and that was with only one soul. "Could all these ghosts be the reason why it's snowing?"

"It's only snowing here and in Bethany," Miles says. I glance over my shoulder to find him showing us his phone screen with a weather app on it. "Ten miles away, it's fifty-nine degrees."

The hospital's front doors glitch, sliding open and closed repeatedly. The Emergency Room sign flickers.

"So, what does this mean?" Miles asks. "Our town is just, like, super haunted now?"

"It's probably fine, right?" I ask. "I mean, as long as the ghosts aren't hurting anybody, it's not a huge problem."

Francesca nods slowly. "I suppose it is all right, as long as they do not hurt anybody."

I don't think they would. Most ghosts are people's dead grandmothers and grandfathers. So what if our town is haunted by a bunch of old people?

Besides, we have the magnets, now, and we know how to defend ourselves. What could a ghost even do to us?

Unexplained Snowstorm Singularly Targets Bethany, Ohio
October 16, 2019

Bethany, Ohio—a town known for its quiet charm—has found itself in the spotlight due to an unexplained meteorological event. Over the past three days, the town has been besieged by a relentless snowstorm, accumulating a staggering 30 inches. Yet, as close as five miles away, neighboring towns are unaffected.

The phenomenon has left meteorologists and climate scientists scratching their heads.

"It's certainly an anomaly," commended Dr. Alice Hammond of the Ohio Weather Center. "We've seen localized weather events before, but nothing this extreme."

The mystery deepens as the town's temperatures plummeted to an almost unthinkable -10°F, breaking all previous records for this time of year.

Local authorities are working tirelessly to provide relief and ensure the safety of the town's residents. Schools and businesses have been temporarily closed, and residents are being urged to stay indoors. The weight of the snow has led to multiple power outages, further adding to the challenges faced by the community.

Social media has highlighted the surreal nature of this event. Images and videos have flooded platforms, showing the stark transition from Bethany's winter wonderland to the clear autumn conditions of its neighboring towns. These posts have garnered attention from national and international media, bringing a flurry of attention to the beleaguered town.

As the snow continues to fall, questions echo through the streets and homes of Bethany: Why is this phenomenon isolated to just one town? And when will it stop?

Post by Sarah McKinney
October 30 at 9:31 AM
[A photo showing a garden with withered crops - once green tomatoes are now shriveled and blackened, leaves on plants drooping and brown.]
Guys, has anyone else's houseplants been looking like this lately? It's like overnight my plants just ... died. I guess it was because of the early snow, but I kept the house warm. Is it just me, or is anyone else having this issue?
52 | 43 comments

Linda Bellview: Omg, same here! I thought it was some new pest or disease, but even the store-bought plants are wilting in my kitchen.

Sophia Yin: I mean, the temperature hasn't risen above freezing since that big storm. Are they too close to a window?

Jordan Rivers: Maybe a new fungus or something?

Rachel Gomez: It's not just plants. The water in my fish tank turned murky overnight. All my fish are dead ...

Post by Mike Alvarez
November 21 at 2:14 PM
[A shaky video clip of his backyard. Chickens are seen with an odd grayish tint to their feathers. A dog is in the corner, panting. Its fur has turned a dull gray, and its eyes have turned white.]
This is really freaking me out. First, it was just the plants, and now my chickens and even Buster?! They're all acting lethargic. Took

him to the vet, and they're baffled. Anyone else's pets going through this?

👍 138 | 💬 97 comments

Derek White: Holy crap, Mike. My cat's fur is changing too! What the hell is happening?

Sophie Langley: Is it contagious?! I've got kids at home. I'm scared to let them near our pets now.

Post by Emma Holt

December 19 at 12:47 PM

 *[A photo of her younger sister's hand - the skin has a subtle grayish pallor, and her veins are black and pronounced.]*
My sister woke up like this today... Her skin... her eyes... I don't know how to explain it. She's been saying she's tired this last week. We're heading to the hospital now. Please tell me we're not the only ones.

👍 302 | 💬 256 comments

Carlos Ortiz: The hospital's packed! My brother's showing the same symptoms.

Natasha Birch: What's happening in our town?

Why are these weird things happening in Bethany, and are the ghosts behind it all? Join Shiloh, Francesca, Miles, and Jonah for the grand finale of the They Stay Series. Scan the QR code below to read the last ghostly adventure:

A Note from Claire

Thank you so much for taking the time to read *They Hunt* and learn to fight ghosts with Shiloh, Francesca, Miles, and Jonah. I love this book. I hope you enjoyed reading it as much as I enjoyed writing it. If you have a second, I'd be so grateful if you told your friends and considered leaving a review to help more readers discover the series.

Could we keep in touch? Claim your free copy of *The Day I Lost My Job at the Bookstore*, a short story from Miles's POV, when you sign up for my newsletter:

Resources

Even though *They Hunt* is a work of fiction and to my knowledge nobody knows whether ghosts are real, the characters in this book deal with many challenges that teens and their families deal with in real life. If you or someone you care about needs information, resources, or someone to talk to, here is a short list of resources that could help.

SAMHSA's National Helpline
A free, confidential, 24/7, 365-day-a-year treatment referral and information service for individuals and families facing mental and/or substance use disorders.
1-800-662-HELP (4357)
https://www.samhsa.gov/find-help/national-helpline

The National Domestic Violence Hotline
A free, confidential hotline available 24/7 for anybody who is experiencing domestic violence or questioning aspects of their relationships.
1-800-799-SAFE (7233)

https://www.thehotline.org/

PACER Center's Teens Against Bullying
A website run by PACER's National Bullying Prevention Center created to help teens learn about bullying, how to respond to it, and how to stop it.
https://pacerteensagainstbullying.org/

National Suicide Prevention Lifeline
The Lifeline provides 24/7, free, and confidential emotional support to people in suicidal crisis or distress.
1-800-273-TALK (8255)
https://suicidepreventionlifeline.org/

RAINN National Sexual Assault Hotline
A 24/7 hotline that connects individuals who have experienced sexual assault, or who know someone who has, with a trained staff member in their area.
1-800-656-HOPE (4673)
https://www.rainn.org/about-national-sexual-assault-telephone-hotline

AcknowLedgments

I loved writing this book. It was very long and at some points seemed like it would never end, but digging into this part of the story was more fun than I could ever imagine.

I have a couple of people to thank for making this book the thing you just read:

As always, the person I need to thank the most is my editor Perry Iles. You breathed life into this story. Thank you for meeting every single chapter with thoughtfulness and enthusiasm. You understand these characters on such a deep level that you just get what I want to do with the story, and I'm immensely grateful for you.

Thank you to the wonderful proofreading team at Pikko's House. You did such an amazing job going through this manuscript and fixing all those pesky typos before publication.

To Mila for such a beautiful cover design. I was blown away by your concepts for this book, and the cover perfectly captures the supernatural ghostly feel of this book. I love it so much!

To Claudia and Rebecca for the amazing Italian translations.

I'm beyond grateful for your help in making Francesca's conversations with her dad sound authentic!

And most of all, thank you to my wonderful family. Tristan, Mum, and Papa—thank you for always being there for me and championing me as I do this thing I love. Thank you for reading the books. Thank you for believing in me always. I love you so much.

And Andrew—you are the best partner a girl could ask for. Thank you for listening to me talk about this series endlessly, being there for me, and giving me a much needed reality check when putting together this plot. The ghost physics would have sounded a lot dumber if it weren't for you.

Lastly, I want to give a big thank you to YOU! Thank you for reading this book all the way to the end. Thank you for supporting this ghostly adventure. You are making my dreams come true.

Claire Fraise is the author of paranormal thrillers about sinister spirits and the brave ghost hunters who bring them down. She won the Grand Prize at the 2023 Writer's Digest Self-Published Book Awards for *They Stay*, and has written four more books in the completed series. When Claire is not sitting behind her computer writing about ghost hunting, you can find her hiking in the mountains, on the back of a horse, or teaching her rescue Chihuahua that it's not nice to bark at people. Even though it goes against every introverted bone in her body, she is on social media. Connect with her on YouTube at Write with Claire Fraise, Instagram and TikTok at @clairefraiseauthor, or visit her website at clairefraise.com.

www.ingramcontent.com/pod-product-compliance
Lightning Source LLC
Chambersburg PA
CBHW061035310726
48969CB00004B/963

9 781960 193025